Praise for Alix Rickloff

The Girls in Navy Blue

"*The Girls in Navy Blue* had me smiling from first page to last! When the US Navy admits women to the ranks during World War I, three intrepid yeomanettes answer the call: Blanche the dashing suffragette, Marjory the German immigrant, and Vivian the preacher's daughter on the run from the police. Friendship, duty, and the struggle of making their way in a man's world will bind the three together, and their secrets will resound through the next fifty years—until Blanche's great-niece, reeling from losses and desperate for home, will pick up the pieces. Alix Rickloff pens a lovely coming-of-age tale: brave women making waves in a war-torn world."

—Kate Quinn, *New York Times* bestselling author

"The unforgettable story of the very first women allowed to join the US Navy in World War I and three friends with their own private reasons for enlisting—reasons that go well beyond duty and patriotism. *The Girls in Navy Blue* is an enthralling story about sisterhood and the secrets we leave behind. A delight from the first page to the last!"

—Lecia Cornwall, author of *The Woman at the Front*

"*The Girls in Navy Blue* is a nostalgic and eye-opening journey into the almost forgotten story of the women who served in the US Navy during World War I. Rickloff has written a riveting reminder that the bonds of found family can be stronger than blood."

—Kaia Alderson, author of *Sisters in Arms*

W9-AZT-256

"*The Girls in Navy Blue* shines a light on the wartime experiences of servicewomen known as 'the yeomanettes,' the first women to join the United States Navy. In this compelling story of groundbreaking women and the dangerous secrets they keep, Alix Rickloff brings the past vividly to life."

—Christine Wells, author of *The Wife's Tale*

Secrets of Nanreath Hall

"In this compelling and heartwarming novel, Alix Rickloff shares with us two women, mother and daughter, whose tragic and triumphant lives intertwine through two world wars. The story pulls us into the universal struggle of all women to find their places in their worlds. I was deeply moved by *Secrets of Nanreath Hall*."

—Karen Harper, *New York Times* bestselling author

"Two women and two wars separated by a generation filled with secrets that kept me turning pages to get to the mysterious truth. At the heart, this is a novel about searching for one's identity. The vivid writing combined with such an intriguing story make Alix Rickloff an exciting voice in historical fiction."

—Renée Rosen, *USA Today* bestselling author

"Alix Rickloff's debut is a delight—beautifully written with fascinating characters, rich historical detail and an intriguing family mystery that keeps the pages turning."

—Hazel Gaynor, *New York Times* bestselling author

"Telling an elegant tale about a mother and daughter trying to find themselves in the midst of two very different world wars, Alix Rickloff establishes herself as an up-and-coming talent in the historical fiction genre."

—Stephanie Dray, *New York Times* bestselling author

"In this engaging and deftly plotted novel, Alix Rickloff introduces us to two heroines who are emblematic of their time yet also manage to transcend its limitations, and who are so memorable and richly portrayed that they all but leap off the page. I loved *Secrets of Nanreath Hall*, Alix Rickloff's first foray into historical fiction, and I eagerly await more from this sensitive and gifted novelist."

—Jennifer Robson, internationally bestselling author

"An emotional and fascinating journey into the hearts of many women. . . . Many will find the soap-opera plotline, likable characters, colorful backdrop, and the quest for answers to decades-old questions as much fun as a *Downton Abbey* episode."

—RT Book Reviews

The Way to London

"A wonderful blend of smart writing, memorable characters, and World War II imagery all centered on the hunger each one of us has to give love and receive it. A great read for not only devotees of period fiction, but anyone who craves a well-told story."

—Susan Meissner, author of *A Bridge Across the Ocean*

"*The Way to London* manages to combine a sense of epic sweep with a very intimate look at one woman's emotional transformation, as the war drives Lucy Stanhope from Singapore to Cornwall to London—and, finally, to the most difficult destination of all: a sense of her own self and the place she belongs. I didn't want the journey to end!"

—Lauren Willig, *New York Times* bestselling author

THE GIRLS
in
NAVY BLUE

THE GIRLS

* * * *in* * * *

NAVY BLUE

A Novel

ALIX RICKLOFF

WILLIAM MORROW
An Imprint of HarperCollinsPublishers

PS™ is a trademark of HarperCollins Publishers.

HarperCollins books may be purchased for educational, business, or sales promotional use. For information, please email the Special Markets Department at SPsales@harpercollins.com.

FIRST EDITION

Designed by Diahann Sturge

Title page and chapter opener art © aksol / Shutterstock

Library of Congress Cataloging-in-Publication Data has been applied for.

ISBN 978-0-06-322749-1

22 23 24 25 26 LSC 10 9 8 7 6 5 4 3 2 1

"Once they are aroused, once they are determined, nothing on earth and nothing in heaven will make women give way; it is impossible."

—Emmeline Pankhurst

I dedicate this book to the "ten thousand girls" who rose up, determined to change the world. And to the generations of women that follow in their footsteps, refusing to give way.

THE GIRLS
* * * *in* * * *
NAVY BLUE

June 1968

A *fifty-year-old mystery is back in the news after a World War I era dog tag was found washed up near Virginia Beach. Sources within the local police department have linked it to a seaman declared missing . . ."*

Peggy turned down the Buick's radio as she made her way off the Virginia interstate and into Ocean View, checking her directions against the foldout map she'd picked up at the Esso station just outside Norfolk. She passed a golf course and a marina. A beachside park where teens played basketball. A library. A grocery store. She rolled the window down and let the breeze off the Chesapeake Bay dry the sweat itching the back of her neck and sticking her legs to the car's leather seats.

She'd barely known her great-aunt Blanche, the black sheep of the family, but her surprise bequest couldn't have come at a better time. Peggy needed a bolt-hole. A place to lick her wounds and start over. A place free of painful memories. Where better than a quiet seaside cottage far from the madness of New York?

Her friends had told her she was crazy to move so far away from everyone and everything she knew, but that was exactly the appeal. How could she come to terms with her grief and her loss when it lay in wait to trip her around every familiar corner? They worried she'd be lonely. How could she explain that was what she wanted; it took so much effort to pretend for the sake of other people. Here she could wallow if she wanted, with no one made uncomfortable.

Besides, it was only temporary, until she got her feet under her.

Then, as the lawyer advised, she could sell the cottage. There was always a market for waterfront property.

She turned off a wide avenue into a neighborhood of sandy yards, tall scraggly pines, and brightly painted houses; some long and low with windows open to catch the bay breezes or perched high on pilings with porches and balconies and slamming screen doors. In one yard a group of children played volleyball. In another, a Sinatra look-alike in plaid Bermuda shorts and a straw sun hat stood watch over a charcoal grill. Peggy made another turn. A few cyclists passed, bells jangling and baskets heaped with damp sandy towels and empty soda bottles. A family made its way home, sandals scuffing, the child whining and red with heat and sun.

It was a nice neighborhood. The kind of neighborhood Peggy might have chosen for herself. Chaz would have hated it; the provincial small-town feel, the distance from any city he considered culturally significant. Not to mention the fact that it was crawling with military and their families. Chaz considered himself a pacifist, the war in Vietnam just the government's latest misguided attempt at imperial opportunism. It wasn't that she disagreed with him. About the war, or anything else, for that matter. But did he have to be so right all the time? Couldn't he leave a little room for doubt now and again?

Maybe if they'd stayed together, all their subtle differences would have expanded into chasms. Maybe it was better they'd collapsed now rather than twenty-five years on. Maybe someday she'd convince herself it was for the best. Right now, missing him still took her breath away.

She shook off her low spirits. This was her fresh start. Her clean slate. She would put New York—and all that went with it—firmly behind her. "She's Leaving Home" from the Beatles' *Sergeant Pepper*'s album came on the radio. Was it a sign she'd made the right decision? She turned it up and pulled onto Bayside Avenue, checking house numbers as she went.

Slowing the car, she glanced at the address she'd scribbled on the back of an envelope. Please let that be a seven and not a two. Please let her house be the pretty Cape Cod two doors down with the striped beach towels flapping on a line and not this overgrown wreck of weathered cedar shingles with the rickety railings and peeling paint. Shoving the car into park, she squeezed her eyes shut, gripping the steering wheel in sweaty palms, clenching her jaw, holding her breath.

So much for an easy sell.

Once upon a time, it must have been lovely. Two stories with a cute dormer window overlooking the front door and a wraparound porch with lots of curlicue woodwork and gingerbread lattice. But that was a long time ago. Now weeds crept along the warped porch floor and twined their way up around the chimney, the dormer window was covered with film and cobwebs, and the screens on the porch were torn. Dead leaves clustered in the corners and caught in the legs of a rusted metal glider.

She left her bags at the front door and followed the sagging porch around to the back of the house where steps descended into a little fenced yard that opened directly onto the beach. She shaded her eyes as she gazed over a low stretch of dunes to the steel gray chop of the bay beyond. So different from their tiny basement apartment in Queens, the clank and bang of trash trucks outside the grilled window, the wail of sirens from the nearby firehouse.

It was a beautiful summer day. A few sunbathers congregated under colorful umbrellas, the scents of suntan oil and charcoal mixing with the briny tang of the sea. Farther down the beach, bathers waded in the low rollers. A transistor radio blared The Turtles' "Happy Together."

Chaz used to sing that one in the shower. Peggy caught herself humming it under her breath.

They'd been happy once. Before the baby. Before the accident.

Or had their happiness been a mirage from the beginning, and she'd been too thick to notice?

The old familiar ache moved from her chest into her temples. This time she didn't have the strength to push it away.

Back at the front door, she fumbled with her bags and the keys while an old man walking his dog watched her from across the street. He chewed on a toothpick while the dog sniffed at a hydrant.

She half expected, half hoped the key wouldn't turn, and she'd have to give up and check into a motel. But then what? Go back to the city with her tail between her legs? Admit she'd been a fool for pretending she could put the pain of the past months behind her? Face all the pitying looks and sympathetic glances that made her want to scream?

The door swung open, and the hot summer scents of outside gave way to must and damp and a house shut up for too long.

Great-Aunt Blanche had passed away four months ago, but the place looked as if it hadn't been touched in years. Light from the French doors at the back poured into a high-ceilinged room cluttered with dusty, old-fashioned furniture. Old flyers, magazines, and advertising mailers pushed through the mail slot, littered a frayed entry rug. To her right, off the kitchen, stairs rose to a landing then up to the second floor.

Upstairs, she found three small bedrooms and a bath. The largest bedroom at the back of the house must have been her aunt's, the furniture handsome despite being layered in dust. Peggy closed the door and inspected the two smaller rooms at the front of the house. The first contained a twin bed, a plain chest of drawers, and a nightstand with lamp. A sewing machine was set up in the second room along with a basket of fabric scraps, a rainbow of thread spools, old dress patterns by Butterick and Simplicity. A cork board hung on one wall, faded magazine photos of models in evening dresses, fashionable day wear, cocktail dresses, trouser sets, all pinned beside swatches of fabric, lists of supplies, a few scrawled notes.

Peggy dumped her bags in the bedroom that looked out over the front porch. The dormer created a small alcove that reminded her of the little reading nook she'd fixed up for herself back home.

No, *this* was her home now. She'd have to make the best of it as she'd had to make the best of so many things over the last months.

Downstairs, she scooped up the clutter of mail on the front carpet. Leaving it on the kitchen table, she found a kettle and a mug and—miracle of miracles—a box of teabags. The lawyer had been good as his word, and there was gas for the stove and electricity humming the squat pink refrigerator.

Taking her mug and the mail, she unlatched the French doors, letting the breeze push through the house. The warmth and the monotonous purr of the waves settled along her bones as she peeled out of her sneakers and curled up on the creaky old porch glider to sort through the mail.

A flyer for a PTA carnival. A notice from a local insurance company. Catalogues from this past Christmas showing Santa and holly and families gathered around great sparkling trees. She'd received this same catalogue. She'd loved looking through it, mooning over all the pages of baby clothes and little toys and decorations for nurseries. Had it only been six months ago?

She dropped the wrinkled catalogue and grabbed up a postcard. The caption on the photo of the gray turreted castle read Richmond City Hall. On the back, a looping feminine scrawl, the words mashed almost corner to corner.

Nov. 1918

Blanche,

Everything was settled as you requested. I'm on a train pulling out of a little country station. The carriage is packed with returning soldiers. Do you remember our long=ago lunch at Broomers? In your uniform, you looked just like the poster girl staring out at me from the Woolworths window. Join the Navy! Do your bit for the war effort! I never thought I'd admit to missing my navy serge and that unflattering hat, but, in this company, I'd feel far less conspicuous than I do in my ill=fitting civilian clothes.

Viv

A sudden wind slammed one of the doors against the house and sent a cold shiver up Peggy's spine. Someone was watching her. She looked up to see the old man across the street staring at her house, his eyes narrowed, his lined face pinched with emotion. After a moment, he turned and walked away, but the crawly feeling along her skin remained.

She glanced once again at the postcard, but this time her gaze settled on the date scrawled at the top corner by the stamp.

November 1918.

That was fifty years ago.

CHAPTER 1

VIV

March 1918
Newport News, Virginia

N ame?"

I paused over the application for only a moment before writing *Vivian Weston* in bold dark ink.

The rest of the answers fell easily off my pen, and I handed the form to the young woman in charge with a smile of confidence. She was a tall, strapping girl. In the fitted blue serge naval uniform complete with shiny gold buttons, clipboard poised and at the ready, she was altogether intimidating. I pushed aside my nerves. Soon enough, I could look like her: clever, efficient, an anonymous uniform among a sea of such. I'd be unrecognizable. Just the way I needed to be.

The girls in line with me all seemed so put together, smiling and chatting as they waited, exchanging hometowns, opinions on the weather, the journey, the war. One or two had tried to start a conversation with me, but I'd been too nervous to make small talk, too self-conscious of my dingy wardrobe, my unkempt hair, my scuffed and pinching boots. They soon drifted away, and I was left alone. Good. Fewer questions meant fewer lies.

She scanned the pages quickly. "Do you have a birth certificate?"

My smile faded. "Will it stop me from enlisting if I don't?"

"Nothing official at all?"

I'd come so far. She couldn't turn me away now, not over something as measly as a birth certificate. "There was a fire a few years back," I explained. "It took all the records with it."

She marked her clipboard, while I held my breath. If she sent me away, where else could I go? I'd burned all my bridges. There was nothing left for me at home. I'd reached the end of the line—literally. To the east lay only the wide Chesapeake Bay opening onto the even wider Atlantic Ocean. War or no war, if I could have swum it, I would.

She handed her clipboard off to a man in summer naval whites who reviewed my paperwork with an even more careful eye. He weighed me up, taking my measure, his long steady gaze unnerving after so many days of trying to be invisible. I stood straighter and held myself with the same confidence I saw in the young woman, but the stretch of healing flesh sent a fire sizzling along new scars, the older ones aching in sympathy. I caught my breath back at the pain and hoped he didn't notice.

"I think we can overlook her lack of documentation. The other information is all in order, and she passed her physical with flying colors."

Since my physical had been conducted by a naval reservist, more embarrassed than me at the thought of the examination, he'd barely done more than make sure I was breathing before passing me along with all the qualifying marks.

"Aye, aye, sir." Her expression of grim efficiency faded, and she answered my obvious relief with a slight smile as the officer pulled a well-used Bible from a desk drawer and beckoned me forward. "Raise your right hand and repeat after me."

I stood as straight as my injuries allowed, my heel no longer pinching, my stomach settling after the sick fear that had followed me halfway across Virginia. "I, Vivian Weston, do solemnly swear that I will bear true faith and allegiance to the United States of America, and that I will serve them honestly and faithfully against all enemies whomsoever; and that I will obey the orders of the President of the United States, and the orders of the officers appointed over me, according to the Rules and Articles of the Government of the Navy."

He thumped the Bible closed with a shouted "Next!"

And that was that.

I was now a yeoman third class in the United States Naval Coast Defense Reserve. No brass bands or parades, just a small dingy room in a building off 24th Street. I had hoped it would make me feel different; braver, more capable. But no amount of governmental paperwork could do that. I was still just as frightened, my old life lurking around the corner waiting to pounce.

I hustled out of the office, making room for the next girl in line, but as I gathered my hold-all, the young woman paused in her interrogation of a short, round dumpling of a girl with blonde curls and a squeaky voice. "Next door, they'll organize your service record and your uniform allowance and offer an advance on this month's pay. Then you'll be told where and when to report."

"I was hoping for a posting somewhere like New York or maybe the West Coast—California maybe."

"You and every other hayseed enlistee looking for excitement. Sorry. You're stuck right here in good old Hampton Roads."

"But I can't stay here," I pleaded. "I just can't."

"That's not up to you. You go where you're told. You're in the Navy now, Weston."

I looked at her blankly for a moment before I realized she was referring to me.

I DIDN'T STAY in Newport News. I left the recruitment office and headed straight for the harbor to catch the ferry across to Norfolk.

Even if the police tracked me this far, they'd lose the trail here. At least that was the hope as I lifted my face to the wind, the glare off the water warming my cheeks and pressing hot on my shoulders through the thin cotton dress I wore.

In the past year, the war in Europe had come to Hampton Roads, the confluence of three rivers and the Chesapeake Bay where it emptied into the Atlantic. Presided over by the bustling cities of Newport News, Norfolk, and Portsmouth, the wide channels swarmed with activity. Ferries crossed back and forth in a never-ending flow of passengers and cargo. A steamer's bellowing horn was answered by the higher-pitched blast from a cargo ship. A school of workboats darted among the freighters and transports anchored farther out in the channel. A Navy cruiser bristling with guns and sailors cut a creamy froth as it pushed its way past the sea of warehouses and wharves, piers and landing stages on its way to the open sea. Smoke and steam rose to mingle with the high clouds.

Alighting at Commercial Place, I headed up from the harbor into the city's busy downtown, the few precious dollars I'd received as an advance on my monthly pay squirreled deep in my purse. For the first time, I had money of my very own. Not parsed out weekly, every penny noted, every expense questioned before being marked down in Father's great ledger. It was a heady sensation, and I couldn't help the zing of liberation along my spine as I lifted my chin just a few inches higher.

The streets were clogged with trucks, cars, and trolleys. A jitney banged and sputtered its way around the corner. A horse and dray blocked an alley as a driver unloaded crates into a storage cellar. Uniforms were everywhere; the dun and drab of Army, the visorless white gob caps of the Navy. I had thought Richmond was busy, but Norfolk's crowds were bigger, louder, more chaotic, and more ominous.

Turning a corner, I found myself among nearly two blocks of fire-blackened ruins, oddly juxtaposed against the new brickwork and green wood of recent construction. What sort of conflagration could have caused such devastation? An unfortunate accident, or something more sinister? Wrinkling my nose at the lingering odors of smoke and mold that hovered like a sour fog, I hurried past until I reached a lunch counter. The menu posted in the window promised a handsome meal for the low price of thirty cents. I'd not eaten since yesterday morning; a few crackers I'd begged off a fellow passenger at the bus station in Port Royal. My stomach growled and my head ached with hunger. I pushed open the door, trying to ignore the curious stares from the smart-looking shop girls and studious clerks. I fought the urge to cringe or drop my eyes. No one here knew who I was or what I'd done.

The place was nearly full. I took a seat by the window where I could watch the afternoon shoppers and let the warm sun relax my nerves. "I'll have the special and a"—my mouth watered as my finger ran down the menu—"a ginger ale, thank you very much."

After lunch, I'd look for a lodging house or hotel, somewhere I could have a bath and rinse out my clothes. I'd overheard some of the girls at the recruitment office discussing the lack of housing and the high prices for the few rooms available, but this morning's success had buoyed my flagging confidence. Surely there had to be space somewhere. I wasn't particular or prudish. And after the last few days of roughing it, I was prepared to accept any hovel or hole so long as it was dry and safe.

The Navy had been a whim—a serendipitous accident. I'd been at the Richmond bus station, a few stolen coins in my pocket, jumping at every word, frightened at any glance that lingered too long, waiting for the clamp of a hand on my shoulder, a policeman's whistle. Where to go? What to do? Then two girls passed me, cases in hand, faces bright with purpose. I heard them talk about employment, opportunity, freedom. All words that drew me after them like a stray puppy on a string.

I'd read the headlines last March when the Navy announced its intention to enlist women for land service duty. I'd seen the posters urging volunteers to join up. Rosy-cheeked buxom girls in sailor suits and cocked white caps. Father had seen those same headlines and railed against the immorality of allowing women to work alongside men; the depravities that would result from such fraternization, the inevitable destruction of the traditional Christian household. But Father was dead, and I'd nothing left to lose and nowhere else to go. Vivian Weston needed a job and a place to hide. The Navy offered both.

As I pondered the menu, the bell over the door jangled and a young woman stood haloed in the light from outside, dark red hair cut scandalously short beneath her brimmed straw hat; her height, uniform, and proud carriage drawing every eye in the place.

A man hurried over, twitching with umbrage. "Didn't you see the sign, miss? It's posted right on the door."

"The one that reads No Sailors?" she asked with a lift of one elegant eyebrow. "I saw it. But I didn't think you really meant it." She faced him down until he crumpled under her steely gaze and retreated behind his counter like a whipped dog.

Ignoring the gawking diners, she sailed across to where I sat, her white button shoes clicking on the linoleum. Who was she, and what did she want? I cleared my throat, hiding the fear infecting me until I was sick with it.

"Mind if I join you?" She didn't wait for an answer but slid in across from me. "Didn't I just see you leaving the recruitment office in Newport News?"

"That's right. I just enlisted." I paused as her question sank in. "Have you been following me?"

"Nothing so nefarious. I'm normally posted to the new naval

operating base at Sewells Point, but this afternoon I had meetings at the recruitment office."

Nerves jumped as I digested this information. I had blithely assumed I'd erased my trail and, within an hour, someone had tracked me down. If one person could do it . . .

Something of my apprehension must have shown on my face.

"You are a suspicious little thing, aren't you?" She laughed. "My streetcar stop is around the corner, but I thought I'd have a bite to eat before I head back to the NOB. The canteen there isn't exactly up to Delmonico's standards. I can leave if you like."

"No, please. I'm sorry." I rushed into the awkward silence that followed, embarrassed at my accusation. I could hardly go about questioning everyone who looked at me twice. "It was rude of me. I shouldn't have doubted you. Please, stay. I wouldn't want you to go back to work hungry."

A whisper from two tables over caught her ear. As I fumbled with my napkin in jittery apology, I watched as she turned with a hard stare that drove the gossips to fall back over their tuna salad with red faces. How did she do that?

She caught me gawking and smiled, mischief in her blue eyes. "You'd think they'd be used to female yeomen by now, but they still behave as if we're one step up from ladies of the evening."

"No one could ever mistake you for that," I gushed. "Your uniform makes you look like a queen."

"I'd rather be an admiral than a queen. More power." I would have laughed at the joke, but she was deadly serious. "The name's Blanche. Blanche Lawrence."

"Viv," I replied, the lie coming more easily now. I wondered how soon before it was second nature.

"Nice to meet you. If you like the uniform, it's Arthur Morris—he's a few blocks south on Plume Street. A decent fit, not like some of the potato sacks the girls are wearing, but I made a few tailoring modifications of my own; the darts in the jacket, for starters, and I shortened my skirt by an inch. Far easier to keep out of the mud."

"You did that yourself?"

"My mother made sure I could sew better than any seamstress. She said I could never be cheated if I knew more about clothes than anyone I hired."

"She sounds very wise."

"I don't know about being wise, but she's definitely opinionated. Luckily, she and Daddy and the rest of my family are far away in Washington, DC, where they can't boss me around." She summoned a waitress with an imperious wave of her hand. "What's this?" she asked, pointing at the menu with a cold look down her aquiline nose.

"Liberty cabbage, miss." The waitress glanced around as if checking for spies, lowering her voice to a whisper. "What used to be sauerkraut."

Blanche shot her a wry look. "I know what sauerkraut is. I'll have some and a hamburger, if you please." She handed the menu over as if daring the waitress to argue.

"You mean . . ."

"I said a ham-bur-ger." She enunciated each syllable, her gaze crackling.

The waitress blushed and scuttled back to the kitchen.

Unmoved, Blanche sipped on her lemonade. "Sorry for that unfortunate episode. I just find some of this showy patriotism a bit much, don't you? As if what we call a hamburger is proof that we love our country."

I'd not given the idea much thought, but she had a point. The day President Wilson had declared war, Father took every book written by a German author from his library and burned it in our backyard. Later he'd organized a group of men from his congregation who met in the rectory study every Thursday and shouted about the evils of a worldwide Teutonic conspiracy. I'd simply been grateful he wasn't shouting at me for a change and dismissed the rest.

"What about you, Weston? Where are you from?"

I used the return of the waitress with our food to delay answering, but I could see Blanche watching me closely. "Richmond," I said finally. I was already juggling so many lies, best stick close to the truth when I could.

"Let me guess." She sat back with a stare that had me squirming. "You aren't here with the family's blessing."

I choked down my panic along with a forkful of salad. "Not exactly."

"You're not the only one. I've heard plenty of stories about horrified parents begging their daughters to reconsider. I think mine were more relieved than anything else. They've never been quite sure what to do with me," she explained around bites of her hamburger. "After I was arrested last year for chaining myself to the White House fence, joining the Navy seemed positively praiseworthy."

"You're a suffragette?"

"A very minor standard-bearer for the cause, I'm afraid." She speared her sauerkraut with murderous gusto. "But this Navy directive brings a whole new dimension to our fight, don't you think?"

Zeal glowed in her face and brightened her eyes. I'd seen suffragettes before. Groups of them gathering on Richmond's Capitol Square or marching in parades with banners urging votes for women. I'd even accepted a leaflet once from a woman speaking in Jefferson Park. I had the scar from Father's belt to prove it. But I'd never had the courage to join those parades or attend the meetings. I'd never had the courage to fight.

Not until a few days ago. And a fat lot of good it had done me.

I looked up from my plate to catch her watching me, a speculative gleam in her eye. "Have you a place to live, Miss Weston?"

"I meant to look this afternoon."

"I know it's out of the blue, but you seem like a nice girl, and, frankly, I'm desperate to find a roomie. What would you say if I offered you a place with me?" She hurried on as if anxious to convince me. "My family has a cottage out on the bay, but there's a trolley runs right into town so it's not too inconvenient."

"That's very kind of you," I said, using my vanilla ice cream to buy time.

Part of me wanted to jump at her offer. Part of me could already tell how dangerous it would be. If I was to keep safe, I needed a place where no one would ask me uncomfortable questions or pry where they didn't belong. Where the girl I had been would simply cease to exist.

Blanche didn't seem to notice my hesitation, or if she did, she didn't care. "I'm not being completely altruistic. I had two roommates, but one was transferred to New Jersey and the other left the Navy to get married, so I'm rattling around the place like a pea in a can. Three dollars a week for your own room, and we even have a proper inside bath. Mother insisted after the summer she found a snake in the outdoor privy. You won't find better than that at the YWCA—and that's if they have space."

"But you've only just met me. I could steal the silver or bash you over the head in the middle of the night."

She sat back, her icy blue gaze seeming to pick me apart. I made my features go blank, easy to do with a mouth full of dessert. "I'm a very good judge of character, and you don't look likely to do either of those things, so what do you say?"

So much for her judgment.

"Here's what we'll do. You go around to the Henrietta and ask for Mr. Morris. He'll get you kitted out with a proper uniform.

Then meet me at the streetcar stop at four. We can ride out to the cottage together. If you decide it's too far from the lights and glamor of downtown Norfolk, you can stay the night and tomorrow be on your way. I promise not to hold it against you."

Maybe she had a point. What if I couldn't find a place to stay that I could afford? Or what if the only place I could find was four to a room with a sink at the end of the hall and a privy at the end of the yard? What if I had to bunk on a bench again? A room of my own meant privacy. And who would think to look for me living in a fancy beach house with a fancy debutante?

"All right." I left money for the meal and, feeling both generous and a little sick from all the food, added a whole nickel for a tip. "I'll see you at four."

AFTER A BUSY afternoon, I was ready and waiting for Blanche at the stroke of four. The day's sun had turned bright and unsettled, the light banging against my temples, the damp in the air frizzing my hair and sticking my blouse to my back. Father would have cursed his bad knee as a sign of impending heavy weather. A ready excuse for a medicinal glass of bootleg whiskey. Not that he ever needed one—an excuse or a whiskey.

I didn't need his gout or his curses to recognize the signs of the storm to come. Black clouds gathered to the west, and the wind kicked up, pushing at skirts and hats, making the cart horses dance in their traces, flapping at the grocer's striped awning farther up the street.

Four fifteen came and went and still no Blanche.

My hold-all slid in my sweaty hands, and the bag from Mr. Morris's shop in the Henrietta knocked against my shins. I'd gone there wielding Miss Lawrence's name like a cudgel, and doors magically opened. I was swept into a workroom where my measurements were taken and bolts of white drill and navy serge brought for my approval. Soon enough, I'd ordered shirtwaists, skirts, and a pair of jackets for summer and winter use. The rest of my uniform had taken a few more stops, but I was ready to report for my first day of naval duty.

Four thirty and the clouds boiled overhead. A rumble of distant thunder bounced between the tall buildings and sent shoppers scurrying for cover. Had I got the time wrong? The street corner? Maybe Blanche hadn't meant what she said. Or maybe she'd changed her mind about my trustworthiness. Maybe she'd found someone who looked better, smelled better, didn't have the law after them . . .

"Yoo-hoo!" Blanche hurried across the street. "Sorry I'm late," she wheezed, catching her breath. "There was a new girl on the switchboards who had the entire base in a tangle of crossed lines. It took all I had to unravel the mess she'd made."

The streetcar ride took us as far as Henry Street where we changed to an electric trolley. Soon enough we left the crowded downtown behind, the smells of asphalt and diesel fumes giving way to a sharper briny tang. The views opened like a gift. A gull rode the uncertain storm winds.

We got off at the end of the line where sky and water met in a hazy gray horizon, the sign on the platform reading Ocean View. Brightly painted buildings and sheds dotted the waterfront ahead of a long, elegant promenade. Beyond that, a wide beach rolled down toward the choppy water. Boats were pulled up onto the sand. The sweet smells of popcorn, toffee, and fried waffles warred with the sour odors of fish and tar and tidal mud. Music wafted from a striped carnival tent and a ticket barker called out for riders to board the Leap the Dip roller coaster where a short train of cars clacked its way five stories up on a rickety track.

"The amusement park is just across the way. I used to love coming down here as a child to ride the carousel and the tunnel of fun.

Sometimes we'd have lunch at the hotel or take a boat out on the bay for an afternoon of fishing."

"You don't anymore?"

"My parents decided to close the cottage for the duration, which worked out wonderfully for me." She headed away from the sounds of a barrel organ. A wedding cake of a building, all gleaming windows and marching pillars, lorded over the beach and the row of bathhouses sheltering under the seawall. "That's the Ocean View Hotel. We're a few streets farther south. Don't worry. It's a lot quieter away from the crowds."

Here, the wide mouth of the Chesapeake opened onto the ocean. To the north, low marshy land clung to the horizon, but to the east, all was choppy gray-green water. A few boats turned into the wind, sails billowed, and, off to the left, I saw the smokestacks of a steamship headed east. The breeze, now speckled with rain, tore at my new brimmed hat. The thunder that had followed us grew closer, the sky licked with lightning.

"Come on!" Blanche grabbed my arm. "We'll need to run if we don't want to get drenched."

She led me along a road where signs swung on creaky chains advertising guest houses and rental cottages with fanciful and nautical names like the Mermaid, the Sand Dune, the Lighthouse. Clotheslines flapped with towels and bathing costumes. Women rocked and sipped lemonade. A pair of sandy sunburnt children walked a dog at the end of a length of rope. After a bit, the modern macadam changed to gravel washed by sand.

"There she is." Blanche pointed to a cottage of gray-weathered shingle with a trellised screened porch that wrapped around the side and across the back. Behind the house, grassy dunes hid the beach, but there was a duckboard path leading between the low sandy hills to the gray line of bay beyond and a border of rose-bushes not yet in bloom.

The heavens opened at that moment, and we made a mad laughing dash through the puddles as the rain thundered around us. Up the steps we flew, flapping our arms and wiping at our faces. "Oh dear. I'm wet right down to my birthday suit," Blanche laughed as she unlocked the door to show me inside, where I dripped on a colorful rag rug and she hung her hat and jacket on a hall tree.

"What do you think?" she asked. "And keep in mind, it was never meant to be lived in every day all year so it's a bit . . ."

"Delightful." It was like a dollhouse, open and bright and furnished sparingly with a few slightly battered but comfortable pieces. The walls were painted a creamy yellow; the floor, wide lacquered pine boards. Silver frames of family members sat propped along a stone mantel alongside collections of seashells and bits of colored glass. A carriage clock ticked the slow steady hours. A set of French doors opened onto a back porch with steps leading right down to the beach. This afternoon, there was little to see as the storm hid everything in a dark torrent of cloud and rain. But on a pretty day, the view would be gorgeous.

I would be safe here. No one would ever think to look for me in such a place.

"It's really just the one big room with a kitchen off there. There are three bedrooms upstairs and the bath I promised." Blanche started for the stairs. "I can show you if you like."

"No need," I said quickly before she could change her mind. "I'll take it."

CHAPTER 2

PEGGY

June 1968

Peggy opened her eyes to a gray rainy morning. A perfect match to her mood. A steady drip in the corner of her bedroom warned of yet another leak in the roof. She'd been here a week and already her list of needed repairs was two pages long and growing with every hour spent in Great-Aunt Blanche's disaster of a house.

No. Amend that—*her* disaster of a house.

She had to start thinking of it as her house. Her house. Her leak. Her disaster.

She rolled over, bunching the extra pillow between her legs, cradling it to her stomach. She closed her eyes and let the sound of the rain against the roof lull her into a semidoze where the worries of today faded into nothing. If only she could stay this way permanently.

A knock at the door woke her. The rain had stopped, though the sky remained overcast. Her skin felt clammy and hot under the pile of blankets, her nightgown stuck to her legs. She rolled over staring up into the ceiling. Maybe whoever it was would go away.

The knock came again. Obviously, they weren't going to take hiding for an answer.

She rolled up to sit on the edge of the bed, taking stock of her appearance in the speckled mirror across the room. Her hair hung loose and limp over her hunched shoulders. Great smudges circled her eyes in a pale shuttered face, her mouth a tight seam, hands gripping the edge of the mattress until the white stood out against the pink flowered sheet.

She was a complete mess. Was it any wonder Chaz had walked out?

She touched the curve of her cheek, her lips, the pulse at her throat. Warmth. Breath. She wasn't a ghost—not yet.

The knock was more insistent this time.

Maybe she was wrong. Maybe this *was* Chaz. Maybe he'd changed his mind and realized how much he still loved her. She imagined him driving through the night, window rolled down and radio blaring The Doors to keep himself awake, wind whipping his hair back off his forehead as he sang along at the top of his lungs.

How many times had they done an all-nighter, taking the Charger on a road trip south to Florida or west into the mountains, once even as far as Colorado? She would curl up beside him on the seat, her legs tucked under her. He'd have one hand on the wheel and one arm draped over her shoulder. In the small hours of the morning on a deserted highway, it was like they were the only two people in the world.

When she got pregnant, the trips had stopped.

After the baby, he'd started going on his own.

It was funny how she could separate her life into parts: before and after. As if a giant knife had sliced it down the middle.

"Hold on. I'll be right there. Don't leave!" she shouted, stomach fizzing, head swimming with nerves. "Please don't leave!"

Throwing a robe on, she hurried downstairs, avoiding the tread with the popped nail. The door's dirty sidelight framed a shadowed figure in a hooded raincoat. Chaz? It had to be Chaz. One of her friends must have given him her new address. Had he been surprised at her move? He'd always told her she was a homebody, a creature of habit. Dependable. Sensible. He'd liked that about her. Now she knew why. It meant he could leave and know exactly where she'd be when he was ready to come back.

Ha! This time, she'd fooled him.

She paused, a hand on the door. "Dignity, Peg," she whispered to herself. "Don't show him you're desperate." Drawing a breath, she opened the door.

Not Chaz.

A stranger in faded paint-stained jeans and a pair of battered work boots leaned against the porch rail. His sun-streaked hair was pulled off his face into a short ponytail, and blond stubble gilded his square jaw. She'd have written him off as a hippie looking for a handout if not for his faint scent of soap and aftershave and the flyer he was holding out for her to take. A camper van with a dented fender and rusty driver door idled at the curb. "David Dyer. Just canvasing the area looking for work and thought you could use a handyman."

She choked down a lump, unsure whether it was relief or disappointment swirling in the pit of her stomach. "Thanks, but I'm not looking to hire anyone right now."

His dubious gaze wandered over the cottage. "You sure? I can do whatever you need—construction, plumbing, wiring, even weeding. No job too small."

Maybe not, but she'd already decided to put the cottage on the market. There had to be somebody interested in buying this place, even if only to knock it down. This move had been a mistake. Maybe Chaz had been right about her. She didn't do change well.

Over his shoulder, Peggy caught sight of the same man from yesterday, his face hidden under a yellow slicker while his dog sniffed at the base of a tree.

"Well, if you change your mind, just give me a call." She accepted the flyer with a nod. The man shifted his feet, cocking his head with a frown. "I don't mean to pry, but are you all right?"

"I'm fine." She ran a hand through her hair, aware of what a mess she must look. "You woke me up, that's all."

She waited for the follow-up question about why she would be just waking up this late in the day, but he seemed to accept her response. "Right. Well, okay then. If you change your mind, my number's on the flyer." With a polite smile, he headed back down the walk as she closed the door.

After a few moments, she peered through the sidelight in time to see the camper grumble away up the street and around the corner. The dog walker watched him go too. She stood at the window until he picked the dog up under an arm and carried it into a neat bungalow across the street.

Awake now, Peggy padded into the kitchen. Afraid of food poisoning, she'd done a quick scrub when she first arrived. The refrigerator had been emptied and washed out and a few essentials from the local Piggly Wiggly brought in to fill the cupboards. The house might be listing on its foundation, but she could at least make coffee and fry an egg without fear of deadly dysentery.

She should have known Chaz wasn't coming to take her back to New York. Like her, he'd moved on. Started fresh. Started over.

The knife severing her old life from her new turned in her chest.

The pain of old habits dying hard.

THE REAL ESTATE agent arrived in a sleek white Corvette convertible, shades down, hair frozen in an eternal Elvis pompadour. Peggy met him on the porch steps wearing her favorite Gay Gibson dress with the Peter Pan collar. Chaz had bought it for her when she'd first told him about the baby. He'd laughed and warned her she'd best wear it while she could still fit into it. Funny, that it hung loose on her these days. Still, after nearly a year of existing in pajamas and sloppy housecoats, it felt odd to dress up. Odd, but good. With her hair styled in a sleek flip and a little powder to go with her cheerful Pink-A-Fling lipstick, she felt almost like the girl she used to be, not the ghost she'd become.

The familiar hollow ache remained deep in the pit of her stomach, but it was a manageable ache. One she could learn to live with.

"Mrs. Whitby?" He flipped up his sunglasses, his gaze traveling up her bare legs as he flashed a Pepsodent smile.

"You must be Mr. Grace," she said, holding out a hand. "Thank you for coming by so soon."

"Call me Barry." His keen gaze reluctantly left her legs to travel over the dilapidated cottage. She could almost see the sums adding and subtracting in his head. "Mind if I . . ." He motioned toward the front door.

"Of course. Please."

He didn't wait for her to lead the way, instead pushing past to head inside. She'd done a hasty cleaning before his arrival; sweeping away cobwebs and washing grime from windows, mopping the knotty pine floor and polishing every surface until it shone. She'd even found an ancient carpet sweeper in a broom closet and run it over the threadbare rugs before it finally died in a grind of belts and a puff of green smoke.

Still, seeing the cottage through another's eyes made her wince at the remaining dinginess as if she, and not Great-Aunt Blanche, was responsible for its state of decay. She forced herself from plumping pillows and tidying shelves ahead of his inspection. "It's not exactly turnkey ready, is it?" he commented.

"But it's solid," she argued. "That's what's important. I had a builder take a look at the place a few days ago." Not a lie exactly. "Nothing a lick of paint can't fix."

He gave a noncommittal grunt and headed upstairs, poking

his nose into cupboards, opening drawers, tapping walls. Was the man a real estate agent or a detective?

Back in the kitchen, he checked under the sink, behind the refrigerator, in the stove. Glanced out the French doors to the back porch. All the while making small noises in the back of his throat as if he was carrying on a private conversation of grunts, tsks, and the occasional heavy sigh. Peggy trailed him back outside where he wandered the fence line, wincing at the overgrown yard and the sagging back porch.

"Shit," he cursed as he carefully untangled his trousers from an enormous overgrown rosebush. "It's a damn jungle back here."

"It's gone a little wild, but that's easy enough to clear out."

He came to halt, rocking back and forth on the balls of his loafered feet, his smile dimmed as he took a final glance around. "So . . . should we wait for your husband before getting down to brass tacks?"

She rubbed at the pale indent on the third finger of her left hand. "If we do that, we'll be waiting a long time. We're divorced." There it was, that stinging sense of shame, of failure. She'd had a good life and she'd let it slip through her fingers. No one said it out loud, but they didn't have to, did they? She'd seen it in their faces, heard it in their gentle platitudes.

And then they wondered why she'd moved three states away.

Would Mom have been one of those who silently chided? Or did she understand those loaded looks all too well herself?

Moments like this made Peggy wish she'd known her better. Had her longer.

"So, what's your assessment, Mr. Grace?"

His smile returned with a vulpine gleam. "It's Barry, remember?" He flipped his sunglasses back down, and she could swear he posed, a hand on the porch railing, one foot on the step, as he raked her from top to toe. "Oh, it's good, very good."

She locked her jaw and glared back. "I meant the cottage."

He shrugged as if he'd lost interest. "Thirty if you're lucky."

"That's it?" She'd not been expecting miracles, but thirty thousand came in much lower than she'd figured last night.

"Nobody's looking for these little turn-of-the-century cottages anymore. They want modern, all new interiors and appliances. They'd be buying to knock this place down. It's the land they want."

"Knock what down? Who the hell are you?" It was the man with the dog, the one from across the street. He stood in the drive, his rangy body practically vibrating. He raised a clenched fist. His other gripped a handful of envelopes.

"Barry Grace from Vallance and Trotter Realty." The realtor put out a hand and flashed a salesman smile.

The man wasn't impressed. His thin lips disappeared into a bushy-browed scowl, which he leveled at her, his bony fist shaking. "Blanche Lawrence would be rolling in her grave if she knew you meant to sell this place. This was her home. And you want to tear it down?"

"Slow down, old man," Mr. Grace said, stepping in front of Peggy. "I'm not sure this is any of your business."

"The name is Symonds"—he poked the realtor in the chest with one gnarled finger—"not old man. And you can keep your nose out of it. This is between me and her." He speared Peggy with a watery glare. "I told Blanche it was a mistake to leave the cottage to you. Told her too much time had passed and too much water under the bridge to make it right now. But she'd not hear a word about it, stubborn to the bitter end."

"I don't understand."

"Here." He thrust a stack of envelopes at her. "These got mixed up with mine. That damn postman is as thick as this smarmy weasel here."

"Wait. Mr. Symonds. What did you mean . . ."

But he'd already stalked back across the street, slamming his front door with a rattle heard up and down the block.

"Nice neighbor," Mr. Grace said with a shake of his head. "Any prospective buyers come across that crazy bastard and the price will drop ten grand at the least."

But Peggy wasn't paying him any attention. Her eyes were glued to the postcard caught between a water bill and a menu from a neighborhood Chinese takeout. The photograph was of a formal garden, the caption underneath reading "Maymont." She flipped it over to read the back.

Nov. 1918

Blanche,

I was rooting through my purse and came across that photograph of you, me, and Marjory that we had taken on the promenade. The three musketeers, she called us. I still can't believe she's gone. I know you said I shouldn't blame myself, but who else can I blame? I brought you both nothing but trouble. Neither distance nor time have eased my guilt. I wonder if they ever will.

Viv

1918. Again.

Was this somebody's idea of a joke? Peggy scanned the street expecting to see Allen Funt lurking behind a bush with a camera crew ready to pounce with a big "Gotcha!"

"Bad news?" Mr. Grace asked.

She felt her cheeks go hot as she feigned a smile. "Just a note from an old friend."

He gave the cottage one last glance from behind his mirrored shades before settling his gaze on her with a smarmy smirk. "If I was you, Peggy—I can call you Peggy, right?" He didn't wait for an answer. "I'd sell up and find myself a nice modern place somewhere. Leave this old house to molder away once and for all. Otherwise, you're likely to wind up as bats as Grandpa over there."

Peggy looked from him back to the postcard. "Who says I'm not already?" she muttered.

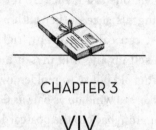

CHAPTER 3

VIV

1918

He came toward me, face twisted and red, the flat of his hand big as a dinner plate, but it was the belt he carried that frightened me. My side still burned from my last hiding. I twisted away as he grabbed for me, his tight hold tearing my dress. The first hit took my breath away. The second dropped me to my knees. I grabbed the first thing that came to hand and swung . . .

"Viv. Viv, wake up."

My eyes flew open to a room grayed with predawn shadows, but it was not the room I expected. No draft across the chilly rectory floorboards, no narrow creaking bed, no hand-stitched sampler scolding me from its place upon the wall; *Whoever heeds discipline shows the way to life, but whoever ignores correction leads others astray.* No snores from down the hall where Father slept off the night before.

"You were having another nightmare." Blanche stood by my bed in her bathrobe and slippers, hair uncombed, cold cream shining her face. She held a steaming mug in her hand that smelled very much like coffee.

I willed my heart rate to slow. "Sorry. I didn't wake you, did I?"

"Are you kidding? I have to be up before the roosters, but this is the third night in a week you've cried out in your sleep."

"What did I say?"

"Nothing that made any sense, but you were thrashing about like you were being murdered."

My body went cold, but I forced my face into a mask of embarrassed self-deprecation. "It was probably that tinned ham we had for supper. Gave me bad dreams." I smiled away her worry until after a few long terrifying moments, she turned away with a tightening of the sash on her robe.

"The iron's hot if you need to press a shirtwaist."

Sweat chilled my skin and my heart galloped unevenly, but there was nothing to be afraid of here. I was safe. I was Vivian Weston. No one could hurt me. Not anymore.

Blanche paused at the door, a hand upon the trim. "You really can trust me, you know." She gave me a last reassuring smile before heading to the bath, the pipes clanking as she turned the taps.

I appreciated her friendship, but there was nothing to tell. Nothing she would understand. She was the kind of girl who attended cotillions and walked out with college boys, her future as bright as a new penny. Her attitude was one of entitled confidence, not hard experience.

Downstairs, I took my coffee out onto the porch as I'd done every morning since I moved in with Blanche. Having spent so many summers here, she didn't even notice the beauty anymore, but I was still in awe each dawn—at the chill in the air that made me cup my mug and inhale the steam off its bitter surface; at the light spreading along the horizon, growing larger and larger until the sky was awash with rose and gold, the sun rising slowly from the water, turning every ripple into a diamond. Small birds raced up and down the beach, darting in and out of the tide in search of breakfast. Sails caught the growing light as watermen headed out for a day of fishing.

This place was magic. And it was mine. I'd not risk losing it with a confession. They'd have to drag me out of here in handcuffs.

"Good luck on your first day!" Blanche called out as she slammed the front door and hurried up the road to catch the bus to the NOB, the new naval operating base, where she worked as a switchboard operator.

I spent a few more minutes drinking in the glorious dawn before retreating inside to get ready for my first official day as a female yeoman or, as the horrid woman at the tailor shop called me, a yeomanette, which set my gritted teeth on edge. It made our work sound frivolous and inconsequential. As if we were dressing up in costume and playing at soldiering. Anyone who saw Blanche drag herself in here at night, worn to a thread, would never presume at such an insult. I began to understand her fervor and her cause.

Standing in front of my mirror, I couldn't help the little thrill of pride that curled like an electric current up my spine. I might have enlisted to escape, but that didn't mean I wasn't proud to pull my oar for the good of the war effort. My gold buttons shone, my black neckerchief was freshly pressed, and my brimmed straw cap regulation to the nearest eighth of an inch. As I checked myself over with a brush of a sleeve and a straightening of a cuff, I stood tall, not hunched and hoping to remain unnoticed. Is this how Blanche felt every day? This sense of belonging she took for granted?

Rummaging through my drawers for a clean handkerchief, my fingers brushed the small tin box I'd hidden away the first morning I arrived. Blanche was gone. I was alone. I sat on the edge of my bed and popped open the lid. Inside, a dried aster; my mother's jet brooch; a bracelet of pink beads; and at the very bottom, a photograph of Tom. It was all I had left of him, his letters safely fed to the kitchen range back in Richmond as soon as I'd read them.

All but the last one. The one that Father found.

A bang of a sputtering motor scared me, and I shoved the tin back into its hiding place among my stockings and cotton combinations. Peering through the curtain, I watched as a young man across the street tinkered under the hood of a delivery van. Pender's Grocery was stenciled along the side. He must have sensed me watching him. He glanced up at my window and waved.

He was still there when I stepped out onto the front porch. His straw blond hair gleamed like corn silk. "Mornin', miss."

I nodded politely and ducked past him, hurrying for the trolley. Blanche was right. Her house *was* at the back of beyond. Not at all convenient for either of us. Maybe I'd have been better off taking a room in town, no matter how dingy or expensive. Yet, even as I hoofed it, out of breath and sticky with sweat, I knew I couldn't leave this little jewel box of a cottage. Not even if I was late every day.

The putter of an engine edged me to the side of the road. "Need a lift?"

It was the boy again, his engine troubles obviously fixed. He sucked on a toothpick around a wide freckled smile.

I shook my head and continued on, hoping he'd take the hint, but he merely followed alongside me in his delivery van. My heart sped up on pace with my stride. Unease stirred low in my gut.

"I heard tell the trolley's broke down. Might be a long wait," he explained. "I can give you a ride into town if you like. I'm headed that way myself."

I slowed, weighing my choices. Ignore him and be late. Accept his offer and be on time.

"I don't bite," he said with another grin and a roll of his toothpick from one side of his mouth to the other. "Ask Blanche. Me and her have known each other forever. The name's Gus."

I couldn't be late my very first day. Reluctantly, I climbed in beside him. "I'm Viv."

"Where to, Viv?"

"The Portsmouth Ferry Dock, please. I'm due to report to the naval hospital." Just saying it filled me with pleasure. I wasn't a nobody scraping by from day to day. I was important; essential even. They needed me. I'd never been needed by anyone before. Not truly. "In an hour, actually."

"An hour? That's loads of time. Heck, I can get you there in twenty minutes easy." He sat up and changed gears, the van leaping forward. "Miss Viv, hold on to your hat!"

GUS WAS AS good as his word, dropping me at the dock with time to spare. Sadly, the ferry was late, and then I took the wrong streetcar and ended up riding all the way to 9th Avenue before turning myself around, so by the time I passed into the hundred-acre campus of the Norfolk Naval Hospital, I was out of breath and fighting a horrid stitch in my side.

A sailor gave me a wink and a smile on my way through the gate. I refused his flirtation with a frown and an imperious look down my nose that Blanche had taught me—unfortunately rather ruined by the sweat beading my brow and my puffing, heaving gasps for air. He pointed me toward an enormous domed and columned hospital building set amid a veritable city of hastily built subsidiary wards, barracks, laboratories, mess halls, and supply sheds. A pair of white-veiled nurses hurried down a road of crushed oyster shell toward another group of wooden buildings set to the northwest of the main campus. A truck idled outside an ambulance shed where a man in dungarees stood smoking. Farther away, a group of sailors in military-issued pajamas and robes sat in wheelchairs in the shade of an oak tree just leafing out. Some smoked. A few read. More stared into the distance, faces blank with hidden strain.

By the time I reached the steps leading up to the entrance, my butterflies were bouncing like cannonballs. How would I ever find my way within this maze of buildings? Or keep names and ranks and faces straight? I'd never held a proper job or been trained in any of the skills necessary for such important work. I was a sham in every way that counted.

A man in faded blue coveralls pushed past me growling about starry-eyed schoolgirls masquerading as sailors. I glared at his back and followed him inside.

Sound bounced and echoed within the enormous main hall. I was directed by an orderly to an office on the second floor where a plain, long-jawed woman sat typing. She was dressed in the same uniform of navy serge that all the female yeomen wore, but below her eagle and crossed quills were three red chevrons to my sad one. Her fingers flashed over the keys in a rapid dance, her round, wire-rimmed spectacles glinting in the light from her desk lamp. I waited patiently as she finished her page, zipping it free of the roller with a flourish. As I opened my mouth to talk, she slid in a fresh sheet and began again, still without even acknowledging my presence.

I cleared my throat. "Weston reporting for duty."

Her hands paused above the keys as she raked me over with a hard unblinking stare. "You're fifteen minutes late."

"I can explain—"

"This is the Navy. Not a visit to your granny's house, Weston. Tardiness is unacceptable. Has no one taught you anything about how we do things?"

"I had a few hours training right after I enlisted."

"From now on, you will be at your desk at the required time. Should you need to make a change in your hours or request liberty, your supervisor—that's me, Chief Yeoman Quarles—will need to approve it. Should you be ill, you'll need to report to the dispensary or have your family doctor call it in. No excuses. No exceptions. Is that understood?"

"Aye, aye, ma'am."

"Good. There are ten of you in your section. Lieutenant Dumfries is the officer in charge."

"Thank you."

"Don't thank me yet. You haven't met him." She resettled her spectacles as I hurried to follow her through rows of desks to an inner office where a middle-aged uniformed gentleman with thinning hair and a dimple in his soft chin pored over a pile of papers. "Weston, I presume?"

With a final better-you-than-me glance, Quarles hustled herself out, leaving me on my own. "Yes, sir."

"You're late!" he barked. Apparently, his chin was the only thing soft about him. He proceeded to filet me with his gaze. I tried to swallow but my mouth was bone dry, my voice barely a whisper.

"Sorry, sir."

This was not going at all how I'd imagined it as I prepared this morning, preening in my new uniform, cocky with excitement.

The lieutenant rose from his desk, coming around to lean his back against it while I remained standing stiff and uncomfortable in front of him. "Let me be perfectly clear, I didn't want you here, any of you. Having women in the Navy is preposterous! First, you all wanted to vote. Then Alice Roosevelt started you smoking cigarettes! Now you're talking about being soldiers. Next thing we know you'll be cutting off your hair and wearing pants! God forbid!"

My earlier confidence oozed out of me with every criticism. I didn't cower or cringe. Even as nasty as his remarks were, he was an amateur compared to some. Instead, I stood silently and let his resentment wash over me. After a few more minutes of explaining why Navy Secretary Daniels would rue the day he allowed girls to join the Navy, he got down to finally explaining what I was supposed to be doing for the next ten hours and the foreseeable future.

"This office maintains all records of patients and staff and is responsible for all correspondence and reports that come from the Navy Department or the 5th District Commandant. Got that?"

"Yes, sir," I said, though I hadn't the foggiest first notion what he was talking about.

There was a tap at the door behind me. Another female yeoman stood there, this one small and dark as a pixie. Her hair was tucked under her cap and her apple cheeks and brown eyes were bright with amusement.

"What do you want?" Dumfries growled.

"Delivery from St. Helena training station, sir." She handed him a ribboned portfolio. "And they asked me downstairs to tell you an ambulance boat from Yorktown just arrived. Ensign Parcell wants you to meet him on Ward F to go over details of the patient transfers."

"Right." He dusted himself off, passing me by as if I were invisible.

After he was gone, the other girl bit back a smile. "He's really not that bad. All bark and no bite. You'll see."

Dumfries' shout echoed back down the hall. "Weston! On the double!"

Ward F turned out to be a roughly constructed building set in a sea of construction mud. Nurses and corpsmen moved quickly and competently between the rows of men, assessing as they reassured the ill and injured they were in the best of hands.

"This time of year it's mostly mumps, scarlet fever, and pneumonia, though we get our share of accidents and injuries," Dumfries explained. "Patients are transferred to the hospital here with all accompanying accounts and records. It's up to our section to make sure all medical and military paperwork is in order. I want everything written down legibly and without question. Afterward, we'll sort through it, transcribing and then typing it all up properly. Six copies on my desk by the end of the day. Understand?"

He didn't wait for an answer but plunged ahead as I trailed after terrified, unprepared, and completely exhilarated.

The ward was a blur of gray feverish faces and whispered names as I checked lists against lists and took pages of scribbled notes. The nurses moved with an expertise I envied, their expressions never anything less than serene.

"Dumfries, sir? Over here." One of the surgeons called the lieutenant away.

I waited, chewing the nub of my pencil, while nearby a corpsman knelt beside a cot, the patient hidden so that only a razored fringe of brown hair and a tanned neck were visible above the blankets. Then he turned, his dark brown eyes staring blankly in his lean angular face. His left hand gripped the blanket. His right wasn't there at all. I stood gaping like a codfish. My heart seized so that I could barely breathe.

"Tom?" I whispered.

It was impossible. I knew it was impossible even as my stomach tightened into a knot. The last I'd heard from Tom, he'd been in aviator training in Ohio. He couldn't be here. But still my hands shook, and I couldn't peel my gaze away.

"Weston!" Dumfries' voice kicked me awake. "Have you heard a word I said?"

"I'm sorry, sir. Can you repeat it? I was—"

"Off with the fairies. Or gawking. Either way, keep up and pay attention. Take these reports to Quarles for her approval. See that copies make it to orthopedics."

I blinked, my vision clearing. This boy wasn't Tom. It was easy to spot the differences now—rounder face, lighter hair, eyes closer together.

Not Tom at all.

"Blast it, Weston! Are you crying?" Dumfries voice dripped with disgust.

"No, sir," I answered, cheeks wet with tears I refused to wipe away. "Just some dust in my eye."

CHAPTER 4

VIV

After my disastrous first day, all I wanted to do was curl up under my blankets and hide, but Blanche wouldn't have it. "That's what they want, Viv. They want us to fail. Then they can use that failure as one more nail in the coffin of women's rights. But you can be just as stubborn and stiff-necked as any bully loud-mouth lieutenant."

I wasn't sure I could, but Blanche had faith in me, so I dragged myself out of bed and was on the trolley before I realized that my new roommate was every bit as stubborn and bullying as Lieuten-ant Dumfries.

Even so, she was right, and in a few days I'd fallen into a routine. Up before dawn and coffee on the back porch, forty minutes on the trolley into downtown Norfolk—twenty if Gus was waiting with his delivery van—a quick ferry ride across the river, and then a street-car to the hospital where I met up with other female yeomen as we filed through the gates. Once in the main building, I climbed the stairs to the rooms housing my section where I called out a cheerful good morning to Chief Quarles who acknowledged my greeting by hammering even harder at her typewriter keys and scowling into her stack of carbon paper. By five minutes to eight, I was at my desk, uniform in order and pen at the ready.

Dumfries' training consisted mostly of demands for me to do

it over, complaints about my slowness, my sloppiness, or my use-lessness, and, now and again, a red-faced cursing fit I assume was meant to provoke me into feminine hysterics. He'd underestimated my upbringing.

After that humiliating shock of the first afternoon, I never again broke down, instead locking my pain away, pushing my grief aside. That life was behind me. I was a new person with a new future. There was no place for Tom anymore. There never had been, really. I'd just been too pie-eyed to see it.

As I learned the ropes, the job grew easier, though no less stren-uous. After ten hours at my desk, I headed to an auxiliary building for classes in naval practices and policies alongside the hospital's other yeomanettes, as we were continually called much to our cha-grin. There were about thirty of us in total; scattered between the hospital and the pay office. Most of the girls were local, but there were a few assigned here from places as far away as Philadelphia, Chicago, and one poor homesick waif from Nebraska whose fea-tures trembled at the edge of tears the entire class, but who gamely completed every task as if her life depended upon it.

It didn't take long for us to grow familiar with the dizzying glos-sary of mysterious Navy terms and the countless pages of strict mili-tary procedures. We were, on the whole, a hardworking, cheerful group, determined to shine. Whatever we were told to do, no matter how tedious or ridiculous, we did as quickly and efficiently as pos-sible. This was our war too, and we wanted to do our part to help.

In our spare time, some of the girls organized a basketball team. Others started a Navy girls' chorus. And there were always those who gathered in the mess to gossip and giggle over every hand-some officer they saw. I quietly declined every invitation with a shy smile until the offers finally stopped coming. But I continued to watch them, envious of their friendships and their laughter. Some-how, I had managed to escape one cage only to trade it for another.

By the time I returned to the cottage each night, I ate a few bites of supper before falling into bed, asleep before my head hit the pillow. Some nights I didn't even bother to eat. Blanche didn't seem to notice or mind. She had her own work and often came home later and more exhausted than me. When she did get off early, she usually headed into Norfolk for one of her suffragist meetings. She'd tried to get me to go with her once, but I put her off with excuses about being tired, being shy, being busy. The last thing I wanted to do was flaunt myself at public demonstrations where the police would be in attendance.

But one evening, I returned to find her at the table, finger running down a page of accounts by the light of an oil lamp.

"Is everything all right?" I asked, removing my hat, shedding my coat, and tearing off my tie to let the breeze dry the sweat creeping up into my scalp. I flopped on the sofa, my blistered feet aching.

Blanche sat back with a sigh and a rub at her temples. "I'm trying—and failing—to make our income and our expenses meet somewhere in the middle. A losing task, it would seem."

"I thought this was your family's cottage."

"It is, but Father makes me pay rent so long as I stay here. I think he's hoping I'll tire of scraping pennies together every month and move back home to work at the Navy Yard. So far, I've held him off, but costs are going up every day. I was thinking of putting a notice up at work. It's always a risk you'll end up with someone who chews with their mouth open or supported Taft for president in the last election, but it's that or raise your rent, and I'd hate to do that. Until we find someone, you won't mind subsisting on rice with cheese and sour-milk corn cake, will you?" She pushed a recipe booklet toward me. On the cover, a smiling aproned woman stood over a stove happily creating healthy wartime meals. "I picked it up outside the mess hall today. Thought it might give us some ideas for stretching our groceries out a bit more, but I get shivers just reading some of these government-sanctioned concoctions."

I glanced through it. "You leave supper to me from now on."

Later that evening when I set the plate down beside her, she looked up, rubbing her eyes. "What's this?"

"Fish cakes—from a tin I found at the back of the cupboard—and roasted new potatoes or what's left of them after I removed all the eyes. I was thinking I might clear a patch in the yard and plant a vegetable garden. What we don't eat, we can trade."

"A good cook *and* thrifty." She dug in, closing her eyes on a smile.

"After my mother died, I took over the housekeeping. My father's congregation is small and there was never a lot of money for extras."

"Your father's a minister? I thought you said he sold insurance."

"Did I?" I frantically searched my brain but couldn't remember what I'd told her. I'd offered up so many lies, it was hard to keep them all straight. "Maybe you're thinking of my uncle. He sells insurance."

Before she could reply, I used the excuse of a hot kitchen to retreat to the back porch where I leaned against the railing gulping in deep steadying breaths. Stupid foolish mistake. I needed to remember who I was and what rested on this lie. How quick would Blanche be to praise my cooking if she knew the truth? My truth?

THE NEXT MORNING, I arrived at the hospital to find Chief Quarles waiting to intercept me before I reached my desk. "Don't sit down. You're to report to the west lawn for parade training."

"But I have a mountain of paperwork." I glanced at the stack of ward reports detailing patients ready for discharge. Dumfries would have my head if they weren't completed in time for his morning meetings.

Quarles scowled through her owlish spectacles. "Get down there on the double, Weston. If we're to be featured in a bond parade next week, we need to be able to march."

"A bond parade?"

"Do you have something against parades, Weston?"

"No, ma'am. Only my marching isn't very good, and I'd be sure to bungle it. I'd be happy to pull double shifts so someone else could go in my place. Maybe Jensen. She's much better at keeping in step."

"All female yeomen are to report. No exceptions." She laid down her red pencil, her expression almost—but not quite—encouraging. "You'll be fine, Weston. That's why we're training. So get a wiggle on and do your best."

Out of excuses, I followed the bewildered nervous group of girls funneling through the buildings toward the parade ground. Twenty of us lined up in four more or less straight lines while a chief petty officer took our names before having us march up and down. For an hour, we fought to remain in step, turn when and where we were supposed to, and halt on command. As the sun grew hotter, the smells more noxious, and the morning sky burned our necks and faces red, the poor CPO first explained then shouted then stood in utter baffled silence as we meandered about like so many dazzled Sunday shoppers.

When a yeoman assigned to the surgical department fainted from the heat, the CPO gave up and sent us away with a sigh and a command we return in the afternoon to try again.

"That was the saddest marching I ever saw." The voice was laced with laughter. "I've seen better timekeeping on a stopped clock."

I turned to find the same apple-cheeked, dimpled girl I'd met a few weeks earlier in Dumfries' office. She was pushing a big black bicycle, a leather satchel slung over her shoulder.

"It wasn't that bad, was it?" I asked, rubbing at a blister on my heel.

"Worse. That poor CPO nearly had a heart attack. I thought he'd foam at the mouth when that girl on the end caught her heel and nearly toppled the whole square."

"That was me."

"Oh. Sorry." She tried to smother her laugher, but the light dancing in her eyes caused my own fit of giggles.

"It's funny now, but Quarles will have my head on a pike if I ruin her moment—and that's if Dumfries doesn't get to me first for falling behind in my work. Maybe I can come down with a surprise case of appendicitis."

"That's right. You're in Dumfries' section. I knew you looked familiar. How are you getting along with old Grumpy Guts?"

"He hasn't cussed at me in over a week. I count that as progress." I eyed her bicycle appreciatively. "You're lucky. Wheels sure would come in handy. I nearly twisted an ankle running for the trolley this morning."

"Thank heavens for old Bessie." She patted the handlebars affectionately. "In the last six months, delivering between here, the NOB hospital out at Sewells Point, the training station at St Helena, and everywhere in between, I've put enough miles on this bicycle to get me to the moon and back." She flashed me a smile and stuck out a hand. "I'm Marjory Kunwald. And before you start eying me with suspicion, I was born and raised in Ohio. I like baseball and apple pie, and three of my brothers serve in the US Army. Okay?"

"Um . . . okay," I answered, hesitant at this unsolicited barrage of information and glancing around for backup in case she threw her bicycle at me. "I'm Viv."

She blinked, and the heat in her eyes flooded her cheeks until they burned scarlet. "Sorry. After a year of being suspected of everything short of outright treason, I tend to lead with my left. I once caught my landlady going through my things. And she charges me three times what she charges her other lodgers for a room barely bigger than a closet and an outhouse at the bottom of the yard."

"Why do you stay?"

"It was the only room I could find. Four other lodging houses I tried wouldn't even speak to me once I told them my last name. Most don't like servicemen to begin with. Tack a German name like Kunwald on to that, and I'm sunk."

"That's horrible. You can't help your last name. And you don't look German."

"You mean horns and a tail?" She gave a tight harsh bark of laughter. "Ask the soldiers you meet on the wards. They'll tell you. The enemy looks and bleeds the same as us." She straddled her bicycle. "Good luck with the marching. Give my regards to Grumpy Guts."

With a twisted cynical smile, she pushed off, pedaling toward the gate.

I stared after her, my brain whirring.

Ever since Blanche had mentioned the danger of being thrown out of the cottage, I'd carried a knot in my stomach. I'd grown to love my little room above the porch with its pink flowered wallpaper, the wide view over the beach as the sun broke above the water, the scent of Blanche's fancy perfume mingled with the sharper, mustier scent of tidal marsh. And the fact that there was always a lamp left burning in the window for me no matter how late I came home.

I couldn't bear the thought of leaving it behind for crowded dingy accommodations in a YWCA hostel or an overcrowded boarding house.

"Wait! Hold on!"

Marjory was in need of a room, and Blanche and I were in need of a roommate. It was perfect. Well, maybe not perfect, but there was something about her I liked. A bracing honesty and an acid sharpness despite her rounded curves and dimpled chin.

I chased her down, my shoes crunching on the gravel, catching her when a truck pulled out and cut her off.

She braked to a stop, her bag banging at her hip. "Be quick. I've got to get these files to the hospital at Pine Beach. The war waits for no man . . . or woman."

"Would you be interested in rooming with me? Me and another yeoman, that is. It's her house actually, but she's looking for a third roommate to split the rent."

Marjory eyed me cautiously. "What's the catch?"

"No catch. Only it's all the way out in Ocean View."

"Aren't you worried I might be building bombs in my spare time or penning seditious leaflets?"

I smiled, offering her the same answer Blanche had offered me. "Not worried at all. I'm a very good judge of character. Besides, I know what it's like to be on the outside looking in. To need friends."

I thought she'd hesitate or ask me more questions. Instead, she grinned, and this time there was no cynicism in her gaze. "Give me the address, and me and Bessie here will be there tomorrow with bells on."

Now I just had to break it to Blanche and hope that Marjory didn't chew with her mouth open.

THE STOCKPOT SIMMERED on the stove as I chopped vegetables. Behind me, Marjory was mixing up a batch of drop dumplings while Blanche read to us from *Little Women*. Putting her in charge of entertainment was the only way I could guarantee she wouldn't burn, spill, or otherwise ruin dinner. Who knew that someone so clever and capable could be such an utter disaster in the kitchen? More evidence if I needed it, that Blanche's life until now had been one of privilege and luxury. And yet, there was no hint of softness in her. She was as hard-boiled as an egg.

"'Laurie, though decidedly amazed, behaved with great presence of mind. He patted her back soothingly, and finding that she was recovering, followed it up by a bashful kiss or two, which brought Jo round at once.'"

"I've never understood what Jo was thinking." Sleeves rolled back, Marjory brushed her dark hair off her forehead with a floury forearm. "Laurie loved her. He was handsome and wealthy. I'm sure he'd have allowed her to continue writing after their marriage."

I needn't have worried about what Blanche would say when presented with my fait accompli. Marjory was tidy and good-natured, and with the addition of her share of the rent, we were no longer reduced to miserly penny-pinching. Her friendly—and generous—baker gentleman friend was an added bonus. Since she'd moved in, our cookie jar was always full, and there was no end to the steady supply of sweet desserts on our kitchen table.

"She couldn't be writing if all her time was taken up with cooking and cleaning and raising babies, now could she?" Blanche argued.

"He was wealthy," Marjory replied. "He'd have servants to do the cooking and cleaning."

"And the babies?" I slid the celery into the pot and began scraping carrots. "Servants for those too?"

Marjory was not going to give up her dream of a Laurie and Jo match without a fight. "Rich people have nannies and nursemaids and governesses to take care of their children." She turned her shrewd gaze on Blanche.

"Why are you staring at me?"

Marjory cocked her a why-do-you-think look.

"Fine, most do, but even so," Blanche shot back, "wealth shouldn't be the only way a woman can command a life beyond the kitchen. There are other options, you know." She slid her gaze back to the page, a knowing smile playing over her lips.

"I think we've wandered off topic, don't you?" I scraped with extra vigor to keep my mind off Blanche's mysterious options, which was not a subject good girls contemplated, much less discussed. "Keep reading." I motioned toward the page with a threatening point of my knife.

Blanche returned to the book with a final sidelong thoughtful glance toward Marjory. "'She lay in that heavy stupor, alike unconscious of hope and joy, doubt and danger. It was a piteous sight, the once rosy face so changed and vacant, the once busy hands so weak and wasted, the once smiling lips quite dumb.'"

"So, what are those options, if you don't mind me asking?" Marjory spoke up, all pink-cheeked innocence.

"Marjory!" I said, nearly slicing off the tip of my thumb.

"What?" she squeaked. "My brothers were Boy Scouts. You know what they say—be prepared." Grinning, she held up a three-fingered salute.

"I don't think that's quite what they had in mind," I replied dryly.

"You don't know my brothers and their friends." Marjory stifled a giggle. "I fear for those poor French mam'selles with that bunch of randy tomcats on the prowl."

So much for the wholesome escapades of Jo, Beth, Amy, and Meg. This conversation had run right off the rails. Maybe chewing with a closed mouth was the least of our worries with our new housemate.

"It's no use burying your head in the sand, Viv," Blanche commented matter-of-factly. "A woman needs to be in control of her own body. You can't trust men to worry about these sorts of things, especially now when the war has normal life and normal courtship turned on its head."

"But Ernst is a gentleman," I argued, my discomfort making my voice high and tight. "He would never . . ." I turned to Marjory. "Would he?"

It was Marjory's turn to go scarlet and splotchy. "I wouldn't think so. I mean it took buying three dozen chocolate *rumkugeln* from his bakery before he plucked up the courage to even speak to me. Three dozen more before he asked me to walk out with him. I think I gained ten pounds just coaxing the man to the starting line. But you never can tell . . ." She shrugged as if the thought wasn't out of the realm of possibility.

"A chivalrous man *and* he knows how to make a smashing *rumkugeln*?" Blanche commented. "Lucky girl! My last suitor turned out to be a two-faced lying cheat with a wife in Nashville."

"Golly!" Marjory gasped at the same time I let out a strangled "Oh no! What did you do?"

Blanche's face was hard, her hands clamped tight around the book. "Wept and screamed and threw things mostly. It was that or murder the scabrous piece of no-good filth. There are times I still think I made the wrong choice."

I waited for the laugh that would turn her words to a joke, but it never came. She remained white-faced and stony, her eyes on fire. I focused on dropping spoonfuls of dough into the simmering broth. "Dinner's almost ready."

"Did someone say dinner?" Gus never bothered knocking, and we'd got used to his turning up at all hours.

Marjory set another place at the table. "Blanche was just telling us what a cad her last suitor was."

"Was she?" Gus and Blanche exchanged a silent look I couldn't decipher.

"It doesn't matter anymore." Blanche looked as if she was sorry she'd mentioned him at all. "He's long gone and I've sworn off men. They're far too much trouble—present company excluded of course." She smiled brightly at Gus, who blushed and dropped his gaze to his bowl of stew.

Marjory bowed her head while I fidgeted with my napkin and focused on the window over the sink and the slice of purple evening sky I could see through the curtains. My father's cold vengeful Lord was one I could no longer worship, not even with a rote prayer.

Blanche seemed to share my reluctance. "I don't know about the rest of you, but I gave up praying when I gave up men."

Marjory lifted her head, a grin cutting deep dimples into her round cheeks. "I had a baseball coach once that said praying was like practicing. You didn't know if it worked until it was too late to do anything about it."

Blanche laughed. "Oh, take my word, Marjory. It's much too late."

CHAPTER 5

PEGGY

1968

G*eneral Westmoreland has been officially replaced as commander of military operations in Vietnam by General Creighton . . . continued fallout from Senator Kennedy's assassination . . . Chief Justice Earl Warren has announced . . ."* Morning headlines dragged Peggy up from a whirl of unsettling dreams, her mouth like cotton, hands trembling as she fought to catch her breath. *"WRVA local news on the hour . . . authorities have confirmed the dog tag found on the beach belonged to a Navy seaman who went missing in November 1918. If anyone has information regarding . . ."*

She smashed her hand down on the alarm clock's button before rolling onto her back, the lumpy mattress catching her square between the shoulder blades, the wafer-thin pillow doing nothing to relieve the steady throbbing in her skull. A cheap bottle of wine and a head full of questions had combined for a troubled sleep.

What did Symonds mean when he said that too much time had passed, that there had been too much water under the bridge to make things right again? Make what right? It obviously all came back to the reason her great-aunt Blanche had left her everything she owned. But Peggy was damned if she knew what it might be.

Blanche had never singled her out for any special attentions before. In fact, she had shunned family get-togethers until her absence was no longer remarked upon, her connection to the family frayed beyond repair. The one and only time Peggy had laid eyes on her had been at her mother's funeral ten years earlier. She wouldn't even have known who she was but for her grandfather's flash of recognition as they passed her standing alone at the back of the church. He'd murmured something under his breath. Blanche had lifted her sunglasses, her blue eyes like chips of ice. By the time they'd gathered at the grave, she was gone. When Peggy had asked, her grandfather spoke of an estrangement that happened long ago when his sister was young, but he'd never elaborated, and, with his death a year later, the last thread between them was cut.

So what changed? What spurred Blanche to reach back out? And why had she waited until after her death to do it? Were these mysterious postcards connected to it? Or just a crazy coincidence?

Was she being paranoid? Whoever the mysterious Viv was, she didn't seem to be threatening in any way, merely nostalgic—or confused. So why then did Peggy get a shiver when she read the postcards? Why did these notes feel like a warning? Like a shadow reaching forward fifty years to darken her crumbling doorstep? Three wars had passed. Nine presidents. A generation growing up and growing old. Another one coming of age. And yet, reading these brief lines, Peggy was pulled back in time and into Blanche's life whether she liked it or not.

Viv's words spoke of guilt she couldn't shake. Peggy knew all about that.

A lukewarm dribble of a shower and two aspirin did little to ease the spin of her thoughts or the bang in her temples.

Sell. Sell and get out. The realtor had put his finger on the only sensible plan. Take what she could get and move on. She didn't know Blanche. She didn't owe her anything. None of this was her concern. Yet, Mr. Grace's condescending advice grated on Peggy's raw nerves. Here was one more person telling her how she should feel, what she should do. Treating her like a child.

Slowly, her scalding cup of coffee smoothed the rough edges and dragged her taut shoulders from around her ears. The beautiful summer weather helped. Outside, the sky was a high milky blue, the day's heat already pushing into the cottage. Far too nice a day to make any monumental decisions. Instead, she'd pack a bag and go sit out on the beach. Choose a book from the tall case by the stairs. Most looked old and dull, but there had to be a paperback stuffed in there somewhere.

As she rummaged through a closet, a wasp flew out of a wooly hat, swooshing dangerously around Peggy's head before careening across the room and up against the window above the desk where it bumped futilely against the glass.

Peggy sympathized.

She tried shooing it toward the door with a rolled-up flyer, but it proved as stubborn as she was, refusing to budge even if it meant freedom.

Abandoning it to its fate, she busied herself with gathering a towel and a thermos of coffee. A wide floppy hat. A bottle of suntan oil. A yellowed copy of *Wuthering Heights* from the bookcase.

Crossing the sand, the sun warmed her bare shoulders and beat against her cheeks, seeping into the cold places. She spread her towel near the dunes. By now, the empty beach was filling with families under wide umbrellas, morning walkers out for a stroll, a group of laughing teens erecting a volleyball net. It was the mother and child that punched the air out of her. The woman dandled her baby in the surf, swinging him high as the waves rippled against the shore. He laughed, his chubby legs kicking the air.

That could have been her. That child might have been her child.

If but for one moment's distraction.

The familiar heart-crashing panic taking hold, Peggy fled back to the cottage, abandoning her bag and everything in it, her chest constricting around the hard knot where she'd locked her loss away.

Stupid. Weak. Useless.

Her thoughts were punctuated by the plink of the leaky faucet, the tick of the old carriage clock on the stone mantel, the bump of that damn wasp against the window. "I'm going to save you if it's the last damn thing I do."

She dragged a kitchen chair over to the desk and climbed up on it, wobbled and braced herself, one hand against the wall, the other on the ancient sash. The wasp swooped in angry circles around her head. Peggy ducked as she adjusted her hold on the sash and gave it a hard yank. There was a crack and a scream of rusted pulleys and weights as the old window groaned upward six inches. The wasp, sensing escape, dove at her one last time. Instinctively, she jerked away. The chair wobbled. Her foot slipped. And, hands windmilling in useless circles, she fell, twisting to avoid the edge of the desk.

She landed hard on the rug, breath punched out of her, the toppled chair lying across her legs along with an avalanche of books, files, and ledgers. Loose papers fluttered around her like confetti. At least the new pain in her side made her forget about the old one squeezing her heart. "You're welcome," she groaned.

She moved first her neck then her arms and legs. Nothing broken. Only bruised. Morning shadows picked out the dingy carpet, the wood floors in need of refinishing, and something else . . . something caught in a floorboard. She lifted her head, catching a gleam of gold through the dust.

Pushing away the chair, she rolled slowly to her knees and reached to the very back of the desk between the skirting and the floorboard. Her fingers closed around something the size of a pebble, flat on one side, nubbed on the other.

A button. A gold button with an anchor pressed into its surface.

Join the Navy, Viv had written. She had mentioned Blanche's uniform. Was this a button off her jacket? Did the two of them serve together in the Navy? Did the Navy even allow women to serve in World War I?

It didn't seem possible. Women couldn't even vote before 1920.

Peggy counted back the years. Blanche would have been in her early twenties in 1918. She'd no idea how old this Viv person would be, but probably about the same age. Were they two young women caught up in the rampant patriotism of the day, wanting to do their bit for the war effort?

No . . . there had been three of them. Viv mentioned someone named Marjory.

Ignoring the mess she'd made, Peggy pushed to her feet and went in search of the postcards she'd shoved into the hall table drawer.

The postmark on both cards was smeared; "Virginia" was easy enough to make out, but the rest was unreadable, maybe an "A" or an "R" and a string of unreadable letters. How many cities and towns started with those letters? And with no last name, even if she did know where the postcards came from, how would she figure out who Viv was? Did she care enough to find out? Or was this just another distraction? A way to not think about the loss of her old life; the collapse of her marriage, the death of . . .

She flinched, her fist closing around the button, its edge digging into her palm, anchoring her here and now, keeping her from falling to pieces.

Drawing a breath in and out, in and out, Peggy rolled the button between her thumb and forefinger. She glanced around at this house, trapped in the past, filled with ghosts.

Viv. Blanche. Marjory.

The three musketeers, she called us. I still can't believe she's gone.

What had happened to these three girls?

Neither distance nor time have eased my guilt.

Peggy had absolutely no answers, but she could agree with the sentiment.

THE STORM STRUCK just after the streetlights flashed on. Peggy had never paid much attention to storms before; the city seeming to dull them into submission. They were an inconvenience of dripping umbrellas and unavailable taxis. Nothing more. But here, they spread in the west, taking over the sky with billowing black-on-black clouds as the dropping air pressure sizzled along her skin and buzzed at the back of her skull. The slow roll of thunder boomed up and down the beach like ancient cannon fire, carried on the waves until the cottage vibrated, the old windows shaking in their crumbling frames. Lightning flashed in a strobe light's blinding flicker, burning the backs of her eyelids with white glare.

Peggy stepped out on the porch, a thrill curling up through her stomach as she watched afternoon turn to night. The beach was empty, abandoned, but for a few forgotten belongings half-hidden in the sand, bits of trash blowing south: a paper cup, a packet of potato chips, a beach ball. Close to the cottage, the dune grasses bent in the wind; farther out, the bay boiled black, flecked with dirty foam. A sudden wind slammed against her, lifting the sleeves of her blouse, tossing her hair around her face. Beneath her, the porch seemed to shudder at the onslaught. The skies opened, a furious deluge steaming against the hot cement, rushing in a torrent of overflowing gutters. The beach was lost behind a thick slashing veil.

As quickly as it erupted, the storm pushed out over the water to the east, the torrent became a drizzle, the world edged in storm-light gold. A lamp shone from a nearby window. Drains rattled and gurgled. The ground around the rosebush in her backyard was strewn with white petals. Peggy drew in a breath of the sweet salty air, her mind swept clean as the empty beach.

She didn't want to go back inside. Not yet. The cottage was dark and quiet. No noisy upstairs neighbors, constant traffic, or Chaz banging in from work with a shout, the apartment fizzing with his presence. She didn't even have a television here to mimic the sounds of a real family and a normal life. She descended the porch steps and pushed through the gate onto the beach.

The sand was cool on her bare feet, the air fresh against her face. She wandered along the tide line, letting the water roll over her feet, splash up her ankles. Across the wide expanse of bay, the storm flickered and boiled over Cape Charles and the far tip of Virginia's eastern shore, but here the wind had died, and a few early stars shone between the fast-moving clouds. House lights spilled out over the beach along with the occasional flash of a passing headlight. A shine of colorful neon from a nearby bar. A car radio blasted an ad for dog food. She kept walking until the slick black pilings of a jetty rose out of the sand, snaking its way into the shallows. Turning back, she saw how far she'd come, her cottage, tucked into the dunes, barely visible.

By now it was full dark, and she had to pick her way carefully over the uneven ground as she headed home.

So intent on keeping her feet, Peggy didn't see the figure until it reared out of the dark, a shape against the night, features lost in the blinding shine of a flashlight. She froze, heart pounding, until the shadows rearranged themselves into Mr. Symonds and his dog. The little terrier sniffed at the bracken washed by the tide until it caught sight of Peggy, ears pricked, body stiffening as it barked ferociously.

"Who's that?" Symonds squinted, spearing her with the flashlight's beam.

"It's me," she said, shielding her eyes. "Peggy. Your neighbor from across the street."

"Enough, Bandit," he grumbled at the dog. "Quit your noise." He switched off his light as the dog subsided into a silent investigation of Peggy's ankles. "What are you doing out here, miss?"

"Same as you. Enjoying the evening."

He lifted his head to the air and sniffed. "Storms'll be back later tonight."

"You can tell that from the wind?"

He gave a gruff bark of laughter. "Weatherman on the radio."

As if in silent agreement, they fell into step together as they made their way back down the beach. "You must have known my great-aunt Blanche pretty well," she ventured.

"Better than most." He turned and called to his dog, who had wandered off after a stick, tail wagging.

"What was she like?"

"She was a good woman. She didn't deserve to be done to the way she was." The dog back at his side, Symonds snapped on the leash, his expression lost in the shadows.

"I don't understand."

"She died in a home, did you know that? Surrounded by strangers. I was away, or I'd have noticed something was wrong. I'd have found her, and maybe she . . . well . . . who knows. At least I was there at the end to see things were done properly. Made sure they didn't hand her body over to the county along with the derelicts and the nameless."

"I didn't know."

"You wouldn't, would you? You and that family of yours wrote her off a long time ago, once you got what you wanted. They're all probably relieved she's dead and can't make any more trouble."

Peggy had no idea what he was talking about or what trouble she might have made. "I'm the only family left."

"No parents?"

"My mom and dad divorced when I was a baby. I never knew him, and she died a while back."

He lifted his pale eyes to her, beetle brows squished in a frown. "It's a hard thing to be all alone in the world."

The understatement of the century.

It was years before she stopped expecting to hear her mother's voice at the other end of the phone, stopped expecting to see her face among a crowd of people. Maybe that's why marrying and starting a family had been so important to her. She didn't want to be alone anymore. And for three glorious years, she hadn't been. Chaz was there: singing in the shower, coming home on a Friday night with Chinese takeout and a bottle of cheap red wine; his dirty laundry piled in a corner, his razor on the sink, his books on the table.

But all his love hadn't been enough to save them.

She was alone again.

They reached the edge of the duckboard path leading to the street. Symonds tucked his dog under his arm, the little terrier licking at his gray grizzled face, its tail wagging like a whip. Peggy's cottage stood on the other side of the faded picket fence, dark and uninviting. The screen door rattled in a fitful wind.

"Do you know if Blanche served in the Navy? Maybe during World War One?"

Was it her imagination or did Symonds seem to stiffen? The moment passed, and she couldn't be sure he hadn't simply stepped wrong in the deep sand. "She did. Proud as a peacock, she was about it too."

"Did she have friends named Viv or Marjory? They might have served with her."

His bushy brows curled low over his forehead, his jaw working back and forth. "That would be a question for her, not me."

"Believe me. I wish I could ask her. I wish I could ask her why she left me this house, someone she barely knew. And now that I'm here, what she thinks I should do. The place is falling apart."

Symonds caressed the little dog's head, scratching it behind an ear, cradling it like a child. "Blanche had her reasons, and no amount of argument could get her to change her mind once it was made up. That's one thing I did know about her."

"Mr. Grace thinks the cottage isn't worth saving."

Symonds' gaze narrowed in his thin face. "Hmph. Anyone with half a brain could see that oily, slick-tongued son of a bitch would say anything to get his hands on Blanche's land—or on you." Peggy shuddered. "So, let me ask you a question, miss. Why did you come here?"

She rubbed at the ache under her breast, though whether it was a stitch from walking so far or something else, she couldn't say. "I didn't have anywhere else to go."

"Same reason Blanche stayed." His lips curled in what almost passed for a smile. "So maybe you and her are more alike than you think. Maybe you got stubborn in you too."

CHAPTER 6

VIV

1918

I glanced at the clock as I raced through the last of my work, before glaring over at Neilson's empty desk. I had started the day with a stack of twenty-five folders while she'd had maybe ten, all of them thin, easily completed. It didn't help that I was abysmal at typing, hunting and pecking my way across the keyboard, and that I had no shorthand experience, which meant the more qualified girls were called away for more interesting tasks while I was left to organize and file and copy out in painful longhand. The sun was setting by the time I closed the last drawer and turned off my lamp. It would be dark when I stepped off the trolley in Ocean View.

I gave a final glance at the clock and groaned.

Blanche was going to kill me.

The three of us were supposed to attend a Red Cross dance at the Ocean View Hotel tonight. We'd been planning it for ages, and now here I was slopping into the cottage, bleary-eyed and ink-stained, with personnel files dancing before my eyes.

"Finally." Dressed in naught but a chemise and petticoat, Blanche glanced up from her seat on the sofa, needle poised, sewing basket at her feet. "We thought you'd never get here."

"Sorry." I pulled off my hat and gloves and hung my jacket up in the closet. Already the cottage wrapped around me like a hug, relaxing my tense shoulders and unkinking the knot in my back. I loved coming up the street, seeing the lamp in the window, smelling Blanche's April Violets perfume, and hearing Marjory's off-key singing. Without trying, I'd made a home here. "There's a staff meeting tomorrow that I had to prepare for and then there was a late request from the nurses in the surgical department for patient records which had already been archived, and then—"

"I don't need a list, just go get ready or we'll be late."

"Is Marjory upstairs?"

"She got here a few minutes ago. Baseball practice ran over. She's washing up now. Ouch!" Blanche sucked at her pricked thumb, rearranging the fabric over her knee.

"New dress?" I asked, rummaging in the kitchen for something to tide me over. There would be a cold buffet at the dance, but I hadn't eaten anything since breakfast, and my head was woozy from hunger.

"Letting out an old one." She licked and rethreaded her needle. "I blame Marjory and that baking-mad beau of hers. This is the second time in a month I've had to let my waists out."

"They say the way to a man's heart is through his stomach. I expect Ernst is hoping the same holds true for the female of the species."

"Well, I don't know about Marjory, but my delight is quickly souring. Why couldn't she have turned the head of a grocer or maybe a druggist? Someone useful."

Blanche might be grumpy over her expanding waistline, but I remained delighted, especially when there were chocolate ginger cookies on offer. "He seems pretty darn useful to me," I said, taking a handful with me upstairs.

As I topped the steps, I paused, a hand upon the banister. Had I left my bedroom door ajar? I pushed the door wider, blinking away a vision of Father rooting through my things, searching out any transgression, any hint of wickedness. I'd learned over the years to be careful, to hide away anything I valued. A habit I had yet to break, which made Marjory's presence on the floor, kneeling amid the scattered contents of my tin, all the more surprising.

"Viv, I can explain," she babbled. "I was looking for a pair of stockings. Mine have a ladder all the way to the knee. Only when I pulled the stockings out, they snagged on the lid and the whole thing fell on the floor and then everything went everywhere. I really am so, so, sorry."

"It's all right. It's fine. You didn't do any harm." Voice brittle, hands trembling, I gathered up my treasures. The aster had lost two of its precious petals. My mother's brooch was caught on the rug. The beaded bracelet was under my bed. And my photograph—Tom's photograph—was clutched in Marjory's hand.

"He's very handsome," she commented with a sidelong apologetic look. "What's his name?"

"Tom," I said through a throat closing around a lump as big as one of Marjory's baseballs.

"Is he in France?"

I snatched the photograph away. "I don't know where he is."

"Marjory!" Blanche called from downstairs. "I repaired the seam on your lilac silk and removed that ruffle that made you look like a cabbage leaf. Come try it on."

Marjory hovered in the door for a moment, her features still troubled with guilt. "I really am sorry, Viv."

"It's all right. I don't mind you borrowing a pair of my stockings."

"I meant about your young man."

Alone, I sat on the edge of my bed, my finger running along the smooth edge of the tin. Marjory was right. Tom *was* handsome;

dark hair and dark eyes in a narrow face of cheekbones and jaw-line. Good breeding obvious in his rangy loose-limbed frame, his careless smile, the jaunty way he posed for the camera.

He'd presented the photograph to me just before he'd stepped aboard the train and told me not to forget him—as if I ever could. He promised he'd come back as soon as his training was over. That we'd be together. That he'd take me away from my life with Father.

I didn't really believe him. The Westons were a well-to-do family with plans for their only son that didn't include the daughter of a Bible-thumping preacher from a poor parish. Besides, Father would never let me go. With Mother dead, he needed someone to keep house for him. He might sermonize about marriage and family, but I was free labor and securely under his thumb. I kept silent, accepting the photograph, kissing Tom one last time, feeling the warmth of him under my lips, taking his courage for my own.

That was nine months ago. Might as well have been a lifetime.

"Hurry up, Marjory. I don't know how you of all people managed to get a job as a courier. You're slow as molasses," Blanche called back over her shoulder. "If we get there too late, everyone's dance card will be filled and we'll be trapped with the foot-stompers, the pinchers, and the hurlers."

"It's *because* I'm a courier that I'm slow as molasses. You try spending all your days on the streets in a blur of bicycle tires. It's nice to slow down now and again." Marjory dawdled, admiring every passing woman's ensemble as we made our way up Virginia Avenue toward the hotel.

"At least you get to see something besides plug holes and wires," Blanche groused. "I wouldn't know if the world ended, squirreled away without so much as a window."

"I'll never understand how you ended up a switchboard operator. I mean you could have had a cushy job trailing after a Washington, DC admiral or something. Going to parties and dinners and balls with all those luscious officers."

"Maybe I wanted to do something more than eat, drink, and smile my way through this war."

"You got your wish," Marjory replied with a cheeky wink as she craned her neck at a couple stepping out of a nearby taxicab. "Did you see that woman's gown? She could poke someone's eye out with all that falderal."

Since Marjory would have worn baseball knickers or a sturdy pair of denim overalls every day if she could, her criticisms were a bit of the pot calling the kettle black. But what she lacked in womanly elegance, she made up for in confidence. I envied her that charisma that drew people to her like flies to honey.

"A woman should understand the occasion and dress appropriately," Blanche replied with a catty swish of her skirt.

"Who knew we were living with our own Edith Ordway?" Marjory joked.

"Despite the current limitations on my attire, I refuse to lower my fashion standards." The cool tone in Blanche's voice was betrayed by the droll smile hovering in the crinkle of her eyes and the curve of her mouth.

"I just like wearing something besides my uniform for a change," I said, loving the soft swish of my borrowed sky blue silk. While we weren't required to wear our uniforms off duty, Lieutenant Dumfries had a strict policy for his section that required prior approval for any changes to the uniform regulations.

"Going out of uniform is permitted only when hunting or fishing," he stated when I first approached him with my request. "But I suppose there will be boys there, so you'll undoubtedly be fishing."

He chuckled at his own joke, and I quickly left his office before he could change his mind.

For the dance, we had replaced our serviceable blue serge for silk, poplin, and lace. Washed and styled our hair. Pinched our cheeks until they ached. And headed up the road, holding our long skirts high to keep them out of the dust.

With the warmer weather, Ocean View's attractions opened to welcome a new season's guests. The hotel dazzled like a fairy-tale castle as if now that the winter's restrictions on lights had finally been lifted, the management meant to make up for lost time. Diners ate the catch of the day on the veranda while the strains of an orchestra could be heard above the din of the nearby amusement park. The carousel's organ played a raucous rendition of "Mary Had a Little Lamb," and colored lanterns adorned the rooftops of carnival booths, holidaymakers wandering wide-eyed among the shooting galleries and painted stalls.

"Let's skip the dance," Marjory suggested, tugging on my arm as she eyed a group of soldiers elbowing and shouting their way up the promenade. "I heard from a chap at the training station, they have a booth where you can win a strand of real Oriental pearls. All you need to do is shoot a bull's eye."

"Maybe Ernst would win them for you." Blanche slid her a sidelong look.

"I can win them myself, thank you very much." Marjory stuck out her tongue. "Come on. What do you say?"

"We got ourselves all dressed up," Blanche said, taking charge. "I'm not wasting all my hard work to be ogled by a horde of locals with nothing better to do with their evening than ride the coaster while they sneak illegal gin from a paper bag."

It was easier to agree with Blanche than to argue, so Marjory and I followed, with one last wistful look at the bright lights of the amusements, before we crossed the street to the hotel where young men in Navy dress blues poured up the steps to avail themselves of Norfolk's hospitality.

"Does Ernst ever worry you'll fall madly in love with a dashing officer and he'll have no one to bake for?" Blanche teased as a young ensign eyed Marjory with an appreciative smile and a tip of his hat.

"You've got cheek. At least Gus isn't following me around like a puppy on a string," Marjory shot back, answering tease for tease. "Or maybe I should say a fish on a line."

Blanche waved her off with a careless smile. "Gus is sweet, but he and I have been friends for too long. It would be like stepping out with my brother, God forbid."

"Just as well. I doubt your parents would approve of a grocery boy for a son-in-law."

"Probably not, but it would be fun making their heads explode," Blanche said, mischief dancing in her blue eyes. "How about you, Viv? Found yourself a handsome surgeon yet?"

"Me?" My stomach tightened.

"Viv's far too loyal to fall for some sly charmer's line. Isn't that right?" Marjory replied stoutly, linking her arm with mine. I appreciated her attempt to defend me against Blanche's ribbing, if not the execution.

"*Loyal*?" Blanche's gaze instantly narrowed with curiosity.

"Let's go. We'll be late." I grabbed Blanche's arm, and together the three of us sauntered up the hotel steps, sweeping all before us.

I'd not had proper friends for so long, I'd forgotten how nice it felt. I wanted so much to lean into that feeling, but letting them in came with a risk. A risk I wasn't yet willing to take.

WE SHED OUR wraps and stepped into the crushed confines of the hotel ballroom to a buzz of conversation underpinning the orchestra's efforts at a Strauss waltz. A woman with graying hair puffed into a cottage loaf style reminiscent of the last century handed us our dance cards with a smile and an admonition to mingle with our gallant brave boys—wallflowers need not apply.

Blanche found a partner almost immediately. A sailor with a cinematic jawline whisked her off for a two-step, her skirt belling around her while he guided her with a sure hand. Marjory eyed the melee, rocking on the balls of her feet, humming under her breath. I eyed the buffet at the far end of the room with a ravenous eye and wondered how soon I could make my way over without looking desperate.

"Ooh, there's Estelle. I was hoping she'd come." Marjory waved to a young woman across the room as if she was backing up a supply truck before ducking into the crowd, my last sight of her the back of her lavender flounce bouncing in time to the music. I was alone. And, chocolate ginger cookies aside, I was hungry.

I sidled along the perimeter of the room, shuttling from shadow to shadow as I made my way toward the food—not an easy feat under the phalanx of electric chandeliers.

"May I have this dance?" I jumped, nearly dropping a cucumber sandwich down my bodice as a young man with the red Geneva cross and single chevron of the hospital corps approached. He gave a small continental bow, the twinkle in his gray eyes and the curve to his lips turning the gallantry into the act of a mischievous little boy.

I glanced around me in panic, hoping for someone . . . anyone . . . to save me, but Blanche was flirting by the punch bowl and Marjory had finagled her way into a group by the doors to the veranda, heads together laughing. "You don't want to dance with me. Honest. I'm a terrible dancer. Two left feet and all that."

His smile widened, a dimple winking at the edge of his mouth. "You won't put me off that easily. Come on. We can be terrible together."

Cornered and unable to come up with another excuse on short notice, I placed my hand in his and was led onto the floor.

"The name's Goode, by the way," my escort said, flashing another smile. "Russell Goode. I'm a pharmacist's mate on the hospital ship *Mercy*."

"I'm yeoman third class Weston, but you can call me Viv."

"Wow. A real Navy girl. I sure do admire you bunch. I have a few sisters who'd make cracking good sailors," Russell shouted over the orchestra as they slid into a new number.

Father hadn't approved of the modern ragtime and two-steps that were all the rage, so I'd never learned them, but Russell, despite his claim, was far from terrible. He guided me carefully, and once I got over counting in my head, I found it rather exciting. By the time the music ended, I was giddy and flushed with heat, my fear of humiliation fading as my skill increased.

Russell brought me a lemonade and bowed over my hand. "Thanks for the dance, Viv. I hope you'll save a waltz on that card for me." He gave me a final wink before being swallowed back into the crowd. And as I stood catching my breath, I realized I was no longer starving or frightened or worried about what others thought of my dance skills or my awkward conversation. I was actually having fun.

An hour later, Blanche and I stood out on the veranda letting the breeze cool our cheeks and our blistered feet rest. I'd danced with a private from New Bedford, a corporal from Baltimore, and twice more with Russell, while Blanche had been at the center of a crowd of young officers most of the evening. She pulled a cigarette from her bag and lit it, exhaling on a long slow breath. "God, I needed that."

She offered me one, but I declined with a wrinkle of my nose. One new vice per night was my limit.

"There you two are. I've been looking everywhere." Marjory reappeared with a pair of naval officers in tow. "Ensigns Neal and Hooper," she said by way of introduction. "They're here awaiting repairs to their destroyer. Boys, this is Viv Weston and Blanche Lawrence."

Blanche shot Marjory a pained look even as she stubbed out her cigarette and graciously extended a hand, her breeding taking over. "How do you do?"

"Are you girls from Norfolk?" Hooper asked, running a finger along his thin pale mustache.

"We're stationed here," Blanche replied. "I'm originally from Washington, DC. Viv's a Richmond girl."

Ensign Neal turned his friendly gaze my direction. "You're from Richmond? Whereabouts? I know the city pretty well."

I silently cursed Blanche for her big mouth and my own stupidity. Why hadn't I chosen some random dot on a map that wouldn't give me away? "Ginter Park," I muttered.

"Really? My aunt has a house off Chamberlain." Consideration narrowed his eyes. "Ginter Park and your last name is Weston. You're not related to Tom Weston, are you?"

The name hit me like a slap. I might even have cringed. "Um . . . yes . . . I mean, he's a cousin. A very distant cousin. We aren't close."

"Did you say his name was Tom?" Marjory asked, her face wearing a puzzled frown. "That's a coincidence. Didn't you say—"

"I think I need a glass of punch." I practically plowed over anyone unlucky enough to be in my way as I escaped inside, ignoring Neal's curious look and Blanche's shrug of confusion.

That should have been the end of it, but no matter how I tried to put it out of my mind, Ensign Neal's innocent question soured the night. My nerves jumped, my stomach an icy swirl of anxiety. My earlier confidence waned, leaving me increasingly out of step and awkwardly fumbling. After crushing the feet of a baby-faced sailor from Pittsburgh, I gave up even pretending my earlier enjoyment.

I slid out of the ballroom, returning to the relative quiet of the veranda, surprised to find Blanche still there.

"Are you feeling all right?" she said as I sank onto a nearby bench. "You look a little off-color. Did some man get fresh? I knew it. A group of them were passing a bottle around out the side when they thought no one was looking. Half the crowd here is probably tipsy."

"What? No. I'm just tired. I think I'll head home." She eyed me with puzzled concern, and I braced for what she might say, what she might ask.

"All right, but Viv . . . about what Marjory said earlier . . ." Her voice trailed off. Worry pinched at her features and clouded her blue eyes.

"Don't, Blanche," I said. "Please."

"All right," she said, placing a hand over mine. "I won't pry. We all have our secrets, don't we?"

I left her sitting alone on the bench, but I knew this wasn't the end of it. Her questions remained. Questions I was not prepared to answer. Questions for which I had no answer.

CHAPTER 7

VIV

Ensign Neals' questions set my raw nerves jangling. I ran through our conversation searching for any sign that I might have slipped up or given something away. Would he check on my story? Would he write to the Westons asking after a cousin named Viv?

During the day it was easy enough to push aside my worries. The hospital's female yeomen had been drilling for weeks in preparation for a bond parade in nearby Hampton as part of President Wilson's national Liberty Day proclamation. All over the country, there would be bond rallies and patriotic exhibitions marking the anniversary of our entrance into the war and demonstrating the nation's continued commitment to beating the Kaiser. The yeomanettes were to be part of the celebration, showing off our military precision to a curious public. It wouldn't be the first time. We were often requested at such events, but this would be our largest crowd by far, and we were all nervous and excited to participate.

Up and down the packed earth of the parade ground, we marched. Dust swirled around our blistered feet, the sun burned our noses and the backs of our necks, all while the CPO shouted and threatened us into proficiency.

But at night, lying in bed with no distractions, my fear of discovery came alive like a monster in the dark, and panic froze me awake until the sky turned gray then pink then gold with dawn.

Dark circles ringed my bleary eyes, my brain muzzy with exhaustion, but as time passed and no policeman knocked on our door, I started to relax. I'd gotten away with it—for now.

I woke the morning of the parade without the creeping dread hanging on me like an anchor, though nerves of a different sort buzzed in my stomach as I dressed and raced to catch the ferry.

We gathered alongside dozens of floats, cars carrying local dignitaries, Boy Scouts, fire companies, and bands from every high school and military camp within fifty miles. The yeomanettes were to take up position between a company of infantry from Camp Hill and a battery of coast artillerymen. A band from one of the Army camps started things off with a raucous "The Stars and Stripes Forever" while the National Soldiers Home Band brought up the rear with "The Liberty Bell" march interspersed with banners and placards and flags urging the purchase of war bonds.

With a flurry of snare drums, we moved into line. They'd decided not to give us guns or sabers—a disappointment to more than a few of our more zealous recruits. Instead, we'd each been assigned a pole with a small American flag at the end that we would shoulder and present as we passed a reviewing stand of dignitaries. I tried setting myself between Bushby and Lester, two tall, sturdy girls I hoped would provide me some protection from the crowds already lining the route. Instead, Quarles placed me on the end of the square with a threat of painful retribution should I embarrass us in any way.

An officer took command, his voice carrying over the noise, and we hustled and shifted into position. The music made keeping the rhythm easy as, eyes forward, we quick-timed it. The weeks of practice paid off. Our button shoes slapped the pavement, our arms swung in unison. Our flags fluttered from the end of our poles.

I tensed as the turn approached. "Right, march!"

My brain went blank. Did I pivot heel first or toe first? Should I slow down? I slid my eyes toward Quarles, who slid her eyes right back. "Right, march," she hissed from the corner of her mouth. "Now."

I did more or less as I was told, and the square made its ponderous way around the corner still in proper military lines. The crowds were thicker here. Men and women lining the route, waving their own paper flags, children on shoulders, dogs on leashes. A boy tried to ride his bicycle between us and was quickly collared by a policeman. My nerves slowly unwound. I lifted my chin higher and stepped out proudly. We made the second turn. The band's drummers matched my heart, which matched my step. Synchronized. A unit.

Another turn completed without error. I would have grinned if I didn't think Quarles would strike me dead. The reviewing stand was near. An enormous stage swallowed in red, white, and blue bunting. Out of the corner of my eye, I caught glimpses of women in spring muslins and men in funereal cutaways and top hats interspersed with military dignitaries glittering with chest medals.

"Eyes, right!"

As one, we looked toward the stage as our parade leader saluted. Eyes unwavering, faces wiped of all but firm determination. We would show them we weren't silly women playing dress-up, but essential participants in the war, as good as—if not better than—any man who served alongside us. They'd have to take us seriously. Have to finally admit we belonged.

Movement at the edge of the crowd caught my attention. A man half in shadow, just inside a doorway. Thick neck. Jowly features. A scouring gaze. My mouth turned to dust. My lungs burned as I fought to breathe. If I could have burrowed into the cement, I would have. But Quarles was beside me, her stare drilling into my back. I had only another few blocks to go. As quickly as he appeared, the man was gone, lost in the swirling laughing shouting holiday crowds. Was it him? Impossible. He was dead and buried a hundred miles away in Richmond. I'd seen the spreading pool of blood, heard the sickening crunch of bone. He'd sprawled at my feet like a puppet with its strings cut, the stove's ash can still gripped in my hand.

Maybe I was going mad or maybe I'd merely seen someone who resembled him. In the uncertain light, it was impossible to tell. But the fear grabbed me by the throat until I could barely breathe. I don't know how I made it to the fairgrounds where the parade broke up, but somehow my legs moved, my heart beat, and I smiled and spoke without giving my panic away. Someone collected my flag. Someone else invited me to stay and watch the rest of the day's events. I declined every invitation, sick and dizzy with tremors I fought to hide. Like a hunted animal, I would go to ground until the danger passed and it was safe to emerge.

I started up the street, hoping to skirt the throng still milling along the parade route. From there, I could find a way down to the ferry landing.

"Weston!" Quarles's voice rang like a gong in my pounding head.

My hand rubbed at a seam on my jacket as a way to distract me from the onrush of nausea and cold sweats gripping me. Whatever Quarles planned to say was lost as soon as I turned. Her features softened from their usual look of grim disapproval. "You look knackered. Go home. Get some rest. We have a busy day tomorrow and I don't want to get a call from sick bay."

I didn't argue.

I didn't recall the trip home, only that it seemed to last forever, every boarding passenger caused my heart to jump and sweat to break out across my back. It couldn't have been him. It must have been a stranger—similar build, similar features. But could I take that chance?

I'd never been so happy to see the little cottage, the pot of rosemary on the porch, the ugly cushions on the painted metal glider.

I let myself in, flipping the dead bolt behind me, pressing my back against the door before I drew my first deep breath since fleeing Quarles at the fairgrounds.

I'd been a fool to think I'd be safe here, that the Navy would shield me. The police would find me sooner or later. They wouldn't give up—not for a crime like murder.

At home, I tried losing myself in busywork. I ironed two skirts and darned my stockings. I washed out my shirtwaists and pegged them to dry on the porch. I polished my shoes. I polished Blanche's and Marjory's shoes. I polished everything that needed polishing. All while telling myself I'd been mistaken, that this afternoon's glimpse of a ghost was my mind playing tricks.

He was dead. Dead and out of my life forever. The crunch of bone and the ringing thwack of the ash can were burned into my memory. He was very very dead.

And yet . . .

I could swear I'd seen him in that doorway. That he'd survived the blow and followed me here from Richmond. That I wasn't as safe as I thought I was.

At last, when everything I owned had either been washed, folded, polished, or mended, I surrendered to the tug of my old life, dropping onto my bed with my tin treasure box open in my lap.

The jet brooch. The bead bracelet. The purple aster. The photo of Tom.

A physical timeline from the child I'd been to the woman I was.

The tap at my door came as I knew it would sooner or later, but it wasn't Blanche. A worried Marjory glanced around the room, her gaze falling on the tin open on my bed. "I knew it."

"Knew what?"

"I knew there was a reason you were acting strange. Blanche told me I was imagining things, but you've never voluntarily polished shoes in your life. You're pining after that Tom fella, aren't you? The one in your photograph." She folded her arms over her chest with a scowl she usually reserved for opposing pitchers and six-foot centers. "Well good riddance, I say. You'll find one ten times better than him. How hard could it be? Norfolk's crawling with single men. Ernst has a friend—"

"No! That is . . ." I swallowed my words. If Marjory believed it was Tom that had me hiding away, all the better. "It wasn't really his fault it didn't work out. My father didn't approve."

She rolled her eyes. "Heaven save us from overprotective parents."

"Are your parents overprotective?"

"Well, no. But my brothers are. Growing up, they made my life a living hell." She laughed. "Do you have brothers, Viv?"

I shook my head.

"Well, I have four of them. Fellas took one look and decided it wasn't worth risking a black eye or a bloody nose from the Kunwald boys just to call on me. Not that I had them beating down the door. Still, there was one chap I sorta liked. He took me to a band concert and bought me an ice cream. Things were going pretty well then one night down by the river he tried to get fresh and that was the end of that."

"Your brothers beat him up?"

"Nah, it was me that punched his lights out. But later when my brothers found out—hoo golly."

"You're lucky to have family that loves you as much as that."

"I'm sure your father *meant* well."

"I'm not. After my mother died, I was more his housekeeper than I was his daughter. It wasn't until I joined the Navy and met you and Blanche that I felt what it was like to be part of a real family, to have a real home." I chewed my lip, looking out at the sky, down at the treasures in my lap, up at Marjory. "I don't want to lose that."

"Who says you'll lose it?" Her sensible tone and down-to-business attitude made my worries seem overblown. "You're stuck with us whether you like it or not. The three musketeers, you know?" She took my hands as if to drag me up off the bed. "Come join us for the fireworks. Gus has promised to pay for a round of root beer floats, and you know what a tightwad he is."

"Thanks, but I think I'm going to stay in tonight. Tell Gus he'll owe me one."

"Ok, but if you change your mind . . ."

I wanted so much to tell her everything. To draw on Blanche's boldness and Marjory's strength when my own courage faltered and the lengthening shadows conjured monsters. "I need to tell . . ." As if sensing my thoughts, she didn't move or speak. The silence widened. "There's something I have to say . . ."

"Marjory Kunwald!" Blanche bellowed up the stairs. "Did you take my last clean shirtwaist? I've warned you about filching my clothes."

The moment snapped with an almost audible twang, and I chickened out, swallowing down my confession. "I only wondered what your brothers did when they found out about that boy."

Her cheeks dimpled in a smile. "The meat-headed idiots claimed that I only had to say the word and they'd beat him to a bloody pulp." She started to leave, but with her hand on the knob, she turned back, a quiet confidence in her eyes that squeezed at my aching chest. "You're right, Viv. We *are* family now, and you only ever have to say the word."

MARJORY AND BLANCHE departed for the promenade with Gus to watch the evening's Liberty Day fireworks while I stayed behind, jumping at every window-rattling cannon shot as the night sky over the bay flashed pink then yellow then blue, kicking myself for not coming clean when I had the chance.

Sinking back onto my bed, I opened the tin again, fingering each item as if they might solve the riddle of what went wrong in my life that left me hiding and on the run.

Every good gift and every perfect gift is from above.

Or so the Bible told us.

Yet these earthly gifts meant more to me than any heavenly bounty.

The brooch was all I had left of my mother. She'd been a gentle soul, no match for Father's violent bullying. When she died in a fall down our cellar stairs, the neighbors were quick to blame it on a loose tread or a heel caught in her skirt hem—an unfortunate accident. Father disposed of her things almost before she was cold in her grave, refusing to speak of her, erasing her as if she'd never been, and any suspicions I'd harbored faded along with her face and the sound of her voice.

The bracelet was my only memento of a bond closer than friend-ship, closer than family. I gripped the pink glass beads until my palm carried the imprint, my heart hollow with a loss I still felt as keenly as I had when I was fourteen and stood at her graveside. I set these aside to roll the aster's dried stem between my fingers, conjuring the memory of a flower crown and a stolen kiss in the Westons' garden. Tom had been thirteen. I'd been eleven. The only secret I'd ever kept from my best friend. I tucked it carefully back into the tin and took up the photo of Tom. He stood under an oak in Richmond's Byrd Park, his Air Corps uniform crisp and new, his crooked smile making my heart do a little flip.

I had hidden the tin under a floorboard at the back of my clothes cupboard. It, and a few coins from Father's change purse, was all I dared take with me when I fled the house that night. The only thing left to remind me of who I really was—not confident, clever, and beloved daughter Vivian Weston at all. Just plain-old, nothing-special me.

Father had told me that often enough, drilled it into me with every scolding over sloppy work and every blow for disobedience. It was a face he hid from the world. To his congregation, he was a bastion of good Christian values. Practical and intelligent, a learned man who could quote scripture at the drop of a hat. Loved and respected for his charity work, his committee involvement. They didn't know him like I did. They never saw his black moods or felt the flat of his hand when he was angry or drunk.

A fool spurns a parent's discipline . . .

Had I been a fool to go against Father's rules when I walked out with Tom?

No. Tom hadn't been the mistake. The error had been in thinking I could keep such a secret. That I'd not be found out and made to pay the price.

. . . But whoever heeds correction shows prudence.

All fine and good until the correction came in the form of a leather belt, the buckle gashing my leg, the bricks of the kitchen floor cold against my bruised back, the leg of the old stove jammed into my thigh as he raised his fist to strike me again. "I'll deal with you same as I dealt with your stupid bitch of a mother."

The words had struck a spark inside me. Whatever doubts I'd buried crashed through years of silence and intimidation. I'd grabbed the first thing that came to hand with no thought other than to stop him before he killed me—as he must have killed her. His eyes narrowed to red slits, his face white and stretched until I no longer recognized him as my father, only as a devil who would brutalize me tonight and tomorrow meet the world with a self-satisfied smile and the oiled words of a saint.

The ash can was empty, but it was still heavy, the cast-iron edge carrying a hammer's crushing power. And I lashed out in fear and fury and desperation.

He'd dropped like a sack to the bricks and lay there beside me, the blood spreading out to soak my skirts, saturate my hair.

He was dead. I knew he was dead.

And I'd killed him.

I'd done what my mother couldn't.

The Bible was pretty clear about murder. *Thou shalt not* and all that.

There wasn't much room for denials and defenses.

So I ran.

But today, for scarcely a moment, in the gloom of that doorway, I'd seen him—alive and breathing.

Terrifying as his survival might be for my future, it also meant that maybe I wasn't a killer after all. Maybe the guilt I carried could finally be laid aside. Did I want to know? Did I need to know?

The clock on the downstairs mantel chimed ten. Blanche and Marjory would be back soon, filling the cottage with laughter and voices, leaving no room for my doubts. I had to know now before they returned to crowd my worries back down into a quiet festering corner.

THE POOL HALL two streets over had a working telephone. The owner was an ex-marine, his clientele on the seedier side, but I hoped my uniform would afford me some protection from any unwanted attention. The place was busy. A gramophone on the counter scratched out a dance tune that nobody could hear over the percussive smack and click of balls and clamor of conversation.

A waitress pointed me to the alcove at the back where the telephone sat on a metal stand. I picked it up carefully, the sleek black column of the candlestick damp under my sweaty grip.

"Richmond 5925A, please," I shouted at the long-distance operator then waited with a knot in my stomach while she connected me. My hand slid up and down the cord. I could hang up now. I could walk away and pretend I'd not seen those bullish shoulders, that long jaw.

"Connecting you now," said the tinny crackle of a voice at the other end.

A series of clicks and I waited, picturing the phone in Father's study, the way it crouched on his desk amid the books and papers, its ring startling the drab solemnity of our house with news of births, deaths, and illness.

A harbinger of drastic upheaval—as it would be now.

"Mount Olive Church. Reverend Prothero speaking."

I nearly yanked the cord from the wall in my haste and shock to hang up. The room tipped then righted itself as I took hold of my shattered nerves.

"Everything all right, miss?"

So focused on the voice at the other end of the line, I'd not heard the waitress approach. "You look as if you've seen a ghost."

Heard one, maybe.

"Yes, thank you," I managed to stammer. "It was a crossed wire. The operator hung up."

She seemed to accept my explanation as I handed over my nickel and stumbled out the door. It hadn't been him at the parade today. All the way back to the cottage, my brain crackled and buzzed like that ill-connected telephone wire. I was innocent. I wasn't a murderer. I drew in my first easy breath in months. Felt a weight I'd not known I carried lift from my chest. I walked home light as air, a bubble of relief making my insides rise. It wasn't until I stepped onto the cottage's front porch into the pool of light cast from a lamp left burning in the window that the weight crashed back, and I nearly sank down onto the floorboards with a small cry of despair, my knees like water.

What was I thinking? He'd all but confessed to killing my mother. He'd never let me go. Not if he saw me as a threat. Someone who needed shutting up.

All this time, it wasn't the police I needed to fear.

It was my father.

CHAPTER 8

PEGGY

1968

Peggy had avoided Blanche's bedroom until today. Not out of any superstition or consideration for the dead; it was self-preservation, pure and simple. One more room that was falling down, falling in, falling apart was one more than she could handle. But this morning, she'd opened her eyes to find that gold button staring at her from the bedside table and the strange conversation with Symonds lurking at the back of her brain.

Chaz used to say she collected odd people. The homeless man who hung in the doorway by the bus station wishing her good morning on her way to work, the elderly Polish lady in the up-stairs apartment who brought them pierogis whenever she made a batch, the pimple-faced checker at the market who called her Mrs. Whitby and insisted on slipping extra coupons into her bag. Chaz would laugh when he said this, as if there was some defect in Peggy's personality that connected her to these people. Maybe he was right. It had drawn Chaz to her, after all, and he turned out to be the oddest of them all.

But Symonds wasn't just odd. He was the only person who might be able to tell Peggy more about her great-aunt. About why she'd left Peggy her cottage. Maybe if she understood that, everything else would make sense. Maybe her life would shift back into focus. She would be able to see the road ahead, which for the last six months felt shrouded in fog.

Unfortunately, he didn't seem inclined to share.

If she was going to find answers to her questions, she'd have to find them without his help, and Blanche's bedroom was as good a place to start as any.

She'd not come in here since the day she arrived, but now she threw open the door and pushed back the curtains on their rings. Loudly and briskly as if noise and light might banish any lingering spirits.

The view was lovely, a wide swath of beach, only now filling up with the morning's sunbathers and beachcombers. Light fell in gold squares over the painted floorboards and across an old faded Persian carpet. A big iron bedstead stood in a corner, the mattresses piled high; an old-fashioned quilt of colorful squares smoothed taut, and heaped at the head with a bank of pillows. There was a highboy and a long-skirted dressing table. Under a window sat a battered armchair and a low bookshelf. Other than a layer of dust, it looked as if Blanche might return at any moment.

Peggy lifted the latch on the closet door and was nearly brained by an avalanche of old shoeboxes. She set these aside to rummage through the jammed rack of clothes, which turned out to be a fashion parade of the last half century. Shirtwaists and ankle-length skirts, pencil lines and shoulder pads, cocktail dresses, cardigans, blouses, trousers. But there, at the very back, was a dark blue jacket bearing two chevrons encircling what looked like a pair of crossed feathers on the sleeve. A bit worn, a bit faded, but clean and neatly repaired with a row of buttons up the front perfectly matching the one she found yesterday. Hung beside it was a jacket of yellowed white with the same insignia. Another hanger produced two navy blue skirts and three white ones.

Peggy moved to the dressing table where dusty bottles of perfume sat on a silver tray scattered with long deadly hair pins, pink plastic rollers, and loose change. She spritzed the air, inhaling a soft, old-fashioned scent of violets. It reminded her of her mother. Peggy spritzed it again, this time on her wrist, rubbing it into her skin where she could enjoy the comforting familiarity.

A pearl necklace hung from the mirror. A tarnished silver frame held a sepia-toned photo of three young women standing shoulder to shoulder. Two of them wore identical dark uniform jackets and long skirts, neckerchiefs, and brimmed hats. They might have been school uniforms if not for the patches and chevrons on their sleeves, the gold buttons at cuff and breast. On the left, a dark-haired, round-faced girl with dimples and a tilt to her head that gave her an impish look. The girl on the right reminded Peggy of the model Twiggy: slender with an almost boyish figure, enormous eyes, and a full mouth. She looked as if a strong wind could blow her away if not for the firm grip of the girl who stood in the center of the frame.

Peggy recognized that expression just as she recognized the curve of the girl's jaw, the long narrow nose, the long-lashed shape of her eyes. She touched her own face, smoothed a hand over her own hair. Ghosts of similarities like a copy of a copy of a copy, faded and just out of focus, but there all the same. This had to be Blanche.

She wasn't dressed like the other two. Instead of a uniform, she wore a loose-fitting, short-sleeved middy blouse with a dark neckerchief and a wide Cracker Jack sailor collar. And she was hatless, her hair cut in a smart bob. She was also taller than the other two, standing chin up, chest out, shoulders back with an arm around each of them, challenge in her direct no-nonsense gaze. A striped

awning bellied out behind them, and there were circus flags along
a roofline to the right.

Was this the photo Viv mentioned in her postcard? The three of
them on the promenade?

She was interrupted by a knock at the front door. This time,
she'd no illusions or hope. Chaz was long gone. This was probably
Symonds with more misdirected mail or maybe a warning to be-
ware smarmy realtors with smarmier intentions.

Wrong again.

"Welcome to the neighborhood!" A young woman held out a
casserole dish. She had tiny, even features, sun-browned skin, and
a dazzling cheerleader smile. But it was her enormous belly that
drew Peggy's unwilling gaze. "I'm Suzanne from down the street."
She indicated the pretty blue house on the corner with a motion of
her stiff blonde bouffant.

"I'm Peggy."

"It's a pleasure, Peggy. Hope you like goulash." She pushed her
way, stomach first, into the cottage. "It's Ron's—that's my husband—
favorite. He says when he goes to heaven he's sure my goulash will
be on the menu." She put the casserole dish on the table, flinging
her dish towel over her shoulder as she gazed round. "Yikes. You got
your work cut out for you here."

Was she seven months? Eight? It was hard to tell. Her red-and-
white-checked blouse billowed out over her stomach. But she wore
that expectant glow, part excitement part exhaustion, that Peggy
remembered from her own pregnancy.

Suzanne noticed Peggy's stare. "I'm a house, right? My youngest
wants to know if I swallowed a beach ball."

"You have more?"

"Two. A girl and a boy. This will be lucky number three."

This woman didn't look old enough to drive much less have
three kids.

"Congratulations," Peggy mumbled, trying to breathe around the lead crushing her chest. "Thank you for the dinner, but I'm kind of in the middle of—"

"Demolition?" Suzanne teased before turning serious. "Now, don't you do a thing until you talk to me. I'm an absolute whiz at decorating. I subscribe to oodles of magazines and stalk the open houses all over Norfolk. Some of the color choices these days, phew!" Her Southern accent was thick as cream and her laugh was high like a bird's.

"I'm not sure about decorating. I don't even know if I'm staying yet."

"But you *have* to stay." She said it so emphatically, Peggy took a step back. "You know how many people would kill for a place right on the beach? It's gorgeous."

"My real estate agent said people don't want old places like this. They'd just knock it down."

"Are you kidding? My mom's a realtor in Texas. She could sell this place ten times over with her eyes shut. It might not be much to look at now, but it would be completely adorable if it was fixed up. Modern fixtures and new furniture. I saw this gorgeous photo spread in *Good Housekeeping* a few months back. I'll have to find it for you. It was all pinks and creams. Don't you let that realtor talk you into anything, you hear?" Her smile by now was practically blinding, her enthusiasm infectious. Maybe restoring the house *would* be therapeutic, more useful than basket weaving, cheaper than a psychiatrist. "Wow!" Suzanne was leaning over the kitchen sink, staring out the small window. "Is that a blanc double de coubert?"

"A blanc double what?" Peggy had lived so long shunning company, she was having a hard time keeping up with Suzanne's whirling conversation.

"The rose in your backyard. My parents have one. They planted it over our dog Toby's grave—white roses signify loss, you know."

Peggy didn't know, but she didn't have time to say so. Suzanne was in full spate.

"It would flower all summer with the most heavenly scent. I used to wrap the petals in cheesecloth and put them in my underwear drawer. Mom was always finding them and throwing them away." She must have noticed Peggy's blank stare because her eyes filled with embarrassed laughter. "Sorry. Don't mind me. Ron says my mouth runs at the speed of sound."

"I don't mind. It's been a little too quiet the past few days."

"Really?" Suzanne beamed. "You *are* a doll." She gave one last glance to the rosebush then at the cottage, not with a hard dollars-and-cents assessment like Mr. Grace, more with a delighted curiosity as if expecting surprises around every corner. It made Peggy warm to her despite her uncertainty. "We're only renting our place, so I can't indulge, but I dream of the day when Ron retires from the Navy and we buy an enormous house that I can decorate any way I want with a backyard where the kids can have a swing set and run around, and I can plant flowers and know I'll still be there to see them bloom."

"It sounds like a nice dream." The kind Peggy had once had. The kind she and Chaz talked about in bed at night when the streetlights burned through the net curtains and Mr. and Mrs. Devender upstairs argued over whose turn it was to take out the trash.

"Well, it's going to stay that way for a while. Ron's shipping out in another month, and then who knows?" For the first time, that eternal sunshine flickered with doubt. "Are you down here scouting things out before the rest of the family arrives?" Something in Peggy's expression must have transmitted itself to her. The doubt became horror. "Oh my God, I just put my foot in it, didn't I? Is he . . . ? No. Don't tell me. It's none of my business. There goes that speed-of-sound mouth of mine again."

It suddenly occurred to Peggy that Suzanne assumed she was a war widow. "Oh no," she hurried to reassure her. "He's not dead. He's just not married to me anymore."

"Oh, thank God. If that's all."

Peggy caught herself smiling at Suzanne's obvious relief. "You're the first person who's treated my divorce as a good thing."

"Oh dear." Her hand fluttered to her collar. "I didn't mean it like that."

"It's all right. Maybe it *is* a good thing. Hard to tell when everyone's piling on the sympathy. It starts to crush you after a while. You forget what good feels like."

Suzanne left soon after, worried over Ron's continued supervision of the kids, but the next morning, Peggy opened her door to find a basket on the front step with a note.

A bottle of wine and a new friend to help you remember.

PEGGY SMOOTHED OUT the wrinkled flyer she'd retrieved from the trash can.

David Dyer.

The sketch below his name was good—like actual art school good. Had he drawn it himself or had someone done it for him? Did it matter? As long as he could assess the cottage and reassure her she wasn't about to have the ceiling fall on her head or the porch crumble into a pile of broken lumber, he could be Andy Warhol himself.

And no, this didn't have anything to do with Suzanne and her neighborly bottle of wine. Or . . . not completely. But it was easier to stay than uproot herself again. And where would she go anyway? She wouldn't run home with her tail between her legs to be coddled and pitied by her friends. Suzanne was right. She needed to remember what good felt like. And right now, for now, this seemed like the best place to do that. It didn't mean anything. She could just as easily change her mind again.

She dialed the number on the flyer, ignoring the jump of nerves in her stomach.

A woman picked up on the first ring. "Lena's Hair Salon."

"Sorry, wrong number." Peggy double-checked the flyer. The phone rang twice before it connected.

"Lena's Hair Salon, this is Lena," the woman repeated around the snap of gum. A chatter of conversation and hair dryers nearly drowned her out.

Peggy cleared her throat. "I'm trying to reach David Dyer. He gave me this number to call."

"Dave?" the woman said with a nauseating snap that reverberated across the wires. "Sure. Who should I tell him is calling?"

"Peggy Whitby—" She paused. "No, make that Peggy Lawrence." This was a new life without Chaz. Maybe if she took back her old name, she'd take back her old self: adventurous, brave, alive. "I need a quote on home repairs, and his flyer says his rates are amazingly reasonable."

"Right." Lena took the message and promised to pass it along, but Peggy hung up less than convinced.

Maybe she should have gone through the yellow pages to find a proper builder with a proper office and a proper receptionist, not gum-cracking Lena jotting notes down between appointments for set and curls and permanent waves. Then again, could she afford someone like that? Probably not. She wasn't sure she could afford Mr. Dyer. Blanche's bequest had been generous but not boundless, and there was no telling what hidden horrors a builder might uncover. But she couldn't walk away and let Barry Grace and his pompadour have the sale. Not quite yet.

It was noon before Mr. Dyer arrived. Time enough for her to take two aspirin and a long hot shower. She fiddled with the taps and settled for lukewarm. She was just wrestling into a pair of clam-diggers and pulling her wet hair into a ponytail when he knocked.

"Decide you might need some help after all?" Still the same scruffy jeans and leather-vested tie-dye, the same stubbled jaw and piercing blue eyes that crinkled at the corners as if he spent a lot of time squinting into the sun . . . or laughing. Maybe both. His was an open, good-natured face.

"Something like that."

"Lena said you had kind of a frantic tone to your voice. Said you sounded just like a customer who's tried to dye their own hair and ended up frying it to a crisp."

"Lena needs to mind her own business."

"Have you ever known a hairdresser who did that? A nose for gossip goes along with the scissors and combs." He eyed the cottage before doing a slow tour of the whole perimeter. "What can I help you with?"

"Take your pick, Mr. Dyer."

"Please . . . it's David. *Mr. Dyer* makes me sound like an expert at actuarial tables. And I'll call you Peggy. I'm not really a last name sort of person. Seems a little formal and old-fashioned, don't you think? And if I'm going to be working here . . ."

"That's yet to be decided."

She was right. His eyes did crinkle when he smiled. "Suit yourself."

"I was told my best option was to tear the place down."

"Really? Who told you that? It needs some work, sure. But I wouldn't condemn it just yet."

"No? What would you do then?"

"I'd set her to rights. Give the old girl a face-lift. New roof. Shore up the porch. Check the plumbing and wiring. Repoint the chimney. New coat of paint. I imagine there's some interior work needs doing?"

"That's putting it lightly."

"Well, the good news is that I can definitely do what you need. The bad news . . ."

"It's going to cost me a fortune I don't have to do it."

"Maybe not a fortune, but . . ." He rubbed the back of his neck, his gaze considering as he eyed the house and the yard before turning back to her, jaw set as if he'd reached a decision. "Look, if you can't afford to pay me up front, maybe we can come to an arrangement."

"What sort of arrangement?" She didn't like where this was headed. Barry Grace was a smarmy tomcat she could easily put in his place. This man with his faded jeans, laughing eyes, and relaxed attitude might not be so easy to brush off.

He seemed to read her thoughts. A smile tipped his mouth. "I'm not hitting on you, if that's what you're worried about. I just need a place to park my camper. The cops don't like me parking at the public lot by the beach, and paying a garage somewhere is too pricey. Let me park it here, and, in exchange, I do whatever work around the place you need doing. You just pay for materials. Labor's on me."

It was a tempting offer, but . . . "What would Lena say to you living in my driveway?"

"I have no idea, but we can ask her if you want." He shoved his hands in his pockets and rocked back on his feet. "So, what do you say?"

Peggy heard the phone ring. It hadn't done that since she'd arrived. Not once. "Just a minute." She raced to pick it up. "Hello? Hello? Is someone there?"

There was only the buzz of a dial tone in response.

"Maybe they'll call you back." David stood in the front hall, holding her mail. She could feel his curiosity as he took in the dust, the clutter, the proof of her pathetic wreckage of a life. "The mailman told me to pass these along." He handed the pile over, a postcard with a photo of Richmond's Monument Row was on top. She snatched it from his hand and turned it over.

December 1918

Blanche,

I dreamt about you last night and woke clammy with sweat wondering whether you were safe. I scour the local papers, but of course there's no news from Norfolk in their pages so I can only pray and imagine you in your usual spot on the back porch looking out over the bay with your sewing basket beside you. I'd do anything to go back to that day and live it over. I'd do anything to make it right between us.

Viv

Make it right—Symonds had used that very same phrase. Blanche was trying to make things right when she left the cottage to Peggy. But what things?

She pictured the three girls in the old photo: arms entwined, smiles as they faced the camera. What had happened to Marjory? Why did Viv blame herself? And why wouldn't Blanche be safe? None of it made any sense, especially why she was getting back in touch now, fifty years later.

"Who's Blanche?" David leaned over her shoulder, a bracing smell of paint thinner and sawdust caught in the folds of his clothes.

Peggy shoved the card between the insurance brochure and the electric bill. "You want a place to park your camper van? If it means I get hot water and outlets that don't spark and a porch I can walk on without fearing for my life, you can park it in my drive from now until the end of time. Deal?"

He surprised her by stretching out a hand for her to shake. His palm was rough, the fingers strong and warm as they curved around hers. "Deal."

CHAPTER 9

VIV

1918

"W eston." Quarles stood over my desk, a puzzled frown behind her glasses. "You have orders to report for ship duty."

"Ma'am?" I said, confused. I'd been battling a rogue typewriter ribbon for a half hour and my fingers were stained purple, my stack of folders still dangerously high. She handed me the papers, which I presented to Dumfries that afternoon.

"You're in the Navy, Weston. Those are your orders. Carry them out."

Was it true? Could this finally be the ticket out of Norfolk I'd been looking for since I enlisted? Serving aboard a Navy vessel would present its own problems—German torpedoes and handsy sailors being one and two on my list. But whatever I faced floating out there in the Atlantic couldn't be half as bad as the threat that hung over me now.

"Aye, aye, sir!" I said grinning with excitement.

The Navy wanted a sailor? I'd be the best darn sailor they'd ever seen—male or female. I could do this. I had to do this.

Blanche thought it was hilarious and ribbed me about it all evening as I pressed my uniform and readied myself for the following day. Marjory demonstrated three different defensive maneuvers should my fellow sailors get fresh.

"Need a break?" She stood over me as I lay on the rug, winded after her wrestler's grapple. "You're looking a bit queer. Maybe you could get them to reconsider. I mean . . . ship duty? You? Are you sure they didn't make a mistake?"

"Are you saying I'm not up to it?" I asked, slightly insulted even as I fought to breathe through the scream in my aching muscles.

"I'm just saying I'd miss you."

I heaved myself off the rug and threw my arms around her, breathing in her smell of witch hazel and lemons. "Is this some sort of new defensive move?" she wheezed. "Because you're doing it all wrong."

"This is a hug, you ninny," I said, a lump in my throat. "I'll miss you too."

Bright and early the next morning, I accompanied Blanche to the naval operating base. Butterflies danced in the pit of my stomach as she straightened my tie and dusted imaginary lint from my shoulders. "Look them in the eye. Speak clearly and with confidence. And whatever you do, don't turn your back or bend down near any of the randy bastards. I had a black-and-blue backside after a month serving here."

"Then what happened?"

"I slugged the next sailor who got impudent. He was too ashamed at being bested by a girl to report me, but it stopped, and word spread that I was a crazy, man-hating bitch." I blushed hot, but Blanche merely smiled as she met my gaze with an encouraging one of her own. "A reputation can be an advantage now and then. Remember that."

If I thought the naval hospital was busy, I was overwhelmed by the size and chaos of the NOB. I skirted a busy road, supply trucks trundling by as I followed directions that took me past troop barracks, offices, staff quarters, and enormous warehouses. Recruits drilled on an enormous parade ground across from the administration buildings, the only holdovers from the old Jamestown Exposition's days. A power plant rose up on my right. Ahead, hangars and shop facilities for the new naval air base were being built alongside a launching pier. Overshadowing everything, long piers jutted out into the water where ships the size of city skyscrapers rocked calmly in enormous slips.

Finding the office and the officer I was to report to, I handed over my orders to the ensign on duty with a snappy salute and a hard stare.

He scanned the pages before handing them back to me with a snort of disgusted laughter. "This is a joke, right?"

"No, sir." I fought down the wobble in my voice. "I'm to report to the minesweeper *SS Guildenhall.*"

He shook his head. "Now I've heard everything. Women serving shipboard duty?" He left me standing while he made a phone call, his voice strained as he offered explanations then excuses then finally arguments. When he hung up, a satisfied smirk sank my earlier nervous optimism.

"As I thought. There's been an error. Women are not, nor will they ever be, assigned to combat ships. Period. End of story." He handed me back my orders. "You're to return to your previous posting."

I felt as if I'd been the victim of one of Marjory's more painful defensive maneuvers. Stomach-punched and left gasping for breath. It had been a wild hope, one I should have known was destined for failure. I tried not to show my disappointment or give in to the tears burning at the edges of my vision. I'd not give this officious popinjay the satisfaction.

"At least it means you get to stay here with us now," Marjory sympathized over dinner that night.

I smiled and agreed, but now I'd seen a glimmer of hope, I wasn't going to let a little thing like a clerical error get in my way. If I could be transferred once, I could be transferred again. And I knew just where I would finally be safe. Free as I could never be free here, no matter how I disguised myself.

Once the idea took hold, I couldn't shake it. In fact, it made more sense as I headed into work the next morning. I crossed the echoing quarter deck at the hospital with a new purpose to my step. Passing Chief Quarles's desk with a firm gaze, I headed straight for Dumfries' office.

He looked up at my knock, his gaze already disapproving before I'd opened my mouth. "Let me guess. The Navy took one look at you and came to its damn senses."

"They sent me back, sir. Apparently, there's no way to tell females from males on the personnel rolls. An oversight, I'm told, that will be remedied immediately."

Disdain flickered over his craggy face. "As it should be."

"That being said, sir," I barreled on while I still had the courage, "there's no restrictions on females being transferred overseas in a clerical and non-shipboard position, therefore I request a proper transfer—to France."

That caught him by surprise. He leaned forward, elbows on his desk as he glared at me over his steepled fingers. As the seconds passed, I fought the urge to shift from foot to foot or chew on my lip.

"You want to serve overseas."

"Yes, sir. I know there are female yeomen serving abroad. I'd like to join them."

"Most of those personnel were already living in London or Paris when the call went out. It's rare for one of you *girls* to be transferred there."

I ignored the snub. I knew he was looking to get a rise out of me. "But it *is* possible," I argued.

"If the yeoman in question has a specific skill or a personal connection who can pull some strings. Do you have either of these, Weston?"

My face fell. "No, sir."

I expected him to kick me out of his office with a bellow to get back to it or else. Instead, he leaned back, a look of encouragement rather than scorn on his face. "Your desire does you credit, but I need you here. What you lack in experience you make up for in grit, so put this idea out of your mind and focus on doing your best at your current posting."

"Maybe I could—"

"Dismissed, Weston."

I knew when I was beaten. "Aye, aye, sir."

I returned to my desk and the usual pile of daily reports. Later, I could hear Dumfries shouting into a telephone and smell the thick scent of his cigar smoke.

"I don't care how, damn it! Just do it!"

I couldn't agree more.

ALL DAY I conjured and discarded plan after plan, no nearer to coming up with a solution to Dumfries' refusal—or more importantly whether I should tell my friends the truth about who I was and what I'd done.

I'd been ruled by secrets for as long as I could remember, great parts of my life lived behind closed doors or in the long silence between the white lies. It was how I survived. How I held my head high despite the bruises on my arms, the marks on my back, the cutting ugly words that lived like spiders in my brain only coming out late at night to spread their doubt and self-loathing.

Only two people had been patient enough—stubborn enough—to gain my trust. One was dead and the other might as well have been.

Sharing secrets was dangerous.

Was I brave enough to be hurt again?

By the time I reached the Portsmouth ferry that night, I was tired, my nerves frayed by disappointment and weeks of holding my breath as I waited for the inevitable.

I couldn't show up at the cottage feeling like this. Blanche and Marjory would know something was wrong as soon as they saw me. Instead, I wandered Norfolk's city streets. Up Bank. Down Plume. Cutting north past City Hall. Back to Monticello. A stitch formed in my side. My legs itched in their wool stockings. When it started to rain, I ducked into a lunch counter, taking a table at the back, out of the way. The last diner had left their newspaper behind, the pages stained with spilled soup and thick pen marks circling help-wanted advertisements for salesmen. I pushed it aside to make room for the waitress to set down a cup of coffee when my gaze landed on a small announcement in a bottom corner. Barely a paragraph, but the words froze me to my seat.

Richmond pastor travels to Hampton Roads to speak Thursday evening at Elizabeth River Community Hall. Admission is free for the lecture and tea to follow.

No name. No reason for the skipping of my heart or the dread slithering cold into my knotted stomach. But leaving behind a nickel for my untouched cup of coffee, I fled the café, racing for the streetcar as if Father was chasing me down.

Maybe he was.

As I CLIMBED the front steps, Blanche was on the porch glider, feet tucked under her skirts, smoking a cigarette. Its red tip glowed bright as the fireflies dancing in the rosebushes and sparkling in the tall pines along the beach path, the scent of her Lucky Strikes mixing with the muddy odor of low tide.

"You're late," she said through a stream of blue smoke. "And you look like hell. Tough day?"

I'd spent the entire ride out to Ocean View telling myself I was being absurd. By the time I stepped off the trolley, I was almost free of the squeezing fist of panic that had me gasping for air as if I was suffocating. Almost.

"You could say that," I muttered.

Blanche's gaze sharpened ever so slightly.

"No National Woman's Party meeting tonight?" I asked, hoping to distract her from whatever gears were groaning to life in her curious brain.

"Not tonight," she replied. "But I have a stack of petitions that need to be folded and stuffed into envelopes if you're so inclined."

Blanche had recently joined the Women's Home Guard run by Mrs. Adams, a devoted local suffragist firebrand she'd met in Washington, DC, the year before. It meant she spent less time at the cottage, and when she was home, she was distracted and preoccupied. Dark smudges circled eyes that had lost their shine, and twice I'd woken in the morning to hear her retching and ill. I'd suggested she report to sick bay, but she always refused, and I was too cowardly to force the issue.

"Stuffing envelopes? I'm sorry I asked."

"That's what Marjory said just before she raced out the door to basketball practice."

My subterfuge worked. Blanche was far too busy grumbling about her housemates' lack of feminist feeling to be curious about why I was gray-faced and rumpled.

We headed inside where two enormous boxes waited for us on the kitchen table. Five minutes in, I was counting every tick of the clock and plotting how I could escape to my bedroom. A half hour in, the methodical process of stuffing and sealing had loosened the last of the kinks in my shoulders and banished the ghost of my father back where he belonged.

"*'. . . how can you plead so earnestly for men, who fight their own fight with a bloody hand, how hold their cause so wildly dear and then, forget the women of your native land?'*" I read before folding it into an envelope.

Blanche grimaced. "Not exactly Shakespeare, but it gets the point across. We're sending copies to President Wilson, every member of Congress, as well as all the men in the Virginia legislature."

"You think it will help?"

"We're fighting a foreign war for freedom from tyranny and oppression, and yet here at home, half the population can't participate in their own democracy."

"Mrs. Pankhurst would be proud."

"Do you suppose she'd write and tell my mother that?"

"Have you received another letter warning you about the risks of eternal spinsterhood?"

Blanche's mother kept up a constant stream of correspondence, filling her in on all the family news as well as the latest country club gossip, which always included at least one recent clipping from the Washington social pages—engagements and weddings were the most frequent, though births had come on strong in recent weeks as the privations of war meant a growing abundance of babies. These needling reminders were supposed to spur Blanche to finally put aside her ridiculous notions, but so far all they'd done was spur her to smoke more than she should and grumble about the smothering patriarchy.

"I wouldn't have been surprised to see her use the term *bluestocking*," Blanche fussed as she licked envelopes. "I love her dearly, but the woman has some positively primeval notions when it comes to femininity."

"I suppose she just wants you to be happy."

"*Her* version of happiness, not mine. She doesn't see what I want. I wonder sometimes if she even sees me at all."

Maybe now was the time to tell Blanche. Maybe she'd understand what had driven me to do what I had done.

Instead, I refilled my mug, fished out the cookie jar for one of Ernst's fruit biscuits. I could face down a hundred browbeating Lieutenant Dumfries. Confessing to Blanche was beyond me.

"At least I have the luxury of a hundred-mile no-man's-land between us. My poor sister-in-law lives just the other side of the river and has to put up with Mother's interference on a daily basis. Today's criticism is my brother's decision to send Iris to Westchester County to stay with family for the summer. How she manages to work Iris's frail health and Gilbert's generous overindulgence into a lament to her own inconvenience is an epistolary tour de force. Iris won't get a moment's peace from my mother until she produces a Lawrence heir. No wonder she's hightailing it to New York. If I was her, I'd run as fast and far as I could too."

"You did."

She laughed. "You're right."

The pile slowly shrank, the time slipping by as we worked. Blanche fell silent, not even my prodding enough to keep a conversation going. Whether she was brooding over her mother's latest long-distance scolding or simply tired was impossible to say. At one point, she lit a cigarette, the smoke encircling her head, the red tip reflected in the dark well of her eyes. "You're a preacher's daughter, Viv. Maybe you can tell me why even when you know the right thing to do, it's still so hard to do it."

"I wish I knew, but I wasn't a very good preacher's daughter. If I was, I wouldn't be here."

CHAPTER 10

VIV

It was near midnight by the time I capped my fountain pen and covered my typewriter. I passed through the hospital gates, exchanging a salute with the guard who warned me of work on the streetcar track. "It's awful late, miss. You might want to hoof it or you'll miss the last ferry for the night."

I thanked him and headed south, more aware than I'd been a moment ago that I was walking alone through dark streets when all respectable people were tucked up in their beds behind safely locked doors. I wasn't completely alone—the business of war ground on around the clock. But at this time of night, most hurried head-down, taking no notice of anything more than the slap of their boots on the uneven bricks, their next shift, their next posting, their next meal.

I headed down Green Street, crossing the tracks when I reached the intersection with London. A few people called out as I passed, crudities I'd long ago learned to ignore. Once, as I passed an alley, I felt the tug of a hand at my jacket, but I wrenched away, sliding into a group of workers in dingy coveralls carrying lunch pails, and the danger fell behind me. As we neared High Street, a noise, sharp and fierce, finally pierced the midnight armor of indifference.

A few of my companions hesitated. Some looked around as if waking from a daze, eyes wide, faces nervous in the light of an occasional streetlamp. I slowed my pace, heart jumping high against my ribcage.

A group of men stood in the street, blocking the way to the ferry. In the dark, they were a mass of indistinguishable caps and jackets, anonymous behind low brims and high collars. A few carried sticks, thick and heavy. One brandished a shovel, the curve of the blade ominous. Another stood with a pail, light glinting off the dented metal. Who were they? What did they want? Somehow, I didn't think they planned on late-night gardening despite the tools they carried.

"Damn American Defense Society," grumbled someone to my left.

"Hush," someone else urged.

Despite being ruled accidental, last winter's devastating fire in downtown Norfolk had spurred a resurgence of groups billing themselves as super patriots whose purpose was rooting out German saboteurs. Marjory had relayed frightening tales from friends and relatives back home in Ohio and Wisconsin of armed gangs meting out vigilante justice to anyone they suspected of aiding the enemy. Until now, our local groups had been more social than anything else, gathering in bars, community halls, or church basements. This was the first time I'd seen any on the streets.

I turned off, hoping I could circle around the long way, but now I was truly alone. The darkness enveloped me, my shoes echoed in the silence. A dog barked in a nearby yard. A rattle of trash cans in an alley made me jump. I quickened my pace, cutting back toward High Street a few blocks over, hoping I'd avoided them.

My stomach gurgled, and a weight slid cold over my shoulders. How long had it taken me to walk this far? Impossible to tell. If I missed the ferry, I'd have to return to the hospital and bunk down there. I didn't relish the thought of Quarles catching me asleep under my desk.

I could smell the tang of the harbor: a mix of fuel oil, mud, and dead fish. I crossed the street again and headed north, following my nose as best I could and hoping I hadn't misjudged in the dark. So caught up in recreating the city's streets in my head, I never heard the shuffle of bodies, the raised voices until I emerged under a streetlamp.

Across the street, the mob had grown, the shifting bodies surrounding a church like Vandals at the gates of Rome. Garish yellow paint splashed over walls and windows. Stained the doors to the vestibule. I could smell the acrid odor of ammonia and lead. Someone held a flashlight. Someone else, a lantern. A third man, his face hidden behind a scarf, carried an actual torch—God only knew what he meant to do with that. Others hung back at the edges, willing witnesses to the destruction, but not yet committed to action of their own. Electricity seemed to charge the scene, the air heavy with fear and rage as the crowd fed on itself, every word tightening the tension that danced over my skin and made my mouth go dry. Someone sang "God Bless America." Another waved an American flag. It would take only a hint of defiance, a careless word or a casual curse to light the match.

As the singing increased, a woman in a cheap print dress stepped forward. My blood ran cold as I recognized pretty Lily Forbes from payroll, her lantern illuminating a face twisted with violence and hate when only this afternoon she'd been laughing over a letter from her sweetheart. "Remember what the good reverend said at his last lecture, 'The German god is a pagan god while our god is a Christian god!'" she shouted.

I ducked my head and broke into a run, hoping she hadn't seen me, hoping to leave the strange ugliness behind. The lights of the ferry terminal rose before me, the familiar rumble of the ferry's engine calmed my jagged nerves. I practically threw my fare at the ticket taker and leapt the gap between shore and ship, nausea rising in my belly. I leaned against the rail, the lights behind me and the lights ahead of me hiding who knew what crimes.

"Smoke?" A yeomanette stood a few feet away. I didn't recognize her, but she held out a pack of cigarettes. "You look like you could use it."

I hesitated only a moment before accepting the cigarette, leaning over as she lit it. The smoke filled my lungs, burned my throat. I was reminded of the church. Was that smoke smearing the night sky of Portsmouth? Or had the police interceded, sending people on their way before events spun too far? I coughed and gagged then inhaled again, and this time the scent and the warmth felt good.

"Thanks," I said to the young woman in her Norfolk jacket and wide-brimmed hat. "I needed that."

I'D NEVER BEEN happier to see the cottage than I was that night; the lamp shining in the front window, spilling light onto Marjory's bicycle leaning against the porch and Blanche's striped beach towel drying on the laundry line. I let myself in as quietly as I could to keep from waking the others only to be met with Marjory's outraged cry of "Five straight games. You have to be cheating!" and Blanche's dry response. "Just because you stink doesn't make me a cheat. You owe me two dollars and that scarf with the flowers on it."

Marjory flung her cards down. Blanche gathered them into the deck with a coy smile. They were both in nightgowns and bathrobes. Marjory's hair was in rags. Blanche wore the polished sheen of copious amounts of Ponds.

"Don't believe her, Marjory," I said, peeling out of my coat before I sank into the couch wishing it was a bathtub. "She cheats worse than the hawkers on the Ocean View boardwalk."

They both looked up from arguing, eyes wide with relief and in Blanche's case, umbrage. "See? I told you she wasn't dead in a ditch."

"You said she *probably* wasn't. Not the same thing at all." Marjory scrambled up to set the kettle on the stove. "I'll make you a cup of coffee, Viv."

Blanche kicked out a chair and beckoned me over. "Join us for a game of rummy and tell us all about it."

"Careful, Viv," Marjory warned, scooping instant coffee into a mug while the kettle heated up. "She's liable to have you in hock for a year's rent by the end of the night."

"You waited up for me?" I asked, blinking and dazed at the commotion after my silent trip home.

"We were worried . . . or rather Marjory was worried and she made me stay up and worry with her."

"Of course I was worried. I'd starve if I had to eat your cooking."

Marjory mothered me with bad coffee and a plate of shortbread, and Blanche dealt me in with the worst hand in rummy history while I danced around the events of the night, falling back on last-minute work and a late-departing ferry as my excuse for my absence. All the while their bickering, their laughter, and the shuffle and slap of the cards dissolved my lingering unease like a stomach tablet in a glass of water until finally I found myself laughing and bickering alongside them.

"Rummy! A set of kings and a run of four." I laid down my hand. "I believe you owe me one dollar plus ironing duty for a week, Miss Lawrence."

Blanche huffed, gathering the deck to shuffle it. "Where did you learn to play like a gambler's-den card sharp?"

I shrugged, remembering a long-ago afternoon, Tom explaining the rules of the game, demonstrating runs and sets and various strategies employed in drawing and discarding cards. I had learned quickly, but his sister had been hopeless, her failure only delighting her more as the three of us laughed and argued and teased one another mercilessly, which only made us laugh all the harder. That had been our last summer together. I'd not played rummy since. I'd not realized I'd missed it until now.

"Suppose it's like riding a bicycle." I couldn't help my sly smile at besting Blanche. It happened so rarely. "Once you learn and all that."

Blanche huffed. Marjory giggled. Another shuffle. Another deal. Another game.

Finally, the clock chimed two. Blanche folded with a sigh and a stretch. Marjory yawned as she nibbled at the last piece of shortbread. I swallowed the dregs of coffee from my mug and rubbed my face, the last ragged edges of tonight's darkness banished, leaving only a comfortable weighted sleepiness. My tired gaze moved between Blanche's racy red curls and Marjory's round cheeks and sparkling eyes.

Maybe it wasn't just the rummy I missed.

AFTER A WEEK that lasted between forever and an eternity, it felt wonderful to pack a lunch and head to the beach for a lazy Sunday afternoon. Summer had arrived in Hampton Roads, the cottages and guest houses around us filling up, the roads growing busier. The scents of taffy apples and popcorn mingled with fish and brine and salt.

"An entire day all to ourselves," Blanche said, stretching her arms over her head, face lifted to the sun. "I feel positively decadent."

The three of us stood at the water's edge, Blanche enveloped in an enormous robe while Marjory and I shivered deliciously in our bathing costumes. The quiet roll of the tide cooled my ankles as my toes dug into the gravely sand. A ship's horn bounced along the waves and echoed back from the houses along the shoreline. A pleasure yacht passed on its way south toward the resorts at Virginia Beach, the crew waving at us from the deck. I blushed, feeling positively exposed in my skimpy wool jersey bathing suit. I tried pulling the skirt farther down over my thighs.

"You'll only encourage them," I hissed as Marjory waved back, her hat flying off in a stray gust, rolling up the beach where it came to rest by our towels, her shining ringlets bouncing in the sun. Her face was brown from endless days pedaling all over Norfolk, the rest of her pale as cream.

"Pooh. Don't fuss." She waved more vigorously. "They're just being friendly."

Shedding her robe at the water's edge, Blanche plunged beneath the waves, surfacing where the far rollers broke against the gray-green water of the Chesapeake. Marjory followed more timidly, submerging herself to her waist, the skirt of her suit ballooning out around her. She shivered theatrically as she made little gasping noises at the cold.

"Come on in, Viv. It's delicious," Blanche called.

"I'm happy right where I am." The sand ground against my feet, the water soaking into my tights.

"Suit yourself." She dove once more beneath the waves while Marjory paddled in the shallows like a carefree child.

I splashed water along my arms and against my neck before retreating up onto the sand to our towels where we'd left our picnic basket and a thermos of cold sweet tea. As I set out plates and cups, I enjoyed the warmth of the sun against shoulders too long hunched over a desk, fingers stained and cramped from too many hours clutching a pen. A seagull fluttered down to investigate, his beady black eyes unblinking in his cocked white head.

I'd kept my mouth shut about the mob I'd witnessed. Marjory would only get upset, and Blanche's schedule had grown more frantic as she split her time between her naval duties and her suffragette work with Mrs. Adams. The whole episode had almost begun to feel like a dream when I'd found myself face-to-face with

Lily Forbes. She'd stood with a group of girls in the mess line complaining about the cost of hair pins and cotton stockings. "Hiya, Weston," she'd chirped, oblivious to my churning stomach, the acrid memory of paint and smoke and rage stinging my nose.

I'd pretended I forgot something and hurried back to my desk where I sat, hands trembling, until it was time to go home. On my way, I'd found myself passing the Lutheran church, its spire defiantly raised to the sky as a pair of men scrubbed the ruined bricks and picked up broken glass.

"Shoo, you dirty beggar." Caught woolgathering, I looked up as Marjory frightened the seagull away, laughing and breathless as she squeezed water from her hair and sank onto her towel with a sigh of contentment. "Delicious. I just might live to pedal another day." She munched on a carrot stick. "You should have at least waded, Viv. It's lovely and refreshing."

"I can't swim."

"Golly! Let me guess—your father thought swimming was immoral and promoted promiscuity."

Ever since I'd opened up to Marjory about my strict upbringing, she'd teased me. Not in a mean way, more in a trying-to-pry-open-a-clamshell way. Twist the knife just the right amount and the soft underbelly would be revealed. It wasn't that I didn't want to open up to her and Blanche. I just didn't know how to start, where to start. How do you explain you've been lying to someone since the very first moment they met you? It had to be done, but it was always easier to put it off to a better moment, another day, next week.

"I don't know about the promiscuity bit, but he believed women were better suited to quiet pastimes like sewing or learning to cook. I took piano lessons when I was young, but they stopped after my mother died. There wasn't time with all my other chores." My churning stomach was back. The last few days, I'd practically lived on a diet of saltines and milk of magnesia.

Marjory poured herself a cup of sweet tea and nibbled the edge of a sandwich. "Is that why you ran away? Because of your father?" She eyed me over her ham and cheese.

Twist. Twist.

"There were a lot of reasons."

Here it was, the perfect opening to spill the beans. I busied myself with arranging napkins, pulling out a jar of pickles, a plate of deviled eggs as I formed the words in my head: *While we're on the subject of my father, my name isn't Vivian and I ran away after hitting him over the head and leaving him for dead. But he's not dead and now I don't know what to do.*

Succinct. To the point.

I could hear myself saying it, see her reaction: shock turning to sympathy and ending in a warm Marjory hug that would reassure me I'd done right by telling her the truth. That all would be well. That our friendship was real.

"Oh, I almost forgot, Viv. Did you hear about Evelyn Salucci?" Her voice dripped with salacious delight.

"What about her?" Evelyn and Marjory were on the same baseball team. She was a tiny stick of a woman who worked in accounts at the shipyard.

"She's been tossed out of the Navy. I heard through the grapevine that the charges against her were so serious they called in the ONI to investigate."

"Naval Intelligence? What on earth did she do? Sell secrets to the Hun?"

"Worse. She lied on her application forms. Then when she was found out, she lied more. And got other people to lie to cover up her first lies."

"Gosh. That's terrible."

"Yeah, she was a really good pitcher. We're going to miss her."

She polished off her sandwich and immediately grabbed a deviled egg from the plate. "Poor Evelyn."

Poor *me*. If Marjory and Blanche found out and told, the Navy would throw me out. And if they kept my secret, they'd be as guilty as I was and risk being thrown out *with* me. I couldn't do that to them. If our friendship was as real as I hoped, keeping silent was the only option.

Blanche continued to swim, her strokes knifelike as she cut through the water parallel to the beach. "Does she never run out of energy?" I asked, wrapping my arms around my drawn-up knees, the sandwich I'd just eaten sitting like a lump.

"I knew a girl at school behaved the same way," Marjory answered. "Poor thing never stopped. Had to be the best in everything. Top marks in all her classes, chair of every committee and club, captain of the girls' basketball and baseball teams."

"Sounds exhausting." Shading my eyes against the sun, I watched Blanche clawing her way north until she was a mere speck against the waves.

"It was worth it when I won the dean's medal my final year over Granville Barker, teacher's pet." She grinned. "Not even my sainted brothers won a medal."

"You?" I studied Marjory with new eyes as if seeing her for the first time, noting a surprising strength to her caramel brown eyes, an unusual severity to the dainty curve of her jaw, a determined pinch to the edges of her cupid bow mouth. How had I never noticed before? Was it her breezy personality, the way she bent every conversation toward laughter, slid through life as if it were a game?

Her expression remained fixed, her features tense. "We do funny things when we're trying to prove a point."

"Is that why you joined up? To prove a point?"

"Me? Heck no." As if aware of my scrutiny, she grinned, and it was the same old Marjory: all good-natured dimples and laughter. No hint of the shadows I'd glimpsed. "I just didn't want to let the boys have all the fun."

By now, Blanche had turned and was heading south, down the beach, her arms pulling strongly at the water, her head cocked with each breath she took. "What point do you suppose Blanche is trying to prove?"

"Can't you guess?" Marjory replied. "She's out to prove she's as capable as any man alive. That's a tall order—even for her. Hopefully, she knows to quit before she sinks like a stone. Otherwise, we'll have to jump in and save her."

"I can't swim. Remember?"

"You'll have to learn fast then." She raided the basket, surfacing with a plate wrapped in grease paper. "Ernst's famous cream-filled *Berliners*. Have one."

"No thank you. I've had to move two sets of buttons since you started seeing him. Any more, and I'll have to ask Blanche for help running up a new skirt."

"You don't know what you're missing." Marjory leaned back in her chair, stretching her legs out in front of her, wiggling her toes in the sand. "Did you know he and his wife left everything they knew to come to Norfolk from Bremen? They set up the bakery together. Had Clara. Then his wife died, and he was left all alone with a daughter to raise and a shop to run."

I hadn't known. In the few times I'd visited the bakery with Marjory, he'd spent most of his time mooning over her like a lovesick schoolboy. And when he called on us at the cottage, his amiable, unflappable personality made it hard to imagine a life of hardship and tragedy.

"I admire that kind of fighting spirit," Marjory continued. "It takes guts to sacrifice everything you've known for a better life. That's what makes me so angry—people whispering because a name isn't American enough or they speak with an accent, or, worst of all, because they have family back in Germany, people they love who are suffering just as much as we are."

"You care for Ernst very much."

She dropped her gaze, lashes long and dark against her sun-tanned cheek. "More than that. I love him. And I don't want to see this wretched war take everything he's gained away from him. It would break his heart." Here came another flash of the new Marjory, a steel-eyed glint in a china doll's face. Her hand curled into a fist around the tea thermos, her knuckles white.

"Is there a reason you think it would?"

It was Marjory's turn to lift her gaze to the water as she stared out at Blanche, tension pooling once more into every curve and angle of her face. Then she looked at me, and it was obvious she'd known about the vandalism at the church all along. "All it takes is a spark and someone to throw the match."

CHAPTER 11

PEGGY

1968

P eggy returned home from an afternoon of shopping, sweaty and yearning for a nice cool bath. She thought summer in Queens was hot, but this sticky, sunbaked humidity that clung like a wet sponge was altogether different—and altogether worse. Thank God for the breeze off the water or she'd have melted into a puddle. She'd unearthed an old rattling box fan in a cupboard under the stairs, but until David gave the cottage's wiring the all clear, she wasn't sure she should plug it in.

Speaking of David—she scanned the street for an open parking space, cursing the camper taking up her driveway and leaving her at the mercy of beach-going day-trippers. There. One spot. Smack in front of Mr. Symonds' bungalow.

She squeezed the Buick between an enormous wood-paneled station wagon heaped with beach paraphernalia and a little yellow convertible with a surfboard sticking out the back. Careful as she was, she still managed to crush an azalea and bump his mailbox with her fender.

"Damn." Praying he'd not seen, she got out to inspect the damage. No real harm done. Just a few broken branches. He might not even notice.

"They teach you to park in those big cities up north or what?"

She practically jumped out of her skin as Symonds came wandering around the side of his house with a watering can, toothpick moving side to side in his mouth.

"Nothing dented."

"Except my shrubbery." He shook his head and continued watering the pots on his front stoop as she slunk chastened across the street.

She had to admit, just a few weeks, and the cottage already seemed brighter, cleaner—more like a home and less like a tomb. Old rotten lumber filled a metal dumpster while a stack of new lumber sat by the front steps. Electric cords snaked over the grass, and an enormous metal toolbox sat open beside a transistor radio. *". . . new information in the case of a World War One yeomanette who disappeared fifty years ago . . ."*

David perched on a ladder against the side of the house. He wore a baseball cap against the sun, but his T-shirt was dark with sweat.

"Why don't you take a break and come inside for some lunch?" Peggy suggested. "Just bought cold cuts and chips." She tempted him with a six-pack. "Even got beer."

"I should really finish this shingling before tonight, in case it rains."

"You won't be much good to me prostrate with sunstroke. Come on. Ten minutes won't kill you."

"Right. You twisted my arm. I'll be right there."

David had been as good as his word, arriving early following their conversation in his rackety camper van to spend every spare hour he had working on the cottage. Also true to his word, he'd never shown interest in exploring anything more than a business arrangement with her. She'd handed over a house key and cleared a shelf for him in the bathroom. Early each morning, she heard him in the kitchen making coffee or in the shower for a quick tepid scrub. Every evening, after knocking off work, he headed for the beach.

Peggy would watch him through the window, crossing the dunes, towel under his arm, dressed in nothing but a pair of ragged cutoffs and sporting a ridiculous farmer's tan. Occasionally he would see her and wave, but he never asked her to join him. As darkness fell, he would sit outside his van in a folding chair, a beer in his hand, the radio on. Sometimes he read the paper. Sometimes he had a book. And sometimes he bent over an enormous pad of paper, pencils in his lap. He barely spoke to her unless it was about the purchase of supplies or her views on whether she wanted him to work on the electrical wiring or the plumbing first. It was exactly what she'd asked for, exactly what she'd wanted. But somehow being alone felt lonelier with him around.

Bags juggled in her arms, Peggy searched for her keys at the bottom of her handbag before realizing the front door was already unlocked and slightly open. She put the groceries down on the kitchen table beside the salt and pepper shakers, the ketchup bottle, and a book—which had definitely not been there when she left the cottage this morning. The blue cover was faded, the binding frayed, but the title's gold lettering shone as bright as the button she'd found all those weeks ago. *The Bluejacket's Manual, United States Navy.*

"Should have the flashing on the dormer done by this afternoon." David came in, wiping his damp hands on a rag. He'd replaced his shirt with a clean one and removed his cap, his sun-streaked hair pulled back in a leather thong. "What's that there?"

"I thought you could tell me. It was here when I got back."

David flipped through the book, reading out, "'Rules regarding salutes.' 'Regulations in regard to uniform.' Looks like a manual for navy seamen." He turned to the flyleaf. "No name or bookplate, just a bunch of squiggles, but the copyright date says 1918."

Of course, it did.

"Did you find it while you were in the attic crawl space?" she asked.

"Wasn't me. Looks like someone's kid got hold of it. There are more squiggles all up and down the margins." He paused on a page. "Here you go—'The duties of lookouts and others specially detailed,'" he quoted. "I'll bet that's guaranteed to keep you glued to your seat."

As she snatched it from him, a yellowed pamphlet fell onto the table from between the fluttering pages. David picked it up, his entire face lighting up with shocked laughter. "Well now, I'd say they didn't cover *this* in any Navy training session."

He handed it over before she could snatch it away too. "*Family Limitation* by Margaret Sanger," she read. "That's not funny."

"Maybe a *little* funny?" He held his thumb and forefinger close together. When she didn't crack a smile, his face fell. "You didn't think our generation invented sex, did you?"

Peggy flushed. "Of course not." She jammed the pamphlet back into the manual and slammed it shut. "So, if you didn't leave it here and I didn't leave it here, that leaves . . ."

"Suzanne?"

As if on cue, she appeared at the screen door bearing a plate of cookies. "Yoo-hoo! Anybody home? Chocolate chip, fresh from the oven." Suzanne's eyes shifted from David to Peggy with a smile that was about as subtle as a smack to the head. "Sorry to butt in. Looks like you two were having quite the conversation."

"We were discussing . . ." Peggy's mind went blank.

"Plumbing," David interjected. For a split second their eyes locked, his thoughts an open book. Her stomach did a nervous flip, and she stifled the impulse to laugh out loud. "I'll come back for that sandwich once you two have had a good gab. Meantime, I'd best get back to work." He snagged a cookie from the plate. "Thanks, Suzanne."

She flipped him a coy little finger wave before getting down to brass tacks after he was gone. "Well?" she hinted. "How's life with the hunky handyman?"

"He's here to do a job. That's all." Peggy sank onto the couch, taking the plate of cookies with her. "Besides, he's already got a girlfriend."

"Since when?"

"Lena from the hair salon. His gum-cracking answering service."

"Hardly competition. Besides, he's living in *your* driveway, not hers. That tells me something."

"That she doesn't have a driveway?"

But Suzanne was off and running. "You're like Richard Burton and Elizabeth Taylor . . . no, wait . . . Elvis and Priscilla . . . ooh, no, Frankie and Annette. Definitely Frankie and Annette. We even have a beach right outside. It's perfect. Maybe I should arrange a barbecue on the sand. We could roast weenies over the fire and have s'mores. Ron even owns a ukulele. Do you suppose David—"

"It sounds wonderful, but I really should do some sorting upstairs. David's supposed to start work inside tomorrow."

"What's this?" Thank heavens. Suzanne had found the blue-jacket's manual, becoming sidetracked from her recitation of famous Hollywood couples and beach-party organizing.

"I think it belonged to my great-aunt Blanche."

"She was in the Navy?" She opened to the front cover, her face broadening into a knowing smile. "I'll bet she was a yeomanette. They took over a lot of the secretarial work so the men were free to go off and fight."

"How do you know so much about them?"

"Ron's grandmother deciphered radio codes or something crazy secret and technical during the First World War. She was barely twenty-one. Anyway, she was one of the reasons Ron decided to enlist in the Navy. All her stories about the good old days inspired him, I guess. Now that I think about it, I wish she'd kept her big trap shut."

"Does she live nearby?"

"New Jersey, but I can give her a ring if you want."

"Would you? I'd love to learn more about them. I never knew Blanche served in the military. It's like finding out you have a spy in the family."

"Or a murderer," Suzanne said as she gave a delicious shudder.

AFTER SUZANNE LEFT, Peggy checked the rest of the house and all seemed just as it should. Nothing moved or shifted. Nothing taken, more was the pity. If Symonds was going to break in, the least he could do was take some of this junk away with him.

Oh yes, she was almost positive it was the old nut across the street. But why? What did an old navy manual have to do with her? None of it made sense, and she was tired of her life not making sense. She'd spent the past six months battered by questions with no answers. When she asked, she was offered platitudes.

"These things just happen."

"It's no one's fault."

"It's time to move on."

The words scraped every nerve raw until she thought she might scream.

Then someone hit her with "It's all part of God's plan."

That one eviscerated her like a knife to the gut.

What sort of miraculous plan called for the death of her child? What good could possibly come from such a tragedy?

No one was able to offer her an answer to that. Not even Chaz.

And if he had questions of his own, he never shared them with her. He didn't share anything. Instead, they moved around each other in awkward uncomfortable silence, the apartment growing smaller as the distance between them increased. By the time he walked out, they were two strangers living under the same roof.

She didn't blame him for leaving. She blamed him for pretending.

For pretending the pregnancy hadn't happened at all. She'd come home from the hospital to an apartment devoid of any sign of a child—their child. Nursery walls painted over. Drawers emptied. Furniture tossed. He'd erased their daughter. Completely. Irrevocably. But in his zeal to forget the past, he'd erased the two of them and any hope they had of a future.

Then she'd come here, to Blanche's cottage where the past consumed everything. This little house was a monument to days long gone. Had her great-aunt been as trapped by her memories as Peggy now was? Was that her reason for leaving the cottage to her? That she sympathized with Peggy's loss? That she saw in Peggy a mirror of her own life? Unmarried. Childless. Alone.

She stood in Blanche's bedroom and gazed around at all that remained of that life and those memories. Cardboard boxes and old fruit crates waiting to be filled; clothes taken from the chest of drawers and skirts and blouses still on hangers, taking up the bed. A dressing table cluttered with knickknacks, old letters, and invitations. The photograph in the silver frame of the three young women standing on the pier, excited and fresh and ready for a grand adventure. The Navy had promised that adventure. The war had been an unexpected invitation to new freedom.

She looked forward to speaking to Suzanne's in-law. To hearing more about these yeomanettes who braved the unknown to serve their country. Such courage should be celebrated, and yet she'd never heard of them. They'd been completely forgotten.

She glanced one last time on that photo—maybe not completely forgotten.

Blanche remembered.

And so did the mysterious Viv who sent those postcards.

Peggy closed the door on the bedroom. That mess—and her questions—would have to wait. The afternoon had grown hotter, the cottage like an oven. She'd put off that cool soak long enough.

The little bathroom off the landing had obviously been carved out of a cupboard. The walls were pink tile and the ceiling sloped down to a tiny pillared sink with a cracked and discolored enamel bowl, the mirror so low she had to bend to see her face in it. The toilet, crushed in a corner, had an old-fashioned overhead tank and chain. The room's only saving grace was an enormous clawfoot tub big enough to stretch out and immerse oneself all the way to the chin.

Dipping a finger in, she shuddered. Cool was one thing. Ice-cold was quite another.

She fiddled with the taps, but the gush of water remained frigid no matter how she spun the hot-water spigot. Had the water heater finally given up? Did she even have a water heater? She wouldn't be surprised if this whole place ran on coal.

Wrapping her robe around her, she headed downstairs, opening and closing closets in hopes of spotting anything that looked like it might shed some light on her problem. She finally found the water heater and the fuse box in a filthy cupboard under the back porch. Trouble was, she'd not the first idea what to do now that she'd found it. She'd always had building managers for that.

Mr. Grace's offer suddenly seemed more than generous. This crazy idea of fixing the place up was spite, plain and simple. He told her she couldn't do it, which of course just made her want to prove him wrong.

She'd married Chaz for the same reason.

Her grandfather had thought he wasn't the right sort, which was code for *He didn't come from old money or have an Ivy League education.* It didn't matter that her family's money had evaporated in the bank crashes of the Depression. Reputation and snobbery were all they had left. She was almost relieved he wasn't alive to see how her marriage had turned out. His I-told-you-so's would have been endless. She'd seen how he needled her mother for *her* failed marriage as if it were some kind of genetic deficiency.

"Problem?"

She grabbed the first weapon to hand and spun around to find David standing just behind her.

"Death by snow shovel?" he said, holding his hands up in surrender.

"There's a problem with the hot water."

He went inside to check the kitchen sink then returned, stepping past her into the cupboard, using a flashlight to examine the heater, which looked like it might have come over on the *Mayflower*. "I'll have to take it apart to be sure, but it looks like your heating coil might be shot."

"Is that bad?"

"Not really, but there's also a leak in one of the lines to the upstairs. And the breaker back here is dicey at best, so I wouldn't use the stove. Not until I get a chance to inspect it. Can you make do until tomorrow?"

"I'll have to, won't I?" She pushed her hair off her face. "Guess it's takeout tonight."

"Didn't you have takeout last night?"

"Keeping tabs on me?"

"Only to notice that you eat like a teamster or a poor college student. Forget ordering out. Have dinner with me tonight. It won't be gourmet, but it'll be better than anything you'll find at any of the places around here."

"In the camper?"

"I promise it's not the den of iniquity you think it is. And I'll be on my best behavior."

She shouldn't accept. It would mean small talk and having to be pleasant, laughing at the right times and saying the right things. As draining as being on stage, caught in a spotlight when all she wanted was to fade into the wings.

She told herself she shouldn't, which of course just made her want to prove she could.

"All right. I'll bring the wine."

CHAPTER 12

VIV

1918

June arrived and brought with it an onslaught of sticky summer heat. At home, we draped ourselves in cool cloths and slept out on the screened sleeping porch in scandalously little. At work, we suffered in our uniforms of white summer drill and counted the hours until we could splash in the tide. Only the passing afternoon thunderstorms offered respite, but these usually brought with them hordes of midges and mosquitoes that buzzed against the screens and gathered around the porch light. Our supply of calamine dwindled.

Occasionally we took our supper down onto the beach where Marjory and I waded in the shallows while Blanche knifed like a dolphin through the deep water, emerging sleek and bright-eyed. Now and then Gus joined us. It turned out his uncle's boat caught more than just striped bass and croaker in the hidden coves and creeks along the Chesapeake's shoreline, so when the fishing was especially good, he would bring us smuggled bottles of bootleg whiskey that he passed around along with a packet of Chesterfields.

While I'd fallen into the habit of smoking, I'd stayed away from the alcohol. Father had been a leader in the temperance movement, railing about the evils of drink from the pulpit and rallying his church ladies to push the state's dry laws even while he indulged his weakness for liquor in the privacy and security of his study every night. To point out his hypocrisy would have been to invite a whipping, so I kept silent and pretended I didn't notice the fumes on his breath, the broken veins on his nose, or the way he downed glasses of Bromo-Seltzer on the mornings after. And on those long twilight beach evenings, when the bottles came to me, I would place the neck to my lips, tasting the woody, sour burn, but never swallowing.

Ernst joined us one evening, his old-fashioned continental manners relaxing under the influence of Gus's illegal hooch, his box of profiteroles perfect after bluefish roasted over the fire and cold potato salad. Blanche took her usual swim, emerging like a mermaid, her red hair slicked back, her skin scented with brine and sand. Gus made room for her on his towel, but she ignored his invitation, and I wondered if our teasing had made her more aware of his lopsided affection.

Ernst and Gus discussed the church vandalism. No one had been arrested, and the city had settled back into a summer stupor. "The laws against all things German have grown strict," Ernst explained, his expression unusually guarded. "Many of the groups I belonged to have disbanded in the last few years. People are afraid of bringing attention to themselves."

"It doesn't help that those who should know better, like Roosevelt, stir up trouble with their blowhard jingoistic speeches," Marjory argued, her face flushed, eyes shining with alcohol and outrage. "It's not right."

Ernst put up a hand as if to placate her. She cut him a look across the fire, a silent message between them that I couldn't read. I didn't blame her for being angry. She and her brothers had enlisted to prove their patriotism to a skeptical country. Yet still their loyalties were questioned.

She took another swig from the bottle and passed it to me. I tipped it to my mouth, lips pressed tight.

"Take a real swallow, Viv," Blanche said, as if she knew I'd been faking it all these weeks, as if daring me to join in. "It'll burn like the devil going down, but you'll feel like a new woman."

"What if I prefer the old?"

Maybe it was the flickering light from the bonfire, but for a moment, those blue eyes of hers sharpened like knives, and there was a watchful stillness in her pose, a strange smile curving that strong chin. "You wouldn't be here if that were the case, would you?"

The hairs lifted on my arms as a chill raced through me. What did she know? Or think she knew? What had Marjory told her? I glanced around the fire, but no one else seemed to take notice of the gleam in her eyes or the challenge in her voice. Was I imagining things? Jittery and quick to leap at shadows?

I lifted the bottle to my mouth, wrinkling my nose at the sickly odor, far too familiar after years of smelling it on my father's breath, his skin, the clothes that I laundered weekly. I took a sip, the taste odd, but not as horrible as I feared.

"See? You weren't struck down by a bolt of lightning," she said, her tone light with amusement, her gaze as open and easy as ever. No hint of anything sinister or suspicious. I took another sip, banishing my ridiculous fears. Blanche was a friend. I'd not waste such a precious commodity on unfounded suspicions and bad lighting. I swallowed more, the heat banging against the back of my throat.

"Steady on, old girl," she warned. "I didn't say toss it back like a cowboy bellying up to the bar."

I gasped and coughed as it sizzled and burned, but, soon enough, a delicious golden warmth oozed its way along my limbs and relaxed my clenched jaw. I could see now why Father might have indulged. There was comfort to be found at the bottom of that bottle.

I met Gus's gaze across the fire. He smiled in a way that made me think perhaps he'd been paying closer attention than I thought. I lifted the bottle in a salute and took another swallow.

There might be courage in that bottle as well.

And I could use all of that I could get.

I WOKE THE next morning with a throbbing head, a belly fragile as a soft-boiled egg, and a huge dose of regret. My mouth was wooly, my throat dry, and the lingering scents of cheap whiskey and bonfire smoke filled my nose. The room was dark, rain pattering against the window, echoing inside my skull like bullets. Rolling over, I fought back a new wave of nausea as I blinked at the clock on the bedside table. Dear God, was it really seven? Had I really overslept by two hours?

I couldn't remember much that had happened after I wiped the neck of the bottle with my sleeve and passed it on. I'd a hazy recollection of Ernst and Marjory walking along the shore, hand in hand. Of Blanche singing "I'm Always Chasing Rainbows" at the top of her lungs while Gus sprawled on his back, elbows propped, watching her indulgently. If I wasn't mistaken, I'd actually joined her in the chorus.

I'm always chasing rainbows
Watching clouds drifting by
My schemes are just like all my dreams
Ending in the sky

Our skirts hitched to our thighs, our toes in the surf.

After that, it was all a kaleidoscopic blur.

I seemed to recall Blanche and Marjory trying and failing to wake me, but they were long gone by the time I had a wash and hurried into my uniform, laddering my stockings as I hopped around on one foot buttoning my shoe. But, good friends that they were, they'd left a pot of hot coffee, a plate of cold toast, and a bottle of aspirin.

I threw on a coat, pulled an umbrella from the stand, and with a scratchy throat and a head heavy as a bowling ball, I sniffled my way to the trolley stop, rain dripping off my hat to slide cold down my neck.

"Just missed it," the man at the turnstile said as he took my money with a lugubrious air and a shrug deeper into his slicker. "Next one's not for a half hour."

By the time I climbed aboard the ferry, I was drenched through, and my head, thick as cotton wool, throbbed all the way down into my neck. The river was choppy, and my stomach rose and fell with the ferry's ponderous wallow. The rest of the passengers huddled out of the weather while I clung like a drowned rat at the rail, praying I didn't humiliate myself. My skin was icy cold with the fear of Quarles's cutting glare and the anticipation of Dumfries' bellow banging in my sloshed brain. Would I be written up? Reprimanded? Charged?

My imagination ran ahead of me all the way to the hospital.

By the time I squished my way through the busy quarterdeck, my watch told me I was an hour late. I didn't need anyone to tell me I was in deep trouble. If only I could reach my desk before—

"Weston!" Quarles's voice shattered the polite murmur of conversations. "Here. Now. On the double."

My heart sank into my shoes. She didn't let me open my mouth before she attacked. "Where have you been? You were to have the weekly reports completed and on my desk first thing this morning, and here you come slinking in late and looking a positive disgrace. I could have you brought up on charges of being absent without leave."

"The rain . . ." I said, dripping on her floor, praying that lightning bolt of Blanche's would kill me now.

"Is no excuse for tardiness. I thought we settled this your very first day." She laid down her pen as she took a closer look at me. "Are you ill?"

If she knew I was hung over, I'd be finished. No hope of gaining a transfer to anywhere but a basement office sharpening pencils for the duration. "A summer cold, Chief. Nothing a cup of hot tea and lemon won't cure."

I wasn't sure if she bought it. She continued to eye me suspiciously. "Sickness needs to be reported to the medical staff. You know that. You can't just wander in whenever you feel like it. That's not how we do things—"

"In the Navy." I finished her sentence. "Yes, ma'am. You're right. It won't happen again."

"I'll let you off with a reprimand this time," she said, the threat very much implied. Then satisfied she'd made her point, she pushed her pages back into order, straightened the blotter, the inkstand, rearranged a pile of paper clips. "Get busy and get those reports completed."

"Aye, aye, ma'am."

"But for God's sake, see someone about that cold. I don't need you infecting the rest of the section."

I did as I was told, ignoring the snickering sideways glances and raised brows as I made my way through the busy office and down to the dispensary. By now, my clothes had dried to a clammy dampness and my hair curled into draggled tails beneath an army of hair pins. The nausea of earlier had lessened, replaced by exhaustion and a teeth-chattering chill.

"You all right, miss?" An orderly, his arms full of boxes, eyed me where I slouched in a stairwell.

"Summer cold," I repeated.

"Right. I have just the thing for those nasty *summer colds*. Guaranteed to put you right." I could almost hear the teasing skepticism. I stayed slumped where I was, too ill to even shoot him a dirty look in response. "Or," he said, "you can continue to prop up that pillar until they figure out you've been enjoying yourself with bootleg liquor."

I heaved a sigh and struggled to my feet.

"That's what I thought." He laughed as I followed him up the stairs to where the majority of surgical services had their offices. Soft-footed staff and earnest interns. Men in white coats who barely looked older than me straight out of training and drafted into service. The orderly turned into a room at the far end of the hall, peering back to make sure I was behind him. "Hurry up. Haven't got all day."

"What will I say if they ask why I'm here?"

"No one will ask. They're way too busy packing."

He was right. Clerks and nurses directed orderlies as they packed files. One unloaded a bookshelf into a series of crates. Furniture had been pushed into the center of the room. A young man sat on the floor sorting papers.

"What's going on?"

The orderly put his boxes down on the floor beside a harried woman in high collar and cardigan before heading to a glass-fronted cupboard. From the very back, he pulled out a brown bottle, an unmarked vial, a teaspoon, and a glass. "Dr. Stewart's been assigned as a battalion surgeon to the base hospital in Brest. He's taking his entire staff with him." He poured a generous amount from the bottle, added three drops from the vial, and mixed it together. "We've been set to organize and pack ahead of his transfer."

I accepted the glass, but once bitten, twice shy, hesitated to swallow it down. "What's in it?"

"Proprietary secret but guaranteed to cure the effects of any summer cold. Drink up."

I took a sniff. Lifted it to my mouth for a taste. "Wait a minute. Did you say Brest? As in France?"

"Are you going to drink it or not? I got work to do."

I tossed it back in one go, the gelatinous sludge sliding down my throat like a raw oyster where it sat in my stomach like a rock.

"Better?"

"I still feel like garbage, but in every other way, I'm better already."

I sang all the way back to my desk.

I'm always chasing rainbows
Watching clouds drifting by
My schemes are just like all my dreams
Ending in the sky

THAT NIGHT, I stared up at the ceiling. Counted dots in the curtains. Cornflowers in the wallpaper. The tick of my clock. Normally, the scrape of crickets and the purr of the bay lulled me to sleep through even the worst of my dreams, but not tonight. Round and round, my brain sped in endless circles as ideas thought perfect one moment were discarded as ridiculous the next.

Sleep was impossible. I rolled over onto my stomach, my back, my side. My fictional cold had turned into an actual cold after a long day spent in damp clothes, and now my scratchy throat and stuffy head made every position uncomfortable. Even a healthy dose of Pro-phy-tol didn't ease my cough or clear my nose, only sat, thick and sour, on my tongue. Finally, I eased myself up, hoping the squeak of bedsprings or the snick of my door latch didn't wake the others. Downstairs, I wrapped myself in a long overcoat against the mist and crept out of the cottage for a walk on the beach.

A fingernail moon hung low in the sky, but I'd made this trip enough times that I no longer needed the light to guide me past the low grassy dunes and out onto the wide shoulder of beach. Sinking into the sand, I slid my feet out of my shoes and carried them as I wandered down toward the slick black water, the soft ripple of surf breaking along the shore bringing with it cold slithery seaweed and a crunch of shattered shells. Ships sat off the coast, looming dark shapes against a darker sky, their lights reflecting off the water.

I knew all about Naval Base Hospital No. 1, which was located in an old convent in Brest. I'd seen the name on documents passing my desk almost daily and could probably type it in my sleep, but tonight, I'd found an atlas among the cottage's books and followed the line of my finger across the Atlantic to the western coast of Brittany where the sea broke against a toothy coast before narrowing into a wide protected bay.

I squinted into the east as if I might see across the miles to the far shores of Europe and the battlefields of Flanders. In my mind's eye, I saw the blinding splash of phosphorescent flares over no-man's land, felt the bone-rattling, ear-bleeding booms of bombardment that rolled on like a storm with no end, experienced the black oozing mud, the stench of death and sewage, the choking taste of cinders and smoke at the back of my throat. I pictured the victims of sinkings; the torn flesh, burns, and broken limbs from exploding mines and U-boat torpedoes; the frostbite, dehydration, and gangrene after days in open lifeboats. I let the worst of the war's violence wash over me like the rising tide, first my toes, then my ankles, then my shins.

None of it made any difference. I wanted to go.

For our boys, France was a place of death and grief and danger.

For me, it would be freedom.

I climbed above the high-tide mark and sat down in a hollow ringed with weeds and a few pieces of driftwood, drawing my knees to my chest under the shelter of my coat. I drew in a deep breath, feeling my chest expand, then blew it out again into my handkerchief with a sneeze.

"Bless you," came a voice from farther down the beach. A lantern bobbed along against the dark. A cold wet nose dug into my side with a snuffle of recognition. I scrubbed the little dog's head as it burrowed into my coat. "Out for a midnight walk, Sparky boy?"

Gus held his lamp up, bathing me in soft light. "What are you doing up so late, Viv?"

"I could ask you the same thing."

"Me and Sparky come out here a lot at night. It's peaceful. Gives a body space to think." The dog wandered down to the water, snuffling out sand-crab holes. Gus joined me, his long skinny body unfolding onto the sand, his gaze as distant as mine. We sat in silence watching the ships, the stars, the turn of the tide.

"I'd go if they let me, you know," he said, breaking the companionable silence. "I'm not afraid."

"I never thought you were."

"People do, though. I can tell. It's not my fault. It's this damn ear." He flashed me a guilty look. "And with my dad ailing and my mom needing help at home, I can't even get proper work at the shipyard or on the docks."

"Has someone accused you of shirking?"

He dug his shoe into the sand, head down. "Remember that conversation we were having last week when Blanche was talking about those women in England . . . the ones who go around handing white feathers to boys not in uniform?"

"Vaguely."

"She said that she wasn't afraid to fight or die so long as the cause was just. I know she was looking at me when she said it."

"I'm sure she didn't mean to imply you were a coward for not enlisting. You know how Blanche gets. Sometimes her enthusiasm outstrips her common sense." Gus hitched a shoulder against my words as if shrugging them off. "You and she are good chums. She'd never hurt you on purpose."

"Suppose you're right," he grudgingly agreed.

"Aren't you the one who told me you two have been thick as thieves since you were little?"

"Yeah, well mostly. You should have been here last winter. We argued and she didn't speak to me for months." I felt the shift of his shoulders, the way he tipped his head. "She always was that way—even when we were kids. The more you told her she couldn't do something, the more she'd set her mind to it."

"What did you tell her she couldn't do?"

He gave another jerk of his shoulder. "Doesn't matter. She didn't listen."

We fell back into silence, but there was a difference, a fellow feeling that made the quiet comfortable, revealing rather than shrouding. It made me bolder than I should have been. "Do you love Blanche?"

Gus combed his fingers back and forth through the sand, but did not answer. The question hung there between us like a bubble over a caricature's head. I wished I could take it back. I didn't want to know. It wasn't my concern. I had spent the past months stepping lightly, holding myself apart as much as I could. And one bad head cold and one sleepless night, I risked it all with a stupid question. "Never mind. You don't have to say anything, Gus. I'm sorry."

The dog growled and barked, breaking the awkwardness between us. We walked back up the beach through the heavy sand. At the gate, Gus waited as I let myself in. "You won't say anything, will you? About what I said? About what we talked about?"

"Mum's the word."

"Blanche was right about one thing. She wouldn't be afraid of the battle." He looked back out to the dark beach. "It's knowing when the fight is over that she has trouble with."

CHAPTER 13

VIV

D idn't I tell you this shop would have what you need?"
The bookstore a few blocks off Church Street was a dark
cavern of a place with crowded aisles, mysterious shadowy nooks,
and shelves upon shelves of books on any topic I could imagine.
It smelled of leather and dust and the tang of old ink and, under
normal circumstances, I could have spent countless happy hours
browsing or curled into one of the battered armchairs.

But I was on a mission today.

To that end, Marjory and I had met up after work. She'd been
waiting with her bicycle when I disembarked from the ferry, her
hat pushed back on her forehead, her neckerchief loosened around
her neck. There was a smudge of chain grease across her knuckles
and dust caked her skirt hems and collar. The two of us had walked
up from the harbor, poking into stores and browsing shelves with
no luck until Marjory had mentioned a bookstore she often passed
on her trips back and forth between the naval base and the hospital
in Portsmouth. She'd propped her bicycle against the wall, and together, we'd wandered up and down the stacks under the guarded
eye of the rail-thin proprietor with a waxed mustache and a weak
left eye.

"Here we are. *Lessons in Pitman Shorthand* by Alice Bemmelmen."
Marjory handed me the instruction book. "Looks rather daunting."

I leafed through it as she continued the hunt for a guide to help me polish my typing skills, which were better than they used to be, but nowhere near the proficiency needed if I wanted to persuade Dumfries that I should accompany Dr. Stewart and his surgical team to France.

"It seems like you're going to an awful lot of trouble. Is going really that important?"

"You said yourself we do funny things when we're trying to prove a point," I said, tucking the manual under my arm. "Hold on. Look at this." I pulled a handsome gold-trimmed volume off the shelf. "A Navy bluejacket's manual."

Together, we flipped through the pages. "Here we go. Page eight-o-nine. Yeomen."

"What does it say?" Marjory peered over my shoulder.

The shopkeeper cleared his throat, mustache twitching. "We ain't a library, miss. Buy it or put it back."

"Right." I quickly found a passable used edition of Mares's *Art of Typewriting* and brought all three books to the counter. "We'll take these."

My package under my arm, we headed up the street toward the trolley stop. Clouds grew in the west, but the sun bleached the sky almost white. Dust swirled in the wake of shoppers crossing Main Street.

"Let's stop in at Ernst's," Marjory suggested.

"I guess it has been a whole four days since you saw him last."

She scrunched her nose at me and stuck out her tongue. "You're just jealous you don't have a beau of your own." Whatever she saw in my face, whatever I gave away, her smile faded like a shadow crossing the sun. "Gosh, Viv. I'm sorry. Really. I didn't mean anything by it. Honest. That Tom fella doesn't know what he's missing."

"He's probably better off for it," I said, offering her my brightest smile to lessen the sting.

Meyer's Bakery was a narrow building squashed between a drugstore and a barbershop and down the block from old St. Paul's Church. A blue and white awning shaded the sidewalk in front of the bakery, a pot of salvia brightened the step. A cat stretched out on an upstairs windowsill, watching us with slitted eyes.

"That's new," Marjory commented at the sight of an American flag hanging beside the red and blue shop sign.

"Very patriotic."

Marjory grunted and pushed her way past.

The bakery smelled warmly of yeast and sugar, the shelves and display case filled with pastries and cakes, baskets of dark bread, and tiny French patisserie like jewels on a cushion. Ernst came out of the back at the sound of the bell over the door, his sober features spreading into a relieved smile when he saw us. "Marjory, my dear," he said, his German accent softened by the years he'd lived in America, but still audible in the occasional clipped consonant. "Viv. It's wonderful to see you both. Where is your third musketeer today?"

"Blanche is guarding a bridge with Mrs. Adams and the Women's Home Guard," Marjory said, stealing a kiss when she thought my attention was on an elegant strawberry and cream tart. "We thought we'd bring her some dessert."

Hearing us, Ernst's young daughter came scampering out of the back. Her brown hair was pulled into two messy braids, her pinafore stained with paint. "Margie! Look at my bird." She carried a wet sheet of paper dripping in watercolors.

Marjory melted under the little girl's gap-toothed smile. "That's lovely, Clara. You're quite the artist."

"Come upstairs." She grabbed Marjory's hand. "I want to show you the new paints Papa got me."

As Clara led Marjory away to the little apartment over the shop where she and her father lived, Ernst boxed us an assortment of pastries from the cases. He was a tall, broad-shouldered man, his lumberjack's build tempered by a pair of twinkling blue eyes in a round pleasant face. But today his gaze seemed uneasy, his smile forced. "You have your choice, and I will even throw in a few extra on the house . . . they will not keep."

I noticed how empty the bakery was and how full the cases. Normally, there was a line out the door on Saturday afternoons, but today only a few passersby glanced in the window before moving on, their features blankly stiff. "Where is everyone?"

His smile faded. "It has been very quiet for the last few weeks." He rallied as he rang me up. "I am sure it's only due to the heat. Who wants heavy sweets and cakes when the weather is so oppressive? Things will improve as the season changes. It always does."

Was he trying to convince me or himself? I followed his gaze as it swept toward the window. Across the street, two men stood watching the shop, sharing a cigarette between them.

"They have been there all day," he said quietly.

"Do you know them?"

"They work nearby. One used to come round for a drink now and then, but I've not seen him for at least a year."

Our conversation was interrupted by Marjory's return. "What is this?" she demanded, appearing out of the back, brandishing a piece of paper.

Ernst winced, his face going positively gray. "It is nothing."

"It doesn't read like nothing." Her eyes scanned the page. "'Go back where you came from. This city is for good, patriotic Americans only.'"

"Someone's idea of a joke. If I worried over every unkind word or suspicious look, I'd be all the time unhappy."

"Is that why you put up the flag?" Marjory asked, anger shining in her face. "Because you're being threatened?"

He puffed out his chest. "I put it up because I am a good American who loves his country."

Marjory continued to fume as I took in the empty shop with new eyes. Were people refusing to buy from Ernst because he was German? Were those men watching the shop for the same reason?

"When were you going to tell me this was going on?" Marjory asked, her calm almost more frightening than her fury.

"It is not your problem, *liebling*, it is mine. And what could you do? You are a strong Navy sailor, but not even you are strong enough for this."

"You're a United States citizen. They can't just bully and threaten you."

"The war drags on. So many killed and wounded. So many missing. I can survive a few unkind words."

"As long as they stay words."

He handed over a box tied with a blue ribbon. "These are my neighbors, my friends. I have lived among them for nearly ten years. They are good people."

I wanted to believe him. After all, how could anyone think Ernst was a threat with his flour-stained apron and cheerful disposition? The way he smelled of sugar and vanilla like other men smelled of bay rum and pomade? I knew better than most that appearances could be deceiving, but no matter how hard I tried, I couldn't imagine Ernst as a German spy.

All it takes is a spark, Marjory had warned.

Maybe she was right to worry.

She was still in the dumps by the time we arrived back at the cottage, kicking at pebbles, pinging them against the bicycle's spokes or clanking off the rim, her gaze lost in thought.

"Ernst is right," I offered, hoping to cheer her up. "It's probably just neighborhood boys having a lark." I didn't tell her about the men. She was upset enough.

"Stop being so naive, Viv," Marjory snapped.

I shrank under her anger, my shoulders unconsciously hunching, my body instinctively bracing for the expected blow, then felt ridiculous for my overreaction. This was Marjory. She wouldn't hurt a fly. She stormed inside and straight up the stairs, leaving me juggling a cake box and my books.

I put my packages down, removed my hat and my jacket, smoothed my hair in the mirror, using each familiar action as a way to calm my racing heart. I picked through the mail, even though I knew there was nothing for me. Breathing in as I read each address. Breathing out as I put each letter back in the rack. One letter had been opened, the pages stuffed awkwardly back into the envelope so that a corner stuck out. I recognized Mrs. Lawrence's stolid square handwriting . . . *lost the baby . . . long rest . . . needed at home . . .*

"Vivian!" Marjory shouted from the top of the stairs. "Quick. It's Blanche!"

THE NEXT MORNING, Blanche and I shared a pot of coffee at the cluttered kitchen table. Other than a new hollowness to her eyes and a bruise on her cheek from hitting a wall when she fainted, she looked the same as always; red hair fluffed into becoming curls that framed her face, dressed in a plain shirtwaist and gray skirt that still probably cost more than my entire closet. Poised. Confident. Queenly, even now.

Strike that—she was like Admiral Mayo himself, minus the mustache.

"What do you think?" I pushed my notebook across the kitchen table toward her. "I copied an article out of the newspaper."

She'd agreed to help me with my shorthand, having taken a course in college. But today's lesson was difficult, and Blanche's thoughts were obviously occupied elsewhere. As were mine, to be honest. I pored over lists of squiggles while she chewed the end of her pen. I read and reread each instruction trying to fix the ideas in my mind as she wrote then scratched out sentences then wrote again. By the time I'd passed my work of the past hour across to her, she'd gone through half a dozen sheets of writing paper and two nibs.

"Blanche?"

My gaze drifted toward her latest attempt at a letter home, but she covered it with her hand.

"I'm sorry," she said with a strained smile. "What were you asking?"

I rubbed the spot between my eyes where a headache was forming, stretched, sighed, and turned from the page of shorthand squiggles to the bluejacket's manual, which was at least written in plain English. There was a test as part of our naval instructions training, and I was determined to get a perfect score.

I dropped my gaze back to my book. "I'll keep working on it."

"You'll master Pitman in no time. If Nora Joyce who couldn't put two sentences together without giggling could do it, you can. I have complete confidence in you."

"Who's Nora Joyce?"

But she'd already returned to her letter with renewed determination, ink soaking into the paper under her pen nib.

I cleared my throat. She shuffled her pages. I stretched and closed my book. She poured herself a fresh cup of coffee.

We might have gone on like this all day if Gus hadn't poked his head around our door. "Mail call."

I waved him inside where he drew up a chair at the table beside us, eying Blanche like a lovesick puppy. Working on his uncle's boat had tanned his face to a weathered brown while brightening his blond hair nearly white. He flung an arm across the chairback, flexing new muscles in his shoulders and ropy arms, clearly hoping Blanche would notice, but she was occupied in sifting through the envelopes and paid him no heed.

"Whatcha doing, Viv?" he asked, eying my shorthand.

"Practicing."

"Viv is hoping to convince the Navy to let her go to France," Blanche explained.

Did Gus notice the chained temper beneath her explanation? I tried to catch his eye, but he was digging at the table with the edge of one thumbnail.

"Seems everyone's going off to do their bit," he grumbled, hurt clear in his gentle gaze. After our conversation on the beach, I felt somehow as if I was betraying him.

"It's not for certain," I explained quickly.

"You going too, Blanche?"

Her face darkened, her brows low over thunderous storm cloud eyes. "Oh don't be a damn fool, Gus. You really do take the cake, you know that?" She flung the pad of paper at the wall and stormed out the doors onto the back porch and was gone, striding over the dunes as if charging into battle.

"What did I say now?" he asked, confusion clouding his expression.

"She's stopped swimming and started sinking," I muttered.

I wanted to follow, but I knew better. She needed to walk off her fear and her frustration. But the moment she returned, I would speak. I understood the weight of secrets better than anyone. They could crush you if you let them.

I wouldn't let them crush Blanche.

It was dusk by the time she strode up the duckboard path and onto the porch where she let herself in through the French doors. I remained where I'd been since she departed, wrestling with shorthand and drowning in cups of weak coffee. She paused when she spotted me, the shadows in the room thick against the encroaching night.

"You'll go blind working in the dark like that," she said, lighting a lamp. Immediately, the cottage, oddly desolate in the late afternoon shade, sprang into cozy comforting brilliance. But the same light picked out every line and hollow in Blanche's pale face. We caught and held each other's stare, neither of us able to break the brittle silence. But this time I didn't allow her to intimidate me. I slammed closed my book with an angry shake of my head. "We need to talk. No more putting it off. It's too important."

Her eyes widened as if surprised at my vehemence. Frankly, I surprised myself. I spent my days fading into the wallpaper, hoping not to be noticed. Blanche was the firebrand, the crusader, the force to be reckoned with.

But that force was all but spent.

I sensed her collapse in the curve of her spine, the clench of her jaw. She turned to the growing darkness, her distant gaze unfocused. "You know, don't you?"

"That you're expecting a child?" She swayed at the punch of my words. "I suspected something was wrong. I didn't know what it was until I loosened your corset after you fainted."

"So much for Mrs. Sanger's expert advice." She gave a sad cough of self-deprecating laughter. "I suppose I should be relieved that ridiculous doctor was in such a hurry. He barely paused to take my pulse and listen to my heart before running out of here."

"That was Marjory's doing. When we realized what was in the works, we had to think quick. She met him on the front porch and by the time she'd escorted him to your bedroom, she had him convinced you were a hypochondriac and a closet tippler. As a result, I have a temperance leaflet for you to read and a bottle of Echam's Medicinal Tonic for your fragile nerves." I offered her an encouraging smile, which she did not return.

"Thank you for not divulging my secret, Viv, though I suppose it's only a matter of time." She glanced down at her stomach. "I can only blame Ernst Meyer's baking skills for so long before the truth of my position is impossible to hide."

"What will you do then?"

"I've been trying to write my mother, but how do you tell the woman who would smack your knuckles over using the wrong fork that you've been knocked up? The words aren't really tripping off my pen." She sank onto the couch, pressing a pillow to her stomach. Her eyes shone with angry tears. "I thought about ridding myself of it. Got as far as making inquiries." She looked up at my swift intake of breath. "Don't worry. I didn't go through with it. Not over any moral quandaries, simply because I took one look at the squalid lack of hygiene and decided I didn't want to die of blood poisoning."

"So what *will* you do?"

"Have it. What else is there to do?" She offered me a brave—if somewhat wobbly—smile. "Don't look so worried. I'll figure something out."

My gaze fell to the Navy manual, the gold lettering, the rules and regulations guiding every enlistee; the advantages to service and the punishments should we fail in our duties. Nowhere among the pages was there talk of fellowship or friendship, but I read it just the same in every sentence. The Navy brought together individuals from every corner of the country and turned them into one cohesive unit. Solidarity and brotherhood—or in our case, sisterhood—were at the heart of that unit. They had to be.

"No," I replied sharply. "We'll figure it out together. All three of us."

Her expression was puzzled but hopeful.

"Friends stick together." I smiled. "First things first. Do you have a ring? Wear it. If anyone asks, you were married at city hall after a whirlwind romance. Who's to call out the lie?"

"Gus might," Blanche replied dryly.

"He knows?"

Why did I ask? Of course he knew—or at least suspected. The quarrel he mentioned. Was that what it had been about? Is that what he meant by her stubborn determination to do exactly what she wished no matter the consequences? Poor Gus. He must have seen what would happen with this man and been powerless to stop it.

"You're safe there. If Gus hasn't spilled the beans yet, he's not likely to." I sat up. "Wait, what about Gus? You don't suppose he might be persuaded to marry you. Everyone knows he's smitten."

Blanche straightened in outrage. "Definitely not. Put that thought right out of your mind, Viv Weston!"

"But . . ."

Her quelling look made me swallow my argument.

So much for that brainwave.

Blanche started to pace, and I could tell she was beginning to believe, to be persuaded we could succeed. "Fine. I tell people I'm married, but what then? Sooner or later, it'll come out. We're just buying time. You know the regs. Once the Navy realizes I'm expecting, husband or no husband, I'm out."

"Well then we'll just have to keep it under wraps as long as possible. You're the best seamstress I know. If anyone can conceal a growing stomach, you can. Wear thick frumpy cardigans and no one will think it odd."

"Accused of a loss of morals or a loss of style, I'm not sure which is worse." She flashed a weary smile, and the cold fear that left my insides raw slowly thawed. The situation wasn't completely hopeless. Blanche still had her sense of humor. That was a start.

THAT NIGHT, WE held a war meeting around the kitchen table. Ernst had sent home a black forest cake, but only Marjory cut herself a slice. Blanche and I mostly stared into our cups of cold coffee.

"Maybe if we just tell the father," she suggested around a forkful. "Maybe he'll come back and sweep you off your feet."

"I don't think that's going to happen," Blanche offered somberly. "Remember the two-timing lowlife with the wife?"

"Oh." Marjory choked into her napkin. "Oh Blanche. I'm so sorry."

"You and me both. I should have known he was too good to be true. Old Boston money. Graduated from Harvard. Dashing. Funny. Handsome. His cousin even lived the next town over from a friend of mine from college. It wasn't until after I'd made the biggest mistake of my life that I learned about the wife."

"He told you?"

"That would be giving him way more credit than he deserves. I wrote to my friend gushing about this new beau. Imagine my surprise when she wrote me back. Unfortunately, by then . . ." She shrugged. "It's a good thing he shipped out the following week or I might not have been liable for my actions. If I'm lucky the Germans will do it for me."

"Blanche!" I exclaimed, shooting a sideways look at Marjory; but she was nodding her agreement, her face grim. "You give me his name. I'll have my brothers put the word out."

"Marjory!" I squeaked. "They can't *kill* him."

"I was only joking," she said gruffly, even as she and Blanche shared a grim look of solidarity.

We talked long into the early hours, but by the time we wandered upstairs to bed we'd agreed on a plan of sorts consisting mostly of silence, resorting to subterfuge only when needed. I didn't explain how I came to know the advantages of sticking as close to the truth as possible, and thankfully neither of them asked.

The following morning, I left for the naval hospital. Blanche had risen before me and was gone before I came down, and Marjory was still banging away in her room, her voice raised high in a chorus of "Over There." All along the dusty walk to the trolley stop and the ride into Norfolk, my mind turned Blanche's problems over in an endless loop, but by the time I reached the ferry and stood out on the deck, the Elizabeth River flashing in a green and silver froth below me, my thoughts turned to my own problems.

Blanche had trusted us with her secret. Maybe it was time to trust them with mine.

I wandered into the offices where my section worked, surprised at the chatter and the group of yeomanettes clustered by Quarles's desk. Normally, she would be there, coffee mug at her elbow, typewriter rattling like a Browning machine gun as she kept a weather eye on those under her charge. But this morning, her chair was empty.

"Anyone seen the chief?" I asked.

"She was here an hour ago. I saw her on the stairs by X-ray."

"If we're lucky, she threw herself over."

Laughter met this remark, and a shrill "You're horrid."

"Good riddance. The woman's a battle-ax in a skirt."

The conversation grew louder as typewriters idled.

"Of course, Weston's worried," someone muttered. "She's teacher's pet."

"Two peas and all," came a whispered answer. "Both dull as mud."

"Weston!" Dumfries finally barked from his office. "What's going on out there? Where's Quarles?"

Face burning, I ducked my head around his door. "She's . . . she's gone to the accounting office, sir," I lied.

"Well get her back here now. I need her reports on auxiliary hospital staffing needs for a meeting I was supposed to be attending"—he checked his watch—"ten minutes ago."

"Aye, aye, sir," I said, snapping him a salute, ignoring the smirks as I hurried out of the office.

A nurse pointed me toward the dispensary. A technician from X-ray sent me toward the staff mess hall. I finally found her in the patients' library, of all places. She sat, knees drawn up into the chair. Her head was lowered, her shoulders bowed and shuddering, her hands clutched under her ribcage as if holding herself together.

"Chief? Is everything all right, ma'am?"

Without her spectacles, she seemed younger, vulnerable. Her pale eyes were red-rimmed and watery with weeping. Her cheeks splotchy where they weren't white as paste. Her hair normally as prim and no-nonsense as her attitude straggled against her neck. I imagined her tearing at it like those women in ancient stories who went mad with grief. She didn't bark at me or demand a reason for my ill-timed intrusion. She simply stared as if struck dumb, her head shaking slowly from side to side in denial.

My gaze dropped from her to the Western Union telegram she held crushed in her hand.

```
33 GOVERNMENT
WASHINGTON DC 632 AM JUNE 6 1918


CHIEF YEOMAN IVY QUARLES
PORTSMOUTH NAVAL HOSPITAL, PORTSMOUTH VIRGINIA


   DEEPLY REGRET TO INFORM YOU THAT PRIVATE
PHILLIP QUARLES INFANTRY IS
   OFFICIALLY REPORTED AS KILLED IN ACTION MAY 17
   HARRIS, THE ADJUTANT GENERAL 645AM
```

"My brother's dead," she said, emotion wiped from her voice.

I didn't know she had a brother. Or a family. Or even a first name. She never spoke of her life outside these walls. I just assumed she bled Navy blue. Or had simply materialized like a specter at her desk back in the spring of '17.

I checked to make sure no one had followed me. It was obvious that there were plenty who would enjoy seeing the tough-as-nails chief yeoman brought low with embarrassment.

"I'm sorry, ma'am."

"He'd only arrived at the front two weeks before he was killed. Can you believe it? Barely time to dirty his uniform in Flanders mud, and now he's gone."

I touched her arm, her muscles taut, her body one live raw wire. I thought she might shatter into a million pieces. Instead, she took a deep breath that was almost a moan, and the grief she'd swallowed in jagged bits and pieces erupted in a gush of weeping.

I held her as she cried. Her body shook until my chest burned with my own tears. Soon her weeping became sobs as exhaustion overcame her. At last, she pushed me away, clearing her throat and straightening her uniform, her face flushed now with embarrassment as well as sorrow. "I apologize, Weston. I should never have lost my composure in such a way. That was unprofessional of me and unbecoming of a Navy chief petty officer."

"He was your brother, ma'am."

She folded the telegram away into her pocket. "And now I'm left to carry on alone. It's a strange feeling, and one I find quite unbearable."

Maybe it was habit, but I immediately thought of Father, of what he would say. "He's with the angels now" was one of his usual bromides when called to a deathbed. "At peace."

I got a hard disbelieving laugh in response. "Save your words for someone who believes." Her voice held a shred of her usual no-nonsense clip. "There is no paradise or heartfelt reunions. He's dead. There's nothing peaceful or angelic about that." She dabbed at her angry eyes with a plain white handkerchief. "I assume you didn't come looking for me to deliver your condolences." She sat up, adjusted her jacket, and met my gaze with one as cool as ice.

"No, ma'am. Lieutenant Dumfries is looking for you. Something about a meeting?"

"Oh." She stood, clearing her throat, adjusting her spectacles. But there was a new fragility to the way she held herself, and her gaze was hazy and unfocused. "Right. Of course. His meeting."

We returned to the office together, the girls back at their desks, though eyes watched us as we passed, and I swear I heard a few snickers and comments about people getting theirs. Did they really see me as a teacher's pet? As dull? I tried not to wonder which girls smiled to my face while whispering behind my back, but my skin crawled with embarrassment and questions.

"Where's the lieutenant?" Quarles asked, her face pale but her voice firm.

"Gone, ma'am," Foyle piped up from her desk by the window. "He said he couldn't wait for you a minute longer."

Quarles collected the pages of reports, stuffed them into a leather case, and buttoned it closed while I stood awkwardly near the door. I had more than enough work to keep me busy, but walking past that row of desks felt beyond me. My knees wobbled and my shoulders twitched with the frightening realization that my attempt at fading into the woodwork had backfired. My standoffishness had been taken as arrogance. My shy silence, as conceit.

"Should we send for a messenger, ma'am?" Norris asked, eager to please, though only last week she'd referred to Quarles as a dried-up old spinster.

"There's no time. The meeting has already started. But—"

"I'll take them." Before she could argue, I grabbed up the case. "Be back in an hour."

"Weston!" Quarles shouted, but I was already out the door.

CHAPTER 14

PEGGY

1968

Peggy and David sat across from each other at the camper's table. Her seat was covered with a paisley throw, all blue and green swirls that reminded her of the bay waters on a sunny day. His seat was piled with cushions, like a sultan's tent. A hurricane lamp hung from a hook in the ceiling between them, shining down on the remains of their dinner. As always, his radio was on, but he'd changed out the American Bandstand Top Forty of that afternoon for a more grown-up jazz sound. They ate to the flutter of a snare accompanied by a soulful trumpet and a singer with a voice like honey while he told her about his travels across the country in his camper, the places he'd seen, the people he'd met. It was the kind of adventurous carefree life she and Chaz had dreamed of once, and she listened hazy with wine, imagining the wide skies of Montana, the red desert terrain of Arizona, the blaze of a Pacific sunset.

"All those wonderful, glorious places, how on earth did you wash up here?"

He shrugged. "A long, boring story, but once I arrived it just felt like somewhere I could call home."

Peggy knew exactly what he meant. She'd felt a similar sensation when she stood with her toes in the sand watching the dawn skies brighten, when she pulled around the corner to see the little cottage waiting at the end of the dusty road, when she lay in bed listening to the tree limbs scratch at the dormer window during a thunderstorm. She'd lived in the city her whole life and never once felt this easy contentment as if a missing piece of herself had finally slotted into place.

Having cleared the dishes away into the camper's sink, David sat back with a satisfied look and a cigarette. Peggy pushed the last crumbs of pie around her plate in between sips of the bitter espresso he'd offered her with dessert. They'd already finished the bottle of wine she'd brought in addition to one he'd pulled from a bucket of ice. A third sat half-full beside the coffee carafe. Peggy was feeling pleasantly relaxed, her bones like butter.

The rain had held off long enough to allow him to prepare the food on the funny little portable cooker attached to one of the van's double side doors, but now it drummed on the roof as they watched the flicker of lightning off to the south.

The camper was far more comfortable than Peggy had imagined. A high shelf bed sat at the back, curtains screening it from the rest of the space, and ingenious little cupboards and shelves were created out of every available nook and cranny. The cushions, throws, and curtains gave it a cozy feel, and far from being a bear's nest of male living, it was neat and smelled of soap and tobacco and aftershave rather than dirty socks and unwashed laundry.

Smoke drifted around David's head as he tapped the ash into his empty coffee cup. "Confess. You're surprised a man can wield a hammer by day and whip you up a gourmet meal by night."

"I concede graciously and gratefully," she replied with a smile. "It was delicious and a welcome change from takeout food. You can only eat so many greasy fries and crack open so many fortune cookies before the novelty wears off."

"Don't you cook?"

"I used to, not great, but I could find my way around the kitchen without embarrassing myself. I just haven't really felt up to it in a while." She ran the tines of her fork up and down her napkin, turned her cup round and round in its saucer, counted the paisley swirls in the throw at her elbow. "I haven't felt up to doing much in a while, really."

"Yeah. I was sorry to hear about your divorce."

"Suzanne told you? I knew I should have kept it to myself." Her gaze swept up to meet his, but there was no pity there and only mild curiosity.

He eased his legs under him as he sat up, but his features looked less relaxed, more alert. As if he knew he trod on thin ice. "Don't be angry. She only hinted you'd had a pretty rough time. I get that."

"Did she say anything else?" she asked, her fork abandoned, her napkin now crushed in one hand. "Any other secrets about me she's spilled to the world?"

"Well, I don't know." The edge of his mouth curved in a teasing smile. "There was an enigmatic mention of Annette and Frankie."

Her anger drifted away like the smoke from his cigarette, and she couldn't help laughing. "The cheeky brat. She ought to know that part of why I fled Queens was to escape meddling friends."

"I think she's taken you on as her personal project."

"You mean her charity case, don't you? You'd think she had enough on her plate. Two kids, a baby on the way, a husband. A house." She couldn't help the resentment that crept into her voice, which made her feel worse. It wasn't Suzanne's fault she'd found the all-American picket-fence life that Peggy had lost.

"You make it sound like her life is perfect," David replied, leaning back, a hand behind his head. "Maybe she's just better at hiding the fact that she's flailing same as the rest of us."

He was right. Now she felt bad *and* wrong.

"We show people what we want them to see," he continued. "'All the world's a stage and the men and women merely players,' or something like that. It's been a while since my high school Shakespeare."

She felt the force of his comment. Hadn't she just dreaded putting on a brave face and pretending through this dinner? Hadn't she laughed and batted the conversation back and forth and smiled while inside the hollow that never left her pinched and ached?

"You said *us*. Are you flailing too?"

"I live in a camper van parked in your driveway. What do you think?" There was no bitterness in his voice; just an almost quizzical tone as if surprised at his life's vagaries.

"I'm sorry. You're right. Suzanne's been kind. I hadn't realized how much I was in need of kindness until I got here."

"What about your family? They must miss you."

"No family. My ex-husband was it. What about you?"

"Too many to count and all of them living within a few miles of one another. The Dyers have deep roots and a long reach. Mom, Dad, grandparents both sides, aunts, uncles, cousins . . . you name it. Leaving home was like attempting a prison break."

"Did you need to leave for any particular reason?"

"You mean like, did I leave trail of dead bodies? Nothing so dramatic. Like you, I just decided I was tired of people telling me they knew better." He crushed out his cigarette in the ashtray and immediately lit another. "Is your plan to stay here in Ocean View?"

Points for the deft way he dodged the question. If she were less hazy with exhaustion and alcohol she might have pushed for an answer, but she knew enough about avoiding interrogations to be sympathetic. "I haven't decided what I'm doing. Not whether to stay or sell or . . ." She slumped back against the bench seat, her head both muzzy with wine and sparking with caffeine. It made for an odd and unsettling combination. "Have you ever felt like you were watching the world through a fun-house mirror—you're on one side of the glass and everyone else is on the other? You can see them and hear them, but they can't touch you and you can't touch them." She shook her head. "I'm not making any sense, am I?"

"Perfect sense. You were hurt so you retreated into your cave—metaphorically—and now, with your move into the cottage—literally. It feels safe. You can't be hurt again if those well-meaning people can't reach you." Their eyes locked, and this time it was David who looked away.

"So what do I have to do to come out of my cave?" she asked, only then realizing how much she wanted—needed—an answer.

David's gaze was steady. "Make a friend." She noticed the diamond sparks in his blue eyes. "Enjoy a dinner." His long pale lashes. "Chip away at that wall brick by brick."

"Is that what *you're* doing?" she asked, her voice suddenly hoarse.

He reached around the coffee for the bottle of wine and poured her another glass.

IT WAS CLOSE to midnight by the time Peggy climbed the front steps and let herself into the darkened cottage. It felt good to be alone with only her thoughts—and the cottage—for company.

The rain had passed and a late-risen moon shone over the scuffed pine floors. In the gloom, the furniture lost all definition, becoming only shapes and patterns and layers of darkness. A faint scent of violets lingered, embedded in the fabrics and the leathers and the very bones of the house. Maybe it was all the talk about family at dinner, but she was suddenly reminded of her mother's perfume. *A lady should always smell like springtime*, she would say as she spritzed herself from the cut-glass bottle on her dresser. Funny, thinking about that after all these years. Obviously her evening with David had jangled all sorts of odd thoughts to the top of her head.

She should have been exhausted after the day—and the amount of wine—she'd had. But she wasn't sleepy, not at all. Maybe David was right—maybe she was chipping away at her walls one conversation at a time. It seemed too simple a solution. After all, how many conversations had people tried to have with her since she'd come out of the hospital? But perhaps that was the difference. She'd been talked at and over, never with. She'd had her problems dissected, interpreted, and explained away by well-meaning people who hadn't the first notion. Or worse, she'd had her pain ignored as if it didn't exist. As if her child didn't exist.

David had done none of that. In fact, other than tales of his travels, he'd barely talked about himself at all, letting her fill the awkward silences. And tongue loosened, she'd prattled along like a windup doll. She'd probably be mortified tomorrow when she woke up hungover, remembering what she'd said. Tonight, she merely felt . . . refreshed.

Would a walk on the beach relax her? Peggy started to slide her feet into a pair of sandals by the French doors but changed her mind. No. In a sudden decision, she headed for Blanche's bedroom and her unfinished sorting.

Up here, the scent of violets was stronger, but there was also a scent of illness and age and a mustiness the rooms downstairs had lost since her arrival. Peggy slid open the curtains. Moonlight silvered the room in a ghostly veil. It shone in the bedside lamp, the lid of a decorative box, the frame on the dressing table. Her skin prickled as if the air were alive with laughter, slamming doors, the scuff of button shoes, and the swish of long skirts. With a shiver, Peggy forced open a window that had been painted shut, letting in a breeze. The scent—and her unease—evaporated in a wash of thick muggy air. She flipped on the overhead light, and the past faded once and for all back into boxes and crates, the plastic of dry-cleaning bags, and piles of old books and useless bits of paper.

Over the next few hours, the chirp of crickets and the quiet purr of the bay slowly worked their magic, and her frenzied activity slowed, her mind unwinding like the spools of colored thread in Blanche's sewing basket.

By the time the clock downstairs chimed three, she'd pulled the last of the clothes from the dresser. Some to be donated, some to be thrown out, and a few—like the old uniforms and two pairs of carefully preserved high-button shoes—stowed back in their plastic and hung back on the rail. There was only the dressing table left to clear.

She sat on the tufted stool, gazing on the clutter of jars and bottles, tubes of ointment and containers of cold cream and witch hazel. In addition to the pearls that hung from the mirror, a drawer held a jewelry box awash in fine brooches and sparkling earrings alongside a few bits and bobs of everyday costume jewelry. But underneath a jangle of gold chains, she came across a flat metal disk with a hole in one end as if it was meant to be worn on a chain. Faint writing had been inscribed on one side—*BR Lawrence*. And underneath, *9-9-93* and *6-17-17*. On the other side was a fingerprint etched into the metal.

She'd found Blanche's ID tag.

Peggy's gaze lifted to the cherished photo, the only one in her aunt's room.

The three girls stood arm in arm, the flap of amusement park flags behind them. Peggy turned the frame over and slid the yellowed photograph free. On the back written in pen were the following words.

V M and B at Ocean View Amusement Park 1918

Pulling free the photo dislodged a small piece of paper that fluttered to the floor. An obituary cut from a newspaper.

U.S.N. yeomanette Marjory Meyer, beloved bride of Ernst
Meyer, died. Funeral will take place at St. Martin's Lutheran Church at 10am. tomorrow.

Was this what Viv meant when she said it all went wrong? When
she said she couldn't forgive herself? That she was to blame?

The bedroom light flickered and went out, plunging the room
into darkness. Peggy jumped with surprise, but not fear. David had
warned her about the faulty breakers. But there would be no more
sorting tonight. She might as well catch a few hours' sleep before
his hammering commenced at dawn.

Feeling her way to her own room and her own bed, she pulled
the sheet up and rolled onto her side, cradling a pillow to her chest.
Questions swirled, but every time she thought she had an answer,
it flitted just out of reach. Symonds would be no help. And Blanche
was dead.

That left Viv.

Decision made, she closed her eyes, letting the steady tick of her
travel clock lull her into a doze. Just as she felt herself falling into
sleep, she gasped as if she were falling. Her eyes flew open to see
the curtains fluttering, the scent of violets on the breeze.

CHAPTER 15

VIV

1918

I took me forty minutes to hoof it down Effingham Street toward the enormous naval shipyard, following the rolling clouds of black smoke from a forest of chimneys to its acres of sheds, warehouses, workshops, and offices—a city within a city.

The warren of brick and steel was the oldest and largest naval facility in the States. Workers in coveralls and heavy boots hurried between buildings. Sparks burst like fireworks from a sheet metal shop, and the noise of riveters and welders was deafening. A coal train stood idle, throwing steam on a rail siding, while ahead in one of the enormous dry docks, a battleship towered over the swarm of mechanics, plumbers, armorers, and shipfitters climbing up and down its sides and along its half-completed hull.

The pace was incredible, and I felt my pulse quicken as I hurried through oily puddles, my shoes slopping and sliding in the mud. I was turned around only once, and that was remedied by a young man in a greasy set of overalls with hands scarred and chapped as he waved me toward the brick building that housed supply and personnel. I thanked him and continued on, passing the marine barracks on my right and the forge on my left, the heat and roar of it blasting like a dragon's breath, a glow like the eye of a demon with a blue heart at its center.

"You lost?" A gruff voice, low and smoky, spun me on my heel. He wore a chief petty officer's stripes, but his uniform was rumpled, and his hands, like the young man's I'd met previously, were rough and broken-nailed. His weathered features spoke of years at sea before assignment to the shipyard. Perhaps age had caught up with him. War was a young man's game. A game all too many of them were losing.

"I'm delivering a package for a staff meeting," I said with a salute.

"Thought you weren't one of our regular gals. You're far too spit and polish. The dirt of the yard gets into everything no matter how careful you are. I'm headed that direction. I'll show you the way," he said with a tip of his cap.

He led me past a row of sheds, and around a corner by the sail shop, when a man came plunging at a run, smack into me. "Fire in welding shed three!" he shouted as we fell in a tangle of limbs, the breath driven out of me, my palms scraped on the gravel.

More men and more shouting.

"Get the hoses!"

"Evacuate! Evacuate!"

"Someone's still in there!"

Fire shot from broken windows, raced along the rooftop. A clanging of fire alarms and men barking instructions billowed around me along with the choking black smoke. Sparks whirled past my face, catching in my jacket where they smoldered in the wool.

"Get back!" my guide shouted. "This place could blow any minute."

A strong whistling crackle blistered my ears. My vision filled with flame, and I was struck as if by a giant slapping hand. I couldn't see. Couldn't breathe. A ringing filled my ears. Then darkness rushed toward me like the locomotive I'd just seen idling at the siding. Then nothing more.

DRIP ... DRIP ... DRIP ...

The plonk of a leaky tap bounced against my skull like a boy's rubber ball before squeezing down onto my neck and spine like a giant vise.

Drip ... drip ... drip ...

My heart met and matched the beat, drowning out the off-key chord sounding between my ears. I winced and tried turning my head, but that only made the note more dissonant, like the piano in my old church in Richmond in sad need of tuning.

"She's coming round."

The voice sounded far away, as if it came through a scratchy radio.

Drip ... drip ... drip ...

"Viv? It's Blanche. Can you hear me?"

Cool fingers linked with mine. The scent of violets made me smile. I blinked against a dim light coming from high above, my eyes scratchy as if gravel had embedded itself beneath my lids.

I looked up into a maze of pipes running overhead. Somewhere in a corner, water dripped into a metal bucket. I was at the end of a row of metal hospital beds, a screen partly shielding me from the room. I could hear the shuffle and squeak of shoes, the rumble of trolleys, the murmur of conversation echoing back to me from the high ceiling, but this wasn't the main ward or even one of the temporary pavilions set up on the hospital's campus. I focused on the brick walls; the scent of cold damp against the stronger odors of sweat, urine, bleach, and illness; the light filtering down from high windows.

Blanche sat beside me, worry shadowing her eyes, pinching her features. Marjory, looking as if she'd come straight from work, shifted uncomfortably from foot to foot. Her gaze seemed to search me out as she fiddled with the strap of her messenger's bag.

"What's happened?" I winced against the pain in my throat. Every breath burned in my chest.

"Try not to talk too much."

"Where am I?" I insisted.

"This is the Navy's idea of separate-but-equal accommodation." Blanche's voice scraped across my brain like nails on a slate. "A dank cell in the hospital's basement."

"You had a nasty knock to the head, my dear." It was only then that I noticed the doctor standing just at the edge of the screen. He scanned my chart before giving me a cool, professional smile. "Quite a few scrapes, some minor burns, and stitches in your leg, but you were lucky. You're young. You'll mend and be good as new in a few weeks."

My head throbbed to the rhythm of the leaky pipe, stars dancing at the edges of my vision. "What happened?" I whispered.

The three of them shared a look.

"There was an explosion at the shipyard. Four men were killed," Blanche answered.

"Do they know what caused it?"

Marjory shook her head. "Not yet, but there are inspectors and officials crawling all over the place. They think it might have been sabotage."

I closed my eyes as if I could blot out the memory of the fire and the blast. But that only seemed to increase the volume of the brain-sloshing drip, drip, drip until I wanted to scream.

The doctor cleared his throat. "I'll check back in when I've completed my rounds. Your friends can stay for a few minutes, then you need to rest."

After he was gone, they huddled closer to my bed. Marjory's chin wobbled. "You've been out cold since yesterday. They weren't sure if you'd ever wake up or if you did, if you'd wake up in your right mind."

"About that . . ." Blanche said, exchanging a glance with Marjory. "The doctor was making all sorts of grim predictions, and we weren't sure if you were going to pull through, so we telephoned your family in Richmond."

I didn't understand at first, my head still buzzing and sloshed with confusion, my battered body aching down to my toenails. "You telephoned them?"

"That's right. Or rather we telephoned the Westons in Ginter Park." Blanche paused to let her words sink in before continuing. "We told them their daughter had been in an accident."

"Oh." I wished I could trade places with the dead men. "I see."

"They were quite shocked at the news. But they would be, wouldn't they?" Blanche let the silence stretch to a breaking point. "Since their daughter died five years ago of diphtheria."

My body flushed hot then cold. My teeth chattered. I rolled over, retching on the floor by my bed until my ribs ached and my throat felt as if someone had slit it open with a dull dagger.

"I could never put my finger on it, but I had a feeling there was something going on with you," Blanche declared with the air of Sherlock Holmes unmasking a villain.

With nothing left in my stomach, I curled into a ball, the stitches in my leg aflame, every bruise on fire.

"Really, Blanche? Now you've gone and upset her," Marjory said as if from down a long tunnel. "Viv? Blanche didn't mean it. We're not angry. We're sure you had a very good reason for lying. Isn't that right, Blanche? Tell Viv you aren't angry."

"Of course, I'm not angry, Viv. Or whatever your name is," Blanche said, her words cutting through the pounding in my head. "But I do think you owe us an explanation."

I TOLD THEM everything. From my suspicions about my mother's death until I gripped the cold metal handle of the ash can. My throat burned and my vision danced and burst at the edges like fireworks, but I left nothing out.

"I can't believe it. It's like something out of a dime novel." Marjory perched on the edge of my bed, her eyes wide with shock, but also excitement. "It's no wonder you ran away."

"Rotten bastard. He's lucky all he got was an ash can to the skull. If I'd been there . . ." Blanche's anger on my behalf was practically palpable. It made my already throbbing head ache even more. I tried to relax and let the noise of the ward wash over me, but my body was strung tight as a wire. My heart banged against my ribs.

"No one would have believed me if I told them what really happened. Father's a pillar in our community. They don't know how he is when he's had too much to drink. And even those who might have suspected, didn't ask. I don't think they wanted to know."

By now my stomach swam as if I were rounding the top of the roller coaster. The specks dancing at the edges of my vision crowded close, the medicine beginning to make me sleepy and sick. "When they handed me that form, I couldn't put my own name down. Vivian's name just popped in my head. I never meant it to go so far."

"She must have been someone very close to you," Marjory said.

"My best friend," I answered softly.

I closed my eyes and there she was—her cloud of brown hair, snub nose in a sun-freckled face, the tiniest gap between her front teeth that made her smile all the more infectious. Even all these years later, I could hear her laugh and the bold way she spoke as if expecting life to fall in with her plans, no matter what. "Vivian was a year older than me. She was clever and beautiful and fun, always getting us into the most ridiculous scrapes. She'd even drag her brother Tom along into our pranks—he was older than both of us and was supposed to be the responsible one, but no one could resist her. She was like a force of nature."

"She sounds like my kind of girl," Blanche said.

Yes. That was it exactly. Blanche *was* like Vivian. Spoiled and headstrong, they shared that same easy confidence that comes with being loved. That charmed assurance that no matter the trouble, they could always land on their feet. Would Blanche's pregnancy be the leap too far? The one sin that could not be overlooked?

"When she died, the Westons were crushed. Tom went away to school. I didn't see him again until we bumped into each other in the park. Then it was as if we'd never been apart—as if his sister was pushing us together again."

Blanche sat back, smoothing out her skirt, adjusting her neckerchief. She glanced around at the activity on the ward as if searching for someone. "So afterward, you became Viv Weston to hide the truth about what you'd done."

I squeezed my eyes shut against the light, against the pain, against that awful sympathetic yet excited look on Blanche's face. "I wanted to tell you both. So many times I came so close to blabbing it all. But then I was afraid if I said anything, the Navy would throw me out. And if they discovered you knew and hadn't reported it, they'd throw you out too. I couldn't have that on my conscience. I've ruined my life. I won't ruin yours too."

"You ninny," Blanche crowed. "What happened to all that talk of sisterhood and facing the world together?"

I barely heard her. "Oh God, what must the Westons have thought when you rang them up?"

I imagined Mrs. Weston picking up the phone, hearing a strange voice at the other end. I imagined her shock then her confusion and then her anger. What had I done?

"So what's your real name?" Marjory asked as if I'd just confessed to nothing more consequential than leaving the milk out or burning the toast. "Is it Emmaline? You look like an Emmaline."

"It's—"

Blanche's head went up like a hound catching a scent. Once again I had the sense she was waiting for someone. Had she turned me in, and this was simply her way of buying time until the authorities arrived?

"You summoned the military police, didn't you?" I struggled up, fighting the nausea and the pain in my head. I wanted to throw up but there was nothing left in my stomach. Blanche put a hand on my shoulder. I struggled against her hold, but she was stronger, and I was weak, my brain sloshed, my limbs quaking with fatigue.

"Hold still before you tear your stitches, you great goon. We haven't called anybody."

My panicked gaze flashed to Marjory, who nodded worried agreement. "She's telling the truth. Honest." Her lips compressed and mischief danced in her eyes. "Well, almost the truth."

I fell back, breath and energy spent, my future slipping away with every moment.

Blanche settled me with a firm word. "You and I and Marjory— we're friends, and someone once told me friends stick together." A voice sounded from beyond the screen. Blanche's face cleared from its previous exasperated frown. "If we can't convince you, maybe he can."

He stepped around the screen, his face incredibly familiar and incredibly dear. "Hiya, sport. Seems like you got yourself in quite a pickle."

Tears swam in my eyes and leaked down my cheeks onto the starched pillow and the thin blanket. I swallowed around a lump. "Tom."

CHAPTER 16

VIV

I had to blink against the sudden blurring of my vision, my heart and my stomach flip-flopping. Tom was here. I had dreamed of him for so long I didn't believe he was real. I wanted to reach out and touch him, feel the pulse in his wrist, smell the woody peppermint scent of his skin even as I shrank from his presence.

At some point Blanche and Marjory melted away, but I barely noticed. All my focus was on Tom. "Is it really you?" Despite his uniform, he looked just the same: thick dark hair, a face angled and thin, all cheekbones and jawline. Eyes a clear sharp hazel and . . . that smile. I used to forget my name when he smiled at me.

"I could ask you the same question." He glanced down at the floor, then back at me. "Vivian."

It had been months since I'd flinched hearing someone address me by that name. But when Tom said it, my body went cold. I couldn't tell from his tone whether he was exasperated or outraged. I swallowed back my fear as I scoured him for clues. Was he angry with me for stealing his sister's identity? Revolted at the idea that I ran away leaving my father for dead on our kitchen floor? Did the wrinkle between his brows signify confusion, frustration, or fury? I'd imagined our reunion so many times. Not once had I pictured myself lying in a hospital bed while he interrogated me over an attempted murder.

"Tom, I can explain everything." I clenched the edges of my blanket as if dangling from a cliff, the whole sordid story spilling out of me, barely a breath between words. When there was nothing left to tell, I waited for the ax to fall, my stomach in knots.

After interminable heart-stopping minutes, he gave a slow, wondering shake of his head. "Clever little fool," he said, the hint of a smile causing the panicked roar in my ears to fade. "You're lucky I happened to be home when the telephone call about my injured sister came through. Mother and Father are away for the summer." He came farther into the room and for the first time, I noticed the shortened gait, the sickbed pallor. He dropped into a chair as if in relief.

"You've been hurt."

"Broke my leg in an air crash. It's healed now, but it still bothers me now and again, especially when I'm tired."

"Will they discharge you?"

He sat up straighter, a proud set his shoulders. "I'd fight them if they tried. I'm down here at Langley Field for a few weeks and then it's off to France."

"How wonderful," I murmured. "I'm sure you'll be brilliant."

He leaned forward as if deciding whether to take my hand. "I wrote to you like I promised, but when I didn't hear back, I assumed your father had convinced you to break it off." I tried not to hear the hurt in his voice. "I even went round to your house last time I was home on leave. I thought maybe if I could talk to him face-to-face, explain things . . ."

"What did he say?" Tom gave a small shake of his head, but I knew him well enough to know he was stalling. "Please, I need to know."

He took a breath as if facing a hurdle. "He claimed you'd attacked him. That he'd caught you stealing money and when he confronted you . . . you bashed him over the head. He was almost gleeful in recounting the incident."

My mouth went dry. I fumbled for the glass of water by my bed. "Did you believe him?"

"I didn't know what to believe, though I found the idea of you bashing anyone, much less your father, pretty impossible. And I was right, or . . . half-right, I guess." He sighed in frustration. "Why didn't you let me know what was going on? I could have helped."

"It would only have tangled you up in my mess. It was better to disappear."

"Become someone else."

I cringed. If only it was Vivian sitting there. She'd have laughed at the joke. Been the first in my corner. Instead, it was her brother, and he wasn't laughing.

I tried to imagine the scene, Father spouting his lies to Tom, who refused to buckle under the weight of his grandiose charm. Would he have told the same story to anyone wondering what had become of me? Or would he have kept my supposed crime to himself? Making it public would mean questions, and questions might mean the truth about what he'd done—to me and to Mother—would finally come out. He couldn't risk that. But he couldn't allow me to remain a loose end either. I wanted to pull the blanket over my head and hide.

"I'm sorry, Tom. It's all I can say, even if it sounds inadequate. Will you tell the authorities who I really am before you go?"

For the first time, anger sparked his gaze and sharpened his voice. "I can't believe you even have to ask me that." He lowered his voice as a nurse passed by with a rickety cart of medicines. "But how long can you keep this lie going? Sooner or later, it's bound to trip you up. Maybe you should tell them yourself."

"No." I surprised myself by the strength of my answer. "I'd be tossed out of the Navy, given a dishonorable discharge—and my friends alongside me. Everything we've worked for would be for nothing."

"But you enlisted to hide. You don't have to anymore."

"I might not be a murderer, but Father's being alive is almost as dangerous. What if he's looking for me? What if he tracks me here?"

"Come with me when I leave. There are jobs in New York same as here. We could be married before I go. You could be Mrs. Tom Weston. That would spike your dad's guns."

My father wouldn't be the only one who'd be disappointed, but I didn't say so.

"What do you say? Marry me?" A corner of his mouth quirked. "I'd get down on one knee, but I'm not sure the leg will let me."

"Please, Tom." I grabbed his hand when he looked as if he might try. "Please don't. Not here. Not like this."

How it hurt to say those words. To turn him down. I ached to fall into his arms and let him take over, make everything all right, put the world back together again. To feel his arms around me, his scent in my nose as he held me, to feel safe and secure like nothing could hurt me. It was the dream I'd carried with me since the moment we parted on the train platform. So why didn't I reach for it with both hands?

Was it because he never once said he loved me?

I BARELY HAD time to register my shock at seeing Tom again when a nurse with a grim face and a voice like thunder poked her head around my screen to declare visiting hours over. As he gave me a last glance before departing, I was relieved then ashamed. What was wrong with me? I'd spent months pining over Tom. I should be over the moon at his proposal instead of thankful I hadn't had to hurt him by turning him down or explaining my reluctance. Not that I had an explanation. Just a sense that even though Tom had asked, he'd done so not out of passion but out of obligation. And even though I ached to accept him, I'd be doing so out of desperation, not love.

I expected him back the very next day, but the hours dragged with no visitors and no messages. Maybe he'd come to the same conclusion I did. Maybe he'd regretted his impetuosity and was just as torn over what words to use that would smooth away the awkwardness. Nurses came and went. The doctor made his rounds. I was poked, prodded, and pronounced satisfactory. In between, I laid in my bed and ran over every mistake, chewed on every regret. Questioned my choices from the moment I first suspected Father's hand in my mother's death to the decision to become Viv and enlist in the USNR.

I should have spoken up, trusted more, risked it all. But I'd let fear rule me. It had kept me quiet, kept me isolated, kept me under control.

The shadows shrank then lengthened into afternoon.

Did I wish that I could turn back time so that none of this had ever happened? Once, maybe. But now? Every choice I'd made or hadn't made had brought me here to Norfolk. To Blanche and Marjory. To the cottage in Ocean View. And to the Navy, where I'd finally been taken seriously, finally been respected for a job well done.

Could I wish all that away if I had the chance?

"Weston?" A nurse in apron and veil appeared at my bedside. "You have a guest."

I braced myself, hoping I could find the right words to make Tom understand, but it was Chief Quarles, spectacles glinting in the light from the overhead bulbs. "Lieutenant Dumfries sends his regards."

"Old Grumpy Guts himself?"

I surprised a chuckle out of her, quickly smothered. "I'll pretend I didn't hear that."

Her features resumed their normal solemnity, but her eyes crinkled with shared amusement. And like sand settling in a jar, the endless loop of questions fell away, leaving a calming certainty. No matter how bad it got, I wouldn't change one single moment.

"He's anxious to see you back at your desk as soon as possible." She pulled up a chair. There was no mark of her recent tragedy but for a slight hollowness to her cheeks and a sunkenness to her gaze. She remained stiff as a board, every crease ironed, every pin in place. Grief for her brother locked firmly away.

"I'm surprised he's noticed I'm missing."

"Well, to be honest his exact words were 'Where's that girl with the frightened-rabbit look? She makes the best coffee,' but the sentiment was sincere."

I wasn't sure how it happened or when it happened or if I was even imagining it—I *was* still a bit light-headed—but somehow Quarles and I had become friends.

Would wonders never cease?

"I'll return as soon as they clear me for duty, ma'am."

"Yes, well let's hope it's soon. With the buildup of troops on the Western front, we need you in fighting form."

"Have you heard any more news about what caused the explosion?"

"Rumors are flying like leaves. Most are accusing German saboteurs. After the fire last winter that swept through downtown, people want answers and they want them now."

"Have they any proof Germans were behind it?" I didn't want to think about what those rumors might mean for Ernst and his friends. Would there be more vandalism and threats? Or worse? Could those vigilantes like the ones in the Midwest that Marjory was always on about turn up here in Norfolk?

"Nothing but conjecture and hearsay, but it's convincing for all that. I'm sure you've heard about the German village that used to be at the shipyard until a year or two ago."

I nodded. Some of the local girls in my unit had told me about the interned sailors off the raiding ships *Kronprinz Wilhelm* and the *Prinz Eitel Friederich*. How the city had treated them like celebrities until America had entered the war, and they were all sent to prison camps down south.

"Surely, *they* couldn't be involved. All those men are long gone."

"Maybe, but there are claims that a few escaped into the city and took refuge with sympathetic friends, biding their time."

"It sounds a bit far-fetched."

"It sounds a lot far-fetched, but people will believe all kinds of rot if they hear it repeated often enough." She rose from her seat, her normally hard-edged features slack, the knife-edge glint in her eye dulled. "Now, enough about that dreadful business. I really came to say thank you. For listening when I needed you and for holding your tongue about it afterward. I know some of the girls find my style of management overly harsh and my manner abrasive. They call me shrill and pushy. A hag. A bitch, even."

"Oh no, Chief. That's not true."

"You're a bad liar, Weston. But I've learned to ignore the names. They can't say I get pushed around or that I let those who serve under me get pushed around either."

I hadn't thought about that, but it was true. Chief Quarles ran a tight unit, but I'd never heard any of the girls complain about the smarmy talk and pinched bottoms so many others griped about. She paused at the edge of the screen. "By the way, I went behind Dumfries' back and spoke to Dr. Stewart. If you play your cards right, maybe you'll get that transfer after all."

"I don't know what to say but thank you."

"It was the least I could do. That could have been me outside that welding shed."

". . . Benny says he's well though the fighting has been fierce around . . . oh that part's blacked out . . ." I reclined on the porch glider, Mrs. Bemmelmen's shorthand primer facedown on my lap listening to Marjory read the latest letter from her eldest brother.

"Probably the town of Vaux," Blanche suggested from her seat where she was knitting socks for the Red Cross.

"Hush and let me read. He says they've given the Germans hell for the past month with their artillery, and the Hun have been clobbering them right back. He lost a pal, someone named Joey who took a shell in the neck."

Blanche and I both winced.

Since my discharge from the hospital, life at the cottage had resumed its normal pattern, but there was a subtle difference to our days, a new camaraderie that didn't bump up against sudden silences or falter against an edged smile. We had risked and grown closer for it.

"'. . . but were pretty lucky regarding casualties,'" Marjory continued. "'Heading off the line for two days leave. Hope to meet up with Albert and Walter'—my other brothers—'if possible at . . .' oh that part's blacked out too."

As Marjory read, I tried to get comfortable on the glider's cushions, wincing at the ache of strained muscles and the sting of blistered skin. Every morning since my return home, I'd scoured the papers for news stories about the explosion, but there had been no mention of my presence. My injuries not worth the typeset. My accounting of the afternoon's events unwanted by any intrepid reporter.

Thank God.

Viv Weston remained intact.

And those who knew the truth remained quiet.

"'Thanks for the pairs of socks and the packs of cigarettes. Both desperately needed. The cake was tops and sure went quick. I shared it around and all the guys say you're the best baker ever. Don't worry, sis. I didn't let on.'" She looked up, going pink at our disbelieving stares. "I sent them one of Ernst's streusel cakes and told them I made it."

"Of course you did," Blanche commented with a laugh.

She stuck her tongue out and bent back over the pages. "'Don't worry about me. I'm keeping safe. Trenches are filthy, awful places but I wouldn't have missed coming for all the tea in China. Tell the Navy hello from us muddy doughboys. Ha. Ha. Love, Benny.'"

Marjory stretched before pulling the rags from her hair. Blanche set aside her knitting to go into the kitchen while I tried decoding the shorthand g hook, but a lingering ringing in my head made focusing on transcribing the brain-teasing dance of squiggles across the page impossible. I gave up, closing my eyes, listening to the droning song of summer cicadas, the clink of glasses, and the running tap as Blanche moved around inside the kitchen, Marjory whistling as she brushed out her curls.

The drowsy heat wrapped around me, the comfortable familiar noises loosened muscles and slid warm along my bones. My breathing slowed. It wasn't until Blanche roused me with a drink and a smile that I realized this was peace. The secrets that had kept me taut and sleepless, the worries I'd carried locked beneath my ribs, they were gone.

Blanche set a glass down on the table next to Marjory, who was rereading her brother's letter for the hundredth time with a teary smile. "I just want this whole rotten war to be over. It feels like it's been going on forever. And every day it goes on, is one more day I have to worry about Benny and Albert and Walter and all the boys from our old neighborhood. My stomach has been in a permanent knot for a year and a half."

"Strictly off the record," Blanche replied, "my brother says sources in the War Department tell him the Germans have been knocked back on their heels by the number of Allies hitting the line. That now the Americans have joined in, it's only a matter of time."

"And would your brother and his sources in the War Department know when that time might come?" Marjory asked.

"No, but I hope it's not *too* soon."

"Blanche! How can you say that?" Marjory cried, practically shouting.

"Because it's true," Blanche replied calmly. "I hate the death and destruction as much as anyone, but once the war is over, you know what will happen. The Navy will tell us thank you for your service but goodbye, and that will be that. The end of the yeomanettes. All our hard work. We'll be right back where we started. Fighting for the scraps. Struggling to get men to take us seriously. It's fine for some, but I refuse to be set aside when I'm no longer wanted—not again." She downed her drink, hands shaky.

The sun sank low over the far trees, setting the sky ablaze. A lamp flickered brightly in Gus's front window. Marjory pulled out a deck of cards.

"Are you meeting Ernst tonight?" I asked.

"He has a wedding cake to finish decorating. He's not had many big orders these past months, so he wants to impress. What about your airman, Viv? Any plans to see him before he leaves for France?"

I hadn't told them about Tom's marriage proposal. Marjory already saw our situation as the epitome of a star-crossed romance. If she found out, I'd never hear the end of it. And Blanche . . . well . . . I wasn't sure how Blanche would react, not with her own future so up in the air. Besides, Tom had been called almost immediately back to Langley. He hadn't repeated his proposal before he went, and, chicken that I was, I'd not brought it up.

"I don't know. So much has happened since I kissed Tom goodbye all those months ago. I'm not sure if we can just pick back up again. It's almost as if he belonged to another life . . . or another person. Not me at all."

"You mean you've been Viv so long, it's hard to think of yourself as anyone else," Blanche suggested.

"Or maybe I don't want to think of myself as someone else."

I hid my sidestepping in a renewed concentration on Mrs. Bemmelmen's shorthand instructions, tracing the tangle of crisscrossing loops. Like Tom and Richmond. So intertwined that it was impossible to think of one without the other, where one left off and the other began. Seeing Tom again meant facing parts of myself I didn't like, parts of myself I'd tried to bury.

I closed my eyes, but the swirls and swoops continued to dance on the backs of my eyelids. Tom loved the old me, the one who jumped at shadows and needed protecting. Would he love this new me just as much? The one who'd embraced her independence too thoroughly to give it up—even for him?

I opened my eyes to Blanche's steady gaze. "I like who I am when I'm Viv. I didn't like myself very much before. That person let awful things happen to her. The Vivian I knew would never just sit back and surrender. She was strong. She was special. That's how I want to be. How I need to be."

"If it's Viv you want to be, it's Viv you shall be." Blanche raised her glass of lemonade. "To Viv Weston, past and present."

"To Viv." We toasted. The long evening shadows fell dreamy and shifting across the porch. It was easy to imagine a fourth girl standing in the corner raising a glass alongside us. I blinked, the shadows shifted once again, and the corner stood empty.

"If she gets to be who she wants to be," Marjory said shuffling her cards, "can I be Florence Lawrence from *Her Ragged Knight*? I loved her in that picture. I snuck into the Palladium back home four times to see it."

I threw a pillow at her. She giggled. Blanche asked if we were playing a hand or what.

The bang and rattle of the Pender's delivery van broke the evening peace of the neighborhood. His flat cap gripped in his hand, Gus crossed the street, his long stride unbroken as he swept through our gate and up the steps. The spring and slam of the screen door gave a snap like a gunshot.

"Did you all hear?" He shoved the day's paper at us. "They arrested somebody for blowing up the shipyard."

CHAPTER 17

PEGGY

1968

Peggy sat at the rolltop desk with the three postcards ranged in front of her. A thorough search through Blanche's address book didn't turn up a Viv or a Vivian, but all the postcards had photos of Richmond landmarks on them and a Richmond zip code. That still only narrowed it down to around a quarter of a million people, but it was a start.

For now, she'd focus on what to say.

Hi. You don't know me, but . . .

Hello. My name is Peggy. I'm sorry to report that my great-aunt Blanche passed away . . .

This may seem strange, but can you tell me who you are and what happened fifty years ago? It's driving me crazy . . .

Peggy scratched through her notepad and tried again, chewing on her pen cap.

There was a tap at the front door. "I'm back from the lumber yard. Figured I'd start on spackling the ceiling in the upstairs hall if that's okay."

She gave a vague wave of assent without looking up.

"Your head is still stuffed in that desk?" David wiped his boots off before coming inside, bringing with him the industrious scents of sawdust, paint, and 2-in-1 oil. "You've been here all day."

"I'm working."

He peered over her shoulder. "I've heard of mail getting lost, but for fifty years?"

She swung around in the chair to catch him looming over her. She'd risen with a headache that only four aspirin could dent. David, on the other hand, looked cool as a cucumber. No bloodshot eyes or waxy pallor. She'd hate him if he didn't look so good. Frankie Avalon? Hell no. Paul Newman or Steve McQueen, maybe. He had that same bad-boy magnetism and raffish charm that spelled trouble with a capital *T.*

She held up the postcard like a shield between her and her thoughts. "This is the third one of these that's showed up. I think Viv must be senile."

"So you're writing a senile woman who thinks she's still fighting the First World War?"

"More or less."

He grabbed her pad, reading her sad attempts out loud. "'Why did my aunt leave me this dilapidated house? Did she hate me that much?'"

Laughing, Peggy grabbed the pad back. "It's a work in progress."

"I'd say."

"Something happened fifty years ago, David. Something here in this cottage. I just know it."

He scanned the postcards quickly. "Do you think you'll achieve anything by interrogating this poor woman like Sergeant Friday? If it's as mysterious as you think, she's more likely to clam up once she knows your aunt is dead."

"Are you suggesting I write back and *don't* tell her Blanche has died?"

"I'm not suggesting anything."

"Maybe I could write back and pretend to be Blanche. How would she know the difference?"

"You can't be serious. That's your great plan?"

"Mr. Symonds told me Blanche—someone I only saw once in my life—left me this cottage for a reason. I want to know what that reason might be."

"You think this Viv woman will know?"

"It's worth a shot."

The phone rang. David was still eying Peggy as if she were crazy as she picked it up. "Hello? Oh. Of course." She held out the receiver. "Lena."

David took the phone while she retreated to the porch out of earshot. A few minutes later he came out, looking far less self-assured than he had before the phone rang.

"Everything all right?"

"Oh yeah," he said brightly. "She needs help unclogging a sink. I told her I'd go over after I finish up here."

"Go now if she needs you. This mess isn't going anywhere."

"No. It's all right. They said . . . that is . . . I'll go when I'm finished here." He stared around him as if he'd forgotten what he'd been doing. Whatever Lena said had jostled him more than he cared to admit.

"You were going to work on the ceiling upstairs," she prompted.

"Right." He started for the camper. "Can you help bring some of this in? Save me a trip?"

He grabbed a bucket of spackle from out of the back while Peggy gathered shopping bags from the cab. If his living quarters were immaculate, the same couldn't be said for the rest of the camper. The seat was strewn with old receipts, empty soda cans, crumpled paper cups, and a pair of work gloves, while two different state highway maps, a rusted coffee can of nails, a set of jumper cables, and part of a jack littered the floor. The ashtray was full of cigarette butts. A lighter on the dashboard sat next to an unwrapped pack of Camels, and a large spiral sketchbook, open to what looked like a building's floor plan and elevations in architectural detail, was stuffed in the door panel.

She'd seen him with it more than once, sketching by the light of the hurricane lamp late in the evening. Carrying it with him out onto the beach after he knocked off work. Whenever she'd asked about it or got too close, he closed the cover and hid it away.

Curious, she leafed through it. Pages of drawings accompanied by copious notes. Here, a house set in an enormous garden. There, a block of apartment buildings. A third page was an elaborate explanation of brickwork on a house in San Francisco. What on earth could be so top secret about that?

"Did you get that box of nails I left?" David stood behind her, a strange look on his face.

"Oh my gosh! You scared me." It was shame, not fear, that had her heart banging against her ribs.

He reached around her to flip the sketchbook closed and grab the pack of cigarettes and the lighter. "I have to get a move on so I can make it to Lena's before she goes bats."

"I didn't mean to pry, David."

"You haven't—yet." Bucket in hand, he headed up the front steps, effectively ending the conversation.

Somehow, she'd mucked it up, and she didn't even know what *it* was.

The afternoon passed. The Crystals shoop-shooping their way through "He's a Rebel" punctuated by the bang of David's hammer and the crumble of old plaster. Dust swirled down the stairs, itching Peggy's nose. She retreated to the glider on the porch where at least the din was muted, but her concentration no better.

She understood prevarication. She was a master at it after six months of dodging well-meaning do-gooders. So David's avoidance was completely understandable—that didn't make it any less distracting. They were roommates, more or less. Their arrangement forced her to trust him. And yet, what did she really know about him? Was he running away from something or running toward something? The same questions that could be asked about her.

The dj faded out and "Nights in White Satin" faded in. She hunched back over her pad of paper with a grumble, but after a few attempts at writing something purposefully vague while digging for information, she gave up.

"Hello! Yoo-hoo!" Suzanne gave the rickety gate a nudge with one hip; as usual, her hands full of a tin-foiled serving bowl. Heavily pregnant in a belted blue and white dress and big hoop earrings, she still looked more stylish than Peggy did on her best day. "You were a million miles away, darlin'." Upstairs, a flurry of banging ended on a shout and a string of cursing. Suzanne's face shone with understanding. "Your hunky handyman hard at work?"

"I choose to ignore that," Peggy grumbled. "Another casserole?"

"Chili con carne. I made enough to feed ten thousand." She headed into the house while Peggy closed her pad. Maybe writing to Viv was a bad idea. Maybe she should leave it alone. If Viv was as lost in her memories as she seemed, she'd be no help.

Suzanne came back out on the porch, hands on hips in a do-as-I-say look Peggy had last seen her use on her four-year-old. "Get yourself a bath and change your clothes. We're going out."

"I can't."

"I'm not taking no for an answer, Peggy. Ron's taken the kids to his mother's for the weekend and you and me are having a girls' night out."

"Should you be partying in your condition?"

"I'm pregnant, not dying. If it makes you feel better, I'll order fruit juice and spring water only, I promise." She crossed her heart.

"I don't know, Suz. I really should keep sorting through—"

"I heard back from Ron's grandmother." She gave me a cool got-cha smile. "I'll tell you everything she said, but only at Captain Lester's Oyster and Tiki Bar."

"That's blackmail."

"Whatever it takes, so slap on some lipstick and curl your hair. We're painting the town."

Make a friend. Enjoy a dinner. Chip away at that wall bit by bit. Peggy closed her notebook. "I guess I'm going out."

LESTER'S TIKI BAR turned out to be a down-on-its-luck nightclub right off the Virginia Beach boardwalk, squeezed between a fish market and an all-night convenience store. Red indoor-outdoor carpet dotted with cigarette burns matched the red and yellow Tiffany-style lamps hanging over scratched and scarred red For-mica tables and sticky red fake-leather booth seats. The walls were covered with travel posters featuring tropical islands, volcanos ris-ing out of lush palm forests, and wide sandy beaches. A forest of fake palms hid the restrooms and the kitchen and clustered at each end of a bar built of bamboo.

A couple clung to each other on the tiny dance floor, the man in uniform, the woman dolled and primped in a long green cock-tail gown and silver earrings that reached her shoulders. A group of sailors in bell-bottoms and square-collared pullovers played a mean game of eight ball at the pool table in the corner.

Peggy surprised the waitress by ordering a scotch and water no ice while Suzanne sipped from a rumless daiquiri that turned out to be cherry Kool-Aid. "It's not exactly the Peppermint Beach Club, but the drinks are cheap and the food isn't half-bad." She'd proved this by ordering an enormous pile of fries, a chili cheese dog, and three slices of pizza. "Besides, with me big as a house, I'd stick out at one of those places like an old married stick-in-the-mud."

"Don't be ridiculous," Peggy said. "You're beautiful. Like a Renaissance Madonna." She was too. In the pinkish glow from the red lampshades, Suzanne's skin looked peachy, her eyes sparkling, and she wore that mysterious half smile reminiscent of Italian paintings and Catholic statuary.

She waved off the compliment, but Peggy could tell she was pleased. "You're crazy. Where do you come up with a line like that?"

"Chaz used to say that to me back when . . ." She cleared her throat and waved the waitress back over for a refill. "Back when we were married."

Suzanne's smile faltered as if she knew she'd said something wrong, her gaze sliding away to a woman in white go-go boots swaying in front of the jukebox to Elvis's "Love Me Tender."

"So," Peggy said before Suzanne could ask the question it was obvious she wanted to ask, "what did Ron's grandmother have to say?"

She tried not to notice the look of relief on Suzanne's face, tried not to feel disappointment when she didn't push it. There had been so many variations on the same awkward conversation about what led to the end of Peggy's marriage, each one worse than the last. Would Suzanne be the one to finally say everything right? Peggy couldn't take that chance. Her recovery was still too fragile.

"She was over the moon to chat about the olden days. I guess Ron's family's tired of hearing her stories. Anyway, she said there were thousands of these gals who signed up when the call went out. Esther, that's Ron's grandmother, joined with her sister. I told you she had some super-secret assignment, and her sister actually loaded ships, but there were jobs for secretaries, clerks, recruiters, some even built bombs or drove trucks. And they were stationed all over, even in England and France."

"How does nobody know about this?"

"It was fifty years ago, sugar. A lot's happened since then—like a whole Second World War. Heck, we're on the fourth war this century. You can see how everyone sort of got busy thinking about other stuff."

"Blanche didn't stop thinking about it. Neither did Viv."

"Well, of course not. For them it was probably the most interesting thing in their whole lives. It was definitely the high point for Esther, if my long-distance phone bill is anything to go by."

"Did she say anything else? How can I find these women? Is there a list somewhere? A group I can get in touch with? The American Legion or the VFW or something?"

"She said a lot of the girls kept in touch after the war, even organized. There's a small group of veterans right here in Norfolk."

"That's fantastic. Maybe they knew Blanche."

Just then, a group of sailors swarmed through the door, voices loud as they ordered drinks at the bar. A couple followed quietly in behind them.

Suzanne sat up. "Ooh, isn't that David? He sure cleans up nice."

In a button-down Oxford stretched across broad shoulders and a pair of jeans, David looked less like a commune escapee and more like—no, definitely not like someone she could find herself interested in. This was Suzanne's fault. All that Frankie and Annette business was getting to her. She shook off those thoughts and focused on the woman with him. She was tall and curvy with long straight dark hair parted in the middle and big mascara'ed eyes in a soft round face. They took a corner booth on the far side of the room, neither one of them glancing their way.

Peggy fished in her purse for her wallet. "We'd better go. Early start and all that."

"What?" Suzanne squawked. "Don't you want to find out who he's with? What he's doing here?"

"Not really."

Suzanne didn't hear her. Or if she had, she decided to ignore her. She sucked down the last of her daiquiri before levering herself up out of her chair. "Let's go say hello."

"He'll think I'm spying on him."

"Pooh. We were here first. Maybe he's spying on *you*." She shook Peggy off, heading over with a smile and a wave. Peggy was forced to follow, wishing she'd worn something more daring than a white blouse and a navy skirt. Beside Suzanne, who radiated fertility goddess, Peggy looked like a virginal schoolgirl. She reached the table just as David was making introductions.

So this was the famous Lena.

She gave Suzanne a friendly smile while she eyed Peggy with caution. "You're the woman whose house is falling down. Not to be rude, but you sounded a complete mess on the phone. I can tell these things a mile away. Comes from one too many home-perm catastrophes."

"That was me. Luckily, David came to my rescue."

Another look, this time it was easier to notice her scrutiny. "I'll bet he did. He's always had an overdeveloped sense of gallantry."

Peggy felt her face redden. Did Lena think she was making a play for David? Was she jealous? Was she right? No. Peggy refused to acknowledge any interest on her part in David Dyer.

"You two make the cutest couple," Suzanne gushed. "Don't they make a cute couple, Peg? We saw you over there and said, Wow that is one cute couple."

"Come on, Suzanne. I think you've had one too many rumless daquiris." Peggy tugged at her friend's sleeve.

"Want to step in here?" Lena asked, shooting an irritated look across the table at David who was sitting back, arms folded, watching the confrontation with a strange unreadable expression.

Suzanne saw it too. She smiled wider if that was possible. "Well, don't let us keep you from feeding the spark, sugar." Then with a twiddly flirty last finger wave, she let Peggy lead her away.

"What was that about?" Peggy asked when they got out to the parking lot.

She laughed. "Did you see him? If he could have drowned himself in his Pabst Blue Ribbon, he would have."

"Just the reaction I was shooting for," Peggy grumbled.

"Oh yeah, he's into you all right."

"You're crazy."

"Like a fox, sweetie." Suzanne grinned. "Like a fox."

They parted later that night at the corner, Peggy walking the rest of the way down the street, an unexpected lift in her chest when she realized the light in the window up ahead was her own. As if the cottage welcomed her back. She let herself in, tossing her purse on a chair, shedding her jacket on the couch. A feeling had been building in her since they'd left the bar, now reinforced by the dark streets, the moon silvering the water like a path from sea to sky. She stood looking out onto the yard at mounds of dirt, lumber, and a dumpster half-filled with broken pipes, old plaster, rotted wood, and leaky shingles.

At the desk, she took out the postcard and began to write.

Dear Viv,

I was shocked to hear from you, but after thinking it over I'm glad you let me know how it went after you left Norfolk. I'm fine, so you can stop your worrying, but I miss you and Marjory and the old days at the cottage on the bay. Write back if you can.

Blanche

PEGGY WOKE TO the slam of a car door and the murmur of voices. The moon had set, and the room was dark, gray-on-gray shapes in the gloom. When the car drove off, she waited for the snick of a latch as David headed into his camper for the night, the bloom of light as he switched on a lamp, the quiet of his radio playing that snare-and-horn jazz he seemed to prefer after the sun went down.

She rose to peer through the curtains. David sprawled in one of the metal folding chairs, the tip of his cigarette glowing red in his hand. He didn't move, not even to lift the cigarette to his lips. Was he asleep? High? Drunk and passed out? She crawled back into bed, but the room was stuffy and airless, the rattling squeak of the fan worse than Chaz's snoring.

After a half hour of tossing and turning, she gave up and headed downstairs for a rummage through Blanche's books. Something suitably dull that would bore her to sleep. The bluejacket's manual was on the table where she'd left it—the perfect antidote to insomnia. She glanced through the front window on her way to the couch. David was still out there, still unmoving. She couldn't tell any more than that in the flickering buzz of the streetlight.

Shaking her head, she settled on the couch, cracking the book open to a random page.

Was he all right?

Maybe he was ill or unconscious.

She couldn't leave him unconscious in her front yard. Suppose the neighbors saw him and reported him to the police. She needed him.

To fix the house, she quickly amended.

She needed him to fix the house.

"David?" She called from the doorway. The porch light was on, bugs batting against the screen door. A spider was building a web between the light and the cedar siding. "Everything okay out there?"

"Sure," he said. "Why?"

"You've been sitting there for an hour without moving."

"I'm stargazing."

"You're staring up into a pine tree."

"Yeah, well . . . all right. I might be a little drunk. Lena drinks like a fish and it only felt polite to keep up."

Peggy came farther out on the porch, leaning on the top step. It was cooler out here, and David was right, the sky was awash in stars, a milky trail of them fading out to the west. "Lena seems really nice."

David shifted in his chair, his face hidden in the dark. "She's one of the few family members that doesn't try to tell me I'm wasting my life every five minutes." There was a long pause as he put his cigarette to his lips followed by the scrape of chair legs on the concrete of the driveway. "You thought she was my girlfriend, didn't you?"

Well, she had up until thirty seconds ago. "Maybe. You two *looked* pretty chummy."

"You're bound to be chummy with someone you've shared a bath with—and before you get any more ideas, we were two at the time." His laugh was gravely, sleepy. "Lena's the one who said I should come to Norfolk. Said it would do me good."

"Did you need good?"

"Don't we all?" he said quietly.

As her eyes adjusted to the gloom, Peggy caught sight of the sketchbook in his lap. "I'll let you get back to stargazing."

He tucked the book out of sight, his hand covering it like a secret. "Wait . . . can I ask you a question before you go?"

She paused at the door.

"Do you consider yourself a brave person?"

"Now I know you're drunk," she said, trying to lighten the mood. "What kind of question is that?"

"An important one—trust me."

And that was the crux of the problem, wasn't it? Trusting him. Trusting herself. She wasn't sure about either. "I've never jumped out of an airplane or gone cave diving if that's what you mean. I don't walk down dark alleys in strange cities by myself. I hate big bugs and scary movies."

"Not that kind of brave. I'm talking more like trying something new even though you might fail spectacularly. Doing something everyone tells you is a mistake. Taking a huge risk when every cell in your body tells you not to."

She watched a moth blunder into the web beside the porch light, its frantic flapping of wings as it fought to escape. "Like leaving all my friends and moving into a rundown old cottage hundreds of miles from anyone and anything I know? That kind of brave?"

"Yeah, that kind of brave," he said. "I guess I have my answer."

She put her hand through the web, and the moth flittered off into the dark. David's voice followed her into the house, raspy and low. "Sweet dreams, Peg."

She grabbed up the bluejacket's manual and headed back to bed, but she'd only read a few dull pages before her eyes were drawn to the doodles in the margins. A squiggle to the left. One that looped downward. Another that looked like an odd cursive letter *f*.

She turned back to the flyleaf where, once again, someone had drawn squiggles all over the page. But they weren't just squiggles. Not the work of some bored child with a pencil. This was shorthand. She'd taken a course when she'd had ideas of working in an office. Then Chaz proposed, and those ideas had been shelved as her occupation became making a home for her new husband and their future children.

She'd have been better off in an office, as it turned out.

Peggy deciphered each symbol slowly, her memories as hazy as some of the marks, but at the end, she'd translated them to read: Vivian Weston. Union Street, Richmond, Virginia.

What were the odds she lived at the same address fifty years later?

Peggy would take that bet.

CHAPTER 18

VIV

1918

D espite Gus's breathless announcement, the man arrested for the explosion at the shipyard was released within a day. Rather than the undercover German spy the authorities thought they had, he'd turned out to be a welder from Georgia brought in by a naval contractor. Anger mounted as the investigation dragged on with no arrests and another worker died of his injuries. A man was taken into custody for asking at the post office how to mail a letter to Germany. A fire at a shoe shop on Main Street had people talking about agents sent by the Kaiser. The newspaper's editorial board ramped up its attacks and innuendo, citing unnamed sources and unofficial accounts. Sabotage? An errant spark? No one knew, leaving everyone on edge.

It was only when reports started coming in from Allied offenses around the city of Aisne, the Argonne Forest, and Rhiems that the newspapers turned to other stories, and the rumors of a German American conspiracy died down. Even then, the fear remained, a hum under the city like a plucked wire. There had been no more occurrences of vandalism, but there remained a sense of unease as palpable as the humid summer haze.

I returned to work at the hospital, my standing raised among the section. Apparently being almost blown up was quite the badge of honor. Even Lieutenant Dumfries marked my return with a small posy of chrysanthemums left on my desk beside an enormous backlog of personnel files, and an awkward "Glad you're back, Weston," before he retreated into his office and closed the door.

I settled in, happier to be back than I thought I would be. Here was order and discipline. Rules and procedures for every eventuality. No problems that couldn't be tackled with a typewriter, a box of carbon paper, and a bottle of ink to go with my trusty fountain pen. It was beyond the walls of the hospital that life grew increasingly complicated and questions banged away at me like moths against a porch light.

A few days after my return, Quarles and a bullish silver-haired gentleman possessing the single star of a warrant officer's rank cornered me at my desk. I immediately straightened, chin up and shoulders square, cursing my flyaway curls and ink-stained fingers.

"We need a group of yeomanettes to attend the Friday evening performance at the Strand. Before the show, during intermission, and after the final curtain, you'll do your part selling war bonds to the audience. Smile, chat them up, show them what you're doing for our boys, make them proud. Turn on your feminine charms"—he eyed me as if I was some sort of carnival oddity—"if you and your pals still know what those are."

I flushed but met his gaze with one equally dismissive. "Aye, aye, sir."

"If you're all going to be underfoot and in the way, might as well make yourself useful," he grumbled all the way out the door.

"Don't mind him," Quarles said after he left. "He knows how valuable we are to the war effort. He just hates to admit it."

"He's hardly alone, ma'am."

"No. But most are better at keeping their opinions to themselves."

Maybe Blanche was right. No matter what we accomplished, how hard we worked, the Navy would never accept us as equals. To them, we were girls playing at sailors. Tolerated so long as necessity dictated, but the end of the war would mean the end of us.

THE YEOMANETTES SELECTED for the bond drive were loaded onto a flatbed truck for the short trip to the theater. We clung to the wooden sides, packed like herrings in a tin, our once crisp uniforms crushed as the driver crawled along City Hall Avenue and around the corner onto Granby Street, threading our way through cars, taxis, and a clanging streetcar.

Signs of rebuilding after last winter's fire were everywhere, but half a year hadn't been enough to clear the air of the sour odors of smoke and damp. Quarles had said more than twenty men were rounded up following the fire. What had happened to them? Had they been guilty of sabotage or innocents simply caught up in the city's panic?

The truck pulled to the curb in front of the elegant Southland Hotel. A doorman stood at attention for the well-heeled guests coming and going. A few paused to ogle us as we jumped off the tail, straightening skirts, smoothing lapels, adjusting our buttons, our belts, the ribbons in our straw hats.

"Form up, ladies."

We jostled into position, marching beneath the Strand's grand arched entryway into the theater, our eyes ahead and our chins up, stepping in unison as if we drilled on the parade ground behind the hospital's main building.

Inside the lobby, we were organized and instructed by our CPO, turning us from soldiers into salesladies. Our patriotic pitches rehearsed, we fanned out in pairs. I was with Loretta, a flirty blonde yeomanette from Cape Charles. We took the right side of the balcony, making our way aisle to aisle and row to row, cajoling, persuading, shaming, and bargaining. Throwing kisses, batting lashes, shaking hands.

"Just one bond could pay for the medicine that might save a soldier's life."

"Your contribution is a gift to our boys overseas who are fighting for our freedom."

"Buy one for yourself and one for your girlfriend. It's an investment in our country."

"Fight the Kaiser. Buy a bond."

The lights dimmed, the newsreel crackled up onto the wide screen, and we retreated back to the lobby to regroup before the intermission. Loretta bought a bag of lemon drops, which we shared as we snuck peeks through the auditorium doors, listening to the orchestra underscore the chase, the kiss, the derring-do accompanied by the rustle of peanut and popcorn bags, the creak of seats, a cough, a sneeze. At the intermission, we all filed in again, but this time I was instructed to head down toward the pit where the glass globes of stage lights flickered along the floor.

A man in the wings motioned for me to come farther. "Miss Weston?"

"That's right."

"The officer in charge pointed you out. If you'd accompany me, please."

Tension crimped my mouth and butterflies banged under my ribs. "Is something the matter, sir?"

"Nothing at all. You're the lady of the hour." He escorted me up onto the stage, where a spotlight pinned me like an insect to a board. He held up his hands, the murmur of conversation quieting. My sister bond-sellers paused in the aisles, an usher shouldered his flashlight. If I'd been standing there in garters and a corset, I couldn't have been more terrified.

"Ladies and gentlemen, if you'll indulge me for a moment," the manager of the theater announced. "It's been brought to my attention that one of these gallant patriotic Navy yeomanettes is fresh out of the hospital—a victim of the recent Portsmouth shipyard bombing."

A ripple of surprise and curiosity spread among the audience. I burned with embarrassment and the heat given off by the enormous lamp trained on my face. My heart hammered against my chest as I resisted the urge to run screaming off the stage. I scanned my surroundings as if I might take refuge behind the candy counter or hide in the ticket office.

"Miss Vivian Weston originally from sister city Richmond, Virginia, courageously joined up to serve her country in its time of need, and now she's here to help raise money for our boys fighting bravely far from home. So open your wallets, get out your purses. Let's help Miss Weston and all our soldiers and sailors defeat the Kaiser and root out his filthy spies and saboteurs infecting our streets, our schools, and our churches."

The house exploded in a roar of applause and stamping feet. I found myself propelled among the crowds, my face aching from the smile frozen like a mask over my fear. Roaring filled my ears, my skin clammy and prickled with goose bumps. People came up to me to offer me a kind word of sympathy or commiseration. They touched my sleeve, patted my back, their faces pressed too close, their words making little sense to my frazzled mind.

"We'll root them out like the vermin they are."

"Dirty foreigners. They don't even try to speak our language."

"What they did to that Prager fella in Illinois, that's what needs to be done to all these traitorous killers."

"They should be arrested at dark, tried at midnight, and shot at daybreak; that's what Pastor Prothero says."

That name.

Knees shaking, I escaped into the lobby, my back slick with cold sweat, my lips trembling. I wanted to believe I'd misheard, that the person had misspoken. That Father's self-righteous malice hadn't spread beyond the tracts he wrote for inclusion in the Sunday circular and the meetings where he railed against the new century's growing immorality. But Prothero was hardly a common name like Smith or Jones, and how many of them had staked themselves to a religious calling? The numbers dwindled as my fear increased.

The door to the auditorium swung open, nearly sending me diving for the steps to the upper balcony. "For someone attempting to lie low, you're doing a rotten job."

"Tom!" I nearly fell into his arms. "I thought you were still training at Langley? How did you know I was here?"

"Marjory told me when I stopped by the cottage. I thought I'd surprise you and take in the feature at the same time."

"Miss Weston." The theater manager barged through the swinging doors closely followed by two ushers. "Miss Weston, I really need to speak with you."

"I'm not feeling very well." I shouldn't leave. We'd not been properly dismissed, and there'd be hell to pay if someone chose to report me to Quarles. But behind them, a shadow flickered in the light of the movie projector. Broad shoulders, long chin, wide cheekbones. I told myself it was all in my head. He wasn't here. He couldn't be here. It was a figment of my imagination just like before. But my hammering heart froze to a painful halt. I gasped and stumbled as if I'd been struck, panic sizzling along my skin. "If you'll excuse me, sir."

Before he could argue, Tom guided me onto the street. "Let's get you out of here before he has you booked every evening and twice on Saturday."

As we passed the Southland Hotel steps, I glanced back, but there was only the theater manager standing arms on hips in the current of evening traffic as he scowled after us.

The shadow, if it had ever been there, was gone.

So why did I feel as if my time was running out?

"You've barely touched your coffee."

We had ended up at a café off City Hall Avenue, the room filled with people enjoying a late supper after the movies or grabbing a quick bite in between sets at the nearby dance halls. The drone of voices and the chink of glasses and cutlery worked to slow my pulse, but I continued to eye the door, inspecting everyone who entered.

"I sound like a skipping record, but you're safe," he said as if reading my thoughts. "You imagined him, I'm sure. Your father is back in Norfolk. And even if he's not, he can't hurt you anymore."

"Easy for you to say. He doesn't have to be standing in front of me telling me I'm a useless waste of a daughter for me to hear his voice. He doesn't have to be standing over me with his fist raised for me to feel the bruises. He lives in here." I tapped my forehead. "All the time. It's only been in the last few months, his words have started to lose their power."

"Since you enlisted?"

"Since I met Blanche and Marjory." I stared into my empty mug. "I forgot how powerful friendship can be."

He reached over to cover my hand with his. His touch sent a zing up my arm. "I miss her too." He smiled. "She'd have been first in line when the call went out, you know."

I smiled. "She never did like a bully."

Vivian in our thoughts, we finished our meal and headed back out into the night.

By now, the sedate and respectable had dispersed to their comfortable homes on Colonial Place or The Hague. The streets were given over to sailors and soldiers, the women on their arms dressed in cheap cotton or oily silk. Lights shone from café doorways and dance hall windows, the tinkle of off-key piano music mingled with the hotter sounds of trumpets and snares. On one corner, the up-tempo slide of a trombone belting out the "Tiger Rag." Down the street, a soulful baritone was warbling his way through "Calling Me Home to You." A pair of policemen passed us at a run followed by the clang of a police wagon. The grunt and shouts signaling a brawl were followed by a shrill scream.

"You come home this way every night?" Tom stepped closer to my side.

"If I'm working late. Maybe it's the uniform, but no one's ever tried anything worse than a few suggestive catcalls or a whistle." I enjoyed the feel of his sleeve brushing against mine, the match of our steps, the handsome curve of his profile. "Would you defend my honor if they did?"

A woman leaned from an upper window, waving down to Tom on the sidewalk with a crudely good-natured invitation. "Maybe you should defend *my* honor."

"Once you're in France, you'll probably have women draped all over you. I hear Paris girls are beautiful and charming."

"Hard to see from a thousand feet up." I could feel him watching me, casting sidelong glances he thought I wouldn't notice. "You never gave me an answer." He paused, kicking a stone like a little boy. "Or maybe that *was* your answer."

Here it was—the conversation I was dreading. How could I explain my reluctance without it sounding like a prompt? And how sincere is such a declaration if it only comes by request? I took a shaky breath, tensing for his anger. "Do you hate me?"

I felt his smile in the way he stepped closer and the loosening of his stride—or maybe it was relief. "I could never hate you, you ninny. That's the whole point, isn't it? But maybe it's for the best. I can come marching back to you after we've won this war. Get a proper hero's welcome." He grinned, the same little boy who'd crowned me queen of the faeries with a wreath of purple asters and a stolen kiss when I was eleven.

I slid my hand into his, and every question that kept me tossing and turning at night, every worry that distracted me as I struggled through endless carbon copies during the day, all of them evaporated in the warmth of his gaze and the shiver up my spine. It was as if we'd never been apart. "I look forward to that."

We wandered aimlessly, up Monticello, past the market building, back through narrow streets toward Granby and down once more toward the trolley stop, past the scene of last winter's fire. Empty windows and skeletal scaffolding made me think of news stories about zeppelins creeping over London's streets, silent as they slid like a black reaching shadow to drop their bombs. The ghostly scenes in newsreels of deserted French villages smashed under competing artillery, nothing distinguishable left but a bent road sign, a crooked steeple.

Maybe Tom had the same thought. His steps slowed. His conversation dwindled.

"Are you afraid of fighting in a war, Tom?"

Torpedo attacks, artillery bombardments, illness and disease—I witnessed the aftermath every day along the hospital's wards, typed it up in triplicate, but it had yet to really touch me. Would that change if I made it to the base hospital in Brest, faced with real war, before the tidying up, the filing away, men reduced to a sum of figures or a penciled list? Would that change once Tom shipped out, and I had someone I cared about in harm's way?

"Afraid of going into battle? Only a brazen liar would tell you no. And I'm no brazen liar. So yes, I'm afraid. But I fear missing out more. Looking back and regretting what I didn't do because fear held me back."

I thought of my conversation with Gus and his thwarted desire to fight. Of Blanche and her frustration at being denied the opportunity simply because of her sex. It wasn't the battle we craved. It was the sense that we were part of something momentous, a fight between good and evil, a turning point in history. "Yes. Yes, that's it exactly."

The wind picked up. The thunder sounded closer as lightning flickered overhead, illuminating the faces of couples running for shelter, a pair of seamen laughing as one's cap went flying. A group of men in Army tan racing for the streetcar. "Enough yammering," he said. "Storm's coming."

He led me around the corner. Rain steamed against the sidewalk, fat cold drops slithering under my collar, plinking in metal downspouts. Just as the skies opened, he took my hand, and we dashed across the street for shelter.

"The Atlantic Hotel? Isn't this where you're staying?"

"It is."

Tom didn't try to lead me inside. Instead, we huddled in a corner of the portico while those arriving behind us flapped drenched overcoats and dabbed at damp faces before heading to the lounge for a late supper or to their rooms for a hot bath and dry clothes.

Tom held me in the warm curve of his body, my head just coming even with his shoulder. I could smell his aftershave and the starch in his collar. Without thinking, I pressed a kiss against his neck. His skin was cool and wet and slightly salty. He tensed against my touch, his arm coming around as his hand reached up under my uniform jacket to cup my side. Even through the fabric of my shirtwaist, I felt every fingertip like a spark. Every brush of his thumb along my ribs sent a little jolt along my trembling limbs and then into the pit of my stomach in a delicious unfamiliar swirl.

"You're different," he whispered, his voice unsteady.

"Is that good or bad?" Here was my chance to know what he thought of the new me, this stranger who had taken the place of the girl he'd left behind. I struggled to keep my voice untouched by the tug of sensations lifting every hair at my neck, raising goose bumps along my arms, pulling at me like the outgoing surf at the beach, solid ground sliding out from under me as the tide rushed past in a dizzying wash of foam.

"I haven't decided yet." Tom's fingers glided up to curve against my breast. "You're definitely not the girl I kissed goodbye last spring."

"Good." Dare I wade deeper? Risk being swept away? There was still time to retreat. I had only to take a single step in any direction, but the idea of moving away from his touch seemed impossible. If anything, I wanted to be closer. "I don't want to be that girl ever again."

"Really? I rather liked that girl."

"And what do you think of this one?" I asked as if uncaring of his regard, though the world seemed to suddenly shrink down to the space between us, the breath we shared, the pause before his answer.

His words were as much sensation as sound, a purr against my ear. "She's growing more interesting by the moment."

I closed my eyes. Was this how Blanche felt last winter in the arms of her soldier? This tumbling landslide of sensations that pushed common sense aside?

It was Tom who came to his senses first.

"I should get you back," he murmured. "Your friends will wonder what's become of you."

He was right. I should go home. Climb into my empty bed. Count sheep until this craziness passed. Instead, I heard my voice, husky with desire, saying, "Blanche and Marjory are attending a dance at the naval base."

"Are they? So no one's expecting you? No ferocious roommates? No domineering father? Not even a disapproving landlady?"

"No one."

Tom was leaving me—again. Would I look back on this night and regret what I didn't do because fear held me back? He'd never mentioned love. That didn't mean I couldn't love him.

Father would be horrified at my boldness.

Marjory would be delighted that I'd been swept away by romance.

I knew which of them I wanted to make proud.

I reached onto my toes once more, and this time I kissed his lips. They were warm and firm and just as I remembered.

"Are you sure?" he murmured, strain tensing his quiet voice.

I nodded.

"Then maybe me and the new you should get acquainted," he replied as we followed the others into the hotel.

CHAPTER 19

VIV

B lanche was reading a letter at the kitchen table when I returned home the next morning. She tucked it back into its envelope to eye me with a cool appraisal that left me squirming. The early edition of the paper was folded so the front page was hidden by a mug of tea, the paper soggy where the milk had spilled. It didn't matter. I'd seen the headlines hawked on the street corners, rustling in the grip of passengers on the streetcar, and whispered over by weekenders, carpetbags filled with beach attire. *800,000 American Troops Now in France. The German Drive Against Paris Halted. American Airmen Attack Behind German Lines.*

One could be forgiven for thinking the war was as good as won; that now that the Yanks had arrived, it was only a matter of time. That if we didn't get into the fighting now, we'd miss our chance for glory.

Almost but not quite, you could overlook the smaller headlines below the fold describing American prisoners being paraded in Germany, U-boats sinking ships off our coast, and at the very bottom corner—hardly noticeable unless you were looking—the smallest headline of all noting the four hundred dead, wounded, and missing on the day's casualty list.

I didn't need a list to tell me there was plenty of war left to fight. Those laughing boys I met on the piers and along the boardwalk with their clean uniforms and eager faces had no idea what waited for them when they stepped onto those ships waiting in the harbor, steaming south past Cape Henry.

Not even Tom.

"We wondered what happened to you last night." Blanche fiddled with the garish diamond newly encircling her ring finger. So far it had done the trick, and other than a few comments of congratulation and surprise, her hasty marriage had been accepted.

Embarrassment scalded my cheeks. "I should have sent word, but Tom—"

"I *thought* your long-lost airman might have something to do with your disappearance. I told Marjory as much. She went all starry-eyed and started yammering on about soul mates and true love. Is that why you did it? Because you love him? Because he said he loved you?"

"Yes. No. I don't know." Avoiding her gaze, I hung my jacket up on the hall tree by the door, removing my hat to smooth a hand through my hastily pinned hair. Tom had sneaked me out of the hotel before dawn this morning. He'd wanted to escort me home, but I'd refused to let him. Tom didn't belong to my life here, and for reasons I couldn't explain, I wanted to keep it that way.

"A baby won't fit in that treasure box of yours, Viv."

My hand unconsciously moved to my stomach, flat as a drum—for now.

"If you're going to play with fire, you need to read this." She pulled a slender pamphlet from under her newspaper and pushed it across to me. "I told you there were ways. Margaret Sanger is a pioneer in family planning. She went to jail for giving women the tools to understand and control their own bodies and thus their lives. The least you can do is learn the basics." She paused. "Or do you want to end up like me?" She spread a hand over her stomach, which, now that I knew what I was looking at, was very obviously carrying a child.

"I won't." My whole body was hot and uncomfortable, a squirrely feeling in my stomach. My night with Tom had been a revelation. I didn't want it reduced to a sordid back-alley tryst.

"How can you be sure?" Blanche replied, her voice cool and clinical as she drove her point home. "Did that father of yours teach you about the birds and the bees? Somehow I doubt it, so as someone older and with experience in that department, it's up to me."

She showed no shame when she said this, and if there was regret, it was carefully camouflaged and passed with barely a flicker. "Read this, then come to me. I can tell you where to go to purchase the proper supplies and answer any questions you might have."

I was embarrassed and curious and outraged and grateful all at the same time. "Do these precautions"—I could barely say the word without stammering—"really work?"

"Do you mean if I'm so damn smart, why am I in the family way?" Her smile was wolfish. "Call me a life lesson. The best laid plans and all that. But you're not me, Vivian. The loads I can bear would crush you flat."

I took the pamphlet, putting my hand over the cover as if hiding it made it less real. "I'll read it, but I don't think I need worry too much. Tom leaves soon for France."

"Lucky bastard."

"Isn't he just?" I looked once more at her letter, at the expensive stationery and her mother's handwriting, both familiar to me now after so many months of living with Blanche. "Are your parents very angry?"

"They would be if I'd told them. But I haven't worked up the courage for that quite yet. Funny, isn't it? I can face down police on the picket line, but my mother's bad opinion completely terrifies me." She slid the letter into her pocket. "Besides, they have other worries right now. Iris isn't eating and barely leaves her room. The doctors are worried, and my brother wants to hire a private nurse."

"Should you take a few days' leave and go home for a visit? Maybe a face-to-face chat would be better."

"Iris wouldn't appreciate my coming. It would take the spotlight off her, and she does enjoy a good bout of melodramatic hypochondria now and then, usually when she thinks Gilbert isn't paying her enough attention. Boys do seem to respond to a damsel in distress. It allows them to polish up their armor."

Her gaze was target sighted on me, and I squirmed under my rumpled uniform. "Is that always such a bad thing?"

"It's all right for some." She picked up her pen and bent back over her letter. "I prefer to rescue myself."

I CLIMBED THE stairs to my room, shutting the door and sitting carefully on my bed. I opened the pamphlet, squirming page by page until embarrassment became something altogether different, and I had to put it away. Memories of Tom and the fumbling breathy nervousness of his stuffy hotel room filled my head. That sense of danger, of getting away with something, had been as much an aphrodisiac as the scent of his cologne and the spread of his hand against the small of my back. Even now, my insides swirled with delicious anticipation.

I undressed, hanging up my skirt and blouse. I unhooked my garters and rolled off my stockings. Slid out of my petticoat. All while remembering Tom's hands in the act of these same small movements, his breath warm on my skin as he undressed me piece by piece as if unwrapping a precious gift. He had marveled at my beauty. He had cursed my scars. Then carefully and nervously we had found each other in the dark of his hotel room.

The Bible was clear on this one. I'd broken the rules. I should feel soiled, shamed, unclean, and fallen in some way.

Flee from sexual immorality. Whoever sins sexually, sins against their own body.

That was just one verse among dozens that warned me of the evils of lust.

Once, I'd have cowered on my knees begging for forgiveness, though in truth it was not God's heavy tread upon the stair I feared nor the sound of His belt as it slid from His trouser loops.

But this morning all I felt was a sense of rightness, of inevitability. Maybe that meant I was already a lost cause. I'd broken so many rules, surely I must be damned a thousand times over. I didn't care.

The sheet was cool against my skin. My muscles ached, but not in the way they used to after a day of scrubbing on my knees or hauling laundry, not even as they had those first weeks of drill when I marched up and down with a broomstick against my shoulder under the Norfolk sun. This was a tenderness that made me feel as if I was the recipient of a delicious secret, and I stretched like a cat on a cushion.

I closed my eyes, sinking deeper into sleep as excitement turned to exhaustion and a sleepless night caught up to me, but it wasn't Tom's face I conjured as I dozed. Not the rough feel of his cheek nor the callused pads of his fingers. It was Vivian who joined me; but not as I'd last seen her, lying white as chalk in a darkened room, but as she would be if she'd survived the diphtheria. Tall and slender, her mane of curls cut ferociously into the same modern bob Blanche and so many of the girls at work sported. Her pointed chin set for battle even while laughter hovered at the edges of her wide dimpled mouth. I could feel the weight of her at the edge of my bed, smell her lemon soap and the scent of her lavender sachets.

I reached for her hand, and it was as warm and real as if she were here beside me. She bent to whisper her blessing in my ear, and even in my happiness, I felt the cold slide of tears against my cheeks.

When I woke, my room was dim with evening shadows. I could sense the cottage's emptiness, the weight of the silence that seemed to fill every corner. The air smelled of rain and wet grass. Someone had left a bouquet of white roses on my bedside table. As I inhaled the delicate scent and admired the velvety petals, I noticed one blossom unlike all the others buried within the snow white blooms, a single purple aster. My insides buzzed. Excitement danced along my skin and prickled my scalp.

He remembered.

Tom AND I stood at the Church Street dock as passengers and workers moved up and down the steamer's gangplank loading luggage and supplies for the trip to New York. The military's frantic buildup of troops on the Western Front was clear in the crowded wharf, the harried porters, the noise and crush of khaki passing through as the embarkation camps of Lee and Hill and Stuart filled with soldiers headed overseas.

"I'm sorry we didn't have more time together." As soon as I said it, I felt the absurdity of my words. It was a pleasantry, something you'd say to anyone. A remark that meant nothing and carried no importance. But true nonetheless. He didn't know how sorry I was. I'd studied Blanche's pamphlet and together she and I had made the embarrassing visit to a small shop off Granby. So much for preparation. I was fortunate to have been granted time to come see him off.

"I am too," he answered just as woodenly.

It was our last farewell replaying itself. Neither of us sure what the future held. Neither of us sure of each other. His silver wings stood out against the drab dun wool of his uniform. His sleeve brushed mine. I could feel the rise and fall of his shoulders, but his expression was closed off, his thoughts lost to me. Even when our eyes met, I knew he was seeing past me to the days and weeks ahead. Once he arrived in New York, he was to take ship immediately for France where he would join other replacement pilots bound for AEF airfields scattered throughout eastern France.

"You'll write?" he asked.

"Every day," I replied, still feeling as if we read from a script, endearments repeated across the country and the world as sweethearts parted, many for the last time. I'd heard the life expectancy of a combat pilot was ten weeks. I pushed that thought away even as I held him closer as if imprinting the feel of him in my memory for the empty nights to come.

The ship gave a blast of its horn. Only a few stragglers remained on the dock, savoring the final moments. Tom gripped his rucksack. His gaze sharpened, body tensing. He grabbed my hand, threading his fingers with mine. "Are you sure you won't come with me?" he blurted.

I started to pull away, but he held me fast.

"Vivian enlisted in the Navy, not you. You could step on board, and Vivian would be a ghost again. It would be like none of this ever happened."

Was it the uniform that gave him a new harder edge? Or had his year of Army life honed the softer edges away? He suddenly seemed taller, broader, more capable, and I almost agreed.

"I told you I can't go back to being that girl again. *She's* the ghost, not Viv. For the first time, I have respect. I have friendship. I can't lose that. Not even for you." He looked stricken but almost relieved. "Just like you have to fly those planes of yours, I have to see this war through to the end. I don't want to look back and regret what I didn't do because I was afraid. I've been afraid for too long."

He stared up into the sky, gray green with cloud and the city lights. "You've always felt you didn't amount to much, but you're one of the strongest most courageous women I've ever known."

The war seemed closer than it ever had. I wanted to hold him, count the constellation of freckles dotting the back of his hand, the splinters of gold in his hazel eyes, the slow rise and fall of his chest beneath my palm. Fear and indecision gripped me. Was I wrong to turn him down? To hold out over a few measly words? Plenty of people said them and didn't mean it. Tom was kind and gentle. We'd known each other forever. He was one of my closest friends. But was that enough? Once it would have been.

But now?

Blanche had shown me possibilities.

Marjory had taught me to trust.

"Don't be too brave." I smiled through watery eyes.

"I'll be just brave enough." He leaned down and kissed me. "I thought I lost you once. I won't lose you again."

"I'll be right here." I placed a palm against his chest. "I promise."

I slipped my free hand into his coat pocket, leaving him a flower to remember me by. I imagined him reaching in when he looked for his wallet or his ticket, in New York or maybe even on the ship to Calais. Finding it and thinking of me.

There was a final shout as we drifted apart, hands then fingertips, then he was jogging up the gangway to join the throng hanging over the railings in a sea of waving white handkerchiefs and tearful shouts of farewell.

Halfway, he turned back, shouting over the din. "I love you!" He must have taken my stunned surprise for confusion. He cupped a hand to his mouth, shouting once more, "I. Love. You!"

Heat bloomed in my cheeks and in my chest. I wanted to cry. He'd said the words, but too late for me to change my mind even if I'd wanted to. "I love you too!" I shouted back.

A ragged cheer went up from the passengers who welcomed him aboard with slaps on the back and grinning salutes. Ropes were cast, engines churned great froth, and the steamer moved free of its mooring as it lumbered out into the river channel. I watched and waited as the wharf cleared, the docks emptied.

Tom was gone.

I was on my own again.

"He loves you, does he? This calls for an enormous popcorn and a huge helping of candy floss." I turned to see Blanche and Marjory standing at the turnstile.

"Come on, Viv." Marjory grinned. "Ride the coaster with me?"

I linked my arms with theirs as we headed back up Church Street.

Maybe I wasn't as alone as I thought.

CHAPTER 20

PEGGY

1968

The sun beat in through the window of the little sewing room at the top of the stairs. Peggy had struggled to open it, but layers of old paint had sealed it tight—add it to her ever-growing to-do list. She'd finally given up wrestling with the intractable sash, resorting to the fan to stir the humid air. The sad breeze fluttered the pattern clippings tacked to an enormous bulletin board alongside fashion photos cut from magazines. Dust clung to Blanche's ancient Singer sewing machine and a long wooden table where parts of a half-finished blouse lay pinned like an intricate puzzle.

Peggy had never had the patience for sewing, despite her mother's insistence she learn. She claimed it was an essential skill, one that would always stand her in good stead. *She'd* been taught by *her* grandmother who'd learned it from hers and so on and so on in a never-ending line, probably back to the *Mayflower*. To a child, the idea had seemed tedious and old-fashioned, the hours painfully dull. Now Peggy wished for even one more afternoon arguing with her mom over uneven stitching and crooked hems.

Obviously, Blanche had been a far better student. She tried to imagine the iron-hard lady she'd glimpsed at Mom's funeral as a young girl toiling away under the watchful eye of Great-

Grandmother Lawrence. Once it would have been impossible. The photograph made it easier. Now she could see that Blanche hadn't always been cold-eyed and grim-faced. She had been young and beautiful. She had laughed, arms flung around friends. She looked like someone Peggy would have enjoyed hanging out with, up for fun and a bit of mischief.

A knock at the door interrupted Peggy's sorting.

She swiped the back of her hand across her sweaty forehead before wiping her hands down her jeans. Just what she didn't need right now—visitors.

Peeking through the front door's sidelight, she spotted a long white Corvette in the drive, Barry Grace leaning against the hood, arms folded, shades down. A second man in rumpled suit and tie stared up at the house with a frown.

"Shit," she muttered before swinging open the door with a wide welcoming smile. "Mr. Grace, what a surprise."

She could feel his smarmy gaze even behind his sunglasses. "Barry, remember?" He came forward, beckoning his guest up onto the porch along with him. "This is Mr. Ebersol. He's in town for a few hours and, when he told me what he was looking for, I immediately thought of you."

Mr. Ebersol was dressed for cooler climes. His face glowed with sweat and there was a desperate thirsty look in his eye. The two of them started toward the door as if she'd already invited them in. Here was her chance to escape. Mr. Grace had a buyer on the line. She could leave this rundown cottage and its uncomfortable memories in the rearview mirror.

She shot a quick look over her shoulder at the canvas tarp blanketing the countertops while David worked on the electrical wiring, the living room wall striped with potential paint colors, a band saw set up on the landing. Not exactly showroom worthy. "Can you come back in an hour?"

Mr. Ebersol offered her an understanding smile. "No need. I'm not interested in the current property as it stands."

"You're looking for land."

"Mr. Grace led me to believe you were open to the idea. I can offer top dollar. You'd be more than satisfied."

As if sensing blood in the water, Mr. Grace added his voice to Ebersol's. "You're wasting your money fixing this place up," he announced with the air of a teacher berating a dim student. "I told you. People don't want these old places no matter how much work you put into them. You're throwing good money after bad."

"Someone will appreciate its charm, I'm sure of it."

His gaze wandered over the house with a dismissive eye before settling on the yard, which was a minefield of construction debris, old and new. A ladder propped against the porch. A trench dug halfway around the foundation. "Just like you women to let sentimentality override good sense."

Peggy's hackles lifted. She felt her smile freeze and her gaze grow hard. Ebersol clearly sensed the change in atmosphere. He offered her an apologetic twist of his mouth while Mr. Grace continued to pontificate. "This place is a white elephant, trust me. The property market in Ocean View is drying up. Everyone's buying in Virginia Beach these days. Accept Ebersol's offer and you can set yourself up in a nice condo down there. I have just the place in mind. Wall-to-wall carpets. Central air-conditioning. A pretty view of the water." He lowered his voice to a throaty purr, his pompadour practically vibrating. "Even a real Jacuzzi."

Skin crawling, she looked up just in time to lock eyes with Mr. Symonds, who stood at his mailbox, pruning broken limbs from his azalea bush. Could she leave now? Walk away without finding out what happened to Blanche, Viv, and Marjory? Turn her back on a place that almost felt like home? Or was this that sentimentality that Mr. Grace warned her about? Air-conditioning sounded awfully nice right now.

She took Mr. Ebersol's card. "I'll think about it."

She could practically hear Mr. Grace's teeth grind, but Ebersol accepted with a businesslike nod. "You can call any time."

After they left, instead of returning to work, Peggy crossed the street to where Symonds had moved on to weeding, his spade stabbing the flowerbed as if he were disemboweling someone—*her* probably. "So you decided to sell," he grumbled. "I shoulda' known."

"Was it you who left that book for me to find?"

He set aside the spade, levered himself to his feet, banging the dirt from his pants. "It was in a box of tat Blanche had with her at that nursing home. Most was junk, but the book . . . you were asking after her Navy days. Figured you'd want it. I knocked, but you were out and that fella of yours was up on the roof. I nipped in and left it."

She was dying to ask if he'd known about the pamphlet stuffed within the book's pages but was too embarrassed to ask. Besides, his quick confession threw her off-balance. She'd expected more cryptic remarks and mysterious evasions. "What did Blanche do in the Navy?"

"Worked at the Navy base as a switchboard operator."

"And Marjory and Viv?"

"Marjory was a courier, if I remember rightly. Viv worked over at the hospital in Portsmouth."

"So, you *did* know them?"

If she thought his owning up to leaving the manual was the start of a beautiful friendship, she was mistaken. He gummed his toothpick as he wiped his hands on an old oily rag. "Never said I didn't, but it wasn't like we were all pals or anything. There were all sorts through here during the war."

"Where's Blanche buried?"

This time he was the one startled silent. He fumbled with his pruners, his thin shoulders working. "Why do you want to know?"

"Because she's family. I want to pay my respects."

His jaw worked, the toothpick moving side to side in his wide mouth. "Forest Lawn."

"How do I get there?"

"I'll show you." He scooped the little dog up under his arm.

"No." She didn't want an audience. She didn't want to make awkward small talk or feel his judgmental eyes on her. She needed to go alone. She and Blanche needed a heart-to-heart. "No, thanks. Just tell me how to get there."

Fifteen minutes later, Peggy was passing the weeping angel Symonds mentioned before arriving at a square slab of granite, rough-cut and flush to the surrounding grass. Simple compared to the monuments on either side, just a name and dates. A hot wind moved through the trees, turning the leaves and whispering over the grass. Nearby, a tent was being erected for a funeral, the red earth heaped and waiting. Farther away, a mower hummed.

She'd not been in a cemetery in years, not since her mother's funeral. That day remained a blur of sad faces, soft words, Grandpa's hand on her shoulder, and Blanche's eyes boring into her back.

"Who is she, Gramps?"

"My little sister, your great-aunt."

"Why haven't I ever met her?"

"There was a family falling out a long time ago. Blanche always could hold a grudge. Stubborn."

"Maybe she's ready to patch things up. Maybe that's why she came to Mom's funeral. Should we go—"

"Stay away from her, Peg," her grandfather demanded. "Hear me? She's trouble. And if she's come today, she's only brought that trouble with her."

Following her grandfather's advice had been easy enough. She'd spent the rest of the day accepting condolences and casseroles as neighbors and friends passed in an endless stream through their living room. She knew Grandpa was disappointed in her. While he'd shaken hands and chatted, Peggy had shrunk into herself, words indistinguishable over the buzzing in her ears, a hole in her chest where her mother used to be. When he'd visited the grave, she'd refused to go. She'd argued there was nothing of her mother under that cold carved stone.

Beloved daughter. Loving mother.

They were just words.

She'd give anything for a stone to visit now. Proof of her heartbreak. Proof she wasn't mad to grieve.

A WEEK PASSED. Peggy checked the mail pushed through the slot—electric bill, monthly bank statement, gardening catalogue, a flyer from Sal's Pizza complete with coupon. She tucked that one away for later. But no postcards. Maybe her hunch about the address had been wrong.

She filed the mail in the front-hall tray to be dealt with later, stepped over the circular saw, shimmied past the paint cans, and headed up to her bedroom, careful not to touch the wiring protruding from the wall on the landing.

Suzanne had been better than her word, and Ron's memaw had phoned a friend who phoned another friend who knew someone from her church group who was in touch with Mrs. Constance Stokes, a member of a local American Legion group who also ran a less-formal social club for former yeomanettes. The ladies met every other Tuesday according to Mrs. Stokes, who welcomed Peggy to join them at their next get-together.

She was due there in—she checked her watch as she stripped for her bath—an hour.

The bathroom had been freshly painted, the floor scrubbed until it shone. David had even installed a small set of shelves beside the sink. The water gushed out of the tap, hot and plentiful. The light over the sink didn't flicker once, and the toilet no longer gurgled incessantly. David was starting to make progress.

Back in her bedroom, she snapped on the radio by her bed as she ran through the few outfits she owned suitable for an afternoon out.

"*. . . authorities now claim the dog tag found washed up on the beach near the Ocean View amusement park belonged to Vivian Weston who went missing in November of 1918 . . .*"

When had she gained so much weight? She'd barely eaten since the accident. Her loss of appetite had only worsened after Chaz left. And now? Her skirts wouldn't zip. Her blouses gapped, and she had the choice of fastening the buttons on her best dress or breathing.

"*. . . further investigation has shown this identity to have been false as the real Miss Weston was found to have died as a young girl in Richmond, Virginia . . .*"

She gasped at the tap on her door, her breath undoing the five minutes of effort it had taken to squeeze herself in.

"*. . . who was this mystery woman and what happened to her . . .*"

She flipped off the radio, shucking off the dress in a fit of despair. "This better be an emergency."

"Sorry to bug you, but I wanted your opinion on the trim for the kitchen."

Slipping her robe back on, she opened the door a crack to find David on the landing with a sample of board in each hand. "I'm sure whatever you pick will be fine."

"Are you sure? The last time I picked something without your say-so, I had to take it back. My back's still griping."

"A refrigerator is different. Believe me, I trust your opinion on floor trim explicitly."

He leaned against the wall, his head cocked in a considering way. "Is today your meeting with the old ladies?"

"The Norfolk Yeomen F Society, yes. But I can't find a damn thing to wear. Too many burgers and pizza pies, I guess. Maybe I should cancel. Maybe this whole idea is crazy. Maybe I'm crazy trying to find out about a woman who obviously didn't want anything to do with me or my family."

"Slow down. You're working yourself into a state. It's coffee with a bunch of grannies. Not tea with the queen."

"Easy for you to say." She slammed the door and sank back onto the bed, scowling at her mirror's reflection.

Gone was the ghost of the last six months. The woman who stared back had color in her cheeks from walks on the beach and limbs tanned and plump from days spent ripping down vines and digging up flowerbeds. Her eyes didn't stare blankly as she struggled to get through the next hour, the next day, the next breath. She hadn't thought about Chaz once in almost a week.

David wasn't the only one making progress.

Half an hour later, Peggy came downstairs dressed in a lemon yellow belted sundress with a collared bodice. A pair of cat-eye sunglasses perched on her hair, which was pulled into a sleek bun at the nape of her neck. "What do you think? I found it at the back of Blanche's closet. It's a little June Cleaver for my taste, but it fits."

"Wow." David stared as she did a slow turn. "I guarantee June Cleaver never filled out a dress like that."

Warmth slid along cold limbs, and she let the smile that bubbled up in her chest escape. It had been a long time since anyone had complimented her. It had been a longer time since she'd *wanted* anyone to compliment her. She'd forgotten how good it felt.

MRS. STOKES LIVED in a snug yellow split-level on a quiet cul-de-sac. Peggy had been led to believe the NYFS gatherings were nothing more than a few old friends swapping stories and reliving their youth over coffee and sandwiches, but by the time she arrived, the driveway was full and the street in front crowded with cars. One even sported out-of-state Maryland plates.

She swallowed down her apprehension, gripped her purse with cold fingers, and ignored the twitch of lace curtains as she headed up the walk to the bright blue front door, which opened before she'd had a chance to even knock.

"You came!" A small woman with big dark eyes and salt-and-pepper hair cut and styled in a becoming helmet of curls welcomed her with a wide smile and a booming voice. On her jacket lapel, she wore a gold pin depicting two crossed feathers and a bronze medal of a winged woman hanging from a rainbow ribbon. "Come in and meet the girls!"

Mrs. Stokes led Peggy into a sunken living room buzzing with blue-haired senior citizens, some holding the expected cups of coffee, but others with large glasses of wine, and a few with tumblers in hand. Most, if not all, wore the same two pins reflecting their military service. A hennaed woman with a striking resemblance to Granny from *The Beverly Hillbillies* stood behind a glass bar cart doling out drinks with the pizazz of a professional mixologist. She sized Peggy up and went straight for an enormous bottle of red.

"I really appreciate you inviting me, Mrs. Stokes."

"Please, honey, call me Connie. I hear you're interested in learning more about us female yeomen. You've definitely come to the right place."

She pointed to one wood-paneled wall covered in framed black-and-white photographs. "My personal hall of fame, as it were. That's me, third row in the back." A line of serious young women stood shoulder to shoulder, all in the same dark jackets, shin-length dark skirts, and wide-brimmed hats she'd seen in Blanche's photo. "And that's me in front of my boarding house." A young woman in the sailor-collared jumper and neckerchief, her hair neatly pinned under a brimmed straw hat, smiled into the camera.

Peggy moved from photo to photo, trying to put herself in the place of these wide-eyed earnest girls, pride and determination shining in every face. Here was one standing arm in arm with a smiling young man in an Army uniform. There was a group in Dixie-cup sailor hats and wide-collared middy blouses having a picnic.

"A thousand of us were stationed just in the Hampton Roads area," Connie explained. "Young and on our own, thinking we were so damn clever. It was an amazing, exhilarating time."

"It's sad," Peggy said as she paused in front of a photograph of rows of uniformed women marching, rifles poised against their shoulders. "You hear about the WAVES and the WACS, but the yeomanettes have been forgotten."

"It wasn't always like that. Right after the war, we were praised for our service and patriotism, offered all the same benefits as the men. They trotted us out for military parades and veterans' rallies. That's when a lot of us joined the American Legion."

"Then what happened?"

Shouts and high-pitched barking coming from what Peggy assumed was the kitchen were followed by "Connie, your dog is in the sandwiches again!"

"Hold that thought, Peggy!" The crowd parted like a wave as she sailed toward the kitchen, shouting orders as she went.

Peggy wasn't left alone long. Granny Clampett appeared at her elbow to hand her a glass of wine. Another woman in a fox stole and a pink pillbox hat moved aside to let her sit down on a long sectional sofa encased in plastic. Both wore the same gold pin of two crossed feathers.

"Connie giving you her yeomanettes' pitch?" Pink Pillbox asked, one hand holding her highball glass, the other stroking her fur with long polished nails.

"Pardon?"

"The performance she puts on for whatever journalist's intern shows up every Veterans Day to do a story on the brave and gallant young women who served their country in the Great War," she clarified.

"She's refined it over the years." Granny Clampett smelled of caramels and talcum powder, her glasses magnifying a pair of sharp eyes decorated in bright blue eye shadow, but her smile was genuine. "It's much better than it was the first few times she recited it."

"Did she get to the part where she laments about how women were eventually barred from service in the reserves?" Pink Pillbox asked. "How the benefits we were promised in the heady days of peace dissolved as politicians' memories lapsed? It's quite affecting."

Granny dabbed dramatically at her eyes. "I tear up every time she tells it."

"I'm not from the paper. My great-aunt was a yeomanette."

Recognition dawned. "Of course! You're Blanche Lawrence's little niece," Pink Pillbox announced, practically spilling her drink in her enthusiasm. "Connie said you might turn up."

"She was a good woman," Granny exclaimed with a lift of her glass. "A real firecracker."

"We were so sorry to hear about her passing." Pink Pillbox laid a ropy, liver-spotted hand over Peggy's. "It was Blanche who was always fighting to get us the recognition we deserved. She wrote letters, made phone calls, lobbied politicians—the NYFS was, in part, her idea. She was a real crusader. We owe a lot to her doggedness and her connections."

"She had connections?"

"Oh yeah, honey," Granny Clampett interrupted. "She was a real mover and shaker in local politics all the way up to the statehouse in Virginia. She always had some cause she was fighting for: women's rights, civil rights, workers' rights. You name it."

"The group wasn't nearly as successful after she dropped out."

"Why did she do that? I mean, if she was so involved."

"Couldn't say. It was quite a while back—maybe ten years?" Pink Pillbox turned to Granny. "Ten years, Marcia?"

"June 1958. I remember because we were planning that trip to Tallahassee and there was a big to-do over the hotel deposit."

"That's right. June of 1958. Connie took over as president after. Haven't been able to unseat her since. Honestly, I always got the impression she resented Blanche's leadership a little. She didn't think it was right that someone who'd served her full enlistment—Connie was discharged in 1921—should be overlooked by someone who'd been dismissed before Armistice Day."

Peggy barely had time to register this remark when Connie returned, a primped and ribboned Yorkie under her arm. "I see you've been ambushed by Mrs. Tilbury"—she glanced at Pink Pillbox—"and Mrs. Gregson." She motioned toward Granny Clampett. "Mrs. Tilbury's a local girl, worked at the shipyard in Portsmouth. Mrs. Gregson was stationed in Rhode Island, but moved here with her husband in 1934."

"What did you do in the Navy?" Peggy asked Mrs. Stokes, who was feeding the Yorkie Vienna sausages from a paper plate.

"I was personal secretary to Admiral Dillingham in operations."

"Did you know Blanche back then?"

"I knew who she was. We all did. That red hair and the way she carried herself, like she was better than everyone and knew it, you couldn't help but notice her. All of us girls were in awe."

"I'm trying to track down more information on the two girls who lived with her—Marjory Meyer and a girl named Vivian, I don't have a surname for her."

"Doesn't ring any bells, sweetie, but I can ask Mrs. Emerson—

she's our corresponding secretary. She might have seen the names pop up in one of the editions of our national newsletter." She scanned the room with a smile. "There she is, by the buffet table as usual. Yoo-hoo, Mrs. Emerson . . ." She dove into the scrum, the Yorkie growling and squirming.

Mrs. Gregson tapped her lips with one manicured finger. "Vivian . . . that name sounds awfully familiar."

"There was a Marjory on my basketball team," Mrs. Tilbury offered, "but I'm afraid I can't remember her last name. It was German-sounding, I think."

"Meyer?" Peggy asked eagerly.

"No, nothing like that. Kallenbach . . . Kaffmeyer. . . . she was a great player, whatever her name was. Had a killer rim shot."

"No luck with Mrs. Emerson, honey," Connie returned. "She doesn't recall that name coming up, but she says you're welcome to sift through our archives."

"You mean the twenty cardboard boxes stowed in Rose's basement behind the Christmas decorations," Mrs. Gregson muttered behind her glass of wine.

Connie shot Mrs. Gregson a hard look, which was returned with one equally belligerent.

"Mrs. Tilbury mentioned Blanche left the Navy early," Peggy stepped in. "Was that usual?"

Connie relaxed back into hostess mode. "I wouldn't say usual, but it happened. Illness. Family complications. Girls usually left when they got married or were expecting. The Navy wasn't quite sure how to treat us—like sailors or like daughters? They split it right down the middle in most cases." By now, she'd run out of Vienna sausages and had moved on to profiteroles, which the little dog snatched from her fingers. "Now where's June? She's meant to show us the slides from her visit to Boston."

The rest of the afternoon was much as Peggy envisioned. She

watched a slideshow then helped fold countless newsletters. The women she met were friendly and eager for a new audience for their stories. But as the first streetlight flickered on, she took up her purse. By now, the room had thinned, only a few diehards left, gathered at the bar cart for a final tipple or by the coat closet gathering hats and purses.

Mrs. Tilbury resettled her stole. By now her pink pillbox had wilted, and her face was flushed from too many cherry-decorated drinks. "I hope you weren't bored to death by a bunch of old weathered warhorses."

"Not at all. It was fascinating, and it was wonderful hearing the stories about my great-aunt. It makes me wish I'd known her better."

"She was a good woman. Smart. Driven. But I wouldn't call her *friendly*. Not like some of the girls. Kept herself to herself, really."

Peggy thought back to the photograph—Marjory, Viv, Blanche.

That may have been the case with *these* women, but once Blanche had known friendship and laughter—and secrets.

She was getting into her car when Mrs. Gregson leaned into the open window. Her eyes gleamed with excitement behind her glasses. "I just remembered where I heard the name Vivian recently—it was in the news about a yeomanette who went missing at the end of the war. Apparently, they never found her body, but her ID tag washed up a few weeks ago on the beach just a few blocks from Blanche's cottage. The name of the yeomanette was Vivian. Vivian Weston."

CHAPTER 21

VIV

1918

August in Virginia slid in like molten gold, slow and hot and cloudless, the air sticky and thick as molasses. American forces were finally in the thick of the fighting, and late summer advances along the Marne at Chateau-Thierry and Belleau Wood were reported in great detail in every newspaper. I scoured articles describing gallant dogfights, rail lines and bridges bombed, German artillery targeted. More slowly would I turn the page to the casualty lists, scanning the names, my stomach in knots, until I reached the end when I could let out my held breath, unclench my fingers from the page.

Tom was alive. More than that, I couldn't say.

It had been two months since he'd stepped aboard the evening steamer to New York. Seven weeks since he'd boarded a troop ship for France. I'd had a postcard from St. Nazaire announcing his arrival. Two from a forward airfield, all pertinent information cut out. And then—nothing. It was as if Europe had swallowed him whole. Every night before bed, I wrote him a letter. Every morning on my way to work, I mailed it. And every evening, I sifted through the envelopes on our front table searching for his familiar scrawl.

I told myself he was busy, fighting was fierce, the mail was probably held up or maybe even lost at the bottom of the sea, a victim of the relentless U-boats prowling the Atlantic. I consoled myself with this mantra during the long days and even into the small hours of the night when the heat made sleep impossible and I tossed and turned on top of my damp sheets. Tom would come marching home when this horrible war was over. Alive and whole and covered with glory.

But would he come marching back to me?

This was the question that lingered, impossible to push away no matter how I tried.

I had turned him down, had sent him away without even an engagement ring to hold him. I had chosen the Navy over his proposal. Maybe in the weeks since we'd parted, he'd changed his mind. Maybe I had lost him—this time for good.

I used hard work and routine to fight my black mood. An old habit from my old life. Up at dawn. Hot coffee. Cool bath. Crisp uniform. Dusty commute. Full desk. Every moment accounted for. Every hour filled. No time to dwell on what I should have done or where I might have gone wrong. But sometimes even those methods deserted me. That's when Marjory would drag me to one of her basketball games.

"Pass me the ball!"

"Open! Open!"

"That's a foul, ref! Clear as day!"

The gymnasium echoed with the squeak of rubber soles and the shouts of two teams of yeomanettes fighting for bragging rights as they elbowed and jostled each other for dominance.

Neither the shortest nor the tallest athlete on the court, Marjory played with the most gusto, flying up and down, shouting orders to her team as she formed them up to attack the basket or defend their own. Her brown hair bounced against her shoulders, the bow on her white cotton blouse wilted, her long navy blue bloomers smudged and stained as she knocked the ball out of the hands of a blonde girl with stork legs then shot for two.

The ball went through the hoop with a swish just as the referee blew the final whistle, but instead of the usual cheering that followed the end of the game, there was a frightened shout from the benches as a crowd gathered around one of the girls.

Marjory darted off the court, shoving people aside as she dug her way to the center of the circle. "Someone get her water!"

Everyone seemed frozen in place, confused and uncertain. Not me. I sprinted for the water cooler by the door where I filled a cup. The knot of worried onlookers had grown, but they moved aside as I approached. Someone had loosened the girl's collar, but her face was pale as oatmeal and slick with sweat while her pulse thrummed wildly in the hollow of her throat. Her eyes fluttered open as Marjory took the cup and held it to her lips.

"We told her not to play. She's been feeling lousy since this morning."

"I'm fine." The girl pushed Marjory aside as she struggled to rise. "Just a little dizzy, that's all."

"You don't look fine."

She hoisted herself to her feet, swaying but upright. "See? Right as rain." She forced a smile, though her gaze remained dull and slightly unfocused. We all knew she lied. None of us called her on it. All of us would do the same in her shoes.

Blanche had been right when she said we were on trial. Born out of desperation and need, the yeomanettes lived on borrowed time. If we didn't prove ourselves now, it wasn't clear we'd ever get a second chance. After all, how many wars could there be in our lifetimes?

I tried not to think about what would happen if the war ended before I made it to France. Where I would go. What I would do.

Instead, I practiced a few simple French phrases amid my ongoing shorthand practice and typing drills.

Despite her show of bravado, the yeomanette didn't shake off Marjory's steadying hand on her arm as the group of players escorted her into the locker rooms.

The excitement over, I headed back to collect my things. One of the players on the opposing team, already changed from her bloomers and blouse into her uniform, passed on her way out of the gymnasium. "I hope I don't get sick. I have a three-day leave next weekend."

"Lucky you," her companion replied. "I'm pulling fourteen-hour days at the base. If they cut me open, I wouldn't be surprised if I bled Navy blue."

Wouldn't we all?

"Good evening, Viv." It was Ernst in his best suit, carrying a small florist's box. "Are you all right? You look . . . as we say in Bremen . . . *besorgt*. Troubled."

He had no idea.

"Going somewhere nice?" I said, hoping to change the subject.

"There is a dance at my social club tonight. My friends have heard so much about Marjory. They are anxious to meet her at last." I noticed the nervous way he handled the box, the way he tapped his foot.

"It sounds serious."

"I hope so," he said quietly. He gave a swift glance toward the locker rooms before stepping closer, lifting the lid to offer me a peek. "Flowers for Marjory," he explained. Nestled in tissue paper was a corsage of violets and blue pansies accented with gold ribbon.

"They're Navy colors."

"I thought they would match her uniform better that way."

He touched the edge of one petal. "They're silk." He looked both pleased with himself and uncertain.

"They're perfect. She'll love them." This was the right thing to say, because he stood straighter and his air of worry receded. "Marjory will be out in a minute. One of the girls took sick."

"Oh dear," Ernst replied, clearly distracted by Marjory's emergence from the locker room and only half listening to me. His face lit up with pride and love as he watched her crossing the gymnasium floor, neckerchief askew, jacket buttoned wrong, wisps of curls haloing her head.

Without warning, envy twisted my gut and made my chest hurt. Is this what the poets meant by *heartbreak*? This actual physical pain that squeezed until I couldn't catch my breath and spots danced at the corners of my eyes? I missed Tom so badly that goose bumps shivered my arms until my teeth chattered.

Ernst finally glanced over at me, his round face wrinkled with concern. "This girl and now you don't look so good. I hope the flu is not coming early this year."

As the number of soldiers and sailors filing through Hampton Roads on their way to France increased, the hospital filled with those returning injured and sick. The names and stories stayed with me, a grim list I typed into letters, forms, requisitions, and in the worst case, telegrams that spread out from the naval hospital like veins from a broken heart.

Some of the yeomanettes had taken it upon themselves to befriend these young men as a way to help with their recovery. They went to movies and dinners. They organized concerts, plays, and dances. I did just the opposite. As the weeks passed with no letters from Tom, I began to avoid the patient wards, keep my head down as I passed through the busy quarterdeck or crossed the grassy campus. I'd been fooled too many times. Seen Tom in too many faces. I should have known Quarles would notice my reluctance.

"Weston." She called me over to her desk one morning, handing me a name on a slip of paper.

"I don't understand."

"The lad's far from home. Confused. Afraid. And trying his damnedest not to show it. I thought you two might have a lot in common."

"I really don't think . . ." I tried to hand it back, but she shook her head, resuming her typing with ferocity.

"That's an order, Weston," she barked over a fusillade of clacking keys.

I stuffed the paper into my pocket, knowing I was beat.

Henry was from Minnesota and the eldest of eight. His father owned a farm that was supposed to come to him after the war, but that was before the U-boat attack that left him blind and without a hand.

Another slip of paper. Another young man. Paul was from Houston, Texas. His parents died when he was small, but his aunt and uncle waited anxiously for word from their nephew. He didn't want to write them about the infection that lost him his leg. He said they'd only worry more.

Eric came next. Before he enlisted, he'd moved from city to city in search of work, but now he thought it would be nice to settle down somewhere out in the country where the air was better. Suffering from tuberculosis, he had maybe five years left—if he was lucky.

Every week Quarles handed me a new slip of paper with a new name. Every week I did what I was ordered. I accepted a shooting gallery's kewpie doll from a Bostonian lieutenant with a heart condition and ate grilled fish from a stall at Buckroe Beach with a torpedoed ensign from Colorado. None of them knew how much I dreaded those outings. Just as with every other task I took on as a yeomanette, I threw myself into this one with determination and gusto.

Then something strange happened. With each young man I met, the knifing pain in my heart eased—just a little. I was able to forget for those few hours. Able to set aside my fear and enjoy swapping laughter and stories. Soon enough the slips of paper from Quarles stopped, but I continued doing what I could for the boys passing through our hospital. Inviting them for suppers at the cottage or meeting them at the amusement park for a stroll on the beach. It was only when talk turned to the sweethearts they left behind and they asked if I had any special someone overseas that I shook my head and changed the subject.

I toyed with the idea of phoning the Westons for news—good or bad. But there was always the risk that my father might find out. That he might find me. If Tom was dead, no amount of worrying would help. If he was alive, I had no reason to worry. That's what I told myself every day. It almost got so I believed it.

One day late in August, I invited a group of boys to the cottage for a picnic on the beach. The summer's tourists had thinned, but the water was still warm and the worst of the heat blown out to sea by a cool shore breeze. I sat on the porch with a bowl between my legs, snapping the last of our garden's summer beans ahead of the night's feast, listening to the screech of locusts in the trees warring with the low trill of crickets. Blanche had bartered her talents as a seamstress for a string of croaker to grill. She was upstairs now, the sewing machine humming. Marjory was on duty, but she had promised to bring a box of Ernst's cream-filled *Berliners* home for dessert.

The clock's chime nearly drowned out the rattle of a motor as

Gus's grocery van careened around the corner, bouncing from rut to rut as it swung to a wild gravel-spitting stop.

"Marjory?" I stood to see better over the rosebushes.

She tumbled out from behind the wheel, her hair disheveled. She'd shed her jacket, and blood spattered her white blouse. "Gus has been hurt!" she shouted as she moved to help someone from the passenger seat.

"I'm fine. Stop fussing," came the plaintive whine even as he let her lead him up the walk, while he held a blood-soaked towel to his forehead, drips of red spotting and staining his shirt.

"What happened? Were you hit by a car?" I abandoned my beans to chase the two of them into the house. "Was it that fella down at the docks, the one with the dog? Don't tell me revenuers finally tumbled to your uncle's sideline."

"Please stop talking, Viv," Gus moaned. "My head is killing me after that drive. Marjory nearly ran over three pedestrians and clipped two mailboxes on her way home."

"I've only ever driven my uncle's Model T," she explained.

"My boss is going to kill me when he sees the van."

Blanche had set aside her sewing to see what all the commotion was about. "I'd think he'd be more concerned with his driver."

We gathered at the kitchen table. Marjory ran for the first aid kit while I boiled water and Blanche peeled away the cloth to inspect the jagged cut slashing its way above his left eye.

"Ouch!" Gus yelped. "Are you trying to skin me alive?"

"Don't be such a baby," she replied, clutching his chin in her hand.

"I'd like to see how you'd feel if someone lobbed a damn rock at your head, thank you kindly."

"Well I wouldn't yell at the person trying to keep me from bleeding to death, now would I?" she snapped back. "It doesn't look too bad. Might need a stitch or two."

"Stitches?" He yanked free of her grip, shielding his head from further inspection. "It's just a little cut."

"A little cut that could have lost you an eye if it was an inch more to the left. One good ear and one good eye. Not so clever then, huh?" The two of them bickered back and forth like an old married couple.

"What happened?" I asked, taking over from Blanche before it came to blows. After a wild-eyed look of panic, Gus allowed me to wash his cut. I dabbed gently, jumping every time he flinched.

"It wasn't anything, some kids joking around," Gus said through gritted teeth. "It got out of hand."

Cheeks flushed with outrage, Marjory stormed back in with a box of bandages, gauze, and a tin of Lesperine antiseptic powder, which she spooned into a glass of hot water. "Stop trying to make excuses for them. This wasn't some childish prank gone wrong. Ernst says—"

"This happened at the bakery?" I asked, trying to sound normal while all I could think about was those men watching the bakery that day, the letter Ernst had received.

"That's right. I saw Marjory on her bicycle coming up from the ferry dock. She said she was headed to the bakery so I offered her a lift in the delivery van." He relayed the encounter in between muttered cusses and quick gasps of pain as I washed out his cut with the dissolved antiseptic. "When we got there, some kids were hanging around, acting tough and bothering folks. Didn't think anything of it, but as we came out, one of them picks up a rock and hurls it at the bakery window. Then all of them hightailed it down the street."

"Damn delinquents," Blanche snipped. "From now on, try to keep that melon head out of range of any projectiles. I prefer it in one piece." Her expression softened, her hand resting on Gus's shoulder for only a moment, but it was long enough for Gus to reach up and cover it with his own. Immediately, she snatched it away, turning her attention to Marjory, her voice fierce, her features flushed. "You'd best go up and change. Viv's guests arrive in a few hours and you look a wreck. And you"—she swung back to Gus—"you need to see a proper doctor and have that cut taken care of. I won't have anyone accuse me of scarring you permanently."

"Too late," Gus muttered.

Marjory's shoulders sagged now that the excitement was over. She clutched the first aid box in her hand like a cudgel. "Sorry about your van, Gus. I'll pay any damages."

"It's all right." He grinned, his blond hair flopping over the top of his bandage. "Hey, maybe you should forget the Navy and join one of those ambulance services. That was some fancy driving."

"I think I'll stick to my bicycle."

He watched as she headed upstairs, his smile fading as soon as she rounded the landing. "I didn't want to say anything, but those boys didn't pick Ernst out just because he has the cleanest windows on Church Street."

"What do you mean?" Blanche had pulled herself together, but there was still an unsettled look in her eye.

"'Dirty Hun.' That's what they yelled when they took off. And I found this on the sidewalk out front." He pulled a knife out of his pocket and set it on the table.

Suddenly that cool wind didn't feel so comforting.

DESPITE GUS'S DESCRIPTION of the vandals, no one was arrested. The police brushed off his suspicions, instead blaming it on common hooliganism and the violent growing pains of a city bursting at its seams. Blanche took to writing scathing letters to the editor, which she read aloud to us from the newspaper every morning with our coffee and toast.

". . . and so I say to the good people of Norfolk, how much more must we endure before our local constabulary steps into the breach to put an end to this pernicious crime wave afflicting our fair city? Or must we take it into our own hands to root out the filth that threatens to destroy all we hold dear . . ." She stood at the head of the table like an orator at her podium, a hand over her heart, her voice raised in condemnation.

"Golly, she's good," Marjory murmured. "Like a general rousing her troops."

"No. She's an admiral," I replied quietly.

Gus snorted his derision. "Go on with both of you. I've seen better acting at the traveling vaudeville show down by the piers," he muttered, though I noticed his gaze was fixed on Blanche as if she were hanging the moon.

When she finished, she sat down to a round of cheering applause. "That's sure to persuade them," Marjory gushed. She grabbed the paper from Blanche's hand. "Look. Yours isn't the only letter either. There are two more complaining about the same thing farther down the page."

"Some of the ladies with the Women's Home Guard agreed to write their own letters. Pressure and public opinion is what will get results." Her gaze slid toward Gus. "Vaudeville show, indeed," she sniffed.

But Gus wasn't listening. He was staring at the paper Marjory was holding. His face splotchy with emotion.

"Gus?" I nudged him. "What's wrong?"

He blinked and cleared his throat. "I reckon I just need another cup of coffee."

Blanche followed his gaze, tearing the page from Marjory's hand and folding it back to the week's casualty list, which ran nearly the length of the page. Heartbreak and tragedy written in bold black printer's ink. And halfway down the right-hand column . . .

Lt Thomas R Weston, Richmond Virginia, missing in action

It wasn't seeing his name that broke me. It was Blanche's whispered "Oh Viv," that did it.

The world fell away. I could no longer hear the locusts rattling in the trees outside or the clomp of Gus's boots across the kitchen floor. I could no longer hear Blanche, though I knew she was speaking. I could see her mouth moving. All was a whirring rush of deafening noise that I realized at last was blood pushing through my veins. Pounding in my ears.

My heart still beat. My lungs still filled. How could that be when I felt turned to stone and frozen through and through?

Somehow, I made my body move. I spoke words, though they came halting and slow. "Excuse me. I have something I need to do."

I felt their hands reach for me, but I brushed them off, fleeing the cottage as if I could flee the knowledge. Tom was missing. Alive? Dead? I hurried up the road, no direction in mind, no intent but the desire to turn back the clock to this morning as I pinned my hair, drew on my stockings, hummed as I washed my face. An ordinary unremarkable cloudless summer day. Not this hurricane of anger and heartbreak and terror.

An hour later, Blanche found me sitting on a bench near the Ocean View Hotel. It was too early for the amusement park to be open, but the smell of cooking grease and hot sugar already filled the humid air. Out on the beach, a few fishermen sat on upturned buckets watching their lines that stretched gossamer thin into the bay. Clouds hung low on the horizon, but here the sky was high and creamy blue, gulls screeching as they rode the breeze.

"I thought I'd find you here."

"I let him go without telling him how I felt. I had everything I wanted and I threw it away."

"You don't know that."

I studied the tops of my shoes, scuffed after my aimless wandering. The pinch on my heel distracted me from the hole blasted open in my chest.

"Let's find a phone and call Richmond," Blanche said, eminently practical even now as the world fell to pieces around me. "We'll call the Westons. They might have more recent news than what's in the paper. It might all be a misunderstanding. Who knows? Tom might even pick up. How about that?"

"And if he doesn't? I can't tell them it's Vivian calling, and I can't tell them who I really am. What if word leaked and my father found out where I was?" My vision burned and blurred. I wiped at my cheeks, surprised to find them damp with tears. "I can't risk that. Not even for Tom."

Blanche pulled me close, letting me rest a head on her shoulder as I wept. "Then we'll have to find another way, won't we?"

CHAPTER 22

VIV

The stifling heat in our office banged against my temples as I typed form after form, the sour odor of carbon paper and typewriter ribbon trapped in my nostrils, my fingertips stained blue from ink and pencil lead. I'd long since had to abandon evenings at the amusement park and the promenade, and our beach parties and bonfires had become an ancient pastime. None of us had the time or the enthusiasm.

War filled the pages of the papers, our troops moving like an inexorable tide of men and machinery. The docks and warehouses groaned with the weight of the effort, the waterways choked with ships. The hospital, too, saw the efforts of our success in harried staff and longer hours.

I stretched, feeling the muscles in my arms scream in protest, the joints in my shoulders pop with relief. Ten hours hunched over a desk. Four hours to go. I took advantage of Quarles's absence from her desk to take a much-needed break, heading downstairs for a smoke.

Despite the hospital's location at the water's edge, there was no respite from the sticky heat that clung damp to my skin and wilted even the most determined starched collar. The sky was a dingy yellow smeared by smoke from the boilers of dozens of ships, the water flat and oily. I headed toward a stand of magnolias, their wide shiny leaves shading one of the wooden pavilions erected at the start of the war. Leaning against the trunk, my shoes dusty in the dry yellowed grass, I smoked a cigarette as I watched a gaggle of nurses pass, their white caps and aprons still crisp with starch.

"Here, doll. Give us a puff." The sailor sat in a wheelchair, the skin of his face taut over sharp bones. One leg missing. One hand curled burned and unusable against his chest. Victim of an exploding boiler as his merchant ship went down.

"I'll do you one better." I fished in my pocket for my pack and a lighter. Lit it and handed it over.

"Thanks." He tipped his head back and closed his eyes on a slow exhale, the rigid haunted look easing from his features. "Shit. I fucking needed that."

He shot me a quick look, but I shrugged him off. After six months of Navy life, I was hardly the sweet virginal maiden he took me for. Ears, or anything else for that matter. Besides, I knew exactly how he felt and took another slow drag of my own.

"Yeoman Weston?" An orderly hovered just outside our cloud of tobacco smoke.

"That's right." My stomach fell at his grim expression and the way he stood as if he wished he was anywhere but here. It couldn't be Marjory. I'd waved to her this morning as we parted ways downtown, her skirts billowing to either side of her big black bicycle. Blanche had gone home to Washington, DC, for her mother's birthday.

"I know I said face-to-face might be better, but now I'm not so sure," I'd said as I walked with her to the train station. "Maybe make an excuse. Tell her you couldn't get leave."

"If you think they'd disown me for getting knocked up without a husband, it would be ten times worse if I missed Mama's annual birthday ball. Everyone who is anyone will be in attendance."

"Maybe they won't notice." Blanche's rough reckoning put her at least six months gone, and while her sewing skills and more than a few carefully dropped remarks about her weight gain due to Ernst's baking had kept the worst of the gossipmongers stifled, I wasn't sure she'd be as successful at hiding the truth from her parents.

"We can't pretend forever, Viv." She'd kissed me on the cheek before stepping on the train like Joan of Arc headed to the stake. "You ought to know that more than most."

Now I wished I'd argued harder.

"Is everything all right?" I asked the young orderly, hating the wobble in my voice.

"Orders to report to the head of surgery," the man said.

I tried not to panic. Instead, I drew a breath and headed inside and up the stairs after my escort. He stopped at a door and gave a jerk of his head. "They're waiting for you."

My stomach fizzed and I wished I'd had time to change my blouse or maybe wipe the gravy stain from my collar.

The office was large with two long windows facing the river. A handsome desk in dark expensive wood sat across from a glass-fronted cabinet filled with leatherbound medical books. The head of surgery was younger than I expected, with thick brown hair and the expression of a kindly uncle. I immediately relaxed, though I ignored his invitation for me to take a seat. Instead, I stood lightly on the balls of my feet, staring solemnly somewhere over his left shoulder.

"I'm told by a reliable source that you're a credible typist, a whiz at shorthand, and most importantly, you're not averse to working in a war zone."

"No, sir. I *want* to serve overseas."

"Commendable, I'm sure. Dr. Stewart's team leaves for France in three weeks. One of his clerks announced this morning that she has decided *not* to accompany him, citing a husband and three small children. Your name was put forward by Chief Quarles as a candidate to replace her."

Quarles had done it. She'd secured me a posting in France. I couldn't help the stupid grin.

"You're single? No children? A saintly old mother who needs you at home?"

Tom's face sprang to mind. Blanche had said we'd find another way to find out what happened to him, and here it was—being handed to me on a silver platter. Once I was stationed in Brest, I could make my own inquiries. Do my own digging. Even if all it turned up was confirmation of his death, it would be better than this weightless limbo I found myself in now.

"No, sir," I said, which was technically the truth.

"Good. Then it's settled. We'll put in the paperwork."

I practically floated back to my office, pausing in front of Quarles's desk. She glanced at me over the rim of her coffee cup. "Something the matter, Weston?"

I glanced around for any sign of Dumfries before leaning nearer. "I wanted to thank you for going around the lieutenant and giving my name to Dr. Stewart."

"Don't thank me. You earned it." Dismissed, I started to walk away when she called out across the office. "But you'd better not make me regret sticking my neck out. Got it?"

Not even Quarles's gruffness could take away from my relief. "Yes, ma'am." I saluted her crisply.

The day passed in a cloud of fuzzy pink optimism not even a last-minute pile of paperwork could diminish.

It was late by the time I stepped off the trolley and headed the three blocks south. The afternoon's summer haze had given way to a cool drizzle. I could almost smell the scent of burning leaves and pumpkin pie. I turned onto our street, following the lamp in the window past Gus's grocery van and the neighbor's rusting crab pots and overturned rowboat resting under the pines by our gate.

I couldn't wait to announce my big news. Without Blanche and Marjory—and Chief Quarles, of course—I'd never have won the post. Blanche had coached me in shorthand until I could read every squiggle and dash like the cleverest of Morse operators. Marjory had quizzed me on naval regulations, the bluejacket's manual marked and underlined until my brain exploded. Their help had not only distracted me when I needed it most, it had earned me a spot on the surgical team.

Stepping onto the porch, the imagined scent of burnt leaves became the very real scent of burnt toast. At least I hoped that was all it was. Marjory had a way of putting things in the oven and walking away. Moths batted at the porch light as I pushed my key into the lock.

No one was downstairs, but Blanche's suitcase was sitting by the front table. I shucked off my jacket and hat. "Anybody home?" I shouted. "You'll never guess what happened!"

A door upstairs closed. There was the sound of running water. Another door clicked open. Marjory thumped down the stairs, taking the last two steps at a dead run. "It's Blanche."

"What's happened? Is it the baby?" My excitement forgotten, I followed Marjory up to Blanche's room. "Should we call a doctor? Get you to a hospital? Hot water and torn sheets?"

But Blanche wasn't in labor. She sat at her dressing table, calmly brushing her hair. She wore a silk robe edged in lace. At her throat, her ID tag had been replaced by a thin gold chain, a ruby pendant nestled in the curve of her breasts.

Marjory perched uneasily on the edge of the bed while Gus, of all people, hovered nearby in a pair of grungy dungarees, smelling slightly of fish and fuel oil.

"What's going on?"

"I've told my parents everything." Blanche's reflection in her mirror was white, her eyes red-rimmed, but dry and hot with some unspoken emotion. "And they, in turn, told the Navy."

I FIXED US a quick supper of scrambled eggs and fried potatoes. Gus produced a bottle of dandelion wine, which he swore he got from a local doctor for medicinal purposes only. Marjory emerged from her room with an emergency tin of Ernst's gingerbread. Blanche didn't touch any of it.

"What exactly did your parents say?" I asked.

"Mother wept and raged. Father just sat there with this horrible look of disappointment on his face. They reminded me of the scandal. The life I would lead with a bastard at my skirts. The shame and embarrassment *they* would encounter as the parents of a fallen woman. Then they offered me a way out." She put a hand to her throat as if expecting to feel the smooth metal of her Navy tag, only to touch the cold stone. "I can stay here at the cottage until the baby is born, at which time I'm to hand it over to Gilbert and Iris to raise as their own."

"Give up your baby to your brother?"

"And if you don't accept this offer?"

Marjory and I spoke over each other.

"Then I'm on my own. They wash their hands of me once and for all."

Marjory sat down with a thud.

"Won't people question if your sister-in-law suddenly turns up with a new baby?" I asked.

"Everyone will question it, but they'll know better than to do it anywhere near my parents."

Gus had been silent up to now, but after a fortifying swig of wine, he cleared his throat and dropped down on one knee. "Blanche Lawrence—"

"Stop! Stop right there, Gus." Panic washed over Blanche's already pale features. For the first time, her voice broke, her face twisted in grief, and she dragged him back to the table. "I know what you're going to ask, and the answer is no. No. No. No." Each word was louder and more frantic as if she was talking herself out of the idea as much as she was Gus.

"Why? Because I'm not high-class enough?" His voice was equally high and tight, but there was such heartsick desperation behind it, I cringed. "Because I smell like fish? I don't plan on hiring on with my uncle forever. I have plans. Big plans."

"Is that why you think I won't marry you? Because I'm better than you?" Her laugh was as sharp as glass, high spots of color on her cheeks; her eyes wild, like a caged thing looking for escape. "Don't be absurd. It's you who is a far better person than I will ever be. And it wouldn't matter if you married me or not. My parents would still cut me off without a penny, but instead of ruining one life, I'd be ruining two." She reached to touch his sleeve before shaking her head and pulling away. "No, Gus. You deserve to follow those dreams of yours without tying yourself to me and a child that isn't yours."

"So will you accept your parents' offer?" Marjory asked.

"I should. Gilbert and Iris have wanted a baby forever, but they've been married five years with nothing but an empty crib to show for it. It would have a good life. A better life than I could ever give it on my own." She changed her mind and took the bottle from Gus, pouring herself a glass of wine. She had lost the gray flat look of despair, but her fingers still trembled and there was a shine to her gaze. "But no. I didn't agree."

"I don't understand." And I didn't. Not her decision. Not her calm acceptance. Not the pain I saw in her eyes when she turned down Gus. "You said yourself the war will be over soon. That you wanted to work with Mrs. Adams, maybe move to Philadelphia and work with the National Woman's Party. You can't do that with a baby on your hip."

"Of course I can. The war has created hundreds, if not thousands, of widows with small fatherless children." She waggled her ring finger at me. "What's one more? Frankly, I'm more upset over the Navy's reaction than I am at my parents. I mean, I understand *their* shock, but as far as the Navy is concerned, it's not like I've lost my ability to type or file or manage an office. My brain hasn't turned to mush. It's not fair. They don't kick men out for having children."

"It's not the same," Gus ventured before the blood drained from his face at the look of complete fury in Blanche's flint-hard gaze. Gone was any hint of regret at hurting his feelings. She looked like she would gladly murder him.

"Says the man with the right to vote," she hissed. "The right to serve on a jury. The right to your own money. Until you've walked a mile in a woman's shoes, the one right you don't have is to tell me how I should feel about the fact that I'm treated like a lesser being simply because of what I lack between my legs."

Blanche rose and left the house, the slam of the porch door breaking the sudden silence that had fallen over the rest of us. Gus and Marjory and I looked from one to the other. Then he got up and followed her. Through the open window, we heard them arguing low and fierce. Whatever was said did little to defuse the situation. Blanche stormed down the steps and through the gate onto the dunes and the beach beyond. Gus turned away and disappeared into the dark, hands shoved into his pockets.

Marjory pushed her greasy potatoes around with her fork. I looked at my cold scrambled eggs with a slow churning stomach.

The silence was thick as cobwebs, but I didn't have the energy to fight my way through it. "You heard her parents' threats," Marjory said at last. "If she doesn't give the baby up, they'll disown her. Talk to her, Viv. She listens to you."

"You said yourself Blanche is out to prove something." I recalled her standing confidently in the café doorway in her crisp uniform, her red hair like a torch, drawing me in like one of those moths on our front porch.

"That she's stubborn as a mule? She doesn't have to prove it to me."

"She's not trying to prove anything to us."

"The world then? Fat lot of good that'll do her."

"Maybe she's trying to prove it to herself."

When I came down the next morning, I found Blanche asleep on the porch glider, an old blanket from the cedar chest in the living room dragged over her bare legs, her feet still dusted with sand. Her hair frizzed with sea air and humidity around her face. One arm curled under her head. One arm curved around her stomach. Her features smoothed out in repose, brows relaxed into gentle curves, her lips parted slightly. As I watched, a frown wrinkled her features, her hand unconsciously moving to spread against her abdomen as if the child quickened within her. I backed away, my heel catching on the lip of the doorway. I put a hand out to catch myself, knocking a lamp and table in the process.

She blinked and opened her eyes. "Viv? Is that you? What time is it?"

"Early. Go back to sleep."

"I couldn't possibly." She winced and sat up, her features settled into their usual shape, closed off, unreadable. "Are you off to work? A little early even for you, isn't it?"

"We're short-staffed."

"At least there's no fear of *you* getting knocked up and complicating the duty roster." She must have seen my pain because she stood, throwing her arms around me. "Oh, Viv. I'm sorry. I'm a beast, I know. You must be worried sick and here I am acting like a bitter old cow."

I couldn't be angry at her. This was Blanche. I owed her too much to hold a grudge over hasty words. I laid my head on her shoulder. She smelled warmly of violets.

"I'm sure he'll turn up," she continued. "Maybe he's been taken prisoner or been injured and doesn't remember who he is. Have you heard anything more about your transfer?"

This was it. The moment I told her that I was leaving. That Dr. Stewart wanted me—shy, dull, little me—to be a part of his surgical team. I had her to thank. I'd never have made it this far without her at my side. I would never have had the courage except that which I borrowed from her.

I opened my mouth, the sentence forming in my head. The explanation, the reasoning, the apology. But when I met her gaze, there was that same blankness to her features I'd seen last night as if she'd been emptied of hope and purpose. I couldn't say it. It would be like rubbing salt in her wound.

"No. Nothing yet," I said, the lie falling all too easily off my lips. Bad habits are hard to break.

Before my blush could give me away, I headed back inside to put the kettle on. I heard the slap of the screen door and the creak of the sofa as Blanche followed behind. As I fixed us both a cup of coffee, we heard the sputter of the grocery van. I glanced out the kitchen window in time to see Gus climb into the driver's seat. His gaze flicked to the cottage, his normally sunny features stormy with emotion. He ignored my wave as he worked the van into gear and pulled away.

"Gus is furious with me," Blanche said, coming up to stand behind me.

"He'll come around."

"I'm not sure. I said some horrible, hateful things to him."

"He knows you didn't mean them."

"Didn't I?" She settled back into the sofa, the rug over her shoulders.

"He only wants to see you happy."

"He thinks I'm making a mistake I'll live to regret." Once again, her hand cradled her stomach. "But that's already happened."

"So maybe giving the child to your brother would be best. It would be a way to mend things. To make it like it never happened."

"Oh no." Her lips pressed tight. "No amount of mending will do that."

She looked around her as if seeing the cottage with new eyes, the comfortable, slightly battered furniture scavenged from the house in Washington, DC, the clutter of shells and driftwood along the mantel, the pale wash of walls faded from years of sun and salt.

"I'll miss this place. I loved coming here as a child, it was like stepping into a different world, one where the normal everyday rules didn't apply."

I knew exactly what she meant. I'd felt the same way when I first entered the cottage, the way it welcomed me like an old, cherished friend. As if I'd known it forever.

"It's a shame my child won't know that same magic."

"Would they really disown you? Kick you out on the street with nothing?"

"Oh yes," she said matter-of-factly. "Even Mother and Father, as indulgent as they are, have their limits. And I've crashed right through all of them. Luckily, I have some jewelry I inherited from my grandmother that I can sell that will keep me in cash for a little while, and maybe I can get a job of some kind. My Navy experience must count for something. Ernst did it. He raised Clara on his own. Why can't I?"

She sounded so confident, assured that she could shape her future just the way she wanted it. I didn't want to burst her dream with practical matters. Maybe I underestimated her. Maybe she could succeed where so many young women in her position couldn't. I clung to that optimistic thought.

"Where will you go when you leave the cottage?"

She sipped her coffee and the question passed without answer.

CHAPTER 23

PEGGY

1968

Peggy had followed Mrs. Gregson's lead here to the library where she'd searched recent newspapers before asking for the librarian's help to access older editions. On a weekday morning, the place was empty, but for a few elderly browsers and a sing-along group meeting in a corner of the kids' section. Peggy locked her eyes on the microfiche viewer and tried to ignore the off-key chorus of "Old MacDonald" coming from half a dozen toddlers and their mothers. But she could still smell baby powder, diaper ointment, and peanut butter from across the room.

She looked up "Marjory Meyer" first, but there was no mention of her to be found in any copy of the *Daily Press*, the *Virginian-Pilot*, or any of the half-dozen local newspapers she sifted through. Nothing but the same small obituary she'd found hidden behind Blanche's photo.

Not so when she looked for "Vivian Weston."

Peggy's heart twisted in her chest as she read the article in an old copy of the *Ledger-Dispatch* from November of 1918.

Yeomanette Vivian Weston reported missing and presumed dead.

Except she wasn't dead, not if she was writing to Blanche fifty years later.

And her name wasn't really Vivian if the more recent news reports were correct.

That person hadn't existed. She'd been a ghost—her identity stolen from a girl in a Richmond cemetery, a girl dead long before 1918.

Peggy fingered the sharp edge of the postcard that had arrived this morning. The stamp crooked in the corner, the handwriting precise and schoolgirl perfect.

Dec. 1918

Blanche,

You don't know how happy I was to receive your postcard. Just to know you're safe is enough to put my mind at ease. Your father was as good as his word. I head to Europe in a week with a list of names—people who might have news about Tom. I try to convince myself that we did what we had to do and that it will all turn out for the best. Maybe someday I'll believe it.

Viv

What had they done? And had it turned out for the best? Nothing made sense.

The singalong group broke into "Eensy Weensy Spider." Peggy made the mistake of glancing over just as a little boy with gold curls pulled himself up against his mother's shoulder. She curved one arm around his chubby body and kissed his forehead with a smile. He laughed and patted her face. Peggy's heart gnawed its way up into her throat. She couldn't catch her breath. Her body shook. She wanted to be sick.

All turn out for the best.

Peggy's stomach turned. Would this ache ever go away completely? Would it subside with each passing year until she could smile and ignore those precious moments she'd missed by one car length? Would she ever find answers to the question of why? Why her? Why her child?

"Did you find what you were looking for?"

The librarian had crept up behind her in her sensible shoes and cardigan, her words hitting far too close.

Without answering, Peggy grabbed her bag and sweater and fled the library, emerging into the sun like a mole, blinking and disoriented. She bent double, head down, until the dizziness passed.

And here she was thinking she was getting better, that her days of falling to pieces were behind her. She barely flinched anymore when she saw Suzanne waddling up the road with her kids in tow. Instead, her eyes passed over them with polite ambivalence, her manner stilted and sickly sweet. Hoping they didn't smell her fear. Praying she could hold it together, that the emptiness didn't swallow her back down as it had so many times before.

She didn't remember the drive back to the cottage. One minute she was waiting at a crosswalk for a group of teens to pedal their bicycles across the street on their way to the beach, the next she was pulling up in front of the cottage. She turned the car off at the curb but stayed in her seat, a hand on the wheel, her mind white noise like the fuzz of a television after the nightly sign-off, just static and buzzing silence.

A tap at the window brought her back with a jolt. David stood outside, a hand braced against the roof of the car. His hair curved along his jaw, silky, bright gold strands tangled with the darker bronzy brown. She'd kill to have hair like that. He hadn't shaved today either, so the gold of his stubble stood out against his tan. She felt herself staring like an idiot teenager with her first crush.

"Suzanne's here with the kids."

Excitement turned to lead in her stomach. Oh God. Did the universe hate her that much?

As if sensing her need for reinforcements, David followed her into the house. Suzanne was at the kitchen table, dabbing herself with a wet paper towel while her kids laid on the rug leafing through Peggy's latest issue of *Cosmopolitan*.

"Hiya, Peg." Suzanne smiled, but there was a strain around her eyes, worry pursing her mouth and digging lines into her cheeks. And no wonder. Ron had left a week ago on a six-month deployment, leaving Suzanne alone with two kids, and a third very much knocking on the door.

"Would it be insulting to say you look exhausted?" Peggy tossed her car keys on the front hall table, stepped out of her sandals.

"Pot very much calling the kettle black," Suzanne shot back.

Drained and head pounding, Peggy fell onto the couch, feeling the wet chill of a glass pushed into her hand.

"Iced tea," David said. "You look like you could use something stronger, but I draw the line at alcohol before noon."

She was both grateful and uneasy at this act of kindness. When had they become so comfortable together? When had the line she'd so clearly defined at his arrival grown so blurred? She should reset the boundaries before things got complicated, but who was she kidding? *Complicated* seemed an understatement at this point. He poured a second glass for Suzanne, so maybe she was reading way too much into a drink.

"I really hate to bother you, Peg sweetie," Suzanne said with pleading eyes, "I know it's a huge imposition and I really wouldn't ask if there was anyone else I could call . . ."

"What's going on, Suzanne?"

"The doctor wants me to come in for some tests. Nothing bad, just routine stuff as I get closer to my due date. Normally, I have

Mrs. Ertz on the corner watch the kids, but she has her bridge club this afternoon, so—"

"We're happy to watch them." David jumped in before Suzanne could finish her sentence.

Peggy wasn't sure how she felt about David volunteering her; and not only that, but making them sound like they were a couple while he did it. But she couldn't argue with the look of relief that passed across Suzanne's weary face.

"Are you sure?" She glanced at Peggy, this time without the teasing smile. "I wouldn't ask, if I wasn't completely out of options, you know that, right?"

A whole day alone with Suzanne's children sounded like hell on earth, but she couldn't tell Suzanne that, not without spilling the whole story; and *that* she wasn't prepared to do. Not because she thought her friend wouldn't sympathize, but because that knowledge changed the way people acted when they were around her. They talked more softly, moved more carefully. They saw her as delicate, fragile—untouchable. The old her would have welcomed the solitude those walls brought with them. The new her found it lonely.

She glanced at David, and her stomach did another of those slow loop-de-loops.

Brick by brick, the wall was coming down.

"Go," Peggy said. "What are friends for?"

"This will be fun," Peggy said, her voice unnaturally high as she helped the kids out of the back seat. "A whole afternoon together."

David cocked her a strange look that she ignored. He'd been shooting her glances since they'd bundled the kids into the car for the short ride to the amusement park. She didn't want his questions. She didn't need his pity.

Nancy immediately grabbed David's hand while Timmy stood stiff and quiet, eyes wandering over the clanking, banging, flashing chaos of the amusement park. A tall steel tower stretched into the sky above the warren of booths and sheds. Beyond was the low stretch of beach, blessedly calm amid the push of people.

"Look at all those rides," Peggy exclaimed, all sugary sweetness. "What should we do first?"

"I don't like rides," Timmy said quietly. "Can we get popcorn instead?"

"Auntie Peggy is at your service," David answered, hefting the beach bag she'd packed with snacks and a thermos of lemonade.

Auntie Peggy? Was he trying to make this harder than it already was?

They followed the steady current of people through the turnstiles and into the park. David headed for a ticket booth while Peggy followed Timmy's guiding hand toward a stall selling food.

Two popcorns and two sodas later, they gathered at Kiddeland. A few moms clustered at the gate to the mini train ride. Some waved. Others snapped photos. A family of four waited in line at the children's coaster, kids dancing around their fathers' legs like puppies. A mother passed with a stroller, an older child chattering away between bites of cotton candy.

Deep breaths. She could do this. She had to do this. She couldn't fall to pieces now.

"You're hurting my hand," Timmy whined.

She quickly loosened her grip with a "Sorry. Don't want you getting lost."

The afternoon passed in a blur of organ music, clacking mechanical rides, and delighted screams accompanied by the scent of grilling hot dogs, French fries, and sugar in every edible form. Peggy felt her body shutting down, going cold. The smiles. The laughter. The happy families. It was like one big pointer finger directed right at her: You had it. You lost it. Your fault.

"Look what David won you!" Nancy jumped up and down, excitement brightening her eyes.

David held out a bracelet of gaudy blue costume gemstones. "I could probably have bought you the real thing for less money than it took to win it."

"It's beautiful, but wouldn't *you* like to have it instead, Nancy?" Peggy suggested.

Nancy giggled and shook her head. "The man said to give it to his girlfriend."

With a sheepish smile, he handed it to Peggy, who slid it onto her wrist—all under Nancy's stern dictatorial gaze.

After that, Peggy barely noticed as the golden afternoon light faded into dusk, the flashing lights and blaring music seeming to intensify as a new, older, more boisterous crowd took over from the families with small children. Her headache blossomed. Timmy plastered himself to her knee while Nancy and David rode the carousel for the gazillionth time.

"Can we go down on the beach, Miss Peggy? It's too loud."

"I thought you'd never ask." The sand was warm on her bare feet. A few diehards remained, but most had headed indoors for showers and dinners and cocktails.

They found a spot and spread their towels. She handed Timmy a spade and shovel while she lit a cigarette to combat her shattered nerves. The darkness spread over the water like ink, a contrail high and heading north in a purple sky. The last waders left one by one. Behind them, the amusement park burned in a blare of gaudy color. She dug her toes into the sand, enjoying the breeze against her legs. Timmy scooped sand into his bucket, turning it out onto his growing pile.

"Mommy says you're sad."

Peggy played with her lighter, the flint striking a spark, her finger lifting off the wheel until the flame died. "Did she?" Scrape. Spark. Flame. Scrape. Spark. Flame.

"I'm sad too." He dug a trail with his spade.

"Really? We had a lovely afternoon. We went on the rides. You ate three bags of popcorn and had two sodas. You even won a bear."

"I miss my daddy." He watched her, his eyes dark and endless like the bay. "Is that why *you're* sad? Do you miss somebody?"

Once she would have answered "Chaz" without hesitation. But somewhere between arriving in Ocean View with nothing to her name but two suitcases and now, the answer had grown murky and more complicated. She missed her mother, her grandparents, her old friends, her old life. But the more she learned about Blanche, the more she found herself missing her—even though they'd never met. She missed Marjory, who she barely knew as more than a name. She missed Viv with her ridiculous postcards. She missed the person she'd been when she was young and thought she had all the answers.

Like the hole Timmy dug with his spade in the soft sand, she felt as if she'd been scooped out, hollowed by every person she'd lost. With shaking fingers, she lit another cigarette.

"Don't you know those are bad for you?" David crossed the beach, Nancy riding on his shoulders, a balloon in one hand, a chocolate bar in another.

"*You* smoke," she argued.

"So I oughtta know." He grinned as he pulled Peggy to her feet. "We'd better get home. Suzanne probably got back ages ago and is wondering what we did with her kids."

The walk to the car was long and quiet. It gave her time to notice that her stomach didn't contract when Timmy held her hand. That she smiled as she wiped off Nancy's sticky face. That she didn't argue when David put a hand out for the car keys. They passed an older couple out for an evening stroll. The wife smiled at them, leaning toward Peggy with a friendly wink. "You have a lovely family, dear."

She opened her mouth to correct her, then thought better of it.

David. Suzanne. Nancy. Timmy. Even Mr. Symonds, though he'd never admit it, and Ron, who was half a world away.

Peggy did have a lovely family.

THE PHONE WAS ringing as Peggy fitted the key in the cottage's front door. David stayed to unload the trunk as she raced to answer, flipping on lamps as she went. "Hello?"

The line was silent.

"Hello? Who's there?"

She waited, palms sweaty, as if she'd conjured him from her earlier thoughts on the beach. "Chaz?" she whispered. "Is that you?"

"Peggy? Thank God. I've been calling for hours."

Her shoulders slid down off her neck, her hands loosening their grip. She was surprised at her relief. "Suzanne? We just got back from—"

"Look," she interrupted. "I know this is completely last-minute, but I didn't know who else to call . . ." Was she crying? Her voice was shrill as it faded in and out.

"Slow down. What's wrong?"

"They admitted me to the hospital. Just for observation, the doctors said, but I don't know what to do." Her voice was shaky, and Peggy had to press the receiver to her ear to hear over David's booming rendition of "Wooly Bully," which was making the children giggle. She waved him off with a shushing motion and a pointed stare toward the kids. He nodded and shuttled them outside with the promise of a tour of his camper.

"Is it the baby?"

"They say my blood pressure is too high. They want to monitor me here tonight and then I'm supposed to rest and stay off my feet for a few days."

"Right. Follow the doctor's orders. Get some sleep. Don't worry about the kids. We'll see you tomorrow."

Peggy filled David in on the change of plans as Timmy sat in the camper's driver's seat pretending to steer and Nancy leafed through a notebook she'd found in the glove compartment.

"Need help babysitting? I have loads of experience. I'm one of the few Dyer men who can change a diaper and knows every verse to 'Froggy Went A-Courtin'.'"

"Your talents never cease to amaze, but I think I can handle two small children," she answered, knowing it sounded curt and ungracious, but she was tired, and having the kids for a whole night terrified her.

She shepherded the grumbling children toward bed in Blanche's room. Despite their protests, they settled under the sheets easily enough, and after a trip downstairs to find Nancy's pressed penny and another to find Tim's carnival bear, she started to close the bedroom door when Nancy called. "Auntie Peg? Is Mommy going to die?"

Her voice, small and thin, twisted in Peggy's gut with the pain of a blade. "Of course not, sweetie. What gave you that idea?"

"We heard you talking on the phone," Timmy explained.

Peggy sat on the edge of the bed, the children hovering close. "Your mother just needs a good sleep like the two of you do. Tomorrow, you'll all be together again, I promise."

That seemed to satisfy Timmy, but Nancy continued to cling. Her dark hair curled around her white face, and there were tears gleaming in her eyes. "If Mommy dies and Daddy's away on his ship, will you take care of us?"

Peggy gathered her into an enormous hug, her slender frame

curving against her body, tucked warm up under her breastbone. "Your mommy is not going to die, you hear me? But I will always be here for you, so no more worrying."

"Pinky promise?" Nancy held up her little finger.

"Pinky promise," Peggy said, the two shaking on it.

Nancy's breathing was shallow as she sobbed, and Peggy felt her own tears tightening her chest, burning her throat, scalding her cheeks. She fought them back, comforting Nancy until she fell asleep. But she was wobbly-kneed and exhausted by the time she headed downstairs. Her nerves jumped and sweat slicked her back.

She curled on the corner of the couch, teeth chattering as if something inside her had been torn wide open. She bent double, the hollowness on the beach an endless emptiness that nothing could fill.

"Peggy? What's happened? Shit, is it Suzanne? Is she okay?" David stood in the doorway, his face striped by shadows, light burning in his eyes.

She couldn't speak, just shook her head as the tears rolled hot down her cheeks.

His gaze narrowed. "Does Suzanne know how hard this is for you?"

Her hands shook as her voice returned. "I don't know what you're talking about."

But she could tell that wouldn't fly. Over these weeks living side by side, David had got close enough to see through the broken parts of her. He might not know the whole story, but he was clever enough to guess and kind enough to care.

"You want to prove to the world that you can make it on your own, I get that," he said. "I do. But strength doesn't always mean going it alone."

He was right. Hadn't she basked in the warmth of new friendship and family just a few short hours ago? And here she was wallowing like a blubbering idiot unable to control herself. But every corner of the cottage felt like it contained a ghost. Every creak of the stairs and every drift of a curtain. The violet-scented air and the whisper of the tide. It was as if the past crowded close, a movement just beyond the edge of her vision.

"Not every person you trust will disappoint you."

Was he right? Or would it be as she feared? Would he watch his words? Keep his distance? Would she lose him? She didn't think she could bear that. But keeping silent meant she was the one keeping them apart.

She wiped her face with the back of her hand, sniffled into a tissue. "It wasn't Chaz's fault, our marriage ending. Not entirely. I relied on him too much. I expected him to always know what to do. And he liked being that guy, it suited him to be the one with all the answers. But he didn't have an answer for why our child died."

She paused, but David didn't jump in with words of reassurance or sympathy. Not even a hitch in his quiet even breathing. It gave her courage. It gave her space to remember and then to speak it out loud.

"I was eight months gone. Chaz was supposed to drive me to a doctor's appointment, but he was away on one of his road trips, Chicago or Tallahassee, I don't even remember anymore. The office wasn't far, but it was raining, and I was running late so I was going faster than I should. Then this dog jumped out in front of me. I slammed on my brakes, but the car slid on the wet pavement. It wasn't bad, a few dents, but . . . I lost the baby. The doctors and nurses all said it was one of those crazy freak accidents, just bad luck. That we could try again in a little while. But I knew they were just being kind. It was completely my fault. If I hadn't been speeding. If I'd been paying closer attention. I couldn't talk about it. I couldn't get past it. I shut down. Guilt ate away at me."

"You were grieving. You were broken and in pain."

"So was Chaz, but I couldn't see that. Not then. In the end, he left. And I let him go. Maybe part of me thought he'd come back eventually, but he never did. Why would he?"

"Because he loved you?"

She fiddled with her ring finger, where only a pale indent remained. All that remained of five years of marriage. "Why did you come back tonight?"

"You forgot this in the car."

It was the bracelet. Instead of setting it on the table, he took her hand in his, sliding the colorful plastic gemstones up over her wrist. His fingers were cool, and she felt a shiver along her skin, a prickle dancing up her spine.

"Good night, Peg." He leaned over to kiss her on the cheek, a sweet press of his lips that sent her insides singing.

"Stay?" She reached for him, catching his wrist. "Please."

She knew how it sounded, like begging, but she didn't care. It had been so long since she'd felt anything at all; these sensations buzzed in her like alcohol. He still seemed to hesitate, so she took the choice from him. "David?"

Her voice, her words, broke through the final bond holding him back. He pulled her to her feet, running his hands up her arms to her elbows, holding her against him. This time, there was nothing gentle or brotherly about his kiss. It was hard and demanding, the strength of him like a drug. They were on the couch then on the floor. His shirt unbuttoned. Her bra unsnapped. His hands followed her curves, slow enough to make her arch closer. Her fingers trailed down his back, pausing at each rib, a scar along his hip. Retracing the trail of her fingers to grip his shoulders, the muscles taut under her touch. His mouth was like silk. She gasped, her breath coming short and shocky with every movement. He blotted out the light, his body above her dark and velvet.

A light flashed on upstairs. A door opened.

She rolled out from under him with a soft "Shit," tugging her shirt down, her jeans up. He leaned back against the couch, breathing hard, hands plowed through his hair.

"Auntie Peggy?" It was Timmy. "I'm thirsty."

She gathered a shaky breath and let it out slowly. Her body vibrated, her skin on fire. "I'll be right up."

She listened as he padded back into the room. Waited another moment before she risked moving or speaking.

"I should go." David tucked his shirt in as he stood, but she could tell he was as off stride as she was. His eyes were large in his dark face. He followed her into the kitchen as she filled a glass from the tap. He brushed a kiss at the back of her neck. "Remember, tonight when you're lying in bed and can't sleep, that I came back."

She closed her eyes, breathing him in, letting herself fantasize. The click of the front door closed. She smiled into the dark.

"Auntie Peg?" The voice was small, but it seemed to fill every corner of her.

"Coming, sweetheart." She climbed the stairs, still smiling.

CHAPTER 24

VIV

1918

I passed through the hospital's main ward, exchanging words with the few men I knew by name, acknowledging those who called out to me or gave me a wave. A few patients detailed for light duties assisted the nurses as they worked, mopping floors and clearing away breakfast trays.

Ernst's prediction from a month ago ended up being more prescient than we could have foreseen. Cases of appendicitis and pneumonia, measles and whooping cough were giving way to those falling prey to a new and deadly strain of influenza. Men healthy one day were falling ill the next. A few here, a few there; but with every day and every ship that steamed into Hampton Roads, we grew more vigilant. Just yesterday, we'd received a directive from the board of medicine detailing signs and symptoms. Too little too late, in my view. Not twenty-four hours later, rumors began swirling about an outbreak at Camp Lee less than one hundred miles away from us.

That afternoon, Lieutenant Dumfries called me into his office—a situation that never boded well. "Bad news, Weston," he said, the growing epidemic over the last few weeks causing deeper lines on either side of his mouth, more wrinkles in the squinting edges of his eyes.

"More flu cases, sir?"

Newport News and Hampton, just across the river, were both home to enormous embarkation centers for soldiers heading overseas. Thousands of them moved through camps Stuart, Hill, Morrison, and Alexander every week. In addition, there were the bases built to defend the busy ports as well as numerous training centers, airfields, and of course, the NOB at Sewells Point.

But these men didn't stay behind barbed wire and palisades. They shopped in our stores and ate at our cafés. They danced with local girls at the YMCA and Norfolk's armory and trolled for prostitutes along East Main Street. They watched movies and shows in crowded theaters and relaxed on our busy beaches. Infection could easily spread between facilities, if not to the communities that hosted them.

"Not that I've heard, but we're preparing for the worst. It's all hands to the pump. Leaves have been cancelled, and everyone is expected to pitch in where we can."

I thought about our troops in France. They'd been hard hit, and I imagined the naval hospital in Brest would be overflowing with influenza cases. There would be plenty of work to keep me busy and distracted from everything and everyone I'd leave behind.

"I have my replacement almost trained, sir," I announced proudly. "When I ship out next week, I'll be leaving the unit fully prepared."

"There won't be any shipping out." Dumfries hadn't been happy to hear I was leaving, so I wasn't surprised by the smug curl of his lip as he delivered his news. "Commander Stewart's surgical team has postponed their departure due to the fluidity of the current epidemic—which means you're staying here for now."

"But Chief Quarles . . ." I stammered.

"Isn't running this hospital last I checked," he growled.

Can someone's heart rise and sink at the same time? For weeks, I'd been watching my back, checking around every corner, counting down the days until I was free of Father and the danger he posed. And for those very same weeks, I'd let one opportunity after another pass without telling Marjory and Blanche about my transfer. I'd wanted to. Every day I came up with a new speech. Every evening the words stuck in my throat. But I couldn't leave it any longer. Tonight, I would do it.

When I arrived at the cottage that night, Blanche was on the back porch, staring out at the lights of countless ships on the bay. She had tried to gloss over her discharge from the Navy, joking that the doctors, in a fit of unflinching accuracy, had written "in the line of duty" on her medical forms. But none of us laughed long. She missed Gus. We all did. We saw the grocery van leave in the morning and arrive back late at night. When it sat there for days, we knew he was out with his uncle, changing the rig over from crab to oyster as the season turned and the mornings cooled. Fishing for striped bass and sea trout when the weather was clear, and whiskey, rum, and gin when the moon was covered by clouds or below the horizon completely. Once or twice I saw him come back early in the morning, a rifle slung over his shoulder, a line of duck hanging from his back. But he never crossed the street to visit. And he never joined our evenings on the beach.

I'd not realized how much I'd come to rely on his easy good humor or how often I hitched a ride into town until he wasn't there. But sides had been set, and if there was a choice to be made, I would always choose Blanche who had chosen me when I needed someone the most.

"You're late," she said as I slumped past her to fall onto the couch, massaging my tired feet, my aching knuckles. "I tried to keep your dinner warm, but I think it's probably burnt to a cinder by now."

"Sorry, work is piling up. I should have sent word."

She pulled the plate from the oven and set it on the table. Whatever it had been, it was now a blackened, dried-out mess. "Maybe you can skip dinner and go straight for a slice of Ernst's strudel."

She washed up the dishes while I ate. Even after all these months, she seemed ill-suited to such domestic tasks. A racehorse hitched to a farmer's plow.

"You look completely flattened," she remarked as she set the last pot on the drainboard to dry. Her face was flushed, and her hair straggled around her face.

"There's been an outbreak of flu nearby," I answered. "The Navy is concerned it could spread."

"How bad can it be? Flu is hardly the black death, is it?"

"This flu is different. Worse. We're seeing more cases in the hospital every day."

"Oof." Blanche winced, a hand going to her stomach. "This child is either going to be a football player or a cancan dancer. I've never felt so much kicking in my life. It's like my insides are being stirred with a stick." She gave a weary, smiling shake of her head.

Here it was. The moment. I would tell her straight-out. "Blanche, I have to tell you something—"

"Is it about your nightmares? You had another one last night." Her hand curled into a fist, her face like stone. Her other hand splayed over her stomach as if she was in pain. "I couldn't sleep, and I heard you call out."

My face grew hot. The nightmares had grown less frequent, but they were still embarrassing. "I'm sorry I woke you." I'd practiced my words all the way home until they rolled off the tongue as easily as any of my lies. Just say it. Spit it out and be done. "About that, you see—"

"You're safe here with us, you know," she said.

I knew she meant it . . . or wanted to mean it, wanted the cottage to remain the refuge it had been all summer; but Tom had promised the same thing, and he'd vanished without a word. How could Blanche protect me? She had her own troubles. There would be no cottage in another few months. We'd be out on the street. No. There was no one I could rely on. Like Blanche said, I would need to rescue myself.

"I was transferred to France." There, I said it. Straight out. No beating around the bush. "I'm leaving Norfolk. Leaving the cottage." *Leaving you* remained unsaid.

"Oh." Her hand moved to clutch the back of a chair, a small flexing of her fingers that caused her fake wedding ring to gleam for a moment. "Congratulations."

"I don't know when exactly." I hurried through my explanation before I lost what little courage I'd mustered. "And I know I should have told you sooner, but . . ." But what? I didn't want to rub my new posting in her face? Didn't want to leave her when she needed me most? Didn't want her to be angry with me when *I* needed her most?

"Are you upset?"

She smiled, and if there was a hint of something darker in her gaze, I chose not to see it. "What? Of course not. This is what you've wanted. What you've worked so hard for. Maybe you'll get that happy-ever-after after all. This calls for a toast." She rummaged in the icebox. "I'm afraid we only have that bottle of Apple-O you bought last week. Without Gus and his contraband alcohol our options have dwindled." By now her voice was high, her movements frantic.

"Juice is fine."

She poured out two glasses. "Have you seen him lately?" She tried to keep her tone casual, but I could tell how much Gus's absence pained her.

"I saw him heading up the beach a few mornings ago."

"I heard he's been missing a lot of work, calling in sick or skipping out early. His uncle's influence, no doubt. Probably has him rum-running. He'll get himself arrested if he's not careful."

"Not Gus. He's smarter than he looks behind that gormless smile."

"He's not the only one." There it was again, that barb within the smiling words. Was it real, or was it my own guilt conjuring it? Blanche smiled and raised her glass. "Here's to us girls in Navy blue."

The door banged open, and Marjory clattered into the house with a whoop, tossing her bag on the couch, her excitement palpable. "You'll never guess."

"You're leaving too?" Blanche asked, this time the bitterness definitely souring the air.

Marjory extended her left hand where a small diamond glittered. "I'm engaged!"

"Come on up! Fun to be had. Prizes. Prizes. Prizes."

"Step right up. Teddy bears. Kewpie dolls. Put the ball through the basket and it's yours."

"Get your photograph taken by the great Nolan Vizzini. Just ten cents to make a memory."

A fresh breeze blew down the Ocean View promenade, past the casino and the dance pavilion. It set the flags over the roller coaster flapping, billowed the grand hotel's curtains and tablecloths, and held gulls aloft as they hovered along the bay's choppy whitecaps. It caught at Blanche's skirt, pulled at Marjory's jacket, and threatened to tear my straw hat from my head.

We didn't care. After the baking heat, the clouds and cooler weather were welcome, and we wandered the midway with our popcorn and lemonade enjoying Marjory's last day of spinsterhood.

Her wedding was tomorrow. City hall. Nine in the morning.

I couldn't get off work, but Blanche would be there. She'd refashioned a tea gown for Marjory to wear along with the hair combs I'd decorated with delicate Queen Anne's lace and late-blooming roses.

"I can't believe you have to report for duty straight after," I said, eying the popcorn stand. "Why didn't you ask for leave?"

"I wasn't sure if the Navy would let me get married, so I figured it was better not to ask," Marjory explained.

I didn't blame her. Some commanding officers were less enthusiastic than others; Dumfries had grudgingly granted a yeomanette in our unit a three-day leave, but only after a lecture on duty to her country that left her in tatters.

"It's not the end of the world," Marjory said around bites of hot dog. "You're taking Clara for the night, so we'll have a little time alone together."

"Not much of a honeymoon," Blanche muttered.

Marjory's cheeks grew pink, her smile wistful. "We have the rest of our lives."

We rode the carousel and explored the fun house and stuffed our faces with cotton candy and hot dogs. We listened to an orchestra playing patriotic marches at the dance pavilion and paid a penny to have our palms read. At last, Blanche sank onto a bench, her face shiny and splotched with too much sun as she grimaced against a pain.

"Is it the baby?" I asked, handing her my lemonade. "Maybe we should head home. I still have a few finishing touches to Marjory's bouquet to make."

A round-faced hawker in a striped apron leaned over his counter. His stall was piled high with trinkets and toys. "Three shots for a nickel, ladies. Step right up. Hit the bull's eye and win a prize."

"I'm fine," Blanche replied. "The moppet's just feeling left out, I guess."

"Win yourself a set of gen-u-ine Oriental pearls." The hawker increased his volume. "Just a nickel."

"Maybe you should call the doctor," Marjory suggested. "That little one's been feeling left out an awful lot lately."

He beat on the counter with a long-handled cane, gesticulating dramatically at the crowds up and down the midway. "All you soldier boys out there, who's got the skills to win a prize? Three shots, and all it takes is one bull's eye."

"Let's get you married off, and then we'll worry about me." Blanche levered herself back to her feet with effort. I didn't like the shine to her gray features, but telling her so was guaranteed to set her off, and her fuse grew shorter every day.

"What about you girls in your fancy uniforms?" The hawker leered our direction, his features greasy with disdain. "You all think you can fight like men. Think you can shoot like 'em?"

Marjory swung around, her face thunderous. "Pardon me?"

Successful in baiting us, he smiled with a wave of his hand over his stall's prizes. "Three shots wins you a set of gen-u-ine pearls. Try your luck?"

The three of us exchanged a look. "Well?" I said. "Better late than never, and a set of pearls would go perfect with your wedding dress."

Marjory handed over her nickel with a face like a gladiator. "I'll show you how we fight, old man."

She took aim. Fired off three quick shots. All three hit the target, but none struck the red center of the bull's eye.

"Go back to the kitchen, ladies," the hawker sneered with a heft of his belt over his paunch. "Let the men win this war."

Marjory's face turned beet red, but before she could say anything, Blanche stepped up to the counter. "I'll have a go."

I knew that smooth tone. I recognized that cool disdainful gaze.

This was the Blanche I'd first met; the one who didn't tolerate bullies and could destroy you with a crook of one superior finger.

The barker handed her a rifle. She weighed it up, sighting along the barrel with a sharpshooter's expert eye. She lifted the gun to her shoulder as if she'd been doing this all her life and squeezed the trigger.

Bang!

The shot ripped a hole dead center.

Bang!

The second shot practically followed the first through the paper and into the barricade of straw bales behind.

Bang!

Number three. Same result.

Blanche set the rifle down on the counter, her gaze like ice. "We'll have those pearls now. They'll go perfect with our stripes."

I chewed my lip to keep from laughing, while Marjory practically snatched the box from the man, and we giggled and elbowed our way down the boardwalk.

"Where did you learn to shoot like that?" Marjory asked, catching her breath and wiping her eyes.

"My brother. I caught him sneaking into the house one night falling down drunk and reeking of hashish. The rest was easy."

"You blackmailed him?" Marjory seemed genuinely impressed by Blanche's cunning.

"I prefer to call it a bargain that suited us both."

"Well, thank heavens for your brother's poor choices. They're lovely." Marjory fastened the strand around her neck.

"Not exactly Cartier." Blanche smiled with a little of her old swagger. "But they'll do in a pinch."

"They're better"—Marjory caressed them—"because they'll always remind me of this day and this friendship and . . . and that we girls can do whatever we put our minds to if we're given the chance."

"No," Blanche challenged. "We can't wait to be *given* a chance as if it's a gift or a handout. We have to grab that chance for ourselves. Grab it and hold on because they'll try to rip it right back out of our hands if we're not careful. We thought enlisting was the prize at the end of the fight. It's just the first punch in the opening round."

I looked up to see a sign for Vizzini's Photography. "Let's go in. I want a photograph."

"I couldn't." Blanche pulled away, suddenly shamefaced and shy. "Not like this. Besides, it's far too expensive."

"Let's splurge." Marjory grabbed her by the arm. "Viv is leaving for France. I'm marrying Ernst. This might be our last chance."

Blanche allowed us to coax her inside, where we pushed through heavy black draperies into a small studio. Light streamed in from above to illuminate a man in a dusty tuxedo fiddling with a camera on a tripod. A small platform had been arranged with a crudely painted mural of the amusement park and the bay as a backdrop.

"Welcome to Vizzini's. You are here for a photograph?"

He didn't wait for us to answer. Instead, from out of the wings, he rolled a long section of white fencing to the center of the stage before arranging the three of us so that we leaned against it as if we were relaxing at the top of one of the promenade's stairs to the beach. Then he stood back, studying us for a long minute.

"Well?" Blanche finally growled.

He went back into the wings and this time he brought with him a dark jacket with gold buttons and a straw hat nearly identical to the ones Marjory and I wore. "Put this on," he told Blanche. "No one will notice a difference, eh? Trust Vizzini."

She shook her head. "Thanks, but *I'll* notice. I'm fine just as I am."

I stood on Blanche's left. Marjory was on her right. Vizzini poked and positioned, a chin up here, a turn just a little to the right there, before he ordered us to look out to the camera "as if you are just coming from a lovely day on the water. Smile big smiles and do not move."

The camera gave a small click, and he was back to usher us out. "Is that it?" Marjory asked, clearly skeptical. It did seem a bit anticlimactic after all his fiddling and fussing.

"It is a good 1A camera from the Kodak company," he asserted. "Takes very good pictures. I promise. You come back tomorrow, and I will have a print for each of you."

"Thank you," we said, handing over our money.

His care-for-nothing demeanor fell away, leaving a grim harshness to his face. "My cousin was killed in Trentino. She was stood against a wall and shot for delivering supplies to the militias in the mountains."

"How horrible," Marjory gasped.

"*Si*. She had no fancy uniform or rank, but she was a soldier, the same as you. A mother bear is the most ferocious, is she not?"

That night, we gathered on the beach. I sat on my towel in the friendly light of the campfire, trying to memorize every moment: the way the sliver of a moon rose over the bay that rippled smooth as black satin and the feel of the sand between my toes. The smoky-sweet smell of Ernst grilling fresh fish over the flames while his daughter, Clara, laughed and splashed with Marjory in the shallows as they hunted for sand crabs. Who knew where the three of us would be by next summer?

Blanche was quiet, and I wondered if the baby was tiring her. She sat on a piece of weathered driftwood, idly tossing small shells and stones into the fire. The flickering light picked out the curve of her lips, the angle of her brow, the deep hollows under her eyes.

"It is a shame that Gus could not join us tonight." Ernst tested the fish with the tips of his fingers, hot grease sizzling as it dripped into the fire. "Clara misses his card tricks."

"I tried to get him to come." I shot a sidelong glance at Blanche. "He said he was busy."

"That's complete bunk," Marjory said with more than a hint of censure in her voice. "He's still sulking over that silly argument. Maybe if you apologized, Blanche. Told him you were sorry."

Blanche threw her a dark scowl. "I'm not keeping him away. He could come over anytime he wants."

"But you know he won't. He's as stubborn and pigheaded as you."

We'd had this argument before. It got us nowhere, and I didn't want to ruin our last night together bickering. But with Marjory's wedding and my transfer, Blanche would be alone just when she needed friends the most. She had to realize she needed Gus, now more than ever. She couldn't hold a grudge forever, could she?

Clara, tired of crab hunting, had come to join us, settling down with pail and shovel. "Digging a hole straight to China," she explained when Blanche asked her what she was doing.

Blanche helped her scoop, the two of them working, heads together. "It must have been hard raising a child on your own after your wife died," she commented to Ernst, sand up to her elbows.

He gazed lovingly on his daughter. "At first. But I had help. There were many in my community who cared for her while I worked at the bakery, brought meals, or made sure she had clean clothes. I tell people she was raised by a committee."

"Do you think without the help you could have managed? I mean, of course you could. People do it all the time, right?" Blanche's gaze met mine, and for a moment, I thought I caught a glimpse of desperation. Then it was gone, and I decided it was only a trick of the flames.

Ernst shrugged. "One does what one must when there is no choice."

"Yes," she said softly. "Yes. You're right."

She jumped up, shaking the sand from her bathing suit before running for the water. Wading out waist deep, her face a pale oval against the dark, she waved to me. "Come in, Viv! It's glorious."

She didn't wait for my answer before she dove beneath the waves, and I counted the seconds as I waited for her to break the surface and start her usual swim north along the beach. But as five seconds became ten then fifteen, my fingers gripped the edge of my towel, a stab of fear deep in my belly.

"Marjory?" I said, my nerves itching as I stared out over the water. "Blanche hasn't come back up."

She dropped Ernst's hand and turned to scan the bay. "Are you sure?"

I barely heard her. I was already up and sprinting into the surf, pushing against the water as I waded deeper, searching the waves. "Blanche! Blanche, where are you?"

The seconds stretched like the taffy they sold on the boardwalk. I couldn't breathe. I flailed, my feet sliding out from under me as the rocks slithered and shifted. The shallows gave way to deeper water, and I went under, the bay closing over my head, filling my ears and my nose. I flailed, coming up spluttering and shaking. "Blanche!"

Another wave hit me, dragging me deeper. I choked as water filled my lungs. My brain was mushy. I moved my arms and legs as I'd seen Blanche do, but it was no good. The little air I gasped each time I made it to the surface wasn't enough, and I felt myself drop back into the blinding darkness, pulled farther from shore. From a long way away, I thought I heard Marjory shouting. Then I sank once again, my chest aching as if an anchor weighted me down.

Through the darkness, faces appeared, ghostly images sliding in and out of the edges of my vision—Tom, my mother, even the Navy seaman from the shipyard with his kind crinkly face. They seemed to reach for me, urging me deeper. I was so tired, my limbs numb, and I couldn't think anymore. It felt easier to follow them.

Something cold slid past my leg. I jerked away. A voice called me; not Marjory this time, but one nearly as familiar. I was scolded, pressed to fight on in the same tone of voice she used to use to coax me to join her in her latest caper. I was shoved hard in the back, up through the tumble of currents where a hand wrapped around my wrist, yanking me to the surface.

Gasping with burning lungs, I continued to struggle as my body took over from my brain, but the hold on my wrist never faltered. An arm clamped around my chest as I was towed toward the beach. "You blasted idiot." Blanche's voice was hard as iron in my ear. "Are you crazy?" she hissed as she pulled me coughing and choking onto the sand. "You could have died."

"She saved me," I whimpered around a throat aching with water. "She told me to keep going."

"*Who* told you? I didn't see anyone out there."

I scanned the water, but the bay slid flat and dark, the surface unbroken. I flopped back on the sand, staring up into the night, roaring in my ears, my temples throbbing. "No one." But if I listened hard enough, I could still hear her voice in my head. "An old friend."

CHAPTER 25

VIV

Our fears about this new influenza turned out to be justified. Despite the precautions taken at Camp Lee, six men died, and by the middle of September, the newspapers were awash in reported cases from Boston to Rhode Island to Minnesota. When more than a hundred sailors at the naval base fell sick, the brass quarantined the place. There was talk of closing churches and schools and movie theaters. The Red Cross and the YMCA cancelled dances, and masks appeared on crowded trolley cars, ferries, and busy city streets.

Leaves were revoked and hours were increased. Aside from our regular duties, the yeomanettes serving at the hospital stepped in to do what we could. We assisted the overworked nurses by spending time on the wards: writing and reading letters, playing cards, or just chatting with the boys to take their minds off their troubles. When the nurses starting falling ill, we took to dispensing pills, changing bed linens, and fetching and carrying until our feet ached and our hands turned red and raw from scrubbing. Occasionally I would pass Dr. Stewart in a hallway or see him from across a crowded ward. No more was said about my orders for France, but I kept my bags packed and ready just in case—though in case of what I didn't dwell on too long.

I'd run before. If need be, I could run again.

Blanche heard nothing more from her family, but their threats hung on her like a weight. She pored over the newspaper's want ads, circling the most promising among the requests for stenographers, typists, and clerks. Each morning, she set out wearing her primmest suit, assured that her experience and education would secure her the position. Each evening, she came home dejected after one potential employer after another turned her away. Out of desperation and boredom, she took to sewing masks, using cloth scavenged from her work basket. Many nights I came through the door close to midnight to find her head bent over her needle. It kept her hands busy and her mind distracted, but it was obvious she grew less confident each day.

At last, Quarles handed me my orders to report to the USS *Madawaska*, causing a roller-coaster lift of my stomach followed by a plummeting drop. The moment I'd both longed for and dreaded had finally arrived. "Remember, Weston"—her granite voice rang with pride as she saluted me—"this is your chance. You're representing all us yeomanettes. Don't let the side down."

Back home, I'd been packed and ready for weeks. My closet was bare, my chest of drawers empty. My whole world was folded into two satchels and a hatbox. If only I could arrange my life with such ease.

Ernst couldn't make it, but Marjory and Clara showed up for a farewell supper from the last of the summer's tomatoes and a loaf of stale bread. It wasn't much, but we had no money for anything better. I tried not to think of how Blanche would fare without my pay to make our increasingly frayed ends meet.

"Give the little one baby kisses from her Auntie Viv when it comes," I said as I washed up for the last time, setting each plate carefully on the dish rack, wiping each glass until it sparkled, scrubbing the pots as if my life depended on it.

"And please, Blanche. Please make up with Gus," I pleaded later as we stood at the water's edge, the lights of the ships like low-hanging stars, my eyes and my mind looking ahead to France as I clasped Blanche's cool hand in my own.

"For God's sake, stop mothering me, Viv." Her expression was lost in the darkness, but I knew her well enough to hear the fear in her voice. She tore herself away and paced a short distance up the beach, ungainly and awkward, her hands stuffed deep in her cardigan's pockets, leaving Marjory and me in awkward silence. When Blanche finally returned to the cottage, climbing the stairs to the porch where we waited, she was contrite and controlled. "I'll be right as rain. Honest."

I wasn't as sure, but there was little I could do about it now. Marjory gave me a hug before she left, her breath soft against my ear as she whispered, "I'll see to her, Viv. Three musketeers, right? All for one and one for all."

That night, I sat on the edge of my bed, my tin open, Tom's photograph held in trembling fingers.

The men on the wards talked of fierce battles south of the Marne and around the city of Rheims, the fight moving from trench to trench in a bloody warfare of inches. Of men who were walking and talking one moment only to be killed the next, victims of snipers' bullets, deadly whizzbangs, and exploding trench mortars. Of ferocious dogfights overhead, planes falling to the earth in flames or exploding into a million pieces of canvas, metal, wood, and bone.

"Where are you?" I whispered to the face smiling up at me. I traced the swagger of his pose, the dimple at the corner of his chin.

The hole in my heart might have callused over, but the wound remained raw, easily torn open by a song, a scent, a face in a crowd, or a laugh from across a room. I glimpsed him in the streets; stepping into a shop, waiting for a bus, or turning a corner just up ahead. Yet no matter how hard I tried, I could never catch up to him. He remained a ghost, a mirage. An elusive oasis in an endless desert.

The pool hall was quiet tonight. Health orders had closed most public establishments, and those that hadn't shut were dark with the resumption of lightless night ordinances that plunged businesses into darkness three days out of the week.

A few brave punters gathered at the back, but they seemed more interested in chewing over the day's news than in playing eight ball. I paid my nickel and hurried to the telephone alcove. My skin crackled with fear as I placed the call. Up to now, I could hope. That hope might be gone depending on what I learned. But I had to do it. Tomorrow I would be gone. It was the only reason I dared risk it.

"Weston household." The voice at the other end of the line was as clear as if she stood in the next room and oh so familiar. Tears gathered in my lashes. "Betty?" I asked. "Betty is that you?"

Betty had worked as housekeeper for the Westons since before I was born. If anyone knew about Tom, she would.

"Who's this calling?"

"It's . . ." In for a penny . . . I'd get no news unless I told her who I was. This was the danger I ran. But it would be worth it if I could finally be certain. "It's Miss Prothero, Betty."

"Miss? Is that really you? Lord, child, I haven't seen you in ages. Are you taking care of yourself?"

"I'm in the Navy now. But—"

"Well, ain't that something. Good on you. I always thought you was a smart girl. Why I said to Mrs. Weston just the other day, I said—"

"Betty, please. Has there been any information about Tom? Anything at all?"

The line went silent. I thought she must have hung up. I gripped the receiver tighter, my hands sweaty with anticipation. "Betty? Are you still there?"

"I'm here." I could feel her grief through the phone line. "We haven't heard nothing. The mister and missus are worried half to death."

No word meant there was still a chance. A hope. Once I reached France, I'd not stop until I found him or found out what happened to him. I could hear the blood roaring in my veins, and my face went hot and then cold. I drew a deep shuddery breath and let it out slowly. "Please, Betty. If you get news, can you send word? You can reach me at"—Blanche's situation was anything but secure, but Marjory wasn't going anywhere—"Meyer's Bakery. Church Street. Norfolk. Can you do that? Please. It's very important."

"Of course, miss. I'll see to it. But, pardon me for saying, shouldn't you be calling your daddy?"

My sweaty hand slid along the candlestick telephone, my heart thudding. What lies was he spreading now? "Why? Has something happened?"

"No, only the pastor was asking the Westons if they'd heard from you. I'm sure he'd be real pleased to hear you're doing so well."

I bet he would.

"Here's Mrs. Weston now. Let me get her for you."

"I have to go, Betty. Bye," I said, hanging up quickly.

It was as I'd expected. My father had kept the truth of that night to himself. He probably only told Tom, hoping he'd wash his hands of me and I'd be left on my own without allies or friends. He'd not anticipated the Navy. I had an entire branch of the military at my back.

Rounding the corner onto Bayview on my way home, I barely noticed the lamp in the window, the brackish tidal air against my cheek, the shiver of silver touching every wave out on the bay. So lost in my own thoughts, I didn't notice the shadow until it fell across mine in the rutted road. "Viv?"

My heart leapt into my throat, and I jumped at the voice in my ear, the hand on my arm. "Gus? What the heck are you trying to do to me?"

"Sorry." The acrid odors of sweat, tobacco, and gunpowder clung to his muddy dungarees, and his hair was tucked under a grease-stained hat. He carried a shotgun, the barrel glinting dull in the moonlight. "I just wanted to know how Blanche is doing."

"She lives ten steps away. You could ask her yourself."

"Yeah, well, I didn't think . . ."

"Oh for God's sake, Gus, are you really going to let one fight blow everything up between you?"

"There *is* nothing between us. That's the problem."

"She might not want you for a husband, but I know she misses your friendship deeply." I thought of Tom, of missed opportunities and lost chances. "Please, Gus. She needs you."

He lowered his head, fiddling with the bill of his cap, digging the toe of his boot into the mud. "Maybe after I clean up. I've been out hunting with the Skiptons. Got a nice haul of canvasbacks. Should bring a good price at the hotel."

"If they don't arrest you for hunting out of season." His smug grin told me he wasn't worried about any overworked game warden. "Fine. Bathe, then come over. She'll be thrilled to see you, I promise."

We parted as I headed up the walk, slowing as I noticed the front door ajar, Betty's words still ringing in my hears. "Hello?" I pushed it open slowly, my heart drumming, to find Blanche on the kitchen floor. Blood soaked her skirts. Her face was deathly white and screwed tight in a grimace of pain. "It's coming. Oh God. The baby is coming."

I rushed to her side, grabbing her hand. "It's not due for a month."

"Tell that to the damn baby." She screamed, a bloodcurdling cry wrenched from deep within her. Her back arched off the floor, her heels flexed. She practically ripped my hand off. "It's too early, Viv. It's too early."

"Hold on." I ran back to the porch. "Gus!" I shouted. "Blanche needs you now!"

"It's a girl." Emotion graveled Gus's voice and there were tears in his eyes.

She was so tiny, smaller than a child's doll, her long thin body barely spilling over the palm of Gus's callused hand. I imagined I could see every threadlike vein beneath her porcelain skin, every flutter of her birdlike pulse as I wiped away the blood and after-birth and wrapped her in a towel. Blanche was still as death, and nearly as translucent as her daughter. I feared the violence of the birth and the blood loss had killed her, but she still breathed, and when I settled her daughter on her chest, Blanche smiled as she held the baby close.

"You did it, Gus," I said, surprised and impressed at his calm demeanor throughout the emergency. What would I have done without him? What would Blanche have done? It didn't bear thinking about.

The doctor came and went with dire predictions and little hope. The baby was too small. Too weak. Born too early, she might have malformed lungs or a dicky heart. She could be deaf or blind or simple. She might not last the night. There was no way to tell. Nothing to be done but pray.

Blanche was quiet after he left. She lay in bed, her features gray with exhaustion, but peaceful, the anxiety of the last months smoothed away as if now that the baby was here, there were no more choices to make, no more questions to ask. She had crossed a line from which there was no going back.

"That man doesn't know what he's talking about," I said, casting an eye on Blanche's sewing basket, which we'd hastily emptied to use for a cradle where the baby now slept.

"What are you going to call her?" Gus filled the doorway, the last few chaotic hours changing him almost as much as they'd changed Blanche. He seemed to stand taller, his face losing its boyishness, his shoulders broader. She had but to put out her hand and he would have been hers forever. Instead, she stared out the window, her thoughts locked away.

"I don't know." She turned to me, and I saw now what I had missed before. It wasn't peace in her gaze, it was resignation. "I didn't think that far ahead."

Later that night after Blanche had fallen asleep, I brought the baby downstairs to the kitchen. Stoking up the stove, I placed the basket nearby, hoping the heat would keep her warm.

"She'll be all right, won't she?" Gus asked. "Her and the moppet?"

He leaned against the railing, a flask in his hand that I didn't question. If anyone deserved a steadying nip, it was him. The clock chimed two. A low moon slid low over the trees to the west.

"I don't know. I work in a hospital. I'm not actually a doctor." The excitement of the evening had left me drained, every muscle aching while my brain spun in useless circles. I held my hand out for his flask.

"You sure you want it, what with all the sickness going round?" Gus asked.

"After tonight, I'll risk it." The brandy was hot and smooth and warmed me from my toes up to my flushed cheeks.

"The doctor wouldn't have just left if he thought Blanche was in danger, would he?" He continued to press, rubbing a nervous hand along the seam of his trousers.

"The flu has everyone working around the clock, Gus. I think we're on our own."

"Damn fool girl," he muttered. "If she'd only . . ." He took back his flask, and this time, he emptied it in one long gulp. "If I'd only . . ." He pushed off from the porch railing, frustration and fear running through him like a live wire. "Shit." He slammed his fist into the side of the house, making me jump, my heart skip. "Shit." He punched the wall again then shook the pain from his bruised and bleeding hand.

I drew my knees up, unsure and a little afraid. There were parts of this new Gus I wasn't sure I liked.

He braced both arms against the porch railing and stared out into the dark. "So, what do we do now?"

But like Blanche, I hadn't thought that far ahead. "I don't know."

Gus finally left, and I climbed the stairs to my bed. Only a few hours until I had to be up and heading across the river for embarkation. The thought nearly made me cry. I checked on Blanche and the baby. The basket was empty, the baby tucked within the curve of Blanche's side. She slept, her skin dry and hot with fever as she tossed fitfully, while the baby lay quiet, her big eyes watching me. She didn't look sickly or disfigured, just hungry.

"Hi, little moppet," I murmured. "Welcome to the world."

I was closing the door when Blanche called to me, her eyes nearly as big and dark as her daughter's in the dim light. "I would have died if it wasn't for you."

"If it wasn't for Gus," I corrected her. "It was his quick thinking that saved the day."

"But who made him come when I was too stubborn? You." She shifted under the blankets, pain lining her face, her eyes sunk within deep shadows. Her voice was quiet, uncertain. "Do you think she'll die? I couldn't bear it if something happened to her."

"If she has any of her mother in her, she's far too willful. She'll live to a ripe old age just to spite that horrid doctor."

This seemed to soothe Blanche. She smiled as she closed her

eyes, already sinking into sleep. "What am I going to do without you, Viv?" she murmured.

"We'll worry about that in the morning."

I tried to follow my own advice, but though my body screamed for sleep, my mind whirred with unanswered questions and half-formed fears.

What *would* she do without me?

I was all she had.

Marjory was still here, but she had her own family to worry over. There was Gus, but, so long as Blanche refused to accept his offer of marriage, he could only do so much.

I was her last hope.

I sat on the edge of my bed, my cases on the floor by the door. Everything ready for my departure.

Would Blanche live to regret her decision to keep the baby? She had so many grand plans, so much ambition. How would she succeed with a child at her skirts? Already, she faced difficulties. Employers who wouldn't look past her circumstances to hire her. Dwindling funds and no way to earn more. I wanted to believe she could do whatever she put her mind to, but even the ablest of admirals foundered when met with hurricane seas. Maybe handing the baby over to the Lawrences was the best answer—for the baby and for Blanche.

The next morning, she remained feverish and weak as a kitten, barely touching her breakfast and rousing herself only long enough to feed the baby who fussed, too small and weak to take more than a few sips. Tearful, Blanche finally gave up, and I took the baby away to try myself with a little milk dipped in a twist of cloth.

One phone call was all it would take. Blanche would get her life back. I could leave for France without worrying. A child would gain a name and a loving home where she would want for nothing. Would Blanche understand? Or would she hate me forever?

This time the pool hall was closed. I banged on the door until the old marine shouted at me through the chained crack. "You again. It's barely sunup. What the hell you want this time?"

"I'll pay you a whole half dollar. I just need to use your telephone."

His eyes widened from their usual bloodshot squint, but he raked the chain free and opened the door wider, blocking my way until I handed over the money. "Be quick about it, girl."

I'd raced the distance here, but now that the decision was upon me, my steps slowed, and I dreaded the moment I'd have to choose. I lifted the receiver, hearing the clicks on the other end, the operator's voice tinny and far away. "Number please."

For all her talk, Blanche had never really had to learn how to survive. She'd always had people who loved her to ease her path. People she loved that she could lean on when times grew tough. Until this last unforgivable scandal, that had always been her family. So, who would be there for her now?

"Number please?" the operator repeated, her voice sharp with impatience.

Not for self, but country. This was the Navy's motto, according to Lieutenant Dumfries who repeated it ad nauseam. But like everything else in the Navy, allowances must be made for the yeomanettes. Not for self, but for sisterhood.

Us Navy girls had to stick together.

"Norfolk Naval Hospital," I said firmly. "Chief Quarles, please. And hurry."

CHAPTER 26

PEGGY

1968

A ribbon of light kissed the horizon when Peggy headed downstairs, still in the old T-shirt she'd been sleeping in since the divorce. One of Chaz's, the collar frayed and a hole under the arm. Early on, it had smelled like him: musky and spicy like the cologne she'd bought him for their anniversary. Now it just smelled of laundry soap.

A quick check of the children showed Timmy and Nancy still fast asleep in a tangle of arms and legs in Blanche's bed, an empty glass of water on the side table. Downstairs, she switched on the coffee and opened the French doors. The temperature was perfect, but by noon, it would be another sticky airless summer day. David had finally bought an air conditioner. Well, *she* had bought it and he'd promised to install it just as soon as he had the time. Cold air at the push of a button sounded wonderful after weeks of rattling fans and dank sheets, but somehow it felt wrong for the little cottage. Out of step with its old-fashioned character, its Victorian charm. She pulled her hair off her neck into a ponytail. No doubt by August, she'd reconsider her principles.

Steaming coffee in hand, she skirted the rotten porch boards to stand at the railing, inhaling the morning off the water. The light spread gold and gray against a cloudless sky while the bay shone soft as satin. A line of gulls skimmed the shoreline heading north. A lone fisherman, pole planted in the sand, sat on an upturned bucket. A few boats worked farther off the coast, decks piled with crab pots.

She'd tucked Mr. Ebersol's business card in the mirror over the front hall table, but every day she found the idea of selling the cottage harder. She'd grown used to the drippy kitchen faucet, the creaks in the stairs, the way the bay's reflection threw shimmering patterns against the walls in the early morning. She'd even made peace with its ghosts.

Could she trade it in for a house where every wall was square and every floor level, but where the only ghosts were the ones she brought with her?

She leaned against a paint-flaked porch column and gazed out on the empty beach, but her mind wasn't focusing on the way the wet sand at the water's edge gleamed gold. Instead, it was grinding through the events of last night in slow motion, dissecting every moment. Rewriting the last hours in her head like a script she could edit.

If she'd been drunk, she'd have an excuse, but she'd been stone-cold sober and still crawled up David like a tree. Thank God for Timmy's glass of water or there was no telling what might have happened.

Wait. Strike that.

She knew exactly what would have happened. She'd wanted it, and David had been more than happy to indulge her. If not for one small thirsty boy, she'd be upstairs in her bed, slack-muscled and content, the scent of good sex in her hair and on her sheets.

So, was it relief or disappointment making her wish for a do-over?

She spun at the scratch of a key at the front door, but it was only David letting himself in to use the bathroom.

"Morning." His voice was thick and sleepy, and made her insides tighten.

"Good morning," she replied, her eyes on the floor, the mug, the light switch inches to his left, anywhere but on his stubbled jaw, his tousled hair, his half-buttoned shirt exposing the glint of gold chest hairs. She felt the awkwardness like a wall, but she'd no idea how to scale it without sounding ridiculous. Maybe if she said nothing at all, they could go back to the way things were between them. Pretend it never happened.

"Peggy—" That sounded ominous.

"There's coffee if you want some," she interrupted before he could finish telling her last night was a mistake, that she was sweet but he wasn't interested. "You said you planned on working on the back porch today. Might want to get a start before it gets too hot."

She was babbling, but it was better than admitting that, twelve hours later, she still vibrated with desire.

"Right," he answered. "Thanks. Guess I better get a move on before the kids wake up."

The bathroom door closed. Peggy heard the rush of water in the pipes as the bath was turned on. The snick of the medicine chest closing. David humming. Normal morning noises. Noises she'd come to expect. Noises she'd not realized she'd missed until now.

Did this mean she was officially over Chaz? She should be happy that, at last, that weight of missing him that she'd carried for so long was finally gone. Instead, it terrified her. If she could get over Chaz, did that mean she might one day get over the death of her child? That she might forget? She'd prayed for the pain to end, but at what cost? With no grave, no funeral, and no mourners but Peggy, if she stopped caring, it would be as if her child had never existed at all.

She hadn't been able to do anything for her daughter. Remembering was all she had left to offer her. She would do it with all her heart.

"You're like Dr. Kimble from *The Fugitive*. On the trail of the one-armed man." Peggy had come to visit Suzanne, who was resting—under doctor's orders—with her feet up on the living room couch. The kids had been banished to the rec room where a television was blasting.

"You think I'm crazy."

"Maybe a little," Suzanne agreed, "but I guess if I was getting postcards from a woman who didn't exist, I'd be a teensy bit curious too. What did the newspaper say actually?"

Peggy unfolded the page she'd photocopied at the library. "Not much. Only what was reported at the time of her disappearance. That it turned out the real Vivian Weston had died as a child and this woman, whoever she was, had used false information when she enlisted in the Navy. Apparently, they questioned all sorts of people, but she never turned up and, eventually, the case went cold."

"Do you suppose Blanche knew who she really was? Maybe that's what Viv's referring to in the postcards." She leaned forward. "Ooh, or maybe Blanche found out and there was a fight and she murdered this girl by accident and hid her body and now . . . now . . ."

"Now this woman has returned from the grave to haunt her with postcards?"

Despite her sarcasm, Peggy appreciated Suzanne's teasing almost as much as her far-fetched ideas. She'd known if anyone could make her look on the lighter side of this mystery, it would be Suzanne, who never seemed to take life too seriously. Not like Peggy, who was always getting lost in her own head. It also helped that looking around at the disaster of Suzanne's house, Peggy could take heart in the fact that David had been right. Suzanne flailed the same as everyone else. It made Peggy like her all the more.

Suzanne picked at the plate of cheese and crackers balanced on her enormous stomach. "No, I don't suppose that makes sense. Still, it would make an awfully good TV show. I see Linda Evans as Blanche and maybe . . . maybe Barbara Eden as Viv. What do you think?"

"I think I want to know what that doctor of yours prescribed you."

Suzanne rolled her eyes. "You want to know what he said? 'Just relax for a few days with those soap operas you ladies like so much,'" she mimicked in a low booming voice. "He went to medical school for *that*? I wouldn't have been surprised if the patronizing son of a gun patted me on the head and gave me a lollipop and a gold star." She leaned back on the cushions, her expression serious and considering. "Have you asked Mr. Symonds about the postcards?"

"I've tried, but he's not exactly forthcoming."

"That just makes him more suspicious—what they call a hostile witness. Ask again. Bribe him with food. That works on even the hardest cases." She cut Peggy a sly hooded glance.

"So, you weren't being neighborly with that casserole, you were worming your way into my confidence?"

"It worked, didn't it?" Suzanne popped a piece of cheddar into her smiling mouth. "Look, Symonds might know what happened to . . . wait a minute, Marjory, the third girl in the cottage. Blanche had her obituary hidden away. I mean, who does that? That's seriously creepy if you ask me."

"What are you saying? That Blanche murdered her *too*? How many bodies do you think my great-aunt has buried in her backyard?"

Suzanne laughed. "Better warn David before he goes poking around back there. No telling what he'll turn up."

"I haven't really talked to David about it . . . or really anything at all lately," Peggy said, suddenly very interested in her soda. "Between working on my place and the few handyman jobs he's picked up, he's been really busy. And he spends a lot of time at Lena's."

"Someone sounds a little irritated." Suzanne sat up, a big goofy knowing grin on her face. "You didn't?" Her smile spread wider at Peggy's blank stare. "Oh my God! You did." She snapped her fingers. "I knew it, Frankie and Annette!"

"You're such a nut." Peggy hid her embarrassment and her laughter in folding the clothes piled in a chair, placing them neatly in a laundry basket to be put away upstairs. "Nothing happened. But yeah, maybe I wanted it to. And now it just feels weird and uncomfortable between us, and I just wish it could go back to the way it was."

"When you were lonely and miserable?" Peggy tried to pass Suzanne's remark off as a joke, but this time she wasn't teasing. "I mean it, Peg. Can you honestly tell me you want things to go back to the way they were when you first arrived in Ocean View?"

"No, of course not." She'd drifted for the last six months without purpose or energy. After Chaz left, she'd shut out the world until the world finally gave up trying. Maybe feeling weird and uncomfortable, as bad as that was, was better than feeling nothing at all.

"Trust me," Suzanne said. "I have a sixth sense about these things and David digs you a lot. No man unclogs a toilet at two a.m. for a woman he's not into."

She'd forgotten about that, but Suzanne was right. Few men would have answered the frantic pounding on their door in the middle of the night, even fewer would have come to her rescue without once complaining or making her feel like a scatterbrained idiot.

"I want to like him. I want to give in to all these crazy feelings I never thought I'd experience again, but it feels wrong somehow."

"It feels wrong to be happy?"

Suzanne had hit the nail on the head. Happiness felt like a betrayal. But she couldn't tell that to Suzanne. Not in a way that made sense.

"It's hard to explain," she said, her hands full of Timmy's T-shirts.

Suzanne must have sensed her discomfort. "Sorry," she said quickly. "I'll back off. Ron says I'm way too pushy and you clearly don't want to talk about whatever it is. I just want to see you as completely contented as I am with my wonderful life."

A crash followed by a yell of "Mom!" came from the rec room. Suzanne rolled her eyes and took a swig from the glass of water at her elbow. At least Peggy assumed it was water. It might have been vodka. One could never tell with Suzanne.

"I see you're living in a veritable paradise," Peggy replied dryly as she set aside the folded laundry to gather two milky bowls of cereal and a coffee mug off the coffee table to add to the stack in the sink.

"Ha. Ha." Suzanne sighed back into her cushions. After a few minutes of watching Peggy cleaning, she ventured, "If you can't talk to Mr. Symonds and the NYFS ladies aren't any help, what next? A road trip to Richmond to track down your mysterious Vivian Weston—fugitive style?"

"I'm not sure my showing up on her doorstep would help. She'd see immediately I wasn't Blanche. She'd figure out I've been lying to her this whole time." Peggy ran hot water into the sink, soaping the dishes while she looked through cupboards for steel wool and rubber gloves. "She'd hardly be likely to open up to a stranger."

A squabble broke out in the rec room. Nancy shouted at her

brother to give her doll back. Timmy shouted that he didn't want to watch *Bugs Bunny*. He wanted to watch *Shazzan*.

Suzanne fell back on the couch with a groan, an arm slung over her face. "Well, if you change your mind, I call shotgun."

Dear Blanche,

Peggy hadn't even had time to respond to the last postcard before this one arrived. It was as if decades of silence had finally pushed Viv over the edge and receiving a response had finally allowed her to unburden herself to the one person who would understand—Blanche.

Have you ever looked back on events and thought how one decision radiates outward in endless ripples? Or maybe how one pulled thread unravels the whole tapestry? I can never decide which metaphor is more accurate.

Oh yeah, Peggy knew all about looking back. That's all she'd done for months, zombie-like in her apartment while well-meaning friends pushed her to get a grip and move on already.

Either way, our choices, good and bad, affect not just one life, but countless lives. If you'd married Gus Symonds when he asked you. If Marjory hadn't stayed at the bakery that night. If I hadn't chosen that cafe on Granby Street to have my lunch. If... if... if...

Peggy understood that endless loop better than most. It ran like a hamster wheel in her head most nights until exhaustion overtook her.

Maybe there is no such thing as choice. No such thing as if. Maybe fate controls everything. It's a comforting thought. It means none of it was our fault.

Viv

There it was again. That sense of guilt and shame. Whatever tragedy had marked these three women continued to haunt even fifty years later. Peggy understood those feelings all too well. She also understood the desire to believe in fate and the controlling tug of destiny. Viv was right—it was a comforting idea. It meant Peggy could set aside the responsibility and the guilt that went with it. Maybe that's what Viv wanted to do too. Why she was reaching out to Blanche all these years later. To expiate old sins. Clear her conscience.

She read the postcard once more as if Viv's enigmatic ramblings might slide into focus.

And there it was like a puzzle piece fitted into the empty space— Gus Symonds.

The name stared her in the face.

She rose to glance out the front window to where his old banger of a station wagon sat in his driveway.

Symonds had claimed that Blanche was just a friend, a woman who lived across the street.

If he lied about that, what else wasn't he telling her?

Sliding the postcard into the bluejacket's manual where she'd hidden the others for safekeeping, she started to head across the street when she was reminded of Suzanne's suggestion. A little bribery might go a long way. She scanned the kitchen for a suitable temptation. There wasn't much. A box of Ding Dongs. A bag of potato chips. A bottle of Glenlivet. She settled on the Ding Dongs, arranging them on a plate as if they'd come straight out of the oven.

A frenzied yapping from inside Symonds' bungalow accompanied her as she crossed the lawn and rapped on the front door.

"I've told you before," came a voice from inside, "I don't need saving. I don't want saving. Go the hell away!" Symonds threw open the door, his scowl lifting only slightly when he saw her on the stoop. "Oh. It's you. Another problem with the mailman? Or is it that slicky realtor fella picking atcha? I got a gun if you want to shoot him."

"I don't want to shoot anyone—yet," she replied. "May I come in?" She didn't wait for his answer. Instead, she pushed past him and into the little house. "I brought food."

She handed him the plate, which he eyed suspiciously. "That's debatable." He closed the door behind her, tucking his shirt farther into his trousers, smoothing a hand through his thinning hair as he carried the plate into the living room. "Best come sit. I'll not be entertaining guests on my doorstep. Might as well be comfortable."

She'd expected clutter and dust, dirty dishes and smelly laundry. Instead, the living room was immaculate. An upright piano stood in a corner. Above it a long wooden shelf held knickknacks, a vase full of early summer blooms, a taxidermy duck with beady glass eyes. A stuffed, antlered deer head stared forlornly down at her from over the television cabinet. In the corner stood a glass-fronted gun case, ancient long guns polished and displayed. She'd obviously interrupted his lunch. A plate sat on a TV tray by a faded BarcaLounger, the television tuned to *The Dating Game*, host Jim Lange interviewing three bachelorettes.

Symonds turned the sound down as he motioned her toward the couch. He offered her a Ding Dong before taking a seat in his recliner. "Well. What's got you all hot and bothered?"

"I've had another postcard from Viv."

"You came all the way over here with god-awful store-bought

baked goods to tell me that? Damn fool girl," he muttered. "I told you already I barely knew her."

She shrank away from his growly irritation, feeling every ounce of ridiculous, but Symonds was her last hope at understanding. David had called her *brave*. She didn't know about that, but she wasn't going to let Gus Symonds scare her off without a fight.

"I don't believe you." She pulled the postcard out of her pocket and slapped it down like a dealer coming up aces high. "I think you knew her, and I think you knew her well."

He scanned the postcard, his hands clasped loosely between his knees. As if sensing his confusion, his dog nudged his leg until he absently scratched him behind one fuzzy ear.

"Is what she wrote true?" Peggy asked. "Did you ask Blanche to marry you?"

He didn't answer right away, but his normal squared-up jaw and furrowed brow smoothed away and for a moment there was a trace of the young man he must have been. "I didn't expect her to accept, but I thought maybe . . . she was desperate, you see. I wanted to help. Thought it might make it all easier if she had a husband."

Illness. Family complications. Married or expecting.

Of course.

"Was the baby yours?"

His face was white, his features flat and angry, but she could see beneath the loose flesh, the rounded jowls, the gray hair, that he would have been a good-looking guy back in the day. A wartime fling with the boy across the street? It seemed possible until she saw the sorrow in Symonds' expression. "No, more's the pity. Though don't think I wouldn't have loved the moppet like my own if I'd had the chance. But Blanche was proud and stubborn. Thought she could flout convention. Shape the world to suit her own wishes."

"What happened to her baby?"

He rubbed his hands together, over and under as if scrubbing them clean. His eyes focused unseeing on the carpet. "She lost it," he said softly.

A punch to the gut. Peggy couldn't breathe. She saw the swirl of furniture, the glare of the TV screen, the flutter of curtains—a dizzying spin of color and light that whirled and burst. Darkness blurred the edges of her vision.

"Here. This'll help." Symonds stood over her, tumbler in hand.

The bourbon burned her throat, but almost immediately the world settled, the darkness receded. She could breathe, even if a new weight seemed lodged somewhere in her lungs.

"Who's Viv, Gus? The newspaper says she went missing at the end of the war. But that isn't right either, not if she never existed."

"What the hell is that supposed to mean? Never existed? You're talking nonsense now. Of course she existed." He snapped off the TV, grabbed up his uneaten dinner, and took it into the kitchen.

Peggy followed, refusing to let him escape. "The woman who served in the Navy and went missing wasn't Vivian Weston. I want to know who she was."

"We only knew her as Viv." He dumped the TV dinner in the trash before pouring his own shot from the bottle on the counter. "If she changed her name, she did it before she arrived in Ocean View."

"Do you know where she went after she left? Why she might be writing to me now?"

He chuckled, his frown smoothing out. "According to that postcard, it's Blanche she's writing to, not you."

Peggy flushed, uncomfortable at being caught in her lie. "You're avoiding the question."

"I told you I don't know. Maybe hearing her ID tag washed up on that beach got her thinking about the old days. Not always a comforting thing to do." His pale gaze settled on her with a cold stare that made her shake. "But I think you already know that."

She tried to grab hold of a conversation that was rapidly slipping through her fingers. "The reports said they never found her body."

His lips twisted in a grim smile as he downed the bourbon. "Guess they didn't look hard enough."

CHAPTER 27

VIV

1918

Even with all the precautions, the flu took hold in Norfolk with a vengeance. Threats of closings and cancellations became a reality. The naval hospital, already crowded, found itself overrun by patients despite new medical facilities at the naval base and the old Pine Beach Hotel, which had been refitted as an auxiliary infirmary by the Red Cross. In a desperate bid, the Navy summoned the hospital ship *Mercy* to Hampton Roads.

Our section worked endless hours typing and retyping the transfers and record requests as patients were moved in and out on their way to convalescent homes or discharged back to their families. It wasn't made easier by the spreading sickness among our own staff. Every morning I arrived early to scrub and disinfect our office, bracing myself against the empty chair, against the grim face that would reveal we'd lost one more to a flu that seemed to ravage the young and the healthy with particular virulence. Every night I made my way home, trying not to see the stacks of coffins standing ready and waiting on the wharves and warehouse platforms.

I waited for Quarles to corner me about my change of heart, but she never did. After our fraught conversation hampered by my refusal to explain my reasoning, she'd reluctantly done what I asked, explaining my decision to Dr. Stewart, arranging for me to rejoin Lieutenant Dumfries' section. But I could tell from her tone of voice, even through the crackling phone wires, that she was infuriated and puzzled by my decision. As far as she was concerned, I'd failed her, and in doing so, I'd failed the sisterhood. Her disappointment bothered me, but it was the loss of her friendship I regretted the most.

Dumfries, on the other hand, seemed pleased to have me stay. Late one afternoon, he paused in front of my desk with a clearing of his throat and odd expression on his face.

"Sir?" I asked, looking up from the five flimsies I was arranging ahead of a new batch of reports.

"Just want to say we're glad you decided to stick around, Weston," he said, clearly unaccustomed to offering praise. "You're a credit to our section."

And with that, he disappeared into his office and closed the door. A few gruff and grudging words, but after the last few weeks, my chest ballooned with unexpected delight. I couldn't wait to tell Blanche and Marjory; if we could change the lieutenant's mind, there was no telling how many minds might swing to our cause. We'd done what we set out to do: we'd proved ourselves.

At home, Blanche recovered more slowly than we expected. It was hard to see her so diminished, her vitality so dimmed. Her old radiance returned only in the moments when the baby was placed in her arms. Then her features came alive with joy, her blue eyes bright as stars, and for a little while she was the old Blanche.

The baby remained frighteningly frail. She slept too much and ate too little. We did what we could, but none of us was sure if it would be enough. Blanche kept her close, the wee mite fussing if anyone but her mother held her.

I'd not told Blanche about my decision to stay. She'd have railed against my sacrifice, told me I was crazy to give everything up for her. But I wasn't looking for guilt or gratitude. And I didn't want either of those things to change our relationship.

Whenever Blanche brought up my transfer to France, I put her off with excuses about delayed orders, missing paperwork, new regulations. My lie was helped along by the reports from overseas, which held everyone's attention. The Germans were on the run. The Italians were beating back the Austrians. The Turks were looking for peace terms. All across the Western Front, the enemy faltered. *Armistice*, a word barely hoped for only a few short months ago, grew more certain every day as newspapers blasted headlines recounting battles won and generals retreating.

Our enlistment had been for four years, but as it looked now, we'd see an end to the war in weeks if not days. Was Blanche right? Would we be sent packing when peace was declared? Our service no longer needed as the boys we replaced came marching home?

I had used the Navy as a place to hide, but for how much longer? With no news of Tom, my future was as hazy as morning fog on the bay. A day at a time. A week at a time. It was the best I could manage. In that, Blanche and I were in complete agreement. She'd yet to inform her parents about Moppet's early birth, assuming that silence bought her time. Time to do what, was the unanswerable question. Even if she could have found work, she remained weak, and leaving Moppet for more than a few hours was impossible. And so the days passed in nervous anticipation—for the war to end, for the ax to fall.

"Has Blanche given any more thought to what to call the baby? She can't keep referring to her as Moppet," Marjory asked.

She had come round with Clara, and I'd fixed us a quick meal from the remnants of my vegetable garden along with a dented tin of corned beef and a broken sack of rice that Gus had brought over—rejects from Pender's inventory. We sat on the screened porch, taking in the last rays of autumn sunlight. Darkness fell earlier these days, and I woke in the mornings to frost icing the grass and the sound of ducks calling as they headed south over the creeks and marshes. The cottage's rosebushes were a thorny tangle of hips and shedding leaves, and the roads of Ocean View were quiet now that the summer season was over.

"Why not?" I asked.

No one had said it out loud, but we all knew why Blanche had yet to choose a name: the doctor's warnings still haunted her. As long as she was "Moppet," she was a doll or a pet, something Blanche could set aside or lose without heartbreak. A name would make her all too real. It would cement her decision in a notary's ink. There would be no turning back or changing her mind.

"How about *Alexandra*?" Marjory suggested while Blanche was upstairs. "It's such an elegant high-class name."

"Elegant, yes. But I don't think the name of the doomed tsarina of Russia is exactly the tone we're going for, do you?"

Marjory grimaced. "Oh. Right. Maybe *Gladys*? I knew a Gladys in school. She wore glasses, but she was a whiz at the cello."

Clara had been reading from a book of *Just So Stories* when she climbed up beside Marjory on the porch glider. "I'm tired, and my head aches."

"Lay down here, love," Marjory said, tucking Clara in beside her. "You'll feel better soon."

"You've taken to family life nearly as well as Blanche," I remarked.

Marjory smiled down on the little girl. "She's a pistol, this one. Reminds me of me at her age, but I'm worried about Ernst. If it's not a request to support a charity, it's a plea to buy more liberty bonds or serve on one more committee. They have him over a barrel and they know it. Prove his patriotism or suffer the consequences."

"What sort of consequences?"

"That's never quite spelled out, but there have been enough stories in the papers of harassment and intimidation that it's pretty obvious. And then there's this group of local troublemakers. We've been to the police about it, but unless something happens, they have too many other issues to deal with."

I tried not to let the shiver curling its way up my spine show in a shudder of my shoulders or a tightening of my face—Marjory was anxious enough—but the stink of smoke and the mob's angry voices played themselves over and over in my head. "The war will be over soon."

"The battles may end, but what damage has been done when neighbors turn on neighbors? What do I tell Clara? She sees the prejudice. She might not understand it, but she understands her life has changed since the war came here." She glanced around her, keeping her voice low. "Speaking of the war, Viv, is it true?"

"Is what true?" I folded my hands in my lap to stop their trembling.

"That you turned down your transfer. That you chose to stay here rather than go to France?"

Once in a while I questioned my decision, usually in the darkest hour of the night when every decision seemed like the wrong one. But the regrets usually faded with the sunrise. "Blanche needed me more than the Navy did."

"More than Tom did?" Marjory asked quietly.

The regrets usually faded. But not always. I squeezed my eyes closed to hold the tears back, unable to answer.

"Viv? Is everything all right?" Blanche carried Moppet in one arm and her sewing basket over the other. She'd spent the last few weeks working on turning one of her old morning dresses into a christening gown, the watered silk spilled over the sides of the basket.

Marjory and I shared a look as I took Moppet from Blanche,

setting the baby against my shoulder. "Everything is just how it's meant to be."

As SOON AS Blanche was well enough, she was forming plans for her future. If she couldn't find employment, she'd create her own. She moved her heavy black Singer sewing machine into Marjory's old bedroom. "An income means independence," she explained, and soon, the space was full of bolts of fabric, shelves of notions, and a small trickle of customers—some old friends from the NOB, a few fellow members of the National Woman's Party—arriving for alterations and fittings. She worked deep into the night, Moppet sleeping in her basket. Making a home and a life for her daughter was Blanche's new crusade and one she took on with all the zeal she'd once put toward the women's movement.

Tonight was no different. I stumbled in well past midnight, hat dripping and cloak soaked through from a cold steady November rain. My eyes burned from long hours crouched over my desk, and a dull heaviness banged at my temples. Blanche was bent over the kitchen table, pinning a pattern to yards of deep forest green fabric. Her fingers moved in and out of the thin tissue, pausing only long enough to puzzle out the best way to arrange the fabric to minimize scraps. I wondered what Mrs. Lawrence would think if she could see how her long-ago advice was helping Blanche now.

Blanche tucked a ruler behind one ear. "You look wretched."

"Thank you. I feel wretched. If you'll excuse me, I'm headed straight to bed."

I started for the stairs, but Blanche called me back. "Wait. You can't go to bed—at least not in *your* bed."

"Why not?"

"Because Clara's in it."

"Why *my* bed?"

"Because Marjory's old bed is covered in Mrs. Tarbutton's new tea gown, and she was afraid to stay down here alone on the sofa—Clara, not Mrs. Tarbutton."

"And what was wrong with *your* bed?"

"I didn't want her waking Moppet. It took me ages to get her down, and I need her to stay asleep if I'm going to ever get this piece finished by breakfast."

"Maybe we should start this conversation over. Why is Clara here in the first place?"

"Marjory dropped her off. Ernst isn't feeling well, and she's worried about Clara catching whatever bug he's got."

A chill that had nothing to do with the rain slid up my spine. "Is it the flu?"

Blanche looked equally concerned. "I don't know. I don't think Marjory does either."

HOURS PASSED WITH no word from Marjory. My heaviness of earlier had blossomed into a full-blown headache, my stomach up near my chest. Until now, I'd been able to push my worries aside, push them down, tell myself to focus on my work and the rest would take care of itself, but this was Ernst. I couldn't push him away or talk myself out of the cold knots slithering in my belly.

"Wait and see," Blanche said, trying for confident, chin up, eyes hard, ready to fight. "Marjory will come banging in here like she always does, and it'll turn out to be nothing—a measly cold and we'll feel silly for worrying."

I wanted to believe that. I wanted Marjory to arrive rolling her eyes at overdramatic men milking every little sniffle for sympathy. I wanted to go back to that day on the boardwalk when the three of us were laughing and happy, and the world—our lives—didn't feel broken and teetering on a dangerous edge.

"He'll be all right, Viv," Blanche continued, as much to convince herself as me. "He has to be. For Marjory's sake. For Clara's. It will all be all right."

"You say it, but you don't know it. Not really."

The last frantic weeks caught up with me all at once. Weeks of being scared and not showing it. Weeks of pretending to be strong when I wasn't. My headache speared down into my neck. My stomach rolled until I wanted to be sick.

"Think of all the men killed in this horrible war or missing"—my voice broke as I swallowed back a ragged sob—"or missing in action. Thousands of them. Hundreds of thousands. Their families told themselves the same thing. It couldn't possibly happen to them. Their loved one would be the lucky one, the one who'd come marching home. They were special."

The words tumbled out of me in a torrent I couldn't stop. Louder and faster until I was almost shouting. The dress pattern forgotten, Blanche met my gaze, her eyes wide and glassy with angry unshed tears that I knew matched my own.

"But nobody's safe, Blanche. Nobody's special when it comes to battle or this god-awful influenza. Not Tom. Not Ernst." My throat burned. I drew in a shuddery breath, my chest tight, a stitch in my side as if I'd been running. My face was hot. My hands curled into fists. "There's nothing we can do but wait and pray, and if Marjory's old coach is right, we won't know if praying works until it's too late."

Blanche crossed the room to where I sat, her arms coming round me from behind as if to keep me from shattering into a million brittle pieces. She was warm and soft and smelled of violets. She kissed my head then rested her chin on my shoulder until my breathing calmed. "Then I guess all we can do is wait."

MAYBE IT WAS the lumpy couch or the drum of rain on the roof, but nightmares I'd thought long banished found me once again that night.

Tom's face . . . Vivian's laughter . . . Mother's song . . . Father's fists . . .

I gasped awake, surfacing like a drowning swimmer. My heart raced. Sweat splashed up my spine and behind my legs. Every breath trembled its way up my throat. At one point, I heard Moppet cry, the creak of floorboards as Blanche rocked her back to sleep. Later, I thought I heard Clara visit the bathroom. I slept again, but this time the dreams that haunted me weren't my own, but fears for my friends.

By the time the clock chimed four, I gave up.

Better to be at work where I was too busy to worry.

That night Clara greeted me at the door when I arrived home. "Oh," she said when she saw me on the stoop.

"And good evening to you too, young lady." I kissed the top of her head.

"She thought you were Marjory," Blanche called from the kitchen.

"She's still not been back? No word at all?"

"Clara love, run upstairs and fetch me a diaper. There's a good girl." Once she was safely out of earshot, Blanche's facade of cheer vanished. "It's not like Marjory to stay away so long and even less not to send a message to explain the delay, unless . . ."

I refused to follow that *unless* to its logical conclusion. "Have you rung around to the bakery? Maybe she's just been busy."

"There's no answer. I telephoned St. Vincent's, but no one will tell me anything, and I don't know if Marjory is even there. I've heard they've begun using schools as makeshift hospitals. I've come up with excuses so far, but Clara's not stupid. She suspects something."

"I should go look for her."

"Would you? I'd ask Gus, but his mother says he's gone on a hunting trip with some friends. No telling when he'll be back or in what state."

I glanced out at the autumn dark. I'd grown more cautious since giving up my place on the ship to France. I kept my head down and stuck close to home when I wasn't at the naval hospital. It hadn't been hard under the circumstances. With so much of the city shut down, there wasn't anywhere to go.

"I want my papa." Clara stood on the landing, tears swimming in her eyes, chin wobbling.

"Right." I pulled my coat back on. "I'll see what I can do."

Back out in the cold, I hoofed it to the trolley stop and headed downtown. Normally, day or night, the streets were alive with soldiers and sailors enjoying their off-duty hours. But tonight, the city was quiet. Most of Church Street's businesses and shops were closed. Only a few automobiles passed me as I made my way to the bakery. An empty streetcar jangled its bell as it rounded a corner. I passed a group of men outside a shuttered café. A couple strolled toward the churchyard, her head on his shoulder.

No lights shone from the bakery. The door was locked, the stars and stripes hanging limp in the cold. I passed down the alley to the outside staircase that led up to the Meyers' apartment, but that door was locked too. "Marjory! . . . Ernst!" I knocked. "Is anyone home?"

A scrape and rattle of a tin can threw every sense on high alert. A figure slid free of the shadows before flicking on a flashlight. It was a boy, no more than fifteen or sixteen. He was a greasy, seedy sort, and I remembered Gus's split head and Marjory's complaints of thievery and vandalism. I channeled Lieutenant Dumfries and gave a bold shout, hoping he didn't see the way my knees trembled. "You! What are you doing here?"

The boy shrugged deeper into his jacket. "Could ask you the same, miss."

"I'm looking for Mr. and Mrs. Meyer. Do you know where they've gone?"

He sniffed and wiped his nose with his sleeve.

"Well?" I continued, descending the staircase one deliberate step at a time. I had no idea what I would do if I reached the bottom and he didn't surrender, but surely something would occur to me. "Should I find a policeman? You can tell him what you're doing lurking in alleys."

The boy's features were petulant, his jaw mulish, but once I reached the bottom step, I could see he was barely taller than me and probably a good ten pounds lighter. Thank heavens. I was sure no policeman would care what I had to say about one vagrant hooligan. "Well?" I barked.

"No skin off my nose, miss. An ambulance came and got Meyer. Don't know where he went. Don't care. He's just a dirty Kraut. Him and that new wife of his. More of that lot die of this flu, the fewer we have to kill for this war to be over."

I stepped toward him, hands balled into fists, my impotent rage clawing its way to the surface. "Mr. Meyer isn't the enemy," I growled through clenched teeth. "He's as much an American as you or me."

"Says you. I got friends who say otherwise."

"What friends?" I bent to scowl into his face, wrinkling my nose at the smell rolling off his jacket, taking evil pleasure in the fear I saw in his beady eyes.

"I told you what you wanted to know, miss." His voice squeaked and broke as he scurried out of my reach. "More'll cost you extra."

I had some change. More than enough to tempt a scrounger like this one. I shoved my hand into my pocket. He looked as if he meant to snatch the money and run, but he stopped short, drawn up as if jerked by an invisible cord. He glanced over his shoulder, eyes widening as if he saw someone. Then, giving me a lip-curl and flashing the middle finger, he beat it back up the alley. "Shove it up your asshole, miss!"

I should have been relieved. Instead, his departure frightened me more than his presence. At least he was company. Now I was on my own and, for the first time ever, not quite sure my uniform would offer me any kind of protection. I hurried back to the relative safety of the street. It might be deserted, but there was traffic and maybe someone to hear me if I screamed.

I took a last cautious look before leaving the shelter of the alley. Halfway down the block in a doorway, the boy stood in conversation with another. A grown man, by the size and build of him. Was this the gang leader? Did his presence signal more trouble for Ernst and his shop? Maybe if they saw me, they'd give up their plotting and go home. Maybe I should find that policeman and tell him what I saw. Trying to will myself invisible, I stepped onto the sidewalk, hugging the wall as much as I could, grateful for once at the light ordinances that kept the street thick with shadows.

So far. So good.

Then a jitney sputtered around the corner, its headlights illuminating me as if I were on a stage. The man looked up, our eyes locking. I froze, unable to move or speak. I couldn't even swallow.

"Well, look who we have here." That honey-smooth tenor had charmed ladies and persuaded men. It terrified me.

With the last of my courage, I tore myself loose of his snaky, mesmerizing stare and ran.

"My father's in Norfolk. I saw him."

It had taken a steaming hot cup of coffee shoved into my frozen hands and ten minutes of cajoling before I could spit it out. I hunched at the kitchen table, holding myself together by the thinnest of threads. The urge to escape was nearly overwhelming. My skin crawled. My heart pounded. I couldn't breathe.

"Where?" Blanche sat across from me in her bathrobe, her face drawn and gray with sleepless nights and the scars of her long recovery. I wondered when she'd lost that cool elegance that had so intimidated me when I first met her.

"Church Street. I'm such an idiot, Blanche. I should never have told the Weston's maid where I was, but I was desperate. I didn't think . . ."

"You didn't think you'd still be here—in America." Her voice was like steel. Her eyes gleamed hard as diamonds. Maybe I was wrong. Maybe Blanche hadn't lost her edge. Maybe I'd just grown accustomed to it.

I forced myself to take slow, even breaths. "What am I going to do? What if he followed me?"

"We're Navy yeomen. First thing we're going to do is not panic. Now tell me everything from the beginning."

Fear ricocheted through me as I told the story, Blanche's features growing darker, almost dangerous. "Do you suppose he was waiting around hoping you'd turn up? What do you suppose he was chatting with that mangy hooligan about? Something doesn't add up."

We had no answers, and I slept that night with a lamp lit and my dresser shoved in front of the door. Just as I hung suspended in that hazy state between waking and sleep, a wisp of a thought brushed my tired brain, something about my father . . . but where had I heard him mentioned? Even as I sought to focus, the thought faded, and I didn't wake until Blanche knocked on my door the following morning.

"Gus left you his rifle, just in case," she said over a breakfast I could barely choke down.

I glanced at the long gun propped amid the umbrellas by the front door with a shudder. "What am I supposed to do with that?"

"Whatever it takes" was Blanche's grim response.

Marjory finally arrived, her face slack with fatigue, her clothes rumpled as if she'd slept in them. We sat her down and plied her with breakfast until color returned to her cheeks and her gaze lost the glassy haze of grief and confusion. "He was burning up with fever. He didn't know who I was. He kept calling out in German." Her fingers curled around a handkerchief stained dark with blood. "The ambulance took hours to come and then we waited hours more before a doctor saw him. The patients were in the aisles and hallways. Propped against walls. I've never seen the like. I was afraid to leave." Her voice broke. "But his fever broke this morning. Hopefully, for good."

"We can keep Clara here for as long as need be." Blanche's gaze passed back and forth between Moppet and Marjory as if assessing the risk of contagion, but her voice held none of her uncertainty. "You focus on Ernst."

"I appreciate the offer, but the Navy's given me compassionate leave," Marjory said, downing her third cup of coffee. "Two weeks and I can apply for more if I need it. Clara will do best at home, and I want to be there in case of trouble."

"What kind of trouble?"

"Hard to say. You read about that riot downtown on Plume Street a few days ago. A bunch of drunken sailors started looting, even shot a policeman. They've got a naval guard patrolling now, so hopefully things will settle back down. I think everyone's just on tenterhooks waiting for news."

Marjory was right. The city seemed to be holding its breath, but it was the excitement of victory that fired them these days. The Germans had been given an ultimatum: accept peace terms by eleven o'clock Monday morning or be crushed on the battlefield by an Allied avalanche. We waited for their decision, aware that every moment of delay meant more American casualties.

All through breakfast, I couldn't sit still. Up and down from my chair. Back and forth to the window where I twitched back the curtain to peer up the street. I picked up then put down the paper. Unable to settle. Unable to push away the thought that all I'd worked toward was unraveling, that any minute now, I would see the bullish figure of my father striding down the street.

Clara clattered down the stairs and threw herself at Marjory. "Where's Papa? Is he here? Can I see him?"

"We'll visit him as soon as the doctors say he's well enough." When Clara's face fell, Marjory gave her chin a chuck. "Bear up, little one. We'll buy him a lovely bouquet to take when we go. That will cheer him up."

Clara turned to me, her watery eyes large and dark as saucers. "Will you take *your* father flowers, Miss Viv?"

I gripped the chairback, flashing panic at Blanche, who met my shock with a pointed frown. What had Clara overheard?

Marjory swung her gaze to me, eyes narrowed. "Your father? He's here?"

Lies bounced through my brain as rapid as machine-gun fire. Laugh it off as a joke. Chalk it up to the exaggeration of small children. All a silly misunderstanding. But I could tell even as the stories formed and dissolved in my head, each one more outlandish than the last, that Marjory wasn't going to be satisfied with anything less than the truth.

"Go on, Viv," Blanche said quietly. "She needs to know."

I'd kept both of them at arm's length for so long. I'd justified it by telling myself it was easier that way, safer, for their own good. I was doing them a favor not involving them in my lies and my problems. But being alone was lonely. And exhausting. Blanche was right. We were clever girls. Together, we could do anything.

By the time I was done, determination hardened Marjory's soft dimpled features, firing her placid brown eyes. "I knew something was bothering Ernst. Maybe this is what it was. Maybe he suspected Prothero of prowling around."

I surprised myself by throwing my arms around her. "Please don't go, Marjory," I urged.

"Fear is what they want, Viv." She held me at arm's length, as if trying to riddle me out. But she was the one who confounded at every turn. Blanche was bold in her strength. She wore it like armor. Marjory's power lay in her goodness, her innate ability to make people love her. "It keeps us quiet and keeps them in charge. I'm done being quiet, aren't you?"

CHAPTER 28

VIV

M y father's arrival in Norfolk scattered my mind so that every minute of the day was a struggle to concentrate on reports and returns that blurred before my eyes. I barely noticed when the clock ticked over to eleven. It wasn't until a cheer went up in the hallways and offices around us that I looked up to see Quarles pause in her typing. The lieutenant stood in the door of his office. Someone sang an off-key rendition of "The Star-Spangled Banner." Farther away, I heard a group belting out "Over There" with wild abandon. From outside came the high blare of truck and ambulance horns and the deep echoing blasts from every boat and ship standing to in the river.

The war was over. Germany had surrendered.

Around me, the men stood and clapped, smiled wide as if they'd fought the Hun to a standstill single-handed. The women were just as enthusiastic, but still we looked to one another as if seeking reassurance, as if wondering what the peace would mean for our Navy service.

That night, I stepped off the ferry, following the line of commuters up from downtown. I jumped at every shadow and startled at every shout like the haunted soldiers I'd met whose minds had been scarred forever by the horrors of battle. I clung to the edges of a rowdy flag-waving crowd, hoping to lose myself among them as I walked the few short blocks to the streetcar stop.

I stepped off the curb just as a van careened around a corner, its tires squealing on the rutted road as I dove for the sidewalk. It skidded to a banging stop, the engine shuddering as Gus leaned out of the window, banging his hand against the door. "Get in. Now!"

"What's wrong? Is it Blanche? The baby?"

I had barely slammed the passenger door closed before he threw it into gear, the van groaning as he accelerated. "The bakery's on fire."

He drove as fast as he dared, but the festival atmosphere only increased the farther up Church Street we headed. Police directed traffic, but spontaneous celebrations broke out on almost every corner, and our climb away from the harbor was painfully slow. By the time we reached the intersection with Nicholson, the traffic became impassible. We abandoned the van and hoofed it the last block, following the sound of a fire truck's claxon. Another fire truck straddled the sidewalk as men unloaded ladders and hooked hoses to hydrants. Smoke poured from the bakery shop's windows to rise black against a greasy gray sky.

"How did it happen?"

"Not sure!" Gus shouted, but I caught him glancing cautiously around at the crowds same as me, at the faces all curious and eager and frightened and wild-eyed as if the fire was just one more way to celebrate the end of the war. It was only when I jerked away from an elbow jammed into my side that I caught sight of my father. He stood at the very edge of the mob where shadows and smoke swirled and faces became indistinguishable, but I recognized him. He wore a long overcoat, his hat covering his balding scalp, pulled low to hide his features. But I would know him anywhere. What was he doing here? Looking for me? No. His eyes were on the fire, not scanning the crowd.

". . . went up like a torch . . ."

". . . think it was arson . . ."

". . . trapped inside . . ."

My heart clenched. I grabbed a fireman's sleeve as he ran by. "There are people in there!"

"We're doing all we can, ma'am." He yanked himself free and kept running.

Gus squinted against the hot smoke that swirled over the street driving people back even as I tugged him forward. "Clara and Marjory are in there. We have to do something."

"Wait here. I'll be right back." He ran off in the direction of one of the trucks, bodies filling the space he vacated until I was pressed in tight, barely able to see over the tops of heads, through the shifting shoulders. I lost sight of my father in the crush, but now my instinct to hide from him warred with my instinct to help Marjory. Every second counted, already smoke poured from the upper windows as the fire spread. Where was Gus? I searched the crowds, growing more frantic with every passing moment.

"Miss Weston? Is that you?" I glanced over my shoulder to see a young man in naval undress blues, his red Geneva cross bright as his cloud gray eyes. It had been months since our dance at the hotel, but I remembered that roguish twinkle and that gentlemanly Southern drawl.

"Russell? Is that you?"

He stood straighter, a tip of a smile at the corner of his mouth. "You *do* remember me. My ship's been assigned to Hampton Roads to help with the epidemic."

"Well, you can start helping right now." I couldn't wait for Gus any longer. I grabbed Russell's hand and pulled him forward. "Come on."

To his credit, he didn't argue or ask questions. He followed me as I led him out of the crowd and down a side lane, ducking back toward the bakery through the coal yards, freight docks, and alleys. Here the roar of the fire was louder, the smoke black and choking. But the back stairway to the apartment was clear. The fire had yet to spread this far.

"Where are we going?" he asked when we finally stopped for breath.

"Up there." I pointed to the stairs.

We took the steps two at a time, my skirts clinging hot to my stockings, my face beading with sweat. Embers fell onto my jacket, which I shed and tossed aside. The apartment door stood open, splintered by a fireman's ax, but within was a black roiling maw.

"Can you see anything?" Russell asked.

"The smoke is too thick!" I stumbled, my throat closing, memories of the shipyard fire burning as bright as the flames before me. I stood on the threshold, every part of me frozen like a block of ice despite the heat. "Marjory!" I shouted, smoke catching in my mouth, my throat. "Marjory, where are you?!" My voice emerged as a gasping croak as I gagged against the acrid taste choking my lungs.

A movement, a flicker within a thousand such, focused my gaze on a far corner of what had been the Meyers' kitchen. "Clara? Is that you?"

Russell pushed past, but his first step set the floor creaking ominously. A snap of singed joists and the whole place would come down. "I'm too heavy."

"I'll go." Even as I said it, my body rebelled, my brain flattening to static like the scrape of a gramophone's needle.

"Are you sure?" Russell shouted, penetrating the buzz infecting my head like a million bees.

I wasn't at all sure, but I nodded and pulled my neckerchief up over my nose and mouth before stepping inside like a cat, uncertain of my footing or what I would find. The smoke was too thick. I couldn't see anything. Dropping to my knees where the air was clearer, I shuffled alongside the wall, keeping the door and Russell in my sight, reaching out to sweep the floor ahead of me in case I missed her in the chaos of smoke and flame. "Clara? It's Viv, love. Where are you?"

I touched the leather of a small shoe, thick tights, the fabric of a skirt. She was behind a table, curled up, her face buried under a cushion. I grabbed her, dragging her unmoving weight inch by terrible inch back toward the door.

"Russell?" I tried to shout, but only a thin gasp of air made it past my seared lungs.

"Here!" he shouted. "This way!"

I adjusted my course, every breath like chewing coals. My knees ached. My skin tightened in the heat. Just as I thought I couldn't go another inch, Russell was there, taking Clara by the arms as I stumbled back onto the landing, drawing in thick sour lungfuls of ash and smoke.

Together, we carried her down the stairs, her body limp, her tear tracks white against the sooty black of her face. Russell laid her down on the bricks, bending over to listen to her chest, feel for her pulse. "She's alive. That's a start. But we need to get her to a doctor."

"You're a medical corpsman. You can help."

"I'm a pharmacist's mate. Not a battlefield medic." He scooped her up in his arms, and we started back toward the street as fast as we could. I could taste the smoke. It filled my head until I was dizzy, the ground rising and falling like the deck of a ship. Russell's voice sounded as if it came from under water. We had just reached the street when a crack split the air. Dust and smoke and flame shot from the roof, which then collapsed in a landslide of shingle and brick and lathing.

We stood dazed and helpless until the crowd noticed us, then we were surrounded. Clara was lifted away. We were questioned and shouted at, shoved and pushed. I couldn't move. Russell gripped my hand as if to hold me steady, yelling for people to stand back or else. A gap opened, and he shoved me in front of him toward the relative safety of a nearby doorway.

"Damn mob," he muttered, but I barely registered his words because I'd caught sight of my father again. He was still there, still watching the building as it burned. For a moment, our eyes locked. He pushed his hat back off his forehead, revealing that square bullish face. His mouth thinned in a knowing smile.

A strange madness took hold of me. Fury burned in my chest, hotter than the flames I'd just escaped. Marjory was right. He wanted me to be afraid, but I refused to continue running and hiding. I refused to live my life always looking over my shoulder.

I pushed my way toward him, but the crowd closed around me like water around a stone. A hand caught me in the small of the back, sending me sprawling on the street, slick with water from spent hoses. My palms stung. My knees ached. A piece of water-sodden paper caught in the folds of my ruined skirt.

A few barely legible words remained, but they were enough for me to curl my fingers into fists.

"No man can serve God and the Allies, Germany and the devil at one and the same time."

I had heard those very words uttered in my father's parlor. Shouted from the pulpit of his church.

This fire hadn't been caused by a faulty wire or an oven left unattended. Marjory was missing. Clara might be dead. Ernst had lost everything.

Father hadn't come to Norfolk for me at all.

BLANCHE AND I huddled together on the sofa while outside fireworks exploded and automobile horns battled pistol shots as all of Ocean View celebrated the Germans' total surrender deep into the night. There was talk of looting and rioters destroying businesses across the river in Newport News, but we saw no sign of that lawlessness here. Just joy and celebration.

If only we could have joined in. Instead, we clung to each other unable to comprehend the enormity of the tragedy. Clara clung to life in St. Vincent's just a few floors down from her father, who was recovering from the flu. Gus was out searching for any word about Marjory. I'd been sent home by well-meaning nurses, Russell escorting me as far as the cottage gate.

"I hope your friend turns up."

I held myself together with extreme effort, sure I would come apart if I even breathed. "Thank you . . . for everything."

He leaned down, giving me a quick brotherly kiss on the forehead. "It turns out we dance pretty well together, Yeoman Weston." My last sight of him was a quick wave as he rounded the corner to head back to his ship.

Time seemed to stutter, the clock on the mantel running in reverse. We started at every sound, hope flickering only to be dashed just as quickly. Blanche tried to nurse a fretful Moppet who twisted, back arched, cries angry as if she sensed our fears. Blanche wrapped her in another blanket and paced the floor, her voice low and quiet as she tried singing her to sleep.

"Hush little baby, don't say a word . . ."

I picked at my bathrobe, twisting a loose thread round and round my thumb. I'd scrubbed until my skin was raw, but I could still smell the smoke. See the flames as if they'd burned themselves into the backs of my eyelids. My lungs worked like a rusty bellows, every breath a sawing wheeze.

"Mama's gonna buy you a mockingbird . . ."

Blanche broke off singing. "What will happen to Clara if Ernst dies?"

The tip of my thumb turned white as the thread tightened. "I don't know. An orphanage, most likely. She has no family in America."

Blanche didn't answer me, but her voice was shakier as she resumed singing. *"If that mockingbird won't sing . . .*

I rose on stiff legs to fix another pot of coffee, the last turning cold and gelatinous in our mugs. Outside, a wind picked up, setting the tops of the pines dancing, pushing a flurry of leaves over the yard. A few fading roses clung to the arbor. Only a few short weeks ago, I'd used them to decorate Marjory's veil. A few short days ago, she'd sat at this very kitchen table, drinking out of this very mug. Oblivious to the tragedy to come. My eyes burned with tears.

"Mama's gonna buy you a diamond ring . . ."

We both heard the automobile's arrival at the same moment. Blanche pushed aside the front curtain. "Whoever it is, they're coming to the door. Could it be news about Marjory? Maybe they've found her."

Before I could stop her, she had flung open the door while I braced myself against a chairback, my eyes searching for anything I might use as a weapon.

He stepped into the cottage, bringing with him the sickening scents of smoke and illicit whiskey. His red-rimmed gaze prowled the room.

"Hello, Father," I said as calmly as my shaking voice would let me.

Blanche's face drained white, and she took an involuntary step back, instinctively cradling Moppet close to her body. "Get out," she demanded.

He dismissed her with a sneering twist of his lip, coming farther into the room, dusting off his hat. My eyes were drawn to the hand he lifted to rake his thinning hair off his forehead as if I might see the long, jagged wound where the ash can had struck him. Instead, all I saw was a silver scar that sliced through his left eyebrow.

"No permanent damage done, you'll be relieved to know." My body went cold, my skin crawling with fear. "Funny thing about head wounds, they bleed like the devil. Even minor ones. If you'd stuck around long enough, you'd have realized that." His voice was like molasses, slow and sweet and dark. It was the voice he used to hold his parishioners in the palm of his hand every Sunday, the charm that captivated committees and opened donors' wallets. That sent him on tour, spewing his hate to a crowd who lapped it up like cream.

"No hug for your father? And you gone so long I despaired I'd ever see you again."

He was like a cat playing with a mouse, batting it gently to see which way it ran. But sooner or later, he'd tire of the game. He always did. Then the claws would come out.

I sent Blanche a silent plea to run and take Moppet with her, but she didn't budge. "I think you should go," she said, her voice holding every scintilla of wealth and privilege her aristocratic ancestors imparted.

"Of course," he answered before turning to me. "Hurry up, girl, and grab your things. I've booked passage for the two of us on tonight's steamer to Richmond. We can be home by lunch tomorrow." His tone was polished smooth, eminently reasonable. In his eyes, I was the inflexible one. The one behaving irrationally. But I knew if I stepped on that boat with him, I'd never step off alive.

My legs were like jelly. I pressed my fingers into the chairback as if it might hold me up. "I'm not going anywhere with you."

A muscle jumped in his jaw, and I knew what little patience he possessed was fraying.

Blanche stepped between us, and I was shocked to see she was slightly taller than my father. "Viv's given you her answer. Now get out."

His smile chilled me to the bone. "That's right. You're Vivian

Weston these days. I remember her; spoiled little thing. I always knew she'd come to a bad end."

My mouth went dry. I couldn't swallow.

"Not like you, a real Navy yeomanette. Serving your country. Doing your bit," he sneered, the first cracks appearing in his showman's cheap veneer. "That'll change soon enough, I expect. I doubt the military looks kindly on cheats and liars."

"What have you done?" I hissed through a jaw clenched so tight, I thought my teeth would crack.

He was faster than he looked, and I was off my game, bruised and sore. Instead of answering, he shoved past Blanche, crossing the room in long angry strides to grab my wrist, the chair going over in a clatter. "The war's over. It's time to come home to your family where you belong."

"This is my family!" I cried out, pushing at him, twisting until my wrist was raw and red; but I slid free. I tried to run, but he snatched my robe's collar, spinning me around, his fist connecting with my chin in a blast of stars. I fell back against the table, my head ringing, tasting the iron bitterness of blood in my mouth.

"Careful, my girl, or you'll end up like that German bitch at the bakery."

The world stilled in that moment. I could hear my blood pushing its way through my veins. It sounded like the soft lap of waves against the beach, like the quiet breathing of Moppet. The memories flooded back. The yeomanette at the church and the young man at the theater, the clues had been there all along. My father's twisted ideas and his angry rants had inspired tonight's violence. It didn't matter whether he'd tossed the match. He'd struck the spark.

"It was you," I hissed. "I know about your horrible lectures, and I saw the pamphlet. You were there at the bakery. Not just tonight but weeks ago. You planned this all along." My body shook. My vision narrowing until all I saw was the hate in his eyes, the violence in his stance. "You killed Marjory." I could barely squeeze the words out. My mouth was dry. My lungs burned. "Just like you killed Mother."

The clock ticked over to the hour, the chime breaking the standoff.

His mouth twitched in grim amusement. "Prove it."

He lunged, his meaty hands circling my throat. My vision narrowed. Black spots danced before my eyes. I struggled to break his hold, but he was stronger, bigger, more desperate. I couldn't breathe, the darkness sucking me under.

"Let her go." I heard Blanche's voice from far away as if speaking down a long tube.

His hands fell away, and I rolled over onto my knees, retching and sucking in precious air.

My father quivered with rage while Blanche stood behind him, Gus's rifle resting inches away from the back of my father's head. There was a stillness to her body, a quiet poise that was far more terrifying than my father's suffused wild-eyed features. I had seen her shoot a target dead center from ten feet away. Six inches would leave nothing left.

My father turned slowly and quietly until he stared the barrel down. "Go ahead."

Her finger moved over the trigger, her gaze hard and terrible. My breath whistled through my damaged throat. I scrambled to my feet. "Don't do it, Blanche. He's not worth it."

Moppet let out a cry. My father's eyes flicked toward the basket as did mine, but Blanche never wavered.

I struggled to my feet, my skirt torn, throat aching with every swallow. "I lost Vivian. I lost Tom and now Marjory. I won't lose you, Blanche," I rasped. "Put the gun down."

"Tom?" Unmoving, Father's gaze settled on me, malice bright

in his dark eyes. "Tom Weston? Are you still soft on that poor bas-tard? You never did have much luck, did you?"

"What do you know about Tom?" I asked, trying not to sound too eager.

Moppet's cries became screams, like nails on a slate.

Blanche lifted the barrel a fraction. "She asked you a question."

His hands twitched and curled into fists. I could feel his fury like heat off a summer road. "He's a prisoner of war. Probably dead by now if half the stories are true. Germans are animals, no better than vermin that should be exterminated."

I thought Blanche would react, but I was the one who flinched. "You're lying."

Father used my involuntary movement to his advantage. Shov-ing Blanche aside, he raced for Moppet's basket. What he meant to do if he'd reached the baby, we'd never know. He dropped in a heap before sliding like a rag doll to the bottom of the steps.

Blanche stood over him, the rifle's barrel fisted in her hands, the stock sticky with blood where she'd smashed it over his head. Shock and disgust haunted her face. "It wasn't loaded."

Waves of nausea washed over me, the past and the present fus-ing within my head. Father on the kitchen floor, blood seeping into the bricks. Father lying motionless on the hall rug, blood soaking into the colorful wool. I met Blanche's horrified gaze. "You killed him."

The knock on the door shattered the moment into a million pieces. "Blanche? Viv? You in there? I have news."

"Don't come in!"

"Go away!"

We both shouted at the same time as the door swung open and Gus surveyed the crime scene. "Well, damn. Guess my news got here before me."

CHAPTER 29

PEGGY

1968

Paint was everywhere. On the drop cloths David had spread over the furniture and floors. On Peggy's jeans and up one sleeve. In her hair. Under her fingernails. If she tried, she could almost taste it in the back of her throat with a tang like bleach. For a week, she'd worked like a dog. But the downstairs looked fabulous. She sat back admiring her handiwork. Suzanne was right. The pale blue she'd suggested made the room feel bigger while the clean white trim brightened the dingy atmosphere.

Peggy leaned back against the couch, browsing the paint chips she'd grabbed from the hardware store. Suzanne had offered more suggestions for the bath upstairs and the three bedrooms.

Peruvian palm green.

Rainbow gold.

Lush apricot.

After a long, hot summer, it was exciting to see the cottage finally come back to life.

"Hold on!" A shout came from outside where David was supervising the building crew he'd hired to help repair the porch's crumbling footers, the final project on his list. He'd approached her last week, warning of collapsing concrete and rotten wood.

Peggy had nodded and agreed, only half paying attention as he presented cost estimates and material lists. Ever since their kiss she'd felt awkward around him. Awkward and a little disappointed.

Both feelings that left their relationship strained—at least her half of it. David didn't seem to have any issues with it at all. He carried on as if they'd not made out like sex-crazed teenagers on her couch. Maybe, to him, it wasn't a big deal. Maybe he was all about free love and live and let live. Maybe once this last job was done, he'd hand over the house keys and that would be that.

Peggy pushed that thought away for another day. Right now, she had to decide between Fantasy orchid and Tiffany blue.

"I said hold on! Don't pull that jack out yet!" David's shout was louder this time and followed by a bang that shook the whole house. Cups rattled on the washboard and the lights flickered. "Shit! What the hell, Claude? Are you trying to fucking kill me?"

Peggy raced to the French doors, which she'd propped open earlier to catch a breeze, sliding to a stop with a frantic grab at the doorjamb just before she nearly plunged through the very new foot-wide gap yawning between the cottage's outside wall and the remains of her back porch which now sagged about six inches lower than it should.

"Everything okay down there?" Fingers clamped to the door, she peered over the edge to the yard below. Deep holes had been dug around the porch, exposing roots, rotten wood, and crumbling cement. Blanche's rosebush had been flattened, branches snapped or crushed, petals scattered among the piles of dirt and lumber. A sawhorse lay on its side. A crowbar had bent the radio's antenna, the speaker still blasting The Byrds, who continued turn . . . turn . . . turning . . . through heavy squealing static.

"Nobody's dead, are they?"

Two men in T-shirts and jeans sheepishly surveyed the wreckage while a third bent over a body lying awkwardly amid the weeds. "Footer collapsed, ma'am. He should be all right—I think." He nudged the body with the toe of his boot. "Will you be all right, buddy?"

A groan was all Peggy heard in response.

Oh my God. Was that David under there? Was he hurt? Dead? Did she really have a dead body in her backyard? She'd been joking, for God's sake.

She ducked back inside, grabbing up the first aid kit from the top of the storage closet. By the time she reached the yard, David was propped against a trash can. He was pale, a goose egg sprouting purple from his forehead, but no protruding bones or gushing blood. That was good. She knelt beside him, frantically trying to remember her Girl Scout training.

"Can you move your arms? Legs? Follow my finger? Are you dizzy? Does this hurt?"

"Not at all. In fact, I'm feeling better by the minute." His slow easy smile turned her insides gooey, which was extremely irritating after the stern talking-to she'd just given herself.

Extremely aware of their audience, she sat back, removing his arm, which had somehow come to rest around her waist. "Good. The last thing I need is you laid up for weeks."

"And here I was beginning to wonder if you really cared."

If *she* cared? Was he really as confused as she was about whatever this was going on between them? Wow, this really did feel like high school.

David's crew hovered as if watching the latest episode of *As the World Turns*. She knew the moment she went inside it would be nudge-nudge wink-wink smiles and atta-boy slaps on the back as they joked about the sex-starved divorcée out to seduce the hunky handyman. Was she that damn obvious? Was she that damn pathetic?

The idea made her sick.

She scrambled up, wiping her hands down her jeans. "Maybe I'm just tired of having your camper van parked in my driveway."

"Peg?" The smile left his face and his voice.

She regretted her dismissive tone almost instantly, which only made her angrier. "I'm not paying you all to stand around." She scowled at the men, all now suddenly interested in the tops of their work boots.

"You heard her, boys," David replied smoothly. "Back to work."

He struggled to his feet, dusting the mud from his jeans, slapping dirt from his sleeves. She tried not to notice the way he leaned on the shovel for support or the tightness at the corners of his eyes. It only made her feel worse than she already did.

She headed back inside, but her earlier satisfaction was spoiled. Why had she been so snippy with David? He'd only ever been kind, and she'd practically bitten his head off. She tried sorting through the sewing room—usually guaranteed to bore her into an empty mind. But after an hour of tossing old spools of thread, fabric scraps, and torn and yellowed patterns, she gave up and headed to the beach. A long walk would clear her head.

Clouds kept the sunbathers away while a stiff wind whipped the bay into whitecaps, dissuading most of the swimmers. Only a few determined beachgoers braved the unsettled weather, beach chairs planted, books in hand. Peggy wandered the shore, following the tracks of terns as they darted up and down ahead of the waves. She sifted through the wet sand for sea glass, but only found a few broken oyster shells and a crushed and rusted soda can. In the distance, she saw Mr. Symonds and his dog. Peggy waved, but he'd already turned away, disappearing between a stand of scrubby trees and a leaning sand fence.

By the time she pushed through the gate into her yard, the crew had departed for the day, but David was still hard at work, up to his knees in a hole with a pry bar. He'd shed his shirt in the late-afternoon humidity. His shoulder-length hair clung to the back of his neck while sweat glistened across wide shoulders that tapered down over a sleek back to his faded jeans. Evidence of his accident was obvious in the bruising along his ribs, and a long bloody scrape on his right arm. Not that it seemed to bother him. He whistled as he worked, still cheerful despite his brush with catastrophe.

Now was her chance to make up for her earlier rudeness. "Looks like you avoided any permanent damage."

He straightened, wiping a forearm across his forehead. "There you are. I wondered where you'd got to."

"I'm really sorry about earlier, David. I don't know what got into me. The last few days have just been so weird."

"*Weird* is an understatement, but before you say anything else, you might want to check this out. Weird might be just the half of it." He dropped his pry bar and climbed out of the hole. She followed him around to the front porch where a wooden box the size of a small suitcase rested on the top step. Once, it must have been varnished and handsome with shiny brass hinges. Now it was dull with dirt, warped and worm-eaten, and only one not-so-shiny hinge remained. "I dug it up from under the rosebush."

"Please don't tell me you found a severed head inside." She fingered the latch, almost afraid to open it.

"Better." He flipped the latch and pushed back the lid. Inside, bundles of letters lay nestled and tied with ribbon. And at the bottom of the box, a cloth bag. A sachet had been laid on top. It smelled of lavender, rosemary, and very faintly of violets. "I think I found your answers."

PEGGY SAT CROSS-LEGGED on the floor, the wooden box open in front of her. David had carried it in, but she stopped him as he started to leave. "Stay?" Experiencing a horrible sense of déjà vu, she quickly added, "I mean, while I go through the box. It's silly, but I don't want to be alone and you were the one who found it. It seems only right."

"You sure?"

"I'm so sorry I made that crack about your camper. It's fine where it is. It's fine you being here. In fact, I couldn't have done any of this without you."

"That's true. I've never seen anyone so confused over a toilet valve, but I won't rub my amazingness in your face too much," he said, taking a seat on the couch behind her, hands clasped loosely between his knees.

And just like that, all was forgiven, and they were back where they'd started. No shouting. No sulking. No slammed doors or silent treatment. A knot in her chest untied itself.

"Well?" David said finally. "The suspense is killing me."

She hesitated, running a hand along the rough edge of the lid, splinters stinging her fingers. Touching the bundle of letters as if they might bite. Smoothing her palm over the folded linen. The lavender and rosemary crumbled at her touch while the scent of violets lingered. "It feels like trespassing. The same as reading her private diary or—"

"Sorting through her private belongings? Which you've been doing for the past few months?"

"Blanche buried these things for a reason."

"She left you this cottage for a reason. Symonds said it himself. Maybe the reason—both reasons—are in that box."

"Maybe now that it comes down to it, I don't want to know the reason."

"Fine." He leaned forward and started to tip the lid closed. "I'll put it back in the hole."

"Wait." She grabbed his wrist.

They stayed that way for a long moment, eyes locked. She could feel the tension in his arm, the jump of his pulse; see the moment his gaze darkened, the iron flecks in his blue eyes, the faint lines fanning the corners where he squinted into the sun day in and day out. She could smell the sweet scent of soil and sweat and laundry soap in his clothes. She remembered how he tasted, how he felt under her hands, how she felt when he kissed her.

"Peggy?" His voice was raspy and soft. Was he thinking the same things about her? Was he remembering what it had been like?

Her mouth went dry, and she swallowed, blinking and looking away before her heart thudded right out of her chest. "Right. Let's do it."

She felt his smile and the laughter he was trying to stifle.

"The box, you idiot," she clarified before lifting out the bundle of letters, leafing through the envelopes, every one of them addressed to "Moppet."

"Who's Moppet?" he asked, leaning over her shoulder.

"I don't know." She felt so stupid. How could she not know her own family? But it seemed like every thread she pulled revealed something new, turned people she'd known her whole life into strangers.

Next she took out a scrapbook, its leather cover cracked. Inside, there were no formal photographs. Instead, the pictures had all been cut from newspapers, the print nearly invisible, the paper yellow.

A baby propped in a rocking chair, legs crossed, curls tied up in an enormous bow. "Moppet at two" handwritten underneath.

A line of little girls in plaid pinafores and blouses standing in front of a brick building. "Moppet's first day of school."

A slender teen in debutante white, long gloves and an orchid for a corsage. "Moppet on her eighteenth birthday."

Wait a minute. Peggy recognized that photo. It had stood in a gold frame beside her grandmother's bed until the day she died. That wasn't anyone named Moppet. That was Peggy's mother.

She turned the page to find a birth announcement cut from the paper; slicked down with glue.

Mr. and Mrs. Lawrence are pleased to announce the birth of a granddaughter. Margaret Iris was born on September 14 . . .

Peggy's stomach knotted. She couldn't breathe. She slammed the book closed, cold infecting every pore.

"Peg?"

"That's me. Margaret Iris. I was named after my grandmother. I was born on September fourteenth."

David slid the book from her trembling grip and placed it on the couch beside him. "Let's see what else there is in here."

She turned to the folded linen bag, but her excitement had soured. Fear coated the back of her throat. Dread gripped her stomach. One corner of the bag was frayed, revealing a glimpse of delicate lace beneath the plain fabric wrapping, a sheen of white silk discolored to a pale yellow ivory.

Was it a wedding gown?

Peggy gentled it out of the bottom of the box to lay it on the carpet. She peeled back one side of the linen, then the other, nearly holding her breath as she revealed the gown underneath. Stale-scented air tickled her nose, camphor and dust and now the soft perfume of violets rose to envelop her. It was as if her mother was here in the room with her, comforting her, reassuring her.

The gauzy silk was trimmed with elaborate embroidery. Lace decorated the collar and the hem, an underdress of simpler but no-less-exquisite silk. She smoothed a hand down the underskirt, her fingertips touching on a spot near the hem where the stitches bunched and curved. She held it to the light and there in gossamer thread was the date October 15, 1918.

Her mother's birthday.

Peggy stood, letting the fabric fall to the floor where it trailed against the rug's fringe. Blanche had crafted this gown with love. It was obvious in every tiny stitch and every embroidered flower.

But it wasn't for a wedding. This was a child's christening gown.

THE GOWN HUNG on the back of the door with a set of cheap paste pearls, the string yellow with age. The scrapbook was open to the last page where Blanche had pasted in Peggy's mother's obituary. The letters lay scattered on the floor around her. Letters revealing the heartbreak of separation between a mother and her child. Hopes. Regrets. Love. Disappointment. Blanche had written one a year for every year of her daughter's life and then buried them all.

She lost the baby.

Mr. Symonds' words echoed down a long tunnel.

Not lost. Simply magicked away like a pea under a shell. Now she's here, now she's gone.

"I don't understand." It was a pleading for answers, but there was no one left to ask. Her mother. Blanche. Her grandparents. None of them were left to explain. "She abandoned her daughter. How could she do that? How could she just walk away?"

"She didn't," David answered. "She gave your mother to people who loved her and cared for her as if she were their own."

"But why keep it a secret?"

"To save face. Protect reputations. You said Blanche never married. If that's the case, a child would have ruined her. The scandal would have tainted the family. They must have thought it best to let the world—and your mother—believe a lie."

Peggy glanced around at the cottage's shabby furnishings then down at the letters dated every year until 1958—the year her mother died, the year Blanche left the Norfolk Yeoman F Society.

What had Suzanne said all those weeks ago when she saw the

enormous rosebush out Peggy's back window? The white rose signifies loss.

Had Blanche planted the rose that year? Buried all her memories in that box and tended it like a grave?

Peggy bowed her head over the letters, her temples throbbing.

"Blanche gave her child away out of love," David said quietly. "Your grandparents accepted her with love. They loved your mother. They loved you."

"It's all you need?" She joked around a tearful lump.

"Something like that," he replied.

She could understand the family wanting to lie to the world. But to lie to her mother? To her? That's what she found hard to forgive. Every memory was suddenly a mirage of hidden motives. Every truth upon which she'd based her life's choices was now torn up and scattered into a million pieces.

David had never lied to her. He'd never promised anything, but he was a rock when everything else in her life shifted under her feet like sand. She let him pull her close, his warmth easing the hollowness in her chest. She felt him kiss her hair. A comforting kiss, a gentle kiss. But she needed more. She needed to fill the emptiness that made her insides hurt. She needed heat to thaw the ice she'd let form around herself.

She spread her palm over his heart. The steady unbroken rhythm and the slow rise and fall of his chest eased her panic. She lifted her head, reaching on tiptoe to kiss his mouth. His gaze was opaque, no way for her to read his thoughts, but he didn't stop her, and when she made to pull away, he caught her, and kissed her back.

This time there was no one to stop them. He shucked his shirt over his head, revealing the long lean lines of a chest paled by a farmer's tan. She slid her hands up over his ribs, jumping at his hiss of indrawn breath. "Sorry. Does that hurt?"

"Not even a little," he murmured.

Her own blouse disappeared in a flurry of loosed buttons, his hand sliding around to unhook her bra, his roughened palm hot against the soft curve of her lower back. They lay on the rug, their bodies skin to skin, and still she wanted him closer. He paused, his hands braced on either side of her head, his gaze blue as the heart of a flame. This was a moment she could have stopped him. She could have come to her senses and asked him to leave. But she didn't. Instead, she pulled him down into a kiss that left no room for second thoughts, and as afternoon faded into evening, she finally felt the last jagged splinter slide loose. Chaz was gone. The smell of him. The taste of him. The way he felt under her hands.

It was only David. And David was exactly who she wanted—who she needed.

Later, she couldn't be sure what woke her up. A quiet conversation? The snick of the front door? A voice in the dark? She'd fallen asleep wrapped in an old blanket David had pulled off the couch, his bunched-up shirt beneath her head. But now a breeze lifted the hairs at the back of her neck and raised goose bumps along her arms. She rose, dragging the rug around her as she tripped over the box in the dark. The letters fluttered like ghosts along the floor, her head filled with the scent of violets and her own damp, sex-scented skin.

She started to close the front window when she saw them on the driveway by the camper van, silhouetted by the streetlamp. She recognized David instantly, but the other figure was impossible to make out until they stepped out of the shadows. It was Lena. Peggy recognized the long spill of dark hair, the sharp-chinned features. She was shaking her head. He was speaking low and quickly. She glanced toward the house, sending Peggy ducking for cover. By the time she risked another look, Lena was getting into her car. He leaned in for a final word, and then she was gone, her taillights bouncing over the potholes.

Peggy closed the window, the sound drawing David's attention. They met on the porch. His jeans were low on his hips, his shirt buttoned unevenly. His feet were bare. Peggy stood on the top step, matching him eye to eye as he stood on the front walk. His hand curved against her ribs as he pulled her close, and she wondered if he needed her heat as much as she needed his.

"Hi," he said softly, his smile making her heart do little flips. Her traitor insides instinctively tightened in delicious expectation.

"Everything all right?" she asked, drawing the blanket closer around her, but her earlier warmth was gone.

He glanced down the street after Lena's car, then up at the cottage, then across the street to Symonds' bungalow, then down at his bare feet.

"Wow. It must be bad. You can't even look me in the eye." She tried to laugh it off as a joke, but he wasn't fooled.

"Peg . . . this is the world's worst timing ever, and it's going to make me sound like a complete ass, but . . ." He scrubbed at the back of his neck, shoulders hunched in apology.

"But?" She knew that look. She'd seen it on Chaz a million times, usually right before he left on one of his road trips to find himself. When had she stopped seeing that freewheeling spirit as boyish charm and started seeing it as selfish self-indulgence?

"Just spit it out, Chaz." David's head shot up, revealing hurt and guilt in equal measure. "I meant David," she corrected herself. "Spit it out, *David*."

After a moment, he nodded and continued. "Lena would have waited till morning to bring it over, but she saw who it was from, and she knew I'd been waiting for it so . . ." He handed her the letter.

Peggy scanned it, her muzzy brain not understanding. "I didn't even know you wanted to be an architect."

"Not many do. It's always been just this crazy idea in the back of my head. A dream that I never really thought could happen.

Ask Lena. She'll tell you. My family's not really big into follow-ing dreams. I love them and all, but they're more the meat-and-potatoes, pull-yourself-up-by-the-bootstraps, get-a-real-job kind of family."

Peggy was reminded of her grandfather's solidly middle-class ideas of what constituted *success*. "I get that."

"So I did what they wanted and got a real job, but I never stopped loving to design and create. It was Lena who kept pushing me to do something with it, but I'm thirty years old. I haven't been in a classroom in years. Look at me. I'm not exactly what you think of when you think *college student*. It seemed insane to even think about—until you."

"Me? What did I do?"

"You showed me what being brave looked like. You gave me the courage to put it all on the line and finally apply to school."

"When do you have to go?" Was it her, or was the temperature dropping? She shivered, goose bumps rising on her arms and legs.

"I can probably grab a morning flight out of DC that can get me to San Francisco in time for the interview, but I need to leave now. Like now . . . now."

"That soon?"

"I'd postpone if I could, but the letter sat in Lena's mailbox for a week while she was away on vacation, so I'm already under the gun."

"Of course. I mean this is your shot. You can't just *not* go."

"I can arrange with the guys to come and finish the porch re-pairs. It'll be good as new."

"Don't be ridiculous. Let me worry about that. You need to get on the road," she said even as every atom in her body was arcing toward him like iron shavings to a magnet.

"And you're sure you'll be okay? I mean this stuff with your aunt . . ." His voice trailed off.

Peggy wanted to tell him no, of course she wouldn't be okay. Her world had just been turned upside down. She was a complete and utter mess.

"I'll be fine." She forced a smile. "One brick at a time, right?"

His laugh was uncertain, as if he wasn't sure whether she was joking or not.

She wasn't sure either.

"Don't worry about me, David. Really." This time her smile was genuine. "It's your big chance. You have to seize it with both hands."

He grabbed Peggy up in a rib-crushing hug. "God, I love you."

She went stiff as a board, swallowing over and over in a mad rush to hold herself together. It was an expression. It didn't mean anything.

"I'll phone you as soon as I get to San Fran. I promise. I know it'll be hard with me on one coast and you on the other, but . . ." He looked around as if trying to find the words. "I mean Suzanne and Ron make it work and he's half a world away, right?"

Her smile made her face ache. "Of course."

Her cowardice had driven Chaz away.

Now her courage was sending David to the other side of the country.

There was something cosmically ironic about that. She'd laugh if she could.

He tried leaning in to kiss her goodbye, but she had already turned away.

"Peg?" he called after her, but she was already closing the front door.

She let Chaz leave. She could let David go too.

CHAPTER 30

VIV

1918

We didn't talk about that night again. It was easy to pretend amid the jubilation and chaos of the war's end—just as it had been easy to hide our crime amid a wild night of smashed windows, overturned automobiles, looted shops, and violent mobs. If a firebrand pastor from Richmond washed up on shore, who was to say he wasn't just one more unfortunate victim? But Gus's knowledge of the bay's lonely coves and hidden inlets came in handy, and the days passed without a raised alarm.

Still, the silence changed things. It infected our friendship as surely as the flu that continued to rage through the city. We grew wary around one another, too many traps waiting to spring, too many dead ends where conversations dwindled away into uncomfortable civilities. We were bound together forever by the events of the night even as the secret of what happened pulled us apart.

Maybe it was easier for me. I'd lived with this guilt before. And while I regretted my part in Father's death, I didn't regret that he was dead. I also had the solace of work to turn my thoughts, though for how long remained unknown. Father's threat of exposure meant that I went to work each morning expecting to be called into Dumfries' office. Each evening, I left exhausted with spent tension, fingernails bitten to the quick. What would happen if they discovered my deception? I would be discharged certainly, but would there be other consequences? Would Blanche be drawn into my lies? Would she suffer for my sins worse than she already had?

She was already growing thin, her round cheeks carved close against her skull, her eyes sunken from long sleepless nights as Moppet's condition worsened. Any money she earned from her sewing seemed to go straight to doctors or for the latest medicines. I came home one day to find her on the couch red-eyed from weeping, Moppet slack and listless in her arms. "She's going to die, isn't she, Viv? She's going to die and it will be all my fault."

"It'll be all right," I said as I poured her a generous glass of Gus's illicit brandy and bundled her into bed. "You'll see." But both of us knew my words rang hollow.

My days worsened as Hampton Roads grew thick with troop ships, the streets of its cities and towns crowded with returning soldiers. I began to see Tom's face around every corner, recognize his way of standing, his uniform insignia, the pitch of his voice. I would touch the shoulder of a young man on the bus or call his name as I hurried after a soldier on a busy street, but they would turn and stare at me without recognition, their confused stranger's gaze slicing through me like a knife.

I reached out to Betty at the Westons' for news, but my letter came back, "Undeliverable" stamped in red across the envelope. When I called the house, no one answered the telephone. I turned to the Red Cross, the YMCA, the Salvation Army, and the War Department for information about repatriated prisoners of war, but I was one among thousands begging for help, and there was little anyone could do. I was shuffled between departments in an endless circle of dwindling hope.

Ernst recovered, but he was no longer the robust contented man of those long summer nights on the beach. Illness, the destruction of the bakery, and Marjory's death had taken their toll. He was thinner, quieter, and when he came to the cottage with Clara to tell us of his move to Ohio, we weren't surprised. The Kunwalds had offered him a new home and a new beginning. I hoped he'd found a new committee to help him raise his daughter.

The day of his departure, we hugged on the front porch, his body hunched against the raw winter wind off the bay. I could feel his bones beneath his coat, the weight of his loss in the new lines upon his face. Clara stood pale and silent, a shabby woolen coat buttoned to her chin, a pair of scuffed oversized boots on her feet. Blanche clutched Moppet, as always, sickly and grizzling within her nest of blankets.

"I found these among the ashes." Ernst handed her a string of paste pearls. "Marjory would want you to have them. You won them, after all." His voice broke as he fought down his grief. "What will we do without her?"

Blanche kissed his cheek, her eyes wet. "We'll do what we must because we have no choice."

His weak sorrowful smile was his only answer.

ONE AFTERNOON IN late November, Quarles came to see me as I was transcribing the scattered pages of a personnel file. "Dumfries is looking for you, Weston. He says it's urgent."

Worry bloomed in my chest when I saw the curiosity behind her thick spectacles. I started for his office when she stopped me. "Not in there. Upstairs in Captain Spratling's office."

The senior medical officer? The man in charge of the entire hospital? This was it. The moment when my lies finally caught up with me.

"Any idea why Spratling and Dumfries want to meet with you?" she asked, stretching out the sentence as if expecting me to crack under the strain. I clamped my jaw shut to keep from babbling everything. She paused on a lift of her eyebrows, the final twist of the rack.

"I've no idea, Chief," I said, eyes wide with feigned innocence.

I must have laid it on too thick. Her curiosity immediately darkened to suspicion. "Oh, I have a feeling you do."

Did she know? Suspect? If I could have sunk through the floor to avoid her narrowed gaze, I would have.

Ever since I'd turned down my overseas transfer, Quarles had kept our interactions sparse and businesslike while her eyes pinned me with reproach. My fellow yeomanettes, sensing blood in the water, needled me about my fall from favor or tried to get me to join them in their Quarles-bashing sessions. I smiled at the teasing and ignored the malice, but both left me bruised and unhappy at the loss of her good opinion—which I'd not realized I valued until it was gone.

"I'll just go up and find out, I guess." Sliding out from under her razor-sharp scrutiny, I dawdled my way upstairs, savoring my last moments in naval uniform. A sharp-featured clerk, sitting behind his desk of compulsively straight edges and symmetrically high piles, eyed me, not unkindly, but as if he barely noticed *me* at all. I was a uniform, a rank of chevrons and insignia, gold buttons and pleated folds. A sailor, same as him in every way that mattered.

Oddly enough, despite my quaking knees and turning stomach, I was filled with pride. I had done my job, and I had done it well. I had proven my worth to a skeptical nation. I had helped, in however small a way, to win this war. They could strip me of my uniform and rank, toss me out of the Navy, but they couldn't take away that achievement. It belonged to me forever.

"Do you need something, yeoman?"

I started to explain my reason for being there, but only managed to stammer a few nonsensical words before something stopped me. *Yeoman*, he'd called me. A smile tugged at my lips. I hadn't joined up out of patriotism like Marjory or out of a need to prove myself like Blanche. I hadn't joined for adventure or opportunity or even money. I had enlisted to hide. I had *become* Vivian. Tom had said it back in June—Vivian enlisted in the Navy, not me. I could disappear and Vivian would be a ghost again. It would be like none of this ever happened.

"I'm sorry. I think I'm in the wrong office."

I felt him staring after me as I turned to leave, but I kept my pace slow as if I'd not a care in the world. I was just passing the stairs when a shout came from behind me. It was the clerk. "Weston? Hold on a minute! They want to talk to you!"

I started to turn when a hand shot out to clamp on my arm, tugging me into the stairwell. "Down here," Quarles hissed.

"What are you doing?" I gasped, shrinking back against the wall as the clerk raced past our hiding place to scour the upper floors.

She ignored my question. "Keep going this way, and you'll come out near the laundries. From there, you can leave through one of the loading docks."

"I don't understand."

"Neither do I, and I don't want to," she said, checking to make sure the coast was clear. "But we yeomanettes need to stick together because *they* for sure aren't going to stick by us. Not now we're no longer needed."

Her words pushed past my confusion to a place where a memory, as real as the corridor's sour smell of bleach and boiled potatoes, shimmered into focus. I'd heard those words before. I'd spoken those words before. We were a sisterhood. "All for one and one for all," I replied, echoing Marjory.

Quarles pushed me onward. "I can give you twenty-four hours then I have to report you AWOL."

Doors were opening and closing above us as the search continued.

"Thank you, Chief."

"You were a damn fine sailor, Weston. Whatever happens, don't forget that."

She turned back to climb the stairs and face the clerk. I hurried down the stairs and through the steamy clatter of the laundries to escape in the confusion of a supply truck's arrival. Keeping my pace relaxed as if it was any other day, I followed the oyster shell road out to Green Street, saluting the guard one last time. I was only postponing the inevitable. The Navy would catch up with me and there would be hell to pay, but for one last night, I was Yeoman Weston.

I was the girl I'd always wanted to be.

BLANCHE FOUND ME late that night on the beach where I stared out on the glittering lights of freighters and barges, converted liners, gunboats, destroyers, and the regular clockwork flow of local ferries and long-distance steamships. The bay was whipped into a froth by a wind that tasted like snow, icy spray off the waves stinging my face. Behind us, up the beach, was a circle of blackened wood where, only a few months ago, we'd grilled fish and passed around a bottle of bootleg whiskey. Our ghosts still seemed to hover like the cold ash swirling in the December breeze.

"It's odd. I knew this day would come sooner or later, that I'd have to stop being Viv, but what now? If I'm not her, who am I?"

"Yourself?"

I shuddered. "I was afraid you'd say that."

Blanche slid her hand into mine, her fingers warm, her touch reassuring. "Where would I be without your strength or your kindness or your . . . your love? That wasn't Viv. That was you. It always was. That hasn't stopped."

I smiled through icy tears.

"Now, enough of this sentimental blubbering," Blanche added briskly. "You've got packing to do."

"I don't understand."

"It's obvious you can't stay here any longer, so you might as well go to France. It's the only way you'll find out what happened to Tom. It's the only way you'll bring him home. My parents will pay for your passage. And Father has the name of a Red Cross contact at the ICRC in Paris who might know where you should start looking."

"Why would your parents help me, just like that?"

She turned to me, her face white against the night. "They *won't* help you just like that."

Comprehension dawned. "Blanche, no. I won't let you give everything up for me."

"Haven't you learned anything by now? No one *lets* me do anything. I do what I want, and I want you to take Moppet to my parents' house in DC."

"You fought so hard to keep her. Why change your mind now?"

"I've been thinking about it for weeks now, and I can't do it. I can't be what Moppet needs, not the way things stand now." Anguish strained her voice. "She's sick. My parents can pay for the best doctors, the latest medicines. She has a chance with them—a future. She doesn't have that with me."

"You're her mother."

"Mothers do what's best for their children. My mother tried when she offered me the chance to start again, and I threw it back in her face. I think I understand her a little better now. Or maybe I understand more about myself."

"I can't, Blanche. I won't."

She grabbed my arms, pulled me in close. "I need you to do this for me, Viv. Please." There was such horrible empty longing in her eyes. I felt it in the tightness of her hold on my arms and in the taut pallor of her face. "I can't bring myself to do it, but it needs to happen. She needs a good home, a home that I can't give her, a home where they can give her the care she needs. If you do this one last thing for me, I'll see that you get to France, even if it is a few months late." Her smile was beautiful and heartbreaking. "You wouldn't disobey your admiral, would you?"

I knew then she wouldn't change her mind. She had charted her course and meant to stick with it, no matter the sacrifice to herself. I wanted to stand firm, refuse to do her bidding, but I already felt myself sliding into surrender, falling under her spell. Maybe she was right. Maybe it was better this way for everyone.

I packed that night, my spirits lifting as a plan took shape. Vivian would do one last thing before she was laid back to rest.

Gus arrived the next morning, grim-faced and as unhappy about this plan of Blanche's as I was. He loaded my luggage into the back of the van while I moved from room to room, the memories thick as cobwebs. When it was time to go, Blanche and I embraced. I felt how delicate she'd become since Moppet's birth, the delicate web of veins running just under the skin of her wrists and throat. She put the baby in my arms, her face scrunched in sleep, her rosebud mouth puckered tight. Blanche kissed her one last time, inhaling the scent of her child, murmuring a promise in her ear.

The van coughed and screeched as Gus set into gear, and I left Blanche and the cottage in Ocean View as snow drifted over the ground, white as the petals off her roses.

"STOP!" WE HAD only driven a short way up the coast before I grabbed Gus's arm, nearly jerking the wheel from his hand.

Gus threw the van into neutral. "Change your mind?"

I wished it was so simple. I wished I could turn the van around and return to the cozy cottage with its garret window and banging screen door, to the long golden days of summer when everything seemed possible, but I couldn't. I'd promised Blanche just as much as she had promised me. We had made a devil's pact, and I would see it through if it killed me.

"Wait here. I won't be a minute." I climbed out of the cab, the snow catching in my cloak like feathers, icy pinpricks melting on my cheeks. Already, it gathered in corners, frosting the grass, whirling in the light from the lamps along the promenade.

Off to my left, the amusement park was shuttered and dark, but the hotel was lit up like a Christmas tree. A few hardy guests milled on the promenade, but the cold and snow kept most people inside.

I crossed the street and hurried down the steps onto the dark beach. The lamps lining the promenade threw dim light over the sand, but the snow was coming faster now, whipped by the wind so that I had to squint to see where I was going. I followed the sound of the waves, stopping at the water's edge where bracken rolled in the quiet tide, the sea foam like frosting. The Chesapeake was wide and dark, the snow blotting out the ship's lights, the far shore, the stars. There was an eerie stillness, the world muffled but for the hiss of the falling snow and my own ragged breathing.

I had no idea what the Navy knew or why they wanted to see me. If Father had revealed my identity or if he'd lied about that as he lied about so much else. But I wouldn't drag my friends any deeper into my mess than I already had. Things might not go back to the way they were with Viv's disappearance, but it might just be enough to point the finger away from the cottage in Ocean View should our crime be discovered.

Blanche was giving me a future. It was only fair I do the same for her.

I drew my ID tag from around my neck, the metal disk warm,

the chain icy cold. Gripping it in one hand, I drew my arm back and hurled it as far as I could out over the water. I saw a flash of silver, heard a slosh as it hit, and then nothing more.

Slowly, I trudged back up the beach and slid into the van, the windows frosting, the headlamps drifted with white.

"You ready now, Viv?" Gus asked. The dim lights fell in long gray shadows over his cheeks, making him appear worn down and older than his years. "It's a long way to Washington."

I tucked Moppet back into the crook of my arm, where she blinked sleepily up at me, her blue eyes fading to green. "The name's not Viv anymore, but yes. I'm ready."

CHAPTER 31

PEGGY

1968

Peggy woke to a splitting headache and a mouth tasting like an old sock. The empty bottle of bourbon on the floor beside the bed might have something to do with that. But obliteration had been necessary. Her brain had been on fire. Spinning out of control. Like her life.

Wait. Not her life at all. She wasn't who she thought she was. She wasn't Peggy Lawrence at all. Not the daughter of Deborah Lawrence. Granddaughter of Gilbert Lawrence and his wife Iris.

Deborah Lawrence was a fiction. Her parents hadn't been her parents at all. Her family had lied about everything. She had gone to her grave never knowing her real mother was out there, loving her from afar.

Did Mr. Symonds know? Stupid question. Of course he knew. He'd known the moment Peggy introduced herself, and he'd spent the following weeks trying to steer her away from the truth.

Did he do it to protect her or to protect Blanche?

Did it matter?

Oh God, the pounding in her head was spinning down into her stomach. She was going to be sick. She rolled over, her eyes falling on the photo of the three yeomanettes, smiling at the beach.

Marjory was dead.

Blanche was dead.

But Viv . . . Viv was still alive and sending her postcards.

Peggy threw on clothes and headed downstairs, blinking against the sunlight. No sounds came from outside. No shouts from builders. No hammering or raunchy conversation. No radio blasting. The driveway was empty except for an oil stain where the camper used to sit. The folding chair leaned against the side of the house.

She'd been right to let David go. Right to think whatever bond connected them had been as ephemeral as the morning mist hanging over the bay. Despite the tiny light that had switched on inside her after six months of darkness, she hadn't really known him at all.

David had left her with a crumbling back porch.

Blanche had left her without once telling the truth about who she was.

Chaz had left her with a heart weighted by loss and grief.

Had she really thought she could pull her life together? That this cottage was somehow the miracle that would bring her back?

She took two aspirin, drank a pot of black coffee, and drowned herself in the shower until the world stopped spinning. Then before she could change her mind, she took Mr. Ebersol's business card off the mirror and dialed the number.

She had just finished her phone call when she heard the door open.

"Peggy?" That voice. That scent of violets. Dizziness hit her like a wave. "Sweetie?"

She spun around, but it was only Suzanne. Peggy put down the receiver, hands shaking. "Still interested in that road trip?"

PEGGY HAD AN eerie sense of déjà vu as she pulled off the expressway, windows rolled down, radio blasting. Only this time it was the Stones' "Stupid Girl" and it was Suzanne wrestling with the gas station map.

What should have taken two hours took nearly four with Peggy spilling the whole story in between Suzanne's frequent potty breaks. "Are you sure you want to sell the cottage? You've worked so hard to fix it up. It seems a shame to hand the keys over to Ebersol just so he can knock it down."

"I never meant to stay. This was just a place to regroup before I decided what to do next."

"Which is?" When Peggy didn't answer right away, Suzanne continued. "This wouldn't have anything to do with David leaving, would it?"

"Of course not. You were the one pushing the Annette and Frankie angle."

Suzanne leaned into the back seat, handing Nancy and Timmy the bag of snacks and sodas she'd bought at the last gas station. All that sugar was likely to haunt them later, but for now it kept the kids content. "Maybe he'll come back."

Peggy gripped the steering wheel tighter. "Maybe."

They crawled along narrow neighborhood streets, eyes peeled for Union Street. It was quiet in the car except for the radio underpinned by the crinkling of snack bags and the hiss of soda-can pull tabs. Did Suzanne even know how to read a map? Three times, they circled the same block.

"What did you name her?" Suzanne asked, talking over a commercial for breakfast cereal.

Peggy didn't have to take her eyes off the road. She could feel Suzanne's stare. She tried to pretend she didn't understand the question, but even now all these months later, the baby's weight, the pain and heartbreak of that day was as real in that moment as the heat of the leather seats, the smell of hot asphalt, the breezy announcer's traffic report.

"I've always liked Barbara for a girl. Barbara Ann"—Suzanne snapped off the radio—"like the Beach Boys, you know. Ron told me I would be subjecting our daughter to a life of ridicule, but in the end, he had to agree it was up to me. He names the boys and I name the girls. That's been our deal."

Peggy gave a pained shake of her head, focusing on reading street signs, tapping impatiently on the steering wheel for the light to turn green, anything to keep from looking over and seeing that dreaded pity in Suzanne's face.

"She didn't have a name," Peggy said finally, hoping that would end the conversation. "She didn't live long enough."

She snapped the radio back on, letting the music fill the emptiness threatening to swallow her. But Suzanne was relentless. She flipped it back off, leaving nothing but the hum of the engine. Peggy could feel her eyes like two laser beams pinning her in place. "Maybe not an official one, but I'm sure you didn't carry her around all those months without calling her something."

Funny, but that didn't sound like pity. It sounded a bit snarky, in fact. When Peggy finally glanced over, she was shocked to see curiosity rather than the teeth-aching sympathy she'd come to despise.

"Knowing you, I'll bet it was something old-fashioned," Suzanne teased. "Maybe Bertha or Hazel or . . . or . . ."

"Rebecca." Peggy could barely speak around the ache in her throat.

She'd never said it out loud. Not once. Not even to Chaz. Maybe she should have, but by then the chasm between them had grown unbridgable.

"I called her Rebecca," she repeated, louder this time.

"It's nice. I like it." Suzanne smiled, her gaze innocent of anything but delight. "And definitely much better than Bertha."

IT WAS ANOTHER half hour of driving in circles before Suzanne pointed to a mailbox with "Weston" painted on the side. "There it is! You were right. The family still lives here." She grinned. "One-armed man, here we come."

She hummed the show's theme song as Peggy pulled into the driveway, which curved up to a covered portico and a set of enormous double doors flanked by riotous late-summer flowerbeds. "Whoever this Viv person is, she used this as her address in 1918 and she's using it now. They *must* know who she really is."

"I just hope they have a bathroom." Suzanne squirmed in her seat.

"Sorry, Suz," Peggy said, pocketing the keys. "I shouldn't have dragged you with me on this crazy quest. You should be home with your feet up, not out chasing ghosts."

"Are you kidding? Forget soap operas. I wouldn't miss this for the world." She stepped out, stretching her legs. "Kids, stay here. We'll be right back."

Peggy was still grappling with what to say when Suzanne banged on the door, shifting from foot to foot. A teenager answered, brown eyes ringed with thick black kohl. She wore a fringed leather vest and a long prairie skirt with a pair of high moccasin boots. Her long blonde hair hung nearly to her waist, a beaded leather thong braided into it. "Can I help you?"

Using every liquid ounce of her saccharine Southern charm, Suzanne explained the reason for their visit. "It sounds crazy, but we're really hoping Mrs. Weston can help us."

"That's so cool." The girl was practically salivating with curiosity. "It's like a real live mystery."

"Ivy?" A voice carried down from upstairs. "Ivy, can you bring me those cookies we had at lunch?"

"That's Gran. I'll see if she's up for guests."

"Before you go, Ivy, if you could show me where the bathroom is . . ." Suzanne said, by now, looking decidedly uncomfortable.

"Oh, I'm not Ivy," the girl replied with a laugh. "My name's Carol. Ivy's my mom. Granny gets confused." Carol took Suzanne down the hall before bounding up the stairs two at a time and disappearing through an archway.

Curious as she waited, Peggy poked her head into an enormous double living room, pocket doors dividing the space. The other side of the foyer let onto a dining room and a smaller study. More doors led toward the back where the kitchen must be. An enormous bouquet of purple asters and white roses sat on a round entry table in the middle of the foyer beneath a chandelier. A grandfather clock ticked off the slow ponderous minutes before striking the quarter hour.

Carol leaned over the upper banister, her hair hanging loose around her face. "Granny says to come on up."

Peggy ascended the wide stair then followed Carol as she was led to a bedroom at the back of the house.

"Like I said, Granny's a little . . ." Carol circled the side of her head with one finger. "She forgets things a lot, so I'm not sure how helpful she'll be, but you never know."

Peggy paused in the doorway. "Does she know what year it is?"

Carol gave a wink. "Depends who's asking."

What struck Peggy about the bedroom, more than the sumptuous furnishings and exquisite artwork, were the photographs. A black-and-white wedding portrait had pride of place by the bed. But on shelves and tables, dressers and desks were a sea of family snapshots: a couple smiling on the deck of a sailboat, posed in front of the Eiffel Tower, under a stone doorway arched with flowers. Here they stood with Big Ben in the background. There, in a gondola on a Venice canal. A child joined the couple. Then another. Then a third, descending in order like stairs. Peggy recognized the Richmond house. The portico out front. The tidy privet hedge. Snaps of different weddings with different couples. More babies, as grandkids entered the scene. There they were as a handsome silver-haired couple amid a crowd of smiling family. But nowhere did Peggy see one of three uniformed yeomanettes arm in arm or any hint of past naval service.

"You wanted to see me?" A tiny woman in a fashionable gray linen suit put down her pen, her white hair arranged neatly to frame her fine porcelain features. She had large doll-like eyes and a tremulous smile. Peggy recognized her immediately. But how did she end up here in the Westons' house with the Westons' name if she wasn't really Vivian Weston?

"This is going to sound crazy, but is your name Viv?"

A line formed between the woman's brows as if she struggled to understand. "Do I know you?"

"No, ma'am. My name's—"

"Blanche." Her eyes grew wide. Her hand moved to cover the postcard she'd been writing, fear taking the place of shock in her eyes. She swung to her granddaughter. "Ivy, go make tea."

"Granny, I told you. I'm *Carol*."

Her face twisted into an irritated frown as she waved her toward the door. "Leave us alone, whoever you are. Blanche and I have to talk."

"I'll let your friend know you'll be down in a minute." Carol shot her grandmother a look, giving Peggy a last twirl of one finger against the side of her head, then left.

Once they were alone, Viv—or whoever she was—lit a cigarette with shaking hands. "I shouldn't have written, Blanche. I know you said not to, that it was better that way, but I couldn't help myself." Her smile was sad, her gaze long. "Tom says what's in the past can't hurt us, but we know better, don't we?"

Peggy glanced at a photo of a young man in an old-fashioned uniform leaning against a tree. "He's very handsome."

Her gaze softened. "If it hadn't been for you, I'd never have tracked Tom down . . . he was so ill, a walking skeleton after those months in the camp at Skalmierschütz. It was almost a year before he was fully recovered."

"Mrs. Weston, it's not 1918. It's 1968, and my name's Peggy. My great-aunt Blanche died last year."

"I don't understand." She looked down at her hands as if seeing the ropy tendons and the bony knuckles for the first time. "Why would you lie?"

"Why did *you*?" Peggy asked quietly.

She sucked on her cigarette, her cheeks sunken, her eyes suddenly darting fearful and nervous.

"Is it because of what happened?" Peggy continued. "I know the truth."

She froze, the cigarette halfway to her lips. "You do?"

"Blanche had a child in 1918—my mother. But instead of raising her, she gave her away. Blanche hid it from my mother, from me, from everyone she knew."

"Like it never happened," Viv said softly. The tip of her cigarette glowed red as she inhaled, but when she blew the stream of blue smoke, the shaking was gone.

"What happened after the war?" Peggy asked. "Why did you let everyone think you were dead?"

Viv frowned, her gaze turned inward as if she was staring deep into the past. Peggy kept as still as possible, but silence seemed to fill the room, press into every corner. Had Viv's mind wandered once again? Had she forgotten Peggy was there? Where the heck was Carol when she needed her?

At last, she seemed to draw back into herself, the light of clarity returning to her eyes. "Why, indeed. For the same reason I became Viv to begin with. It was easier to start over." Peggy could understand that impulse. It was what had driven her to Norfolk. "Tom's parents died of the flu so there was no reason for us to come back to Richmond right away. We stayed in Europe. Twenty years. It was a good life. A safe life. By the time we got back to the States, we were up to our ears in a new war. The last one felt like a dream. I told myself it was best to let the past stay where it was."

Her grandfather's warnings.

Blanche's box under the rosebush.

Gus Symonds' stonewalling.

Viv wasn't the only one who had wanted the past to stay buried, yet her postcards had set Peggy on to the truth. "So what changed?"

Even as she asked the question, she followed the flick of a cigarette against an ashtray, her gaze falling on the newspaper folded beside it: *Missing Yeomanette Presumed Drowned in Suicide.*

The old woman stood, walking to the window to look down on the back garden, but Peggy had the sense she wasn't seeing the trim boxwood hedges, the brick paths, the two-car garage. "A friend convinced me it was time."

A smile tipped her lips, and she raised her hand as if waving to someone below. Was it Suzanne or Carol? No. Peggy could hear their voices downstairs. Out of the corner of her eye, she saw a flash of color, heard a young girl's shouting laughter, but when she looked, there was no one there.

THE RIDE HOME was completed mostly in silence. The kids had fallen asleep in the back seat and Suzanne stared out the window, her sunny features shadowed with fatigue. At one point, Peggy looked over to see her friend's eyes closed, her breathing slow and deep.

She'd underestimated Suzanne and her perky cheerleader attitude. She'd known exactly what to say to smash that last stubborn brick in Peggy's wall to dust.

As they neared Newport News, Suzanne opened her eyes and

stretched. "Sorry for zonking out. Guess I was more tired than I thought."

"Do you want to pull off and get some dinner?"

Suzanne rubbed the wide expanse of her stomach under her cute summer maternity top. The fading light threw greenish shadows across her face. "My indigestion is acting up. I think I just need to get home."

Ahead, Peggy saw signs for the ramp to Hampton and the bridge tunnel. "Not long now."

Suzanne leaned the seat back. "Are you sure I can't change your mind about the cottage? I'll miss you. Who else will eat my casseroles if you leave?"

"Mr. Symonds could use some fattening up . . . and a good friend."

Suzanne sighed. "You have an answer for everything."

"I don't have *any* answers. That's the problem." Peggy checked her rearview and changed lanes. "Just when I think I have hold of one, it slides right through my fingers."

"You found the answer to why Blanche left you the cottage."

"Yeah. Guilt."

"Was it?" Suzanne gripped the armrest and, even in the darkness, Peggy could see her discomfort, the jut of her clenched jaw. "Blanche sacrificed her happiness so that her child—your mother—could have the chance for a good life. And she made sure you—her granddaughter—had a home when you needed it." She gave a small, stretched grimace of a smile, a hand against her side, lips pressed tight. "Blanche did exactly what good mothers do."

Peggy's chest ached. Her back was tight, but there were no tears and only a squeeze of the usual sorrow around her heart. "She did, didn't she?"

Suzanne reached out and gripped Peggy's hand, releasing her on a wincing gasp as she cupped her stomach.

"Suz?" Peggy asked. "What's wrong?"

"I don't know." Pain clouded her features, and she stiffened in her seat. "Could be just false contractions. I got them all the time with the other two. Or . . ." She gasped again, her breathing shallow and fast. "I don't feel so good, Peggy."

"We're almost there." She tried to sound encouraging, but traffic had slowed to stop-and-go as everyone funneled down to one lane.

"Something's not right. This doesn't feel like the others." Suzanne hunched over, her face truly green now.

"Just another few miles," Peggy said, trying to remain calm even as her pulse ratcheted up to a mile a minute.

"It hurts so much, Peg. I can't . . ." Suzanne panted in between groans then let out a small cry. She touched her wet skirts, a puddle dripping onto the floor of the car. "Oh my God. My water broke."

"You are *not* having this baby in my car. Do you hear me?" Flicking on her emergency flashers, Peggy hit the gas, peeling onto the shoulder with a spit of gravel. An opening in the traffic appeared to her right. She took it with a screech of brakes and a press of her horn. Another lane change into the left. Back again, weaving in and out like a driver at Indy. By now the kids were awake and wide-eyed, and Suzanne was cussing and moaning with increasing volume and intensity.

Someone leaned out of a passenger-seat window with an insult directed at lady drivers. Peggy responded with a very unladylike middle finger as she laid on the horn. "She's having a baby in here, so get out of my way or so help me . . ."

The car let her in, and she shot the gap with a roar of her engine as they hit the bridge. "Could you find *every* pothole?" Suzanne hissed, her back arched off the seat.

"Complain to Virginia state roads!" Peggy shot back as the highway descended under the water, the walls of the tunnel closing around them.

Suzanne's face flashed green and yellow in the arc of overhead lights. "Peggy?" Her voice was high and breathless. "Do you know where you're going?"

Ahead, the highway rose again toward the surface. As they burst back out onto the second bridge span, she could see a sliver of moon to the east over the bay, the lights of Ocean View strung like jewels just ahead. "Not even close, Suz. But I'm beginning to figure it out."

CHAPTER 32

PEGGY

Peggy's nose stung with the smells of disinfectant, rubber, and stale coffee and she winced at the nails-on-a-blackboard squeak of trolleys being pushed by hushed-voiced nurses. At the far end of the hallway, a man shouted into a pay phone while a couple huddled together by the vending machine debating the merits of chips over candy bars.

She counted floor tiles. Three black. Two gray. Three black. She watched the minute hand on the clock over the nurse's station inch with excruciating slowness twice around. Mrs. Ertz came to collect the children. She tutted over them with grandmotherly concern and dish-soap scented hugs. As they were ushered out, little Nancy looked back over her shoulder at Peggy. "Don't forget your promise."

As if she could. As if her spinning brain would allow her to think of anything else, now that Suzanne was lost behind those swinging doors.

She knew what disaster lay in wait behind those doors. She wanted to be sick.

Her eyes grew scratchy. She tapped a foot. She paced the entire hallway and back again—three times. She sang every song on the *Deliver* album's side one. But not even the Mamas & the Papas could drag her mind away from the whirl of memories so vivid they made her want to throw up.

Each circuit, she stopped to ask for news; and each circuit, they simply checked their charts and shook their heads. No news was good news. That was the saying. Peggy clung to it one more hour before a nurse finally met her gaze. "Why don't you go home, ma'am? It's nearly three in the morning. Come back tomorrow. I'm sure we'll know something by then."

"Not until I know she's safe."

Though at this point, Peggy wasn't even sure who "she" was— Suzanne? Her baby? Or was "she" Peggy's baby—the silent bloodied scrap they'd rushed out of the room without ever once letting Peggy hold her?

She was so jumbled up inside, past and present moving like mirrors in a fun house. The nurse gave up arguing and Peggy returned to picking at a cigarette burn in the plastic chair arm.

The swinging door to the ambulance bay opened, a man pushing through to the whirl of red lights. She immediately stiffened and sat up as he scanned the waiting room, before heading in her direction. He stopped in front of her, hands on his hips, a hardness to his jaw. It took all she had not to throw herself into his arms. "What are you doing here?" she asked as if accusing him of something. "You're supposed to be in California."

"I'm looking for you," David replied. "When I saw you weren't home, I swung by Suzanne's. Mrs. Ertz explained the situation and that you were still here. Any news?"

"I don't know. No one will tell me anything." A strip of plastic from the chair came off in her hand. She rolled it round and round between her thumb and forefinger. "That explains why you're here in the hospital, but not why you're here in Norfolk. You left."

"Guess you can't get rid of me so easily." He scrubbed at the back of his neck before sitting down, clearly noticing when she inched to the farthest edge of her chair, eying him cautiously. "I got as far as my plane change in Chicago. I was sitting in the lounge listening to them announcing arrivals and departures, and the longer I sat there, the more California seemed like a fool's errand. I kept thinking to myself, What am I doing here?"

"I thought my bravery inspired you to take a risk."

"It did." He was looking at her with that stare that made her stomach do flips and her insides fizz like soda pop. "So, I'm taking one now. I called the university from O'Hare and explained the situation. They were very polite about it."

"About what?"

"About my turning them down to stay in Virginia. They even went so far as to suggest a few programs closer to home where I could apply."

"Home?"

He took her hand. "Home."

She hadn't realized how much grief weighed her down until it was lifted from her shoulders. She felt like she was floating three feet above the floor—for exactly three minutes—then her legs gave out under her. "David! What have I done?"

Before he could answer, a nurse with a clipboard came through the doorway marked Maternity. "Miss Lawrence?" She looked around the room. "Is there a Miss Lawrence here?"

"That's me." Peggy stood. "Is Suzanne . . . is Mrs. Anderson all right? Is the baby . . . ?" She couldn't say it. Her throat closed around her words.

"Mrs. Anderson's out of surgery, and both she and her new daughter are doing well. She's resting, but she wanted me to deliver a message. I believe her exact words were"—she checked a note pinned to her board—"'Tell the damn idiot to go home already and tie one on for me.'" The nurse smiled. "She was still suffering from the aftereffects of the anesthesia at the time."

"I'll bet she was," David muttered, laughing under his breath.

The nerves and the worry that had held Peggy together through the hours of waiting snapped like rubber bands. She felt her muscles unclench, her head start pounding, her teeth start chattering. "The baby's alive. Did you hear that, David? She's alive."

"I heard." He took Peggy in his arms. She felt him kiss her head, his voice soft and low. "Thanks to you."

The nurse gave a discreet clearing of her throat. "If you'd like, the nursery's just down the hall through those doors. You can see the baby for yourself. Look for a pink card attached to the bassinette. Should read 'Rebecca Ann.'"

Her arms still wrapped around David, Peggy smiled into the soft, faded folds of his shirt. "Rebecca Ann," she whispered. "I like that."

THE SHADOWS WERE long and the light hazy by the time Peggy blinked the grit out of her eyes and sat up. Outside the streetlights buzzed on as moms hollered for their kids to come for dinner. Had she really slept the day away?

The odors of cafeteria coffee and bleach clung to her hair and clothes, and her face felt tight from crying. She vaguely remembered David stripping her down to bra and panties before tucking her into bed with a kiss on the forehead. When she came downstairs wrapped in a robe, he was still there, a beer on the coffee table in front of him, his pencil flying over a page in his notebook.

"Hey sleepyhead," he said with a slow smile that lit her up like a firefly. "How ya feeling?"

"Embarrassed. Did I really cry all over you last night?"

"Technically, it was this morning, but yeah. Not a problem. I hadn't had a shower so . . ." he teased, pushing aside sofa pillows to make room.

"What are you drawing?"

He tipped the page so she could see.

"Oh." She felt her cheeks go hot and couldn't stop a stupid grin.

This wasn't a floor plan or an annotated drawing of a building, the doors and windows all measured and marked. Instead, he'd sketched her face while she'd slept. Quick pencil strokes created light and shadow: the curve of her cheek, the fan of her lashes. Her hair spilled along her neck, a few strands caught on her lips. She studied it closely, seeing the ghost of Blanche in the high arch of her brows, the width of her mouth.

"It's beautiful," she whispered.

He looked at her closely, the iron flecks in his eyes like shards of summer lightning. "*You're* beautiful."

That soda-pop fizz was back in her stomach. A chill raced up her spine, a sweet warmth settled over here. She quickly rose and busied herself in the kitchen, ignoring the indulgent smile that followed her.

"Suzanne called while you were asleep," he said. "She'll be in the hospital for a few more days, but mother and child are doing fine. Her mom arrived an hour ago to look after the kids."

"So just like that, it's all back to normal. Like it never happened."

"Well, not exactly. There's still the little matter of Ebersol."

She dropped her head in her hands. "Good Lord. He's supposed to come around today with Mr. Grace to discuss terms for the sale. They're going to think I'm the worst kind of dim-witted female for wasting their time."

"Did you mean what you said last night?" David asked. "That you'd changed your mind about selling the cottage?"

She looked down to their linked hands then up into his face. "I'm willing to take a chance if you are."

"Then I think you're safe from Ebersol and Grace."

He pointed to the front window. Outside, Symonds stood at the front gate barring the way like a medieval sentinel, his ropy body still powerful enough to deter Barry Grace, who shrank back against his Corvette as if attempting to protect it. Mr. Ebersol showed more pluck, but even he maintained a safe distance from Bandit, who strained at the end of his leash like a dog possessed.

"Miss Lawrence isn't interested, so you two slimy carpetbaggers can go back to wherever you came from," Symonds growled, chewing the end of his toothpick.

"This doesn't have anything to do with you, old man," Barry Grace blustered.

"Old man, is it?" Symonds' face turned an ugly wild-eyed shade of red, bony fists clutched as if he might explode any moment.

"Barry, perhaps we should go." Ebersol cleared his throat, obviously coming to the conclusion that he didn't need this particular bayfront property that badly.

"I can see you have strong feelings on the subject, sir." Mr. Grace's face smoothed into a mask of salesman's charm. "But take a look around. This community isn't exactly the hottest real estate market. If Miss Lawrence wants to get the best price, she needs to sell now. The good old days of mom and pop and the kiddies taking the jalopy on a Sunday outing are long gone."

"Not so long as there are those of us who remember." Symonds released Bandit, who shot toward Barry Grace's ankles as he leapt into the car—sunglasses going one way, briefcase going the other—shouting about scratched paint, damn mutts, and legal action.

Ebersol joined Grace in the car, adjusting his bow tie. "Tell Miss Lawrence we wish her all the best," he said over Bandit's frenzied snarling and yapping as Grace shoved the car into reverse with a roar of his engine.

Peggy turned away from the window, doubled over with laughter. "Did you see that? I wasn't sure Barry Grace would escape with his life. Symonds looked angry enough to do murder."

"That old buzzard? Nah." David shook his head. "He's all talk, I guarantee it."

THIS TIME, WHEN she arrived on Symonds' doorstep, she brought the Glenlivet.

"Trying to bribe me?" he grumbled around his toothpick, though Peggy noticed his tone didn't possess its usual bite. She'd call that progress.

"Trying to thank you. For dealing with Mr. Grace and for . . . well for lots of things." Handing him the bottle, she made herself at home on the living room's flowered couch while the dog spun circles around her legs, his back end vibrating a hundred miles an hour.

Symonds seemed to accept his defeat. He didn't complain, merely poured two glasses.

"Water, no ice," she said, but he was already handing her a glass, a glint in his eye she'd not seen before.

"Blanche drank hers the same way," he grumbled.

Peggy tried not to shudder at the odd ways in which her aunt made her presence felt, hiding her reaction behind appreciation of her drink. The alcohol's burn became a warmth that filled her belly before spreading out to her fingertips. Liquid courage to see her through the next few minutes.

"So, you've thanked me," he said. "Was that all?"

"No." Her gaze slid to the deer's head on the wall, the taxidermy duck, Symonds' dog who met and matched her stare for stare. All those eyes watching her. It was like being on stage. One more swallow for luck before she blurted out, "I found Viv."

There was a long pause while Symonds poured himself another drink, a frown forming between his brows. "Did you now?" She couldn't help but notice the way he sloshed the whiskey onto the sideboard or the way his jaw worked as if he was chewing over his response before settling on "How is she?"

Even now, he was going to make her work for every inch. Blanche couldn't have asked for a more stalwart knight in shining armor. As protective of her in death as he had been in life.

"Vague at times, but she told me what happened to Marjory." Peggy finished off her whiskey and held out her glass for more. "About the bargain that got Viv to France."

He downed his second whiskey before settling into his recliner, his face smoothing back into its usual taciturn lines as if relieved. "It was all a long time ago."

"That's what she said. But it still matters. To Viv. To you. And now, to me."

He stared into his empty glass as if it were a crystal ball. "There are mornings I wake up and it's as fresh as if it happened yesterday. I expect to look out my window and see those girls, bold as brass, in their uniforms, striding down the street arm in arm." His gaze grew soft with memory. Bandit, as if sensing the wistful turn of his thoughts, crawled up into the chair beside him. After a minute, he cleared his throat and drew a breath, banishing the ghosts with a loud blowing of his nose into his handkerchief.

"What was Blanche like, Gus? Viv told me about the girl she was, but what about the woman she became?"

"What do you want to know?"

"Are you kidding? Everything!"

He gave a rough scrape of laughter. "That might take more than one bottle."

She obliged by pouring out two more hefty glasses before he could change his mind.

"She was strong," he said after taking a fortifying swallow. "Had to be, didn't she? Stubborn as hell when she thought she was right. Most of the time even when she knew she was wrong."

Glancing up at her from his chair, his face striped by afternoon shadows, Peggy caught a hint of the young man beneath the old exterior. She could see why Blanche had leaned on him. There was formidable strength under all that gruffness and swagger.

"Blanche had a big heart and a smart mouth. She couldn't cook worth a damn, but she could sew better than any fancy fashion designer. Was always on the go with one cause or another. Never stopped. Life was good. *We* were good." He paused, his features softening. "Better than good." Flushed, he polished off his third whiskey, waved his glass for a fourth. "Then your mom died, and it was like the air went out of her."

"She still had her causes," Peggy replied. "Her work. She still had you."

"Wasn't the same. I knew that. Even so, I kept an eye on her as best I could. I reckon by then, me and her had got to be a habit we couldn't break." He looked up, his eyes glistening. "I see Blanche in you, you know. Out on the beach that first night, I could have sworn you were her for a minute. Gave me a start, like seeing a spook." He leaned forward in his chair. "You might think I'm crazy, but every now and then I catch a whiff of her perfume like she's still here."

"Violets?" Peggy said through a held breath.

"That's right. She wore that same scent every day her entire life. How'd you guess?"

Peggy looked to the front window where, framed by chintz curtains, the cottage stood in its sandy lot across the street. Where it would continue to stand, if she had anything to say about it. "Just a hunch."

IT WAS A beautiful day for a funeral.

A few rows over, under a tall sheltering willow, a long shining hearse stood, doors open, while six marines unloaded a flag-draped coffin. A knot of mourners in black surrounded the grave, a stunned young woman clutching a handkerchief with a child on her lap sat in the front row.

The war in Vietnam, playing out on television sets across the country, hit far closer to home in this community where everyone knew someone who was serving. Peggy glanced at Suzanne, wondering what her best friend was thinking, but her eyes were all for the baby she held. If she noticed the nearby service, she kept her fears locked up tight.

Here, there was no taps playing, no honor guard, no symbolic folding of the flag. But Blanche Lawrence, Yeoman Second Class of the Naval Coast Defense Reserve Force, was being honored by those she knew: Symonds, looking odd in a double-breasted suit and a pair of squeaky new shoes; the women of the NYFS, including Mrs. Stokes, Mrs. Gregson, and Mrs. Tilbury still sporting her fox stole and a pillbox and veil in funereal black. And those Blanche had never met, like Suzanne, the soft glow of new motherhood exhaustion paling her cheeks; David, his hair clipped short as a new recruit's as he prepared to start classes; and Peggy, who stood not at the front by the simple white stone marker, but at the back, her gaze moving between the minister and the cemetery's gravel drive.

A car pulled in. A handsome, silver-haired gentleman got out to open the passenger door for his wife who emerged dressed in an elegant suit of navy blue, white lace at her throat. Peggy watched as Symonds approached Viv Weston, for even after all this time, Peggy couldn't think of her as anyone else.

There was a moment when the two of them stood close, his head bent to hers, his hand on the sleeve of her jacket, her face pale as chalk. Peggy couldn't hear what was said, but almost immediately light bloomed in her face, his features broke into a smile that could only be described as boyish, and they threw their arms around each other.

Her companion crossed the grass toward Peggy. "Tom Weston," he said, holding out a hand. He glanced back at his wife and her old friend with an indulgent smile. "Thought I'd give the two of them a few minutes to reminisce. They've got fifty years to catch up on."

Soon after, Symonds escorted Viv to the gravesite and the group.

"You came," Peggy said. "I wasn't sure you would."

"Blanche?" Once again there was that moment of confusion as Viv's mind wandered before the focus reentered her gaze. "Silly me. Not Blanche at all. You're the other one." She drew a shaky breath as she took in the group, all here to pay their respects.

"She touched a lot of people," Peggy said.

Viv's answering smile held as much sadness as joy. "She always said she'd rather be an admiral than a queen. More power." She dropped Gus's arm, attaching herself to Peggy, who led her through the gathered crowd. "I've thought about her every day since I left here fifty years ago."

"Why didn't you ever visit?"

"Blanche and I came to the end of our road together a long time ago. My coming back here would only have reminded her of what—and who—she'd lost."

"My mother?"

"Among others."

Viv bent to place a bouquet of asters on the stone, the blue flowers with their yellow centers bright against the white marble. Her face relaxed, the lines smoothed away. She looked eighteen again as she stood before them, a light shining in her pale eyes.

"I ain't a yeomanette, no more. I'm just a plain civilian as before. Wish I could ship another cruise; Hate to doff my navy blues. Can't walk in these French-heeled shoes, no more."

Her voice was almost inaudible, but as she spoke there was a shifting among the other women, a stirring as shoulders straightened and chins lifted. Some smiled. Some dabbed at watery eyes.

"Nothin' is the same, no more! I just go to town and not 'ashore.' No longer is my dinner 'chow.' I must punch a time clock now; No wonder smiles adorn my brow—no more."

A few voices joined her. At first rusty and uncertain, but with each verse, the chorus grew louder, the yeomanettes of the NYFS moving closer together as if joined by an invisible bond. The sunlight burned brighter. The air felt swept clean by a breeze off the water.

"When a gob goes marching by, no more. Dare I look him in the eyes on shore. For no longer will he see. Just a 'sister gob' in me. Bound by fellowship are we—no more."

Peggy shivered as the voices came together in a swelling of resolve and purpose. From every walk of life, these women had come together to serve their nation. They had, with skill and pluck and unwavering enthusiasm, surpassed every expectation, and in doing so forged a path that others who came behind followed without ever recognizing these trailblazers.

Peggy took Viv's hand, and the two stood shoulder to shoulder.

"No! I ain't a yeomanette no more. And though I hate the very thought of war. If Uncle Sam should ever say, 'I need ten thousand girls today.' Would he get 'em? Well, I'll say! And more."

ACKNOWLEDGMENTS

Bringing the story of the US Navy's yeomanettes to readers has been a labor of love, faith, and determination. But it was a labor shared by many, starting with my agent, Kevan Lyon, who has been in my corner for as long as I've had a corner. Her guidance, support, and enthusiasm have never wavered, and for that I will be forever grateful.

I would also like to give a huge shout-out to the Lyonesses, my amazingly brilliant writer pride who have supported me every step of the way, including authors Christine Wells and Kerri Maher for offering their time and energy to read early chapters, Natasha Lester and Kaia Alderson for helping me pull together a coherent proposal, Laura Kamoie for coming up with the perfect title, and Eliza Knight for taking that all-important last look before submission.

Patricia Clark, reference librarian extraordinaire at Kansas City Public Library, went above and beyond to track down every obscure research book I asked for—even making phone calls when libraries weren't so enthusiastic about sending their materials out of state. Shelley Kay at Webcrafters took my scattered, half-formed notes and turned them into a gorgeous website, and Do Leonard and Maggie Scheck, who have been a part of my writing journey since I first had this wild idea of being a published author, shared encouragement, advice, laughter, and mad editing skills even when it all had to be done virtually due to COVID.

Writing the book is only the first step. Making it the best it can be requires a team of experts, beginning with editor Tessa Woodward at William Morrow who saw my vision and made it her own. Madelyn Blaney answered all my questions, no matter how trivial; John Simko double-checked that all my *i*'s were dotted and all my *t*'s were crossed; Elsie Lyons created the most gorgeous cover art; Diahann Sturge made sure the inside looked as fabulous as the outside. I want to thank them and everyone at William Morrow and HarperCollins who shepherded this book from vague idea to finished product.

Five years separate the release of my last novel from the release of this one. Five very long years where I began to fear I had no more words left to write and no more stories left to tell. But here we are, and I couldn't be happier and more grateful to all those who had a hand in seeing this day come.

About the author

About the book

Read on

Insights,
Interviews
& More . . .

Meet Alix Rickloff

Creative Focus Portrait Photography

ALIX RICKLOFF is a critically acclaimed author of historical fiction. Her two previous books, *Secrets of Nanreath Hall* and *The Way to London*, were both published by William Morrow. She lives in Maryland in a house that's seen its own share of history, so when she's not writing, she can usually be found trying to keep it from falling down.

Author's Note

I stumbled on the story of the Navy's yeomanettes quite by accident. Reading an article about Joy Bright Hancock's involvement with World War II's Navy WAVES, I discovered that she actually began her military service as a yeomanette in the Naval Coast Defense Reserve in 1917. This was the first I'd ever heard of these women despite the fact that over ten thousand of them served between March 1917 and January 1922.

Secretary of the Navy Josephus Daniels could be said to have been the mastermind behind this unprecedented idea. Seeing war on the horizon and realizing how badly undermanned the US Navy was, he noted that nowhere in the regulations for land service did it state the recruit had to be male. Well aware of the number of women already working in clerical positions within the government, he chose to open the doors to them as a way to free up men for ship duty and more closely control the allocation of these women where they would be most valuable.

In March 1917, the announcement was made. Within a month, hundreds had raced to join up becoming yeomen (f), or, as they were nicknamed much to their chagrin, "yeomanettes." The bulk of these new recruits were assigned to clerical positions, but they also served as switchboard operators, couriers, supply drivers, munitions workers, fingerprint ▶

3

Author's Note *(continued)*

experts, and camouflage designers, and they even worked in naval intelligence.

There were many reasons why women raced to join the Navy. Some viewed it as a chance for adventure and new opportunities. Others joined in solidarity with husbands, brothers, or sons already off fighting. Those involved in the suffrage movement hoped the success of the yeomanettes would push the government toward finally granting women the right to vote. But all of them were driven by patriotism and a desire to do their bit for the war effort.

Ocean View, the small bayside resort community outside Norfolk, Virginia, was an obvious choice to set the story. Hampton Roads, Virginia, already had a long proud naval history, but the war brought a rapid expansion to the area with the opening of the Naval Operating Base (NOB) at Sewell's Point north of Norfolk and the construction of five Army embarkation camps where over half a million soldiers took ship for France. Over one thousand yeomen (f) scattered mainly between the Portsmouth shipyard, the naval hospital, and the NOB served as part of the 5th Naval District.

The anti-German sentiment that drives much of the conflict in the story, while far more virulent in the Midwest, was a nationwide issue amplified by groups like the National Security League and the American Defense Society. These groups saw the German communities' strong sense of cultural identity as a threat. Local groups formed to "monitor" their German neighbors and root out any possible spies, saboteurs, or anyone seen as not "patriotic" enough.

Many used this super-patriotism as a way to gain power in political circles. One such leader was Reverend Newell Dwight Hillis, a New York Congregationalist minister who made a name for himself as a crusader against immorality and whose virulent anti-German speeches packed theaters and lecture halls. Pastor Prothero was very loosely inspired by Pastor Hillis, and the words I've attributed to Viv's father in the book are taken directly from some of Hillis's speeches and writings.

While I invented the explosion at the Portsmouth shipyard and the vandalism of the German church, the fire in downtown Norfolk did occur in January 1918 and destroyed nearly two city blocks. More than twenty-three men were arrested in the panic that followed as officials hunted for German saboteurs, though it turned out the fire was accidental in origin.

In writing this book, I took great inspiration from the wonderful stories told by the yeomanettes themselves and collected by historians Jean Ebbert, Marie-Beth Hall, and Regina Akers, and even my initial inspirational yeomanette Joy Bright Hancock. Where I could, I've included many incidents prompted by actual experiences, including the frustration and disarray of early parade practices, the confusion over shipboard ▶

Author's Note *(continued)*

assignments, and the animosity shown to the female recruits by some naval officers.

Lieutenant Dumfries is an amalgamation of many of these officers who were skeptical of these new women recruits. Both his behavior and many of his words, including blaming poor Alice Roosevelt, were taken from one yeomanette's description of an interview with her commanding officer. Later, he gives his permission to allow Viv to attend a dance out of uniform with a quip about hunting and fishing. This quote was taken from Gavin's *American Women in WWI* and was too good not to include. The mix-up in orders for ship duty actually happened to Joy Bright Hancock during her time as a yeomanette stationed in New Jersey. The uncertainty around marriage that makes Marjory sneak off to the courthouse without telling anyone was commented on by more than one yeomanette interviewed.

My own family history also inspired a character in the book. While I was researching and writing the story, my mother came across my grandfather's World War I ID tag. Russell Goode served as a pharmacist's mate on a hospital ship during the war. While I never met him, I was overwhelmed by the sense of connection I felt upon receiving such a treasure and knew immediately he deserved a part in my story. I hope he doesn't mind my dramatic liberties, but I'm sure that if placed in such a situation, he would surely have risen to the occasion.

I end the book with a poem. This melancholy ode to the yeomanette's gallantry and courage was penned in 1919 by yeomanette E. Lyle Macleod, discovered in yeomanette Helen Dunbar McCreary Burns's scrapbook, and published in Lettie Gavin's book *American Women in World War I: They Also Served*. The words beautifully sum up the experience of these women who looked back on their service with pride in a job well done and wistfulness at a time gone by. ∽

Reading Group Guide

1. The yeomanettes were the first women to serve in the US military in a non-nursing capacity. Did you know about them before reading this book? If not, what most surprised you about their service? If you were already familiar with them, did you learn anything that you didn't know before?

2. Which of the three yeomanettes did you most connect with: Viv, Marjory, or Blanche? Why? What drew you to them?

3. Sisterhood and the importance of "found family" is a major theme in the book. Can you think of scenes where this was best illustrated by the author? What did you think of the various female relationships in the book?

4. Peggy and Viv both wrestle with lost faith. Did you understand their reasons? Did you feel it was restored by the end?

5. The beach cottage becomes a refuge for Viv, Blanche, and Peggy. Do you have a favorite place that signifies home and family? Explain why.

6. We see prejudice in various forms throughout the book; from subtle sexism to deadly violence. How did these acts of intolerance affect and change the characters? Were there

moments when they could have fought back? Why do you think they didn't?

7. Blanche begins the book as the strong one of the three. Was there a specific scene in which you saw that begin to change? Did you still feel she was the strongest by the end? Why or why not?

8. For many women, their service in the Navy was a first taste of independence. What was your first taste of independence? Discuss how it made you feel.

9. A family secret lies at the heart of the story, but many of the characters keep secrets. Did you understand why they kept silent? Which of the secrets surprised you the most? Were everyone's secrets revealed by the end?

10. The book deals with a deadly pandemic as well as bigotry and ethnic violence; both issues that remain timely today. Where do you see parallels? Where do you see differences? ∾

More From Alix Rickloff

ALIX RICKLOFF, THE AUTHOR OF *SECRETS OF NANREATH HALL*, RETURNS WITH ANOTHER GRIPPING, BEAUTIFULLY WRITTEN HISTORICAL FICTION NOVEL SET DURING WORLD WAR II

Impetuous and overindulged, Lucy Stanhope, the granddaughter of an earl and stepdaughter of one of Singapore's wealthiest businessmen, is living a life of pampered luxury until one reckless act will change her life forever. Exiled to England to live with an aunt she barely remembers, Lucy could never have foreseen that she would be one of the last to escape before war engulfs the island, and that her parents would disappear in the devastating aftermath, leaving her alone and unhappy as she copes with the realities of a grim and gray battle-weary England. Then she meets Bill, a young evacuee sent to the country to escape the Blitz, and in a moment of sherry-induced weakness, Lucy agrees to help him find his mother in London. The unlikely runaways take off on a seemingly simple journey across country, but things grow complicated when she is reunited with an invalided soldier she knew in Singapore. It's then that Lucy must finally confront the choices she's made if she's ever going to gain the future she desires.

***SECRETS OF NANREATH HALL*, A
FASCINATING DEBUT HISTORICAL NOVEL BY
ALIX RICKLOFF, IS THE GRIPPING STORY OF
A YOUNG MOTHER WHO FLEES HER HOME
ON THE ROCKY CLIFFS OF CORNWALL AND
THE DAUGHTER WHO FINDS HER WAY BACK,
SEEKING ANSWERS**

Cornwall, 1940. Back in England after the harrowing evacuation at Dunkirk, World War II Red Cross nurse Anna Trenowyth finds herself unexpectedly assigned to Nanreath Hall—her dead mother's childhood home. All Anna has left of her mother, Lady Katherine Trenowyth, are vague memories that tease her with clues she can't unravel. Anna knows this could be the chance for her to finally become acquainted with the family she's never known—and to learn the truth about her past.

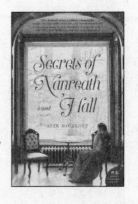

Cornwall, 1913. In the luxury of pre–World War I England, Lady Katherine Trenowyth is expected to do nothing more than make a smart marriage. When Simon Halliday, a bohemian painter, enters her world, Katherine begins to question the future that was so carefully laid out for her. Her choices soon lead her away from the stability of her home and family toward a wild existence of life, art, and love. As Anna is drawn into her newfound family's lives and their tangled loyalties, she must decide if the secrets of the past are too dangerous to unearth . . . and if the family she's discovered is one she can keep. ⌁

Discover great authors, exclusive offers, and more at hc.com.